RICHARD ADAMS, the son of a country doctor, was born in Newbury in England in 1920. He was educated at Bradfield College and Worcester College, Oxford. He served in the Second World War and in 1948 joined the Civil Service. In the mid-1960s he completed his first novel, *Watership Down*, for which he struggled for several years to find a publisher. It was eventually awarded both the Carnegie Medal and the Guardian award for children's fiction in 1972. In 1974 he retired from the Civil Service and published a series of further novels, including *Shardik*, *Tales from Watership Down*, *Maia*, *The Plague Dogs* and *The Girl in a Swing*. Richard died on Christmas Eve, 2016.

Books by Richard Adams

WATERSHIP DOWN
TALES FROM WATERSHIP DOWN

RICHARD ADAMS

WATERSHIP DOWN

Illustrated by David Parkins

PUFFIN

PUFFIN BOOKS

UK | USA | Canada | Ireland | Australia
India | New Zealand | South Africa

Puffin Books is part of the Penguin Random House group of companies
whose addresses can be found at global.penguinrandomhouse.com.

www.penguin.co.uk
www.puffin.co.uk
www.ladybird.co.uk

Penguin
Random House
UK

First published by Rex Collings 1972
Published in Puffin Books 1973
Reissued with new illustrations 1993
Published in this edition 2018
001

Text copyright © Richard Adams, 1972
Illustrations copyright © David Parkins, 1993

Front cover illustration copyright © Watership Down Television Limited 2018
Based on the Watership Down BBC and Netflix TV mini-series © Watership
Down Television Limited 2018
Licensed by ITV Ventures

The moral right of the author and illustrator has been asserted

Set in 10.5/14.5 pt Sabon LT Std
Typeset by Jouve (UK), Milton Keynes
Printed and bound in Great Britain by Clays Ltd, Elcograf S.p.A.

A CIP catalogue record for this book is available from the British Library

ISBN: 978-0-141-37894-7

All correspondence to:
Puffin Books
Penguin Random House Children's
80 Strand, London WC2R ORL

Master Rabbit I saw

– WALTER DE LA MARE

*To Juliet and Rosamond, remembering
the road to Stratford-on-Avon*

Acknowledgements

I acknowledge with gratitude the help I have received not only from my family but also from my friends Reg Sones and Hal Summers, who read the book before publication and made valuable suggestions.

I also wish to thank warmly Mrs Margaret Apps and Miss Miriam Hobbs, who took pains with the typing and helped me very much.

I am indebted, for a knowledge of rabbits and their ways, to Mr R. M. Lockley's remarkable book, *The Private Life of the Rabbit*. Anyone who wishes to know more about the migrations of yearlings, about pressing chin glands, chewing pellets, the effects of over-crowding in warrens, the phenomenon of re-absorption of fertilized embryos, the capacity of buck rabbits to fight stoats, or any other features of Lapine life, should refer to that definitive work.

Acknowledgements

Note

Nuthanger Farm is a real place, like all the other places in the book. But Mr and Mrs Cane, their little girl Lucy and their farmhands are fictitious and bear no intentional resemblance to any persons known to me, living or dead.

Contents

Contents

PART II   ON WATERSHIP DOWN

PART III   EFRAFA

PART IV   HAZEL-RAH

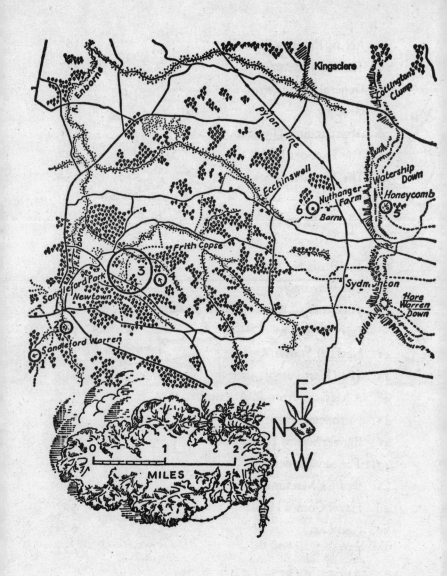

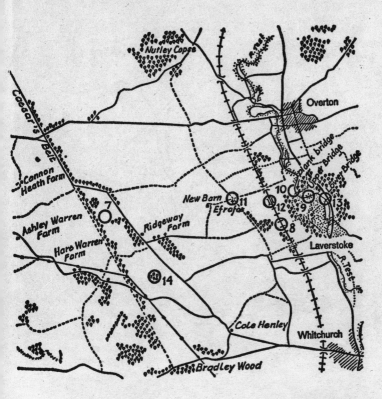

PART ONE

The Journey

1. The Notice Board

CHORUS: Why do you cry out thus, unless at some
            vision of horror?
CASSANDRA: The house reeks of death and dripping blood.
CHORUS: How so? 'Tis but the odour of the altar
            sacrifice.
CASSANDRA: The stench is like a breath from the tomb.

Aeschylus, *Agamemnon*

THE PRIMROSES were over. Towards the edge of the wood, where the ground became open and sloped down to an old fence and a brambly ditch beyond, only a few fading patches of pale yellow still showed among the dog's mercury and oak-tree roots. On the other side of the fence, the upper part of the field was full of rabbit-holes. In places the grass was gone altogether and everywhere there were clusters of dry droppings, through which nothing but the ragwort would grow. A hundred yards away, at the bottom of the slope, ran the brook, no more than three feet wide, half-choked with king-cups, water-cress and blue

3

brook-lime. The cart-track crossed by a brick culvert and climbed the opposite slope to a five-barred gate in the thorn hedge. The gate led into the lane.

The May sunset was red in clouds, and there was still half an hour to twilight. The dry slope was dotted with rabbits – some nibbling at the thin grass near their holes, others pushing farther down to look for dandelions or perhaps a cowslip that the rest had missed. Here and there one sat upright on an ant-heap and looked about, with ears erect and nose in the wind. But a blackbird, singing undisturbed on the outskirts of the wood, showed that there was nothing alarming there and in the other direction, along the brook, all was plain to be seen, empty and quiet. The warren was at peace.

At the top of the bank, close to the wild cherry where the blackbird sang, was a little group of holes almost hidden by brambles. In the green half-light, at the mouth of one of these holes, two rabbits were sitting together side by side. At length, the larger of the two came out, slipped along the bank under cover of the brambles and so down into the ditch and up into the field. A few moments later the other followed.

The first rabbit stopped in a sunny patch and scratched his ear with rapid movements of his hind-leg. Although he was a yearling and still below full weight, he had not the harassed look of most 'outskirters' – that is, the rank-and-file of ordinary rabbits in their first year who, lacking either aristocratic parentage or unusual size and strength, get sat on by their elders and live as best they can – often in the open – on the edge of their warren. He looked as though he knew how to take care of himself. There was a shrewd, buoyant air about him as he sat up, looked round and rubbed both front paws over his nose. As soon as he was satisfied that all was well, he laid back his ears and set to work on the grass.

His companion seemed less at ease. He was small, with wide, staring eyes and a way of raising and turning his head which suggested not so much caution as a kind of ceaseless, nervous tension. His nose moved continually and when a bumble-bee flew humming to a thistle bloom behind him, he jumped and spun round with a start that sent two nearby rabbits scurrying for holes before the nearest, a buck with black-tipped ears, recognized him and returned to feeding.

'Oh, it's only Fiver,' said the black-tipped rabbit, 'jumping at blue-bottles again. Come on, Buckthorn, what were you telling me?'

'Fiver?' said the other rabbit. 'Why's he called that?'

'Five in the litter, you know: he was the last – and the smallest. You'd wonder nothing had got him by now. I always say a man couldn't see him and a fox wouldn't want him. Still, I admit he seems to be able to keep out of harm's way.'*

---

* Rabbits can count up to four. Any number above four is *Hrair* – 'a lot', or 'a thousand'. Thus they say *U Hrair* – 'The Thousand' – to mean, collectively, all the enemies (or *elil*, as they call them) of rabbits – fox, stoat, weasel, cat, owl, man, etc. There were probably more than five rabbits in the litter when Fiver was born, but his name, *Hrairoo*, means 'Little thousand', i.e. the little one of a lot or, as they say of pigs, 'the runt'.

The small rabbit came closer to his companion, lolloping on long hind legs.

'Let's go a bit further, Hazel,' he said. 'You know, there's something queer about the warren this evening, although I can't tell exactly what it is. Shall we go down to the brook?'

'All right,' answered Hazel, 'and you can find me a cowslip. If you can't find one, no one can.'

He led the way down the slope, his shadow stretching behind him on the grass. They reached the brook and began nibbling and searching close beside the wheel-ruts of the track.

It was not long before Fiver found what they were looking for. Cowslips are a delicacy among rabbits, and as a rule there are very few left by late May in the neighbourhood of even a small warren. This one had not bloomed and its flat spread of leaves was almost hidden under the long grass. They were just starting on it when two larger rabbits came running across from the other side of the near-by cattle-wade.

'Cowslip?' said one. 'All right – just leave it to us. Come on, hurry up,' he added, as Fiver hesitated. 'You heard me, didn't you?'

'Fiver found it, Toadflax,' said Hazel.

'And we'll eat it,' replied Toadflax. 'Cowslips are for *Owsla**–don't you know that? If you don't, we can easily teach you.'

---

* Nearly all warrens have an *Owsla,* or group of strong or clever rabbits – second-year or older – surrounding the Chief Rabbit and his doe and exercising authority. Owslas vary. In one warren, the Owsla may be the band of a war-lord: in another, it may consist largely of clever

Fiver had already turned away. Hazel caught him up by the culvert.

'I'm sick and tired of it,' he said. 'It's the same all the time. "These are my claws, so this is my cowslip." "These are my teeth, so this is my burrow." I'll tell you, if ever I get into the Owsla, I'll treat outskirters with a bit of decency.'

'Well, you can at least expect to be in the Owsla one day,' answered Fiver. 'You've got some weight coming and that's more than I shall ever have.'

'You don't suppose I'll leave you to look after yourself, do you?' said Hazel. 'But to tell you the truth, I sometimes feel like clearing out of this warren altogether. Still, let's forget it now and try to enjoy the evening. I tell you what – shall we go across the brook? There'll be fewer rabbits and we can have a bit of peace. Unless you feel it isn't safe?' he added.

The way in which he asked suggested that he did in fact think that Fiver was likely to know better than himself, and it was clear from Fiver's reply that this was accepted between them.

'No, it's safe enough,' he answered. 'If I start feeling there's anything dangerous I'll tell you. But it's not exactly danger that I seem to feel about the place. It's – oh, I don't know – something oppressive, like thunder: I can't tell what; but it worries me. All the same, I'll come across with you.'

---

patrollers or garden-raiders. Sometimes a good story-teller may find a place; or a seer, or intuitive rabbit. In the Sandleford warren at this time, the Owsla was rather military in character (though, as will be seen later, not so military as some).

They ran over the culvert. The grass was wet and thick near the stream and they made their way up the opposite slope, looking for drier ground. Part of the slope was in shadow, for the sun was sinking ahead of them, and Hazel, who wanted a warm, sunny spot, went on until they were quite near the lane. As they approached the gate he stopped, staring.

'Fiver, what's that? Look!'

A little way in front of them, the ground had been freshly disturbed. Two piles of earth lay on the grass. Heavy posts, reeking of creosote and paint, towered up as high as the holly trees in the hedge, and the board they carried threw a long shadow across the top of the field. Near one of the posts, a hammer and a few nails had been left behind.

The two rabbits went up to the board at a hopping run and crouched in a patch of nettles on the far side, wrinkling their noses at the smell of a dead cigarette-end somewhere in the grass. Suddenly Fiver shivered and cowered down.

'Oh, Hazel! This is where it comes from! I know now – something very bad! Some terrible thing – coming closer and closer.'

He began to whimper with fear.

'What sort of thing – what do you mean? I thought you said there was no danger?'

'I don't know what it is,' answered Fiver wretchedly. 'There isn't any danger here, at this moment. But it's coming – it's coming. Oh, Hazel, look! The field! It's covered with blood!'

'Don't be silly, it's only the light of the sunset. Fiver, come on, don't talk like this, you're frightening me!'

Fiver sat trembling and crying among the nettles as Hazel tried to reassure him and to find out what it could be that had suddenly driven him beside himself. If he was terrified, why did he not run for safety, as any sensible rabbit would? But Fiver could not explain and only grew more and more distressed. At last Hazel said,

'Fiver, you can't sit crying here. Anyway, it's getting dark. We'd better go back to the burrow.'

'Back to the burrow?' whimpered Fiver. 'It'll come there – don't think it won't! I tell you, the field's full of blood –'

'Now stop it,' said Hazel firmly. 'Just let me look after you for a bit. Whatever the trouble is, it's time we got back.'

He ran down the field and over the brook to the cattle-wade. Here there was a delay, for Fiver – surrounded on all sides by the quiet summer evening – became helpless and almost paralysed with fear. When at last Hazel had got him back to the ditch, he refused at first to go underground and Hazel had almost to push him down the hole.

The sun set behind the opposite slope. The wind turned colder, with a scatter of rain, and in less than an hour it was dark. All colour had faded from the sky: and although the big board by the gate creaked slightly in the night wind (as though to insist that it had not disappeared in the darkness, but was still firmly where it had been put), there was no passer-by to read the sharp, hard letters that cut straight as black knives across its white surface. They said:

THIS IDEALLY SITUATED ESTATE, COMPRISING SIX ACRES OF EXCELLENT BUILDING LAND, IS TO BE DEVELOPED WITH HIGH CLASS MODERN RESIDENCES BY SUTCH AND MARTIN, LIMITED, OF NEWBURY, BERKS.

2. The Chief Rabbit

The darksome statesman, hung with weights and woe,
Like a thick midnight-fog, moved there so slow,
He did not stay, nor go.

Henry Vaughan, *The World*

IN THE darkness and warmth of the burrow Hazel suddenly woke, struggling and kicking with his back legs. Something was attacking him. There was no smell of ferret or weasel. No instinct told him to run. His head cleared and he realized that he was alone except for Fiver. It was Fiver who was clambering over him, clawing and grabbing like a rabbit trying to climb a wire fence in a panic.

'Fiver! Fiver, wake up, you silly fellow! It's Hazel. You'll hurt me in a moment. Wake up!'

He held him down. Fiver struggled and woke.

'Oh, Hazel! I was dreaming. It was dreadful. You were there. We were sitting on water, going down a great, deep stream, and then I realized we were on a board – like that board in the field – all white and covered with black lines.

There were other rabbits there – bucks and does. But when I looked down, I saw the board was all made of bones and wire; and I screamed and you said, "Swim – everybody swim'; and then I was looking for you everywhere and trying to drag you out of a hole in the bank. I found you, but you said, "The Chief Rabbit must go alone," and you floated away down a dark tunnel of water.'

'Well, you've hurt my ribs, anyway. Tunnel of water, indeed! What rubbish! Can we go back to sleep now?'

'Hazel – the danger, the bad thing. It hasn't gone away. It's here – all round us. Don't tell me to forget about it and go to sleep. We've got to go away before it's too late.'

'Go away? From here, you mean? From the warren?'

'Yes. Very soon. It doesn't matter where.'

'Just you and I?'

'No, everyone.'

'The whole warren? Don't be silly. They won't come. They'll say you're out of your wits.'

'Then they'll be here when the bad thing comes. You must listen to me, Hazel. Believe me, something very bad is close upon us and we ought to go away.'

'Well, I suppose we'd better go and see the Chief Rabbit and you can tell *him* about it. Or I'll try to. But I don't expect he'll like the idea at all.'

Hazel led the way down the slope of the run and up towards the bramble curtain. He did not want to believe Fiver, and he was afraid not to.

It was a little after *ni-Frith*, or noon. The whole warren were underground, mostly asleep. Hazel and Fiver went a short way above ground and then into a wide, open hole in a sand patch and so down, by various runs, until they were thirty feet into the wood, among the roots of an oak. Here they were stopped by a large, heavily-built rabbit – one of the Owsla. He had a curious, heavy growth of fur on the crown of his head, which gave him an odd appearance, as though he were wearing a kind of cap. This had given him his name, *Thlayli,* which means, literally, 'Furhead', or as we might say, 'Bigwig'.

'Hazel?' said Bigwig, sniffing at him in the deep twilight among the tree-roots. 'It is Hazel, isn't it? What are you doing here? And at this time of day?' He ignored Fiver, who was waiting farther down the run.

'We want to see the Chief Rabbit,' said Hazel. 'It's important, Bigwig. Can you help us?'

'We?' said Bigwig. 'Is *he* going to see him too?'

'Yes, he must. Do trust me, Bigwig. I don't usually come and talk like this, do I? When did I ever ask to see the Chief Rabbit before?'

'Well, I'll do it for you, Hazel, although I'll probably get my head bitten off. I'll tell him I know you're a sensible fellow. He ought to know you himself, of course, but he's getting old. Wait here, will you?'

Bigwig went a little way down the run and stopped at the entrance to a large burrow. After speaking a few words that Hazel could not catch, he was evidently called inside. The two rabbits waited in silence, broken only by the continual nervous fidgeting of Fiver.

The Chief Rabbit's name and style was *Threarah,* meaning 'Lord Rowan Tree'. For some reason he was always referred to as '*The* Threarah' – perhaps because there happened to be only one threar, or rowan, near the warren, from which he took his name. He had won his position not only by strength in his prime, but also by level-headedness and a certain self-contained detachment, quite unlike the impulsive behaviour of most rabbits. It was well-known that he never let himself become excited by rumour or danger. He had coolly – some even said coldly – stood firm during the terrible onslaught of the myxomatosis, ruthlessly driving out every rabbit who seemed to be sickening. He had resisted all ideas of mass emigration and enforced complete isolation on the warren, thereby almost certainly saving it from extinction. It was he, too, who had once dealt with a particularly troublesome stoat by leading it down among the pheasant coops and so (at the risk of his own life) on to a keeper's gun. He was now, as Bigwig said, getting old, but his wits were still clear enough. When Hazel and Fiver were brought in, he greeted them politely. Owsla like Toadflax might threaten and bully. The Threarah had no need.

'Ah, Walnut. It is Walnut, isn't it?'

'Hazel,' said Hazel.

'Hazel, of course. How very nice of you to come and see me. I knew your mother well. And your friend –'

'My brother.'

'Your brother,' said the Threarah, with the faintest suggestion of 'Don't correct me any more, will you?' in his voice. 'Do make yourselves comfortable. Have some lettuce?'

The Chief Rabbit's lettuce was stolen by the Owsla from a garden half a mile away across the fields. Outskirters seldom or never saw lettuce. Hazel took a small leaf and nibbled politely. Fiver refused, and sat blinking and twitching miserably.

'Now, how are things with you?' said the Chief Rabbit. 'Do tell me how I can help you.'

'Well, sir,' said Hazel rather hesitantly, 'it's because of my brother – Fiver here. He can often tell when there's anything bad about, and I've found him right again and again. He knew the flood was coming last autumn and sometimes he can tell where a wire's been set. And now he says he can sense a bad danger coming upon the warren.'

'A bad danger. Yes, I see. How very upsetting,' said the Chief Rabbit, looking anything but upset. 'Now what sort of danger, I wonder?' He looked at Fiver.

'I don't know,' said Fiver. 'B-but it's bad. It's so b-bad that – it's very bad,' he concluded miserably.

The Threarah waited politely for a few moments and then he said, 'Well, now, and what ought we to do about it, I wonder?'

'Go away,' said Fiver instantly. 'Go away. All of us. Now. Threarah, sir, we must all go away.'

The Threarah waited again. Then, in an extremely understanding voice, he said, 'Well, I never did! That's rather a tall order, isn't it? What do you think yourself?'

'Well, sir,' said Hazel, 'my brother doesn't really think about these feelings he gets. He just has the feelings, if you see what I mean. I'm sure you're the right person to decide what we ought to do.'

'Well, that's very nice of you, to say that. I hope I am. But now, my dear fellows, let's just think about this a moment, shall we? It's May, isn't it? Everyone's busy and most of the rabbits are enjoying themselves. No elil for miles, or so they tell me. No illness, good weather. And you want me to tell the warren that young – er – young – er – your brother here has got a hunch and we must all go trapesing across country to goodness knows where and risk the consequences, eh? What do you think they'll say? All delighted, eh?'

'They'd take it from you,' said Fiver suddenly.

'That's very nice of you,' said the Threarah again. 'Well, perhaps they would, perhaps they would. But I should have to consider it very carefully indeed. A most serious step, of course. And then –'

'But there's no time, Threarah, sir,' blurted out Fiver. 'I can feel the danger like a wire round my neck – like a wire – Hazel, help!' He squealed and rolled over in the sand, kicking frantically, as a rabbit does in a snare. Hazel held him down with both forepaws and he grew quieter.

'I'm awfully sorry, Chief Rabbit,' said Hazel. 'He gets like this sometimes. He'll be all right in a minute.'

'What a shame! What a shame! Poor fellow, perhaps he ought to go home and rest. Yes, you'd better take him along now. Well, it's really been extremely good of you to come and see me, Walnut. I appreciate it very much indeed. And I shall think over all you've said most carefully, you can be quite sure of that. Bigwig, just wait a moment, will you?'

As Hazel and Fiver made their way dejectedly down the run outside the Threarah's burrow, they could just hear, from inside, the Chief Rabbit's voice assuming a rather sharper note, interspersed with an occasional 'Yes, sir,' 'No, sir.'

Bigwig, as he had predicted, was getting his head bitten off.

3. Hazel's Decision

What am I lying here for? ... We are lying here as though
we had a chance of enjoying a quiet time ... Am I waiting
until I become a little older?

Xenophon, *The Anabasis*

'BUT, Hazel, you didn't really think the Chief Rabbit
would act on your advice, did you? What were you
expecting?'

It was evening once more and Hazel and Fiver were
feeding outside the wood with two friends. Blackberry, the
rabbit with tipped ears who had been startled by Fiver the
night before, had listened carefully to Hazel's description
of the notice board, remarking that he had always felt sure
that men left these things about to act as signs or messages
of some kind, in the same way that rabbits left marks on
runs and gaps. It was another neighbour, Dandelion, who
had now brought the talk back to the Threarah and his
indifference to Fiver's fear.

'I don't know what I expected,' said Hazel. 'I'd never been near the Chief Rabbit before. But I thought, "Well, even if he won't listen, at least no one can say afterwards that we didn't do our best to warn him".'

'You're sure, then, that there's really something to be afraid of?'

'I'm quite certain. I've always known Fiver, you see.'

Blackberry was about to reply when another rabbit came noisily through the thick dog's mercury in the wood, blundered down into the brambles and pushed his way up from the ditch. It was Bigwig.

'Hullo, Bigwig,' said Hazel. 'You're off duty?'

'Off duty,' said Bigwig, 'and likely to remain off duty.'

'How do you mean?'

'I've left the Owsla, that's what I mean.'

'Not on our account?'

'You could say that. The Threarah's rather good at making himself unpleasant when he's been woken up at ni-Frith for what he considers a piece of trivial nonsense. He certainly knows how to get under your skin. I dare say a good many rabbits would have kept quiet and thought about keeping on the right side of the Chief, but I'm afraid I'm not much good at that. I told him that the Owsla's privileges didn't mean all that much to me in any case and that a strong rabbit could always do just as well by leaving the warren. He told me not to be impulsive and think it over, but I shan't stay. Lettuce-stealing isn't my idea of a jolly life, nor sentry-duty in the burrow. I'm in a fine temper, I can tell you.'

'No one will steal lettuces soon,' said Fiver quietly.

'Oh, that's you, Fiver, is it?' said Bigwig, noticing him for the first time. 'Good, I was coming to look for you. I've been thinking about what you said to the Chief Rabbit. Tell me, is it a sort of tremendous hoax to make yourself important, or is it true?'

'It *is* true,' said Fiver. 'I wish it weren't.'

'Then you'll be leaving the warren?'

They were all startled by the bluntness with which Bigwig went to the point. Dandelion muttered, 'Leave the warren, *Frithrah!*' while Blackberry twitched his ears and looked very intently, first at Bigwig and then at Hazel.

It was Hazel who replied. 'Fiver and I will be leaving the warren tonight,' he said deliberately. 'I don't know exactly where we shall go, but we'll take anyone who's ready to come with us.'

'Right,' said Bigwig, 'then you can take me.'

The last thing Hazel had expected was the immediate support of a member of the Owsla. It crossed his mind that although Bigwig would certainly be a useful rabbit in a tight corner, he would also be a difficult one to get on with. He certainly would not want to do what he was told – or even asked – by an outskirter. 'I don't care if he is in the Owsla,' thought Hazel. 'If we get away from the warren, I'm not going to let Bigwig run everything, or why bother to go?' But he answered only, 'Good. We shall be glad to have you.'

He looked round at the other rabbits, who were all staring either at Bigwig or at himself. It was Blackberry who spoke next.

'I think I'll come,' he said. 'I don't quite know whether it's you who's persuaded me, Fiver. But anyway, there are too many bucks in this warren, and it's pretty poor fun for any rabbit that's not in the Owsla. The funny thing is that you feel terrified to stay and I feel terrified to go. Foxes here, weasels there, Fiver in the middle, begone dull care!'

He pulled out a burnet leaf and ate it slowly, concealing his fear as best he could; for all his instincts were warning him of the dangers in the unknown country beyond the warren.

'If we believe Fiver,' said Hazel, 'it means that we think no rabbits at all ought to stay here. So between now and the time when we go, we ought to persuade as many as we can to join us.'

'I think there are one or two in the Owsla who might be worth sounding,' said Bigwig. 'If I can talk them over, they'll be with me when I join you tonight. But they won't come because of Fiver. They'll be juniors, discontented fellows like me. You need to have heard Fiver yourself to be convinced by him. He's convinced me. It's obvious that he's been sent some kind of message, and I believe in these things. I can't think why he didn't convince the Threarah.'

'Because the Threarah doesn't like anything he hasn't thought of for himself,' answered Hazel. 'But we can't bother with him any more now. We've got to try to collect some more rabbits and meet again here, *fu Inlé*. And we'll start fu Inlé, too: we can't wait longer. The danger's coming closer all the time – whatever it is – and besides, the Threarah isn't going to like it if he finds out that you've been trying to get at rabbits in the Owsla, Bigwig. Neither is Captain Holly, I dare say. They won't mind odds-and-ends like us clearing off, but they won't want to lose you. If I were in your place, I'd be careful whom I picked to talk to.'

4. The Departure

Now sir, young Fortinbras,
Of unimproved mettle hot and full,
Hath in the skirts of Norway here and there
Sharked up a list of lawless resolutes
For food and diet to some enterprise
That hath a stomach in't.

Shakespeare, *Hamlet*

FU INLÉ means 'after moonrise'. Rabbits, of course, have no idea of precise time or of punctuality. In this respect they are much the same as primitive people, who often take several days over assembling for some purpose and then several more to get started. Before such people can act together, a kind of telepathic feeling has to flow through them and ripen to the point when they all know that they are ready to begin. Anyone who has seen the martins and swallows in September, assembling on the telephone wires, twittering, making short flights singly and in groups over the open, stubbly fields, returning to form longer and even

21

longer lines above the yellowing verges of the lanes – the hundreds of individual birds merging and blending, in a mounting excitement, into swarms, and these swarms coming loosely and untidily together to create a great, unorganized flock, thick at the centre and ragged at the edges, which breaks and re-forms continually like clouds or waves – until that moment when the greater part (but not all) of them know that the time has come: they are off, and have begun once more that great southward flight which many will not survive; anyone seeing this has seen at work the current that flows (among creatures who think of themselves primarily as part of a group and only secondarily, if at all, as individuals) to fuse them together and impel them into action without conscious thought or will: has seen at work the angel which drove the First Crusade into Antioch and drives the lemmings into the sea.

It was actually about an hour after moonrise and a good while before midnight when Hazel and Fiver once more came out of their burrow behind the brambles and slipped quietly along the bottom of the ditch. With them was a third rabbit, *Hlao* – Pipkin – a friend of Fiver. (Hlao means any small concavity in the grass where moisture may collect, e.g. the dimple formed by a dandelion or thistle-cup.) He too was small, and inclined to be timid, and Hazel and Fiver had spent the greater part of their last evening in the warren in persuading him to join them. Pipkin had agreed rather hesitantly. He still felt extremely nervous about what might happen once they left the warren and had decided that the best way to avoid trouble would be to keep close to Hazel and do exactly what he said.

The three were still in the ditch when Hazel heard a movement above. He looked up quickly.

'Who's there?' he said. 'Dandelion?'

'No, I'm Hawkbit,' said the rabbit who was peering over the edge. He jumped down among them, landing rather heavily. 'Do you remember me, Hazel? We were in the same burrow during the snow last winter. Dandelion told me you were going to leave the warren tonight. If you are, I'll come with you.'

Hazel could recall Hawkbit – a rather slow, stupid rabbit, whose company for five snow-bound days underground had been distinctly tedious. Still, he thought, this was no time to pick and choose. Although Bigwig might succeed in talking over one or two, most of the rabbits they could expect to join them would not come from the Owsla. They would be outskirters who were getting a thin time and wondering what to do about it. He was running over some of these in his mind when Dandelion appeared.

'The sooner we're off the better, I reckon,' said Dandelion. 'I don't much like the look of things. After I'd persuaded Hawkbit here to join us, I was just starting to talk to a few more, when I found that Toadflax fellow had followed me down the run. "I want to know what you're up to," he said, and I don't think he believed me when I told him I was only trying to find out whether there were any rabbits who wanted to leave the warren. He asked me if I was sure I wasn't working up some kind of plot against the Threarah and he got awfully angry and suspicious. It put the wind up me, to tell you the truth, so I've just brought Hawkbit along and left it at that.'

'I don't blame you,' said Hazel. 'Knowing Toadflax, I'm surprised he didn't knock you over first and ask questions afterwards. All the same, let's wait a little longer. Blackberry ought to be here soon.'

Time passed. They crouched in silence while the moon shadows moved northward in the grass. At last, just as Hazel was about to run down the slope to Blackberry's burrow, he saw him come out of his hole, followed by no less than three rabbits. One of these, Buckthorn, Hazel knew well. He was glad to see him, for he knew him for a tough, sturdy fellow, who was considered certain to get into the Owsla as soon as he reached full weight.

'But I dare say he's impatient,' thought Hazel, 'or he may have come off worst in some scuffle over a doe and taken it hard. Well, with him and Bigwig, at least we shan't be too badly off if we run into any fighting.'

He did not recognize the other two rabbits and when Blackberry told him their names – Speedwell and Acorn – he was none the wiser. But this was not surprising, for they were typical outskirters – thin-looking six-monthers, with the strained, wary look of those who are only too well used to the thin end of the stick. They looked curiously at Fiver. From what Blackberry had told them, they had been almost expecting to find Fiver foretelling doom in a poetic torrent. Instead, he seemed more calm and normal than the rest. The certainty of going had lifted a weight from Fiver.

More time went slowly by. Blackberry scrambled up into the fern and then returned to the top of the bank, fidgeting nervously and half-inclined to bolt at nothing. Hazel and Fiver remained in the ditch, nibbling half-heartedly at the dark grass. At last Hazel heard what he was listening for; a rabbit – or was it two? – approaching from the wood.

A few moments later Bigwig was in the ditch. Behind him came a hefty, brisk-looking rabbit, something over twelve months old. He was well-known by sight to all the warren, for his fur was entirely grey, with patches of near-white that now caught the moonlight as he sat scratching himself without speaking. This was Silver, a nephew of the Threarah, who was serving his first month in the Owsla.

Hazel could not help feeling relieved that Bigwig had brought only Silver – a quiet, straightforward fellow, who had not yet really found his feet among the veterans. When Bigwig had spoken earlier of sounding out the Owsla, Hazel had been in two minds. It was only too likely that they would encounter dangers beyond the warren and that they would stand in need of some good fighters. Again, if Fiver was right and the whole warren was in imminent peril, then of course they ought to welcome any rabbit who was ready to join them. On the other hand, there seemed no point in taking particular pains to get hold of rabbits who were going to behave like Toadflax.

'Wherever we settle down in the end,' thought Hazel, 'I'm determined to see that Pipkin and Fiver aren't sat on and cuffed around until they're ready to run any risk just to get away. But is Bigwig going to see it like that?'

'You know Silver, don't you?' asked Bigwig, breaking in on his thoughts. 'Apparently some of the younger fellows in the Owsla have been giving him a thin time – teasing him about his fur, you know, and saying he only got his place because of the Threarah. I thought I was going to get some more, but I suppose nearly all the Owsla feel they're very well off as they are.'

He looked about him. 'I say, there aren't many here, are there? Do you think it's really worth going on with this idea?'

Silver seemed about to speak when suddenly there was a pattering in the undergrowth above and three more rabbits came over the bank from the wood. Their movement was direct and purposeful, quite unlike the earlier, haphazard approach of those who were now gathered in the ditch. The largest of the three newcomers was in front and the other two followed him, as though under orders. Hazel, sensing at once that they had nothing in common with himself and his companions, started and sat up tensely. Fiver muttered in his ear, 'Oh, Hazel, they've come to –' but broke off short. Bigwig turned towards them and stared, his nose working rapidly. The three came straight up to him.

'Thlayli?' said the leader.

'You know me perfectly well,' replied Bigwig, 'and I know you, Holly. What do you want?'

'You're under arrest.'

'Under arrest? What do you mean? What for?'

'Spreading dissension and inciting to mutiny. Silver, you're under arrest too, for failing to report to Toadflax this evening and causing your duty to devolve on a comrade. You're both to come with me.'

Immediately Bigwig fell upon him, scratching and kicking. Holly fought back. His followers closed in, looking for an opening to join the fight and pin Bigwig down. Suddenly, from the top of the bank, Buckthorn flung himself headlong into the scuffle, knocked one of the guards flying with a kick from his back legs and then closed with the other. He was followed a moment later by Dandelion, who landed full on the rabbit whom Buckthorn had kicked. Both guards broke clear, looked round for a moment and then leapt up the bank into the wood. Holly struggled free of Bigwig and crouched on his haunches, scuffling his front paws and growling, as rabbits will when angry. He was about to speak when Hazel faced him.

'Go,' said Hazel, firmly and quietly. 'Or we'll kill you.'

'Do you know what this means?' replied Holly. 'I am Captain of Owsla. You know that, don't you?'

'Go,' repeated Hazel. 'Or you will be killed.'

'It is you who will be killed,' replied Holly. Without another word he too went back up the bank and vanished into the wood.

Dandelion was bleeding from the shoulder. He licked the wound for a few moments and then turned to Hazel.

'They won't be long coming back, you know, Hazel,' he said. 'They've gone to turn out the Owsla, and then we'll be for it right enough.'

'We ought to go at once,' said Fiver.

'Yes, the time's come now all right,' replied Hazel. 'Come on, down to the stream. Then we'll follow the bank – that'll help us to keep together.'

'If you'll take my advice –' began Bigwig.

'If we stay here any longer I shan't be able to,' answered Hazel.

With Fiver beside him, he led the way out of the ditch and down the slope. In less than a minute the little band of rabbits had disappeared into the dim, moonlit night.

5. In the Woods

These young rabbits ... must move out if they are to survive. In a wild and free state they ... stray sometimes for miles ... wandering until they find a suitable environment.
R. M. Lockley, *The Private Life of the Rabbit*

IT WAS getting on towards moonset when they left the fields and entered the wood. Straggling, catching up with one another, keeping more or less together, they had wandered over half a mile down the fields, always following the course of the brook. Although Hazel guessed that they must now have gone further from the warren than any rabbit he had ever talked to, he was not sure whether they were yet safely away: and it was while he was wondering – not for the first time – whether he could hear sounds of pursuit that he first noticed the dark masses of the trees and the brook disappearing among them.

Rabbits avoid close woodland, where the ground is shady, damp and grassless and they feel menaced by the undergrowth. Hazel did not care for the look of the trees.

Still, he thought, Holly would no doubt think twice before following them into a place like that, and to keep beside the brook might well prove safer than wandering about the fields in one direction and another, with the risk of finding themselves, in the end, back at the warren. He decided to go straight into the wood without consulting Bigwig, and to trust that the rest would follow.

'If we don't run into any trouble and the brook takes us through the wood,' he thought, 'we really shall be clear of the warren and then we can look for somewhere to rest for a bit. Most of them still seem to be more or less all right, but Fiver and Pipkin will have had as much as they can stand before long.'

From the moment he entered it the wood seemed full of noises. There was a smell of damp leaves and moss, and everywhere the splash of water went whispering about. Just inside, the brook made a little fall into a pool and the sound, enclosed among the trees, echoed as though in a cave. Roosting birds rustled overhead; the night breeze stirred the leaves; here and there a dead twig fell. And there were more sinister, unidentified sounds, from further away; sounds of movement.

To rabbits, everything unknown is dangerous. The first reaction is to startle, the second to bolt. Again and again they startled, until they were close to exhaustion. But what did these sounds mean and where, in this wilderness, could they bolt to?

The rabbits crept closer together. Their progress grew slower. Before long they lost the course of the brook, slipping across the moonlit patches as fugitives and halting in the bushes with raised ears and staring eyes. The moon was low now and the light, wherever it slanted through the trees, seemed thicker, older and more yellow.

From a thick pile of dead leaves beneath a holly tree, Hazel looked down a narrow path, lined on either side with fern and sprouting fire-weed. The fern moved slightly in the breeze, but along the path there was nothing to be seen except a scatter of last year's fallen acorns under an oak. What was in the bracken? What lay round the further bend? And what would happen to a rabbit who left the shelter of the holly tree and ran down the path? He turned to Dandelion beside him.

'You'd better wait here,' he said. 'When I get to the bend I'll stamp. But if I run into trouble, get the others away.'

Without waiting for an answer he ran into the open and down the path. A few seconds brought him to the oak. He paused a moment, staring about him, and then ran on to the bend. Beyond, the path was the same – empty in the darkening moonlight and leading gently downhill into the deep shadow of a grove of ilex trees. Hazel stamped, and a few moments later Dandelion was beside him in the bracken. Even in the midst of his fear and strain it occurred to him that Dandelion must be very fast: he had covered the distance in a flash.

'Well done,' whispered Dandelion. 'Running our risks for us are you – like El-ahrairah?'*

Hazel gave him a quick, friendly glance. It was warm praise and cheered him. What Robin Hood is to the English

* The stresses are the same as in the phrase 'Never say die'.

and John Henry to the American Negroes, Elil-Hrair-Rah, or El-ahrairah – The Prince with a Thousand Enemies – is to rabbits. Uncle Remus might well have heard of him, for some of El-ahrairah's adventures are those of Brer Rabbit. For that matter, Odysseus himself might have borrowed a trick or two from the rabbit hero, for he is very old and was never at a loss for a trick to deceive his enemies. Once, so they say, he had to get home by swimming across a river in which there was a large and hungry pike. El-ahrairah combed himself until he had enough fur to cover a clay rabbit, which he pushed into the water. The pike rushed at it, bit it and left it in disgust. After a little, it drifted to the bank and El-ahrairah dragged it out and waited a while before pushing it in again. After an hour of this, the pike left it alone and when it had done so for the fifth time, El-ahrairah swam across himself and went home. Some rabbits say he controls the weather, because the wind, the damp and the dew are friends and instruments to rabbits against their enemies.

'Hazel, we'll have to stop here,' said Bigwig, coming up between the panting, crouching bodies of the others. 'I know it's not a good place, but Fiver and this other half-sized fellow you've got here – they're pretty well all in. They won't be able to go on if we don't rest.'

The truth was that every one of them was tired. Many rabbits spend all their lives in the same place and never run more than a hundred yards at a stretch. Even though they may live and sleep above ground for months at a time, they prefer not to be out of distance of some sort of refuge that will serve for a hole. They have two natural gaits – the gentle, lolloping, forward movement of the warren on a summer evening and the lightning dash for cover that every human has seen at some time or other. It is difficult to imagine a rabbit plodding steadily on: they are not built for it. It is true that young rabbits are great migrants and capable of journeying for miles, but they do not take to it readily.

Hazel and his companions had spent the night doing everything that came unnaturally to them, and this for the first time. They had been moving in a group, or trying to: actually, they had straggled widely at times. They had been trying to maintain a steady pace, between hopping and running, and it had come hard. Since entering the wood they had been in severe anxiety. Several were almost *tharn* – that is, in that state of staring, glazed paralysis that comes over terrified or exhausted rabbits, so that they sit and watch their enemies – weasels or humans – approach to take their lives. Pipkin sat trembling under a fern, his ears drooping on either side of his head. He held one paw forward in an awkward, unnatural way and kept licking it miserably. Fiver was little better off. He still looked cheerful, but very weary. Hazel realized that until they were rested they would all be safer where they were than stumbling along in the open, with no strength left to run from an enemy. But if they lay brooding, unable to feed or go underground, all their troubles would come crowding into their hearts, their fears would mount and they might very likely scatter, or even try to return to the warren. He had an idea.

'Yes, all right, we'll rest here,' he said. 'Let's go in among this fern. Come on, Dandelion, tell us a story. I know you're handy that way. Pipkin here can't wait to hear it.'

Dandelion looked at Pipkin and realized what it was that Hazel was asking him to do. Choking back his own fear of the desolate, grassless woodland, the before-dawn-returning owls that they could hear some way off and the extraordinary, rank animal smell that seemed to come from somewhere rather nearer, he began.

6. The Story of the Blessing of El-Ahrairah

> Why should he think me cruel
> Or that he is betrayed?
> I'd have him love the thing that was
> Before the world was made.
>
> W. B. Yeats, *A Woman Young and Old*

'LONG ago, Frith made the world. He made all the stars too and the world is one of the stars. He made them by scattering his droppings over the sky and this is why the grass and the trees grow so thick on the world. Frith makes the brooks flow. They follow him as he goes through the sky and when he leaves the sky they look for him all night. Frith made all the animals and birds, but when he first made them they were all the same. The sparrow and the kestrel were friends and they both ate seeds and flies. And the fox and the rabbit were friends and they both ate grass. And there was plenty of grass and plenty of flies, because the world was new and Frith shone down bright and warm all day.

'Now El-ahrairah was among the animals in those days and he had many wives. He had so many wives that there was no counting them and the wives had so many young that even Frith could not count them and they ate the grass and the dandelions and the lettuces and the clover and El-ahrairah was the father of them all.' (Bigwig growled appreciatively.) 'And after a time,' went on Dandelion, 'after a time the grass began to grow thin and the rabbits wandered everywhere, multiplying and eating as they went.

'Then Frith said to El-ahrairah, "Prince Rabbit, if you cannot control your people, I shall find ways to control them. So mark what I say." But El-ahrairah would not listen and he said to Frith, "My people are the strongest in the world, for they breed faster and eat more than any of the other people. And this shows how much they love Lord Frith, for of all the animals they are the most responsive to his warmth and brightness. You must realize, my lord, how important they are and not hinder them in their beautiful lives."

'Frith could have killed El-ahrairah at once, but he had a mind to keep him in the world, because he needed him to sport and jest and play tricks. So he determined to get the better of him not by means of his own great power but by means of a trick. He gave out that he would hold a great meeting and that at that meeting he would give a present to every animal and bird, to make each one different from the rest. And all the creatures set out to go to the meeting-place. But they all arrived at different times, because Frith made sure that it would happen so. And when the blackbird came, he gave him his beautiful song, and when the cow came, he gave her sharp horns and the strength to be afraid of no other creature. And so in their turn came the fox and the stoat and the weasel. And to each of them Frith gave the cunning and the fierceness and the desire to hunt and slay and eat the children of El-ahrairah. And so they went away from Frith full of nothing but hunger to kill the rabbits.

'Now all this time, El-ahrairah was dancing and mating and boasting that he was going to Frith's meeting to receive a great gift. And at last he set out for the meeting-place. But as he was going there, he stopped to rest on a soft, sandy hillside. And while he was resting, over the hill came flying the dark Swift, screaming as he went, "News! News! News!" For you know, this is what he has said ever since that day. So El-ahrairah called up to him and said, "What news?" "Why," said the Swift, "I would not be you, El-ahrairah. For Frith has given the fox and the weasel cunning hearts and sharp teeth and to the cat he has given silent feet and eyes that can see in the dark and they are gone away from Frith's place to kill and devour all that belongs to El-ahrairah." And he dashed on over the hills. And at that moment El-ahrairah heard the voice of Frith calling, "Where is El-ahrairah? For all the others have taken their gifts and gone and I have come to look for him."

'Then El-ahrairah knew that Frith was too clever for him and he was frightened. He thought that the fox and the weasel were coming with Frith and he turned to the face of the hill and began to dig. He dug a hole, but he had dug only a little of it when Frith came over the hill alone. And he saw El-ahrairah's bottom sticking out of the hole and the sand flying out in showers as the digging went on. When he saw that, he called out, "My friend, have you seen El-ahrairah, for I am looking for him to give him my gift?" "No," answered El-ahrairah, without coming out, "I have not seen him. He is far away. He could not come." So Frith said, "Then come out of that hole and I will bless you instead of him." "No, I cannot," said El-ahrairah, "I am busy. The fox and the weasel are coming. If you want to bless me you can bless my bottom, for it is sticking out of the hole."

All the rabbits had heard the story before: on winter nights, when the cold draught moved down the warren passages and the icy wet lay in the pits of the runs below their burrows; and on summer evenings, in the grass under the red may and the sweet, carrion-scented elder bloom. Dandelion was telling it well and even Pipkin forgot his weariness and danger, and remembered instead the great indestructibility of the Rabbits. Each one of them saw himself as El-ahrairah, who could be impudent to Frith and get away with it.

'Then,' said Dandelion, 'Frith felt himself in friendship with El-ahrairah, because of his resourcefulness, and because he would not give up even when he thought the fox and the weasel were coming. And he said, "Very well, I will bless your bottom as it sticks out of the hole. Bottom, be strength and warning and speed for ever and save the life of your master. Be it so!" And as he spoke, El-ahrairah's tail grew shining white and flashed like a star: and his back legs grew long and powerful and he thumped the hillside until the very beetles fell off the grass-stems. He came out of the hole and tore across the hill faster than any creature in the world. And Frith called after him, "El-ahrairah, your people cannot rule the world, for I will not have it so. All the world will be your enemy, Prince with a Thousand Enemies, and whenever they catch you, they will kill you. But first they must catch you, digger, listener, runner, prince with the swift warning. Be cunning and full of tricks and your people shall never be destroyed." And El-ahrairah knew then that although he would not be mocked, yet Frith was his friend. And every evening, when Frith has done his day's work and lies calm and easy in the red sky, El-ahrairah and his children and his children's children come out of their holes and feed and play in his sight, for they are his friends and he has promised them that they can never be destroyed.'

7. The Lendri and the River

Quant au courage moral, il avait trouvé fort rare, disait-il,
celui de deux heures après minuit; c'est-à-dire le courage de
l'improviste.

Napoleon Bonaparte

AS DANDELION ended, Acorn, who was on the
windward side of the little group, suddenly started
and sat back, with ears up and nostrils twitching. The
strange, rank smell was stronger than ever and after a few
moments they all heard a heavy movement close by. Suddenly,
on the other side of the path, the fern parted and there looked
out a long, dog-like head, striped black and white. It was
pointed downwards, the jaws grinning, the muzzle close to
the ground. Behind, they could just discern great, powerful
paws and a shaggy, black body. The eyes were peering at
them, full of savage cunning. The head moved slowly, taking
in the dusky lengths of the wood-ride in both directions, and
then fixed them once more with its fierce, terrible stare. The
jaws opened wider and they could see the teeth, glimmering

white as the stripes along the head. For long moments it gazed and the rabbits remained motionless, staring back without a sound. Then Bigwig, who was nearest to the path, turned and slipped back among the others.

'A *lendri*,' he muttered as he passed through them. 'It may be dangerous and it may not, but I'm taking no chances with it. Let's get away.'

They followed him through the fern and very soon came upon another, parallel path. Bigwig turned into it and broke into a run. Dandelion overtook him and the two disappeared among the ilex trees. Hazel and the others followed as best they could, with Pipkin limping and staggering behind, his fear driving him on in spite of the pain in his paw.

Hazel came out on the farther side of the ilexes and followed the path round a bend. Then he stopped dead and sat back on his haunches. Immediately in front of him, Bigwig and Dandelion were staring out from the sheer edge of a high bank, and below the bank ran a stream. It was in fact the little river Enborne, twelve to fifteen feet wide and at this time of year two or three feet deep with spring rain, but to the rabbits it seemed immense, such a river as they had never imagined. The moon had almost set and the night was now dark, but they could see the water faintly shining as it flowed and could just make out, on the further side, a thin belt of nut-trees and alders. Somewhere beyond, a plover called three or four times and was silent.

One by one, most of the others came up, stopped at the bank and looked at the water without speaking. A chilly breeze was moving and several of them trembled where they sat.

'Well, this is a nice surprise, Hazel,' said Bigwig at length. 'Or were you expecting this when you took us into the wood?'

Hazel realized wearily that Bigwig was probably going to be troublesome. He was certainly no coward, but he was likely to remain steady only as long as he could see his way clear and be sure of what to do. To him, perplexity was worse than danger; and when he was perplexed he usually grew angry. The day before, Fiver's warning had troubled him, and he had spoken in anger to the Threarah and left the Owsla. Then, while he was in an uncertain mood about the idea of leaving the warren, Captain Holly had appeared in capital time to be attacked and to provide a perfect reason for their departure. Now, at the sight of the river, Bigwig's assurance was leaking again and unless he, Hazel, could restore it in some way, they were likely to be in for trouble. He thought of the Threarah and his wily courtesy.

'I don't know what we should have done without you just now, Bigwig,' he said. 'What was that animal? Would it have killed us?'

'A lendri,' said Bigwig. 'I've heard about them in the Owsla. They're not really dangerous. They can't catch a rabbit that runs, and nearly always you can smell them coming. They're funny things: I've heard of rabbits living almost on top of them and coming to no harm. But they're best avoided, all the same. They'll dig out rabbit kittens and they'll kill an injured rabbit if they find one. They're one of the Thousand, all right. I ought to have guessed from the smell, but it was new to me.'

'It had killed before it met us,' said Blackberry with a shudder. 'I saw the blood on its lips.'

'A rat, perhaps, or pheasant chicks. Lucky for us it *had* killed, otherwise it might have been quicker. Still, fortunately we did the right thing. We really came out of it very well,' said Bigwig.

Fiver came limping down the path with Pipkin. They, too, checked and stared at the sight of the river.

'What do you think we ought to do now, Fiver?' asked Hazel.

Fiver looked down at the water and twitched his ears.

'We shall have to cross it,' he said. 'But I don't think I can swim, Hazel. I'm worn out, and Pipkin's a good deal worse than I am.'

'Cross it?' cried Bigwig. 'Cross it? Who's going to cross it? What do you want to cross it for? I never heard such nonsense.'

Like all wild animals, rabbits can swim if they have to: and some even swim when it suits them. Rabbits have been known to live on the edge of a wood and regularly swim a brook to feed in the fields beyond. But most rabbits avoid swimming and certainly an exhausted rabbit could not swim the Enborne.

'I don't want to jump in there,' said Speedwell.

'Why not just go along the bank?' asked Hawkbit.

Hazel suspected that if Fiver felt they ought to cross the river, it might be dangerous not to. But how were the others to be persuaded? At this moment, as he was still wondering what to say to them, he suddenly realized that something had lightened his spirits. What could it be? A smell? A sound? Then he knew. Near-by, across the river, a lark had begun to twitter and climb. It was morning. A blackbird called one or two deep, slow notes and was followed by a wood-pigeon. Soon they were in grey twilight and could see that the stream bordered the farther edge of the wood. On the other side lay open fields.

8. The Crossing

The centurion ... commanded that they which could swim
should cast themselves first into the sea and get to land. And
the rest, some on boards and some on broken pieces of the
ship. And so it came to pass, that they escaped all safe to land.

The Acts of the Apostles, Chapter 27

THE TOP of the sandy bank was a good six feet above
the water. From where they sat, the rabbits could look
straight ahead upstream, and downstream to their left.
Evidently there were nesting holes in the sheer face below
them, for as the light grew they saw three or four martins
dart out over the stream and away into the fields beyond.
In a short time one returned with his beak full, and they
could hear the nestlings squeaking as he flew out of sight
beneath their feet. The bank did not extend far in either
direction. Upstream, it sloped down to a grassy path
between the trees and the water. This followed the line of
the river, which ran straight from almost as far away as
they could see, flowing smoothly without fords, gravel

shallows or plank bridges. Immediately below them lay a wide pool and here the water was almost still. Away to their left, the bank sloped down again into clumps of alder, among which the stream could be heard chattering over gravel. There was a glimpse of barbed wire stretched across the water and they guessed that this must surround a cattle-wade, like the one in the little brook near the home warren.

Hazel looked at the path upstream. 'There's grass down there,' he said. 'Let's go and feed.'

They scrambled down the bank and set to nibbling beside the water. Between them and the stream itself stood half-grown clumps of purple loosestrife and fleabane, which would not flower for nearly two months yet. The only blooms were a few early meadow-sweet and a patch of pink butter-bur. Looking back at the face of the bank, they could see that it was in fact dotted thickly with martins' holes. There was a narrow foreshore at the foot of the little cliff and this was littered with the rubbish of the colony – sticks, droppings, feathers, a broken egg and a dead nestling or two. The martins were now coming and going in numbers over the water.

Hazel moved close to Fiver and quietly edged him away from the others, feeding as he went. When they were a little way off, and half-concealed by a patch of reeds, he said, 'Are you sure we've got to cross the river, Fiver? What about going along the bank one way or the other?'

'No, we need to cross the river, Hazel, so that we can get into those fields – and on beyond them too. I know what we ought to be looking for – a high, lonely place with dry soil, where rabbits can see and hear all round and men hardly ever come. Wouldn't that be worth a journey?'

'Yes, of course it would. But is there such a place?'

'Not near a river – I needn't tell you that. But if you cross a river you start going up again, don't you? We ought to be on the top – on the top and in the open.'

'But, Fiver, I think they may refuse to go much further. And then again, you say all this and yet you say you're too tired to swim?'

'I can rest, Hazel, but Pipkin's in a pretty bad way. I think he's injured. We may have to stay here half the day.'

'Well, let's go and talk to the others. They may not mind staying. It's crossing they're not going to fancy, unless something frightens them into it.'

As soon as they had made their way back, Bigwig came across to them from the bushes at the edge of the path.

'I was wondering where you'd got to,' he said to Hazel. 'Are you ready to move on?'

'No, I'm not,' answered Hazel firmly. 'I think we ought to stay here until ni-Frith. That'll give everyone a chance to rest and then we can swim across to those fields.'

Bigwig was about to reply, but Blackberry spoke first.

'Bigwig,' he said, 'why don't you swim over now, and then go out into the field and have a look round? The wood may not stretch very far one way or the other. You could see from there; and then we might know which would be the best way to go.'

'Oh well,' said Bigwig rather grudgingly, 'I suppose there's some sense in that. I'll swim the *embleer** river as many times as you like. Always glad to oblige.'

---

* Stinking – the word for the smell of a fox.

Without the slightest hesitation, he took two hops to the water, waded in and swam across the deep, still pool. They watched him pull himself out beside a flowering clump of figwort, gripping one of the tough stems in his teeth, shake a shower of drops out of his fur and scutter into the alder bushes. A moment later, between the nut-trees, they saw him running off into the field.

'I'm glad he's with us,' said Hazel to Silver. Again he thought wryly of the Threarah. 'He's the fellow to find out all we need to know. Oh, I say, look, he's coming back already.'

Bigwig was racing back across the field, looking more agitated than he had at any time since the encounter with Captain Holly. He ran into the water almost headlong and paddled over fast, leaving an arrow-head ripple on the calm, brown surface. He was speaking as he jerked himself out on the sandy foreshore.

'Well, Hazel, if I were you I shouldn't wait until ni-Frith. I should go now. In fact, I think you'll have to.'

'Why?' asked Hazel.

'There's a large dog loose in the wood.'

Hazel started. 'What?' he said. 'How do you know?'

'When you get into the field you can see the wood sloping down to the river. Parts of it are open. I saw the dog crossing a clearing. It was trailing a chain, so it must have broken loose. It may be on the lendri's scent, but the lendri will be underground by now. What do you think will happen when it picks up our scent, running from one side of the wood to the other, with dew on it? Come on, let's get over quickly.'

Hazel felt at a loss. In front of him stood Bigwig, sodden wet, undaunted, single-minded – the very picture of decision. At his shoulder was Fiver, silent and twitching. He saw Blackberry watching him intently, waiting for his lead and disregarding Bigwig's. Then he looked at Pipkin, huddled into a fold of sand, more panic-stricken and helpless than any rabbit he had ever seen. At this moment, up in the wood, there broke out an excited yelping and a jay began to scold.

Hazel spoke through a kind of light-headed trance. 'Well, you'd better get on, then,' he said, 'and anyone else who wants to. Personally, I'm going to wait until Fiver and Pipkin are fit to tackle it.'

'You silly blockhead!' cried Bigwig.' We'll all be finished! We'll –'

'Don't stamp about,' said Hazel. 'You may be heard. What do you suggest then?'

'Suggest? There's no suggesting to be done. Those who can swim, swim. The others will have to stay here and hope for the best. The dog may not come.'

'I'm afraid that won't do for me. I got Pipkin into this and I'm going to get him out.'

'Well, you didn't get Fiver into it, did you? He got you into it.'

Hazel could not help noticing, with reluctant admiration, that although Bigwig had lost his temper, he was apparently in no hurry on his own account and seemed less frightened than any of them. Looking round for Blackberry, he saw that he had left them and was up at the top of the pool, where the narrow beach tailed away into a gravel spit. His paws were half-buried in the wet gravel and he was nosing at something large and flat on the water-line. It looked like a piece of wood.

'Blackberry,' he said, 'can you come back here a moment?'

Blackberry looked up, tugged out his paws and ran back.

'Hazel,' he said quickly, 'that's a piece of flat wood – like that piece that closed the gap by the Green Loose above the warren – you remember? It must have drifted down the river. So it floats. We could put Fiver and Pipkin on it and make it float again. It might go across the river. Can you understand?'

Hazel had no idea what he meant. Blackberry's flood of apparent nonsense only seemed to draw tighter the mesh of danger and bewilderment. As though Bigwig's angry impatience, Pipkin's terror and the approaching dog were not enough to contend with, the cleverest rabbit among them had evidently gone out of his mind. He felt close to despair.

'Frithrah, yes, I see!' said an excited voice at his ear. It was Fiver. 'Quick, Hazel, don't wait! Come on, and bring Pipkin!'

It was Blackberry who bullied the stupefied Pipkin to his feet and forced him to limp the few yards to the gravel spit. The piece of wood, hardly bigger than a large rhubarb leaf, was lightly aground. Blackberry almost drove Pipkin on to it with his claws. Pipkin crouched shivering and Fiver followed him aboard.

'Who's strong?' said Blackberry. 'Bigwig! Silver! Push it out!'

No one obeyed him. All squatted, puzzled and uncertain. Blackberry buried his nose in the gravel under the landward edge of the board and raised it, pushing. The board tipped. Pipkin squealed and Fiver lowered his head and splayed his claws. Then the board righted itself and drifted out a few feet into the pool with the two rabbits hunched upon it, rigid and motionless. It rotated slowly and they found themselves staring back at their comrades.

'Frith and Inlé!' said Dandelion. 'They're sitting on the water! Why don't they sink?'

'They're sitting on the wood and the wood floats, can't you see?' said Blackberry. 'Now we swim over ourselves. Can we start, Hazel?'

During the last few minutes Hazel had been as near to losing his head as he was ever to come. He had been at his wits' end, with no reply to Bigwig's scornful impatience except his readiness to risk his own life in company with Fiver and Pipkin. He still could not understand what had happened, but at least he realized that Blackberry wanted him to show authority. His head cleared.

'Swim,' he said. 'Everybody swim.'

He watched them as they went in. Dandelion swam as well as he ran, swiftly and easily. Silver, too, was strong. The others paddled and scrambled over somehow and as they began to reach the other side, Hazel plunged. The cold water penetrated his fur almost at once. His breath came short and as his head went under he could hear a faint grating of gravel along the bottom. He paddled across awkwardly, his head tilted high out of the water, and made for the figwort. As he pulled himself out, he looked round among the sopping rabbits in the alders.

'Where's Bigwig?' he asked.

'Behind you,' answered Blackberry, his teeth chattering.

Bigwig was still in the water, on the other side of the pool. He had swum to the raft, put his head against it and was pushing it forward with heavy thrusts of his back legs. 'Keep still,' Hazel heard him say in a quick, gulping voice. Then he sank. But a moment later he was up again and had thrust his head over the back of the board. As he kicked and struggled, it tilted and then, while the rabbits watched from the bank, moved slowly across the pool and grounded on the opposite side. Fiver pushed Pipkin on to the stones and Bigwig waded out beside them, shivering and breathless.

'I got the idea once Blackberry had shown us,' he said. 'But it's hard to push it when you're in the water. I hope it's not long to sunrise. I'm cold. Let's get on.'

There was no sign of the dog as they made haste through the alders and up the field to the first hedgerow. Most of them had not understood Blackberry's discovery of the raft and at once forgot it. Fiver, however, came over to where Blackberry was lying against the stem of a blackthorn in the hedge.

'You saved Pipkin and me, didn't you?' he said. 'I don't think Pipkin's got any idea what really happened; but I have.'

'I admit it was a good idea,' replied Blackberry. 'Let's remember it. It might come in handy again some time.'

9. The Crow and the Beanfield

With the beanflower's boon,
And the blackbird's tune,
And May, and June!

Robert Browning, *De Gustibus*

THE SUN rose while they were still lying in the thorn. Already several of the rabbits were asleep, crouched uneasily between the thick stems, aware of the chance of danger but too tired to do more than trust to luck. Hazel, looking at them, felt almost as insecure as he had on the river bank. A hedgerow in open fields was no place to remain all day. But where could they go? He needed to know more about their surroundings. He moved along the hedge, feeling the breeze from the south and looking for some spot where he could sit and scent it without too much risk. The smells that came down from the higher ground might tell him something.

He came to a wide gap which had been trodden into mud by cattle. He could see them grazing in the next field, further up the slope. He went cautiously out into the field, squatted down against a clump of thistles and began to smell the wind. Now that he was clear of the hawthorn scent of the hedge and the reek of cattle dung, he became fully aware of what had already been drifting into his nostrils while he was lying among the thorn. There was only one smell on the wind and it was new to him: a strong, fresh, sweet fragrance that filled the air. It was healthy enough. There was no harm in it. But what was it and why was it so strong? How could it exclude every other smell, in open country on a south wind? The source must be close by. Hazel wondered whether to send one of the rabbits to find out. Dandelion would be over the top and back almost as fast as a hare. Then his sense of adventure and mischief prompted him. He would go himself and bring back some news before they even knew that he had gone. That would give Bigwig something to bite on.

He ran easily up the meadow towards the cows. As he came they raised their heads and gazed at him, all together, for a moment, before returning to their feeding. A great, black bird was flapping and hopping a little way behind the herd. It looked rather like a large rook but, unlike a rook, it was alone. He watched its greenish, powerful beak stabbing the ground but could not make out what it was doing. It so happened that Hazel had never seen a crow. It did not occur to him that it was following the track of a mole, in the hope of killing it with a blow of its beak and then pulling it out of its shallow run. If he had realized this, he might not have classed it light-heartedly as a 'Not-hawk' – that is, anything from a wren to a pheasant – and continued on his way up the slope.

The strange fragrance was stronger now, coming over the top of the rise in a wave of scent that struck him powerfully – as the scent of orange-blossom in the Mediterranean strikes a traveller who smells it for the first time. Fascinated, he ran to the crest. Near-by was another hedgerow and beyond, moving gently in the breeze, stood a field of broad beans in full flower.

Hazel squatted on his haunches and stared at the orderly forest of small, glaucous trees with their columns of black-and-white bloom. He had never seen anything like this. Wheat and barley he knew, and once he had been in a field of turnips. But this was entirely different from any of those and seemed, somehow, attractive, wholesome, propitious. True, rabbits could not eat these plants: he could smell that. But they could lie safely among them for as long as they liked, and they could move through them easily and unseen. Hazel determined then and there to bring the rabbits up to the beanfield to shelter and rest until the evening. He ran back and found the others where he had left them. Bigwig and Silver were awake, but all the rest were still napping uneasily.

'Not asleep, Silver?' he said.

'It's too dangerous, Hazel,' replied Silver. 'I'd like to sleep as much as anyone, but if we all sleep and something comes, who's going to spot it?'

'I know. I've found a place where we can sleep safely for as long as we like.'

'A burrow?'

'No, not a burrow. A great field of scented plants that will cover us, sight and smell, until we're rested. Come out here and smell it, if you like.'

Both rabbits did so. 'You say you've seen these plants?' said Bigwig, turning his ears to catch the distant rustling of the beans.

'Yes, they're only just over the top. Come on, let's get the others moving before a man comes with a *hrududu** or they'll scatter all over the place.'

Silver roused the others and began to coax them into the field. They stumbled out drowsily, responding with reluctance to his repeated assurance that it was 'only a little way'.

They became widely separated as they struggled up the slope. Silver and Bigwig led the way, with Hazel and Buckthorn a short distance behind. The rest idled along, hopping a few yards and then pausing to nibble or to pass droppings on the warm, sunny grass. Silver was almost at the crest when suddenly, from half-way up, there came a high screaming – the sound a rabbit makes, not to call for help or to frighten an enemy, but simply out of terror. Fiver and Pipkin, limping behind the others, and conspicuously undersized and tired, were being attacked by the crow. It had flown low along the ground. Then, pouncing, it had aimed a blow of its great bill at Fiver, who just managed to dodge in time. Now it was leaping and hopping among the grass tussocks, striking at the two rabbits with terrible darts of its head. Crows aim at the eyes and Pipkin, sensing this, had buried his head in a clump of rank grass and was trying to burrow farther in. It was he who was screaming.

Hazel covered the distance down the slope in a few seconds. He had no idea what he was going to do and if the

---

* Tractor – or any motor.

crow had ignored him he would probably have been at a loss. But by dashing up he distracted its attention and it turned on him. He swerved past it, stopped and, looking back, saw Bigwig come racing in from the opposite side. The crow turned again, struck at Bigwig and missed. Hazel heard its beak hit a pebble in the grass with a sound like a snail-shell when a thrush beats it on a stone. As Silver followed Bigwig, it recovered itself and faced him squarely. Silver stopped short in fear and the crow seemed to dance before him, its great, black wings flapping in a horrible commotion. It was just about to stab when Bigwig ran straight into it from behind and knocked it sideways, so that it staggered across the turf with a harsh, raucous cawing of rage.

'Keep at it!' cried Bigwig. 'Come in behind it! They're cowards! They only attack helpless rabbits.'

But already the crow was making off, flying low with slow, heavy wing-beats. They watched it clear the farther hedge and disappear into the wood beyond the river. In the silence there was a gentle, tearing sound as a grazing cow moved nearer.

Bigwig strolled over to Pipkin, muttering a ribald Owsla lampoon.

> *'Hoi, hoi u embleer Hrair,*
> *M' saion ulé hraka vair.**

'Come on, Hlao-roo,' he said. 'You can get your head out now. Having quite a day, aren't we?'

---

* 'Hoi, Hoi, the stinking Thousand, We meet them even when we stop to pass our droppings.'

He turned away and Pipkin tried to follow him. Hazel remembered that Fiver had said he thought he was injured. Now, as he watched him limping and staggering up the slope, it occurred to him that he might actually be wounded in some way. He kept trying to put his near-side front paw to the ground and then drawing it up again, hopping on three legs.

'I'll have a look at him as soon as they're settled under cover,' he thought. 'Poor little chap, he won't be able to get much further like that.'

At the top of the slope Buckthorn was already leading the way into the beanfield. Hazel reached the hedge, crossed a narrow turf verge on the other side and found himself looking straight down a long, shadowy aisle between two rows of beans. The earth was soft and crumbling, with a scattering of the weeds that are found in cultivated fields – fumitory, charlock, pimpernel and mayweed, all growing in the green gloom under the bean leaves. As the plants moved in the breeze, the sunlight dappled and speckled back and forth over the brown soil, the white pebbles and weeds. Yet in this ubiquitous restlessness there was nothing alarming, for the whole forest took part in it and the only sound was the soft, steady movement of the leaves. Far along the bean-row, Hazel glimpsed Buckthorn's back and followed him into the depths of the field.

Soon after, all the rabbits had come together in a kind of hollow. Far around, on all sides, stood the orderly rows of beans, securing them against hostile approach, roofing them over and covering their scent. They could hardly have been safer underground. Even a little food could be had at a pinch, for here and there were a few pale twists of grass and here and there a dandelion.

'We can sleep here all day,' said Hazel. 'But I suppose one of us ought to stay awake; and if I take the first turn it'll give me a chance to have a look at your paw, Hlao-roo. I think you've got something in it.'

Pipkin, who was lying on his left side, breathing quickly and heavily, rolled over and stretched out his front paw, underside turned upwards. Hazel peered closely into the thick, coarse hair (a rabbit's foot has no pads) and after a few moments saw what he had expected – the oval shank of a snapped-off thorn sticking out through the skin. There was a little blood and the flesh was torn.

'You've got a big thorn in there, Hlao,' he said. 'No wonder you couldn't run. We'll have to get it out.'

Getting the thorn out was not easy, for the foot had become so tender that Pipkin winced and pulled away even from Hazel's tongue. But after a good deal of patient effort Hazel succeeded in working out enough of the stump to get a grip with his teeth. The thorn came out smoothly and the wound bled. The spine was so long and thick that Hawkbit, who happened to be close by, woke Speedwell to have a look at it.

'Frith above, Pipkin!' said Speedwell, sniffing at the thorn where it lay on a pebble. 'You'd better collect a few more like that: then you can make a notice board and frighten Fiver. You might have poked the lendri's eye out for us, if you'd only known.'

'Lick the place, Hlao,' said Hazel. 'Lick it until it feels better and then go to sleep.'

10. The Road and the Common

Timorous answered, that they ... had got up that difficult place: but, said he, the further we go, the more danger we meet with; wherefore we turned, and are going back again.

John Bunyan, *The Pilgrim's Progress*

AFTER some time, Hazel woke Buckthorn. Then he scratched a shallow nest in the earth and slept. One watch succeeded another through the day, though how the rabbits judged the passing of the time is something that civilized human beings have lost the power to feel. Creatures that have neither clocks nor books are alive to all manner of knowledge about time and the weather; and about direction too, as we know from their extraordinary migratory and homing journeys. The changes in the warmth and dampness of the soil, the falling of the sunlight patches, the altering movement of the beans in the light wind, the direction and strength of the air currents along the ground – all these were perceived by the rabbit awake.

The sun was beginning to set when Hazel woke to see Acorn listening and sniffing in the silence, between two white-skinned flints. The light was thicker, the breeze had dropped and the beans were still. Pipkin was stretched out a little way away. A yellow-and-black burying beetle, crawling across the white fur of his belly, stopped, waved its short, curved antennae and then moved on again. Hazel grew tense with sudden misgiving. He knew that these beetles come to dead bodies, on which they feed and lay their eggs. They will dig away the earth from under the bodies of small creatures, such as shrew-mice and fallen fledglings, and then lay their eggs on them before covering them with soil. Surely Pipkin could not have died in his sleep? Hazel sat up quickly. Acorn started and turned towards him and the beetle scurried away over the pebbles as Pipkin moved and woke.

'How's the paw?' said Hazel. Pipkin put it to the ground. Then he stood on it.

'It feels much better,' he said. 'I think I shall be able to go as well as the others now. They won't leave me behind, will they?'

Hazel rubbed his nose behind Pipkin's ear. 'No one's going to leave anyone else behind,' he said. 'If you had to stay, I'd stay with you. But don't pick up any more thorns, Hlao-roo, because we may have to go a long way.'

The next moment all the rabbits leapt up in panic. From close at hand the sound of a shot tore across the fields. A peewit rose screaming. The echoes came back in waves, like a pebble rolling round a box, and from the wood across the river came the clattering of wood-pigeons' wings among the branches. In an instant the rabbits were running in all directions through the bean-rows, each one tearing by instinct towards holes that were not there.

Hazel stopped short on the edge of the beans. Looking about him, he could see none of the others. He waited, trembling, for the next shot: but there was silence. Then he felt, vibrating along the ground, the steady tread of a man going away beyond the crest over which they had come that morning. At that moment Silver appeared, pushing his way through the plants close by.

'I hope it's the crow, don't you?' said Silver.

'I hope no one's been silly enough to bolt out of this field,' answered Hazel. 'They're all scattered. How can we find them?'

'I don't think we can,' said Silver. 'We'd better go back to where we were. They'll come in time.'

It was in fact a long time before all the rabbits had come back to the hollow in the middle of the field. As he waited, Hazel realized more fully than ever how dangerous was their position, without holes, wandering in country they did not know. The lendri, the dog, the crow, the marksman – they had been lucky to escape them. How long would their luck hold? Would they really be able to travel on as far as Fiver's high place – wherever it might be?

'I'd settle for any decent, dry bank, myself,' he thought, 'as long as there was some grass and no men with guns. And the sooner we can find one the better.'

Hawkbit was the last to return and as he came up Hazel set off at once. He looked cautiously out from among the beans and then darted into the hedgerow. The wind, as he stopped to sniff it, was reassuring, carrying only the scents of evening dew, may and cow-dung. He led the way into the next field, a pasture: and here they all fell to feeding, nibbling their way over the grass as easily as though their warren were close by.

When he was half-way across the field, Hazel became aware of a hrududu approaching very fast on the other side of the further hedge. It was small and less noisy than the farm tractor which he had sometimes watched from the edge of the primrose wood at home. It passed in a flash of man-made, unnatural colour, glittering here and there and brighter than a winter holly tree. A few moments later came the smell of petrol and exhaust. Hazel stared, twitching his nose. He could not understand how the hrududu could move so quickly and smoothly through the fields. Would it return? Would it come through the fields faster than they could run, and hunt them down?

As he paused, wondering what was best to be done, Bigwig came up.

'There's a road there, then,' he said. 'That'll give some of them a surprise, won't it?'

'A road?' said Hazel, thinking of the lane by the notice board. 'How do you know?'

'Well, how do you suppose a hrududu can go that fast? Besides, can't you smell it?'

The smell of warm tar was now plain on the evening air.

'I've never smelt that in my life,' said Hazel with a touch of irritation.

'Ah,' said Bigwig, 'but then you were never sent out stealing lettuces for the Threarah, were you? If you had been, you'd have learned about roads. There's nothing to them, really, as long as you let them alone by night. They're elil then, all right.'

'You'd better teach me, I think,' said Hazel. 'I'll go up with you and we'll let the others follow.'

They ran on and crept through the hedge. Hazel looked down at the road in astonishment. For a moment he thought that he was looking at another river – black, smooth and straight between its banks. Then he saw the gravel embedded in the tar and watched a spider running over the surface.

'But that's not natural,' he said, sniffing the strange, strong smells of tar and oil. 'What is it? How did it come there?'

'It's a man-thing,' said Bigwig. 'They put that stuff there and then the hrududil run on it – faster than we can; and what else can run faster than we?'

'It's dangerous then? They can catch us?'

'No, that's what's so odd. They don't take any notice of us at all. I'll show you, if you like.'

The other rabbits were beginning to reach the hedge as Bigwig hopped down the bank and crouched on the verge of the road. From beyond the bend came the sound of another approaching car. Hazel and Silver watched tensely. The car appeared, flashing green and white, and raced down towards Bigwig. For an instant it filled the whole world with noise and fear. Then it was gone; and Bigwig's fur was blowing in the whack of wind that followed it down the hedges. He jumped back up the bank among the staring rabbits.

'See? They don't hurt you,' said Bigwig. 'As a matter of fact, I don't think they're alive at all. But I must admit I can't altogether make it out.'

As on the river bank, Blackberry had moved away and was already down on the road on his own account, sniffing out towards the middle, half-way between Hazel and the bend. They saw him start and jump back to the shelter of the bank.

'What is it?' said Hazel.

Blackberry did not answer and Hazel and Bigwig hopped towards him along the verge. He was opening and shutting his mouth and licking his lips, much as a cat does when something disgusts it.

'You say they're not dangerous, Bigwig,' he said quietly. 'But I think they must be, for all that.'

In the middle of the road was a flattened, bloody mass of brown prickles and white fur, with small, black feet and snout crushed round the edges. The flies crawled upon it and here and there the sharp points of gravel pressed up through the flesh.

'*A yona*,' said Blackberry. 'What harm does a yona do to anything but slugs and beetles? And what can eat a yona?'

'It must have come at night,' said Bigwig.

'Yes, of course. The yonil always hunt by night. If you see them by day they're dying.'

'I know. But what I'm trying to explain is that at night the hrududil have great lights, brighter than Frith himself. They draw creatures towards them and if they shine on you, you can't see or think which way to go. Then the hrududu is quite likely to crush you. At least, that's what we were taught in the Owsla. I don't intend to try it.'

'Well, it *will* be dark soon,' said Hazel. 'Come on, let's get across. As far as I can see, this road's no good to us at all. Now that I've learnt about it, I want to get away from it as soon as I can.'

By moonrise they had made their way through Newtown churchyard, where a little brook runs between the lawns and under the path. Wandering on, they climbed a hill and came to Newtown Common – a country of peat, gorse and silver birch. After the meadows they had left, this was a strange, forbidding land. Trees, herbage, even the soil – all were unfamiliar. They hesitated among the thick heather, unable to see more than a few feet ahead. Their fur became soaked with the dew. The ground was broken by rifts and pits of naked, black peat, where water lay and sharp, white stones, some as big as a pigeon's, some as a rabbit's skull, glimmered in the moonlight. Whenever they reached one of these rifts the rabbits huddled together, waiting for Hazel or Bigwig to climb the further side and find a way forward. Everywhere they came upon beetles, spiders and small lizards which scurried away as they pushed through the fibrous, resistant heather. Once Buckthorn disturbed a snake, and leapt into the air as it whipped between his paws to vanish down a hole at the foot of a birch.

The very plants were unknown to them – pink lousewort with its sprays of hooked flowers, bog asphodel and the thin-stemmed blooms of the sun-dews, rising above their hairy, fly-catching mouths, all shut fast by night. In this close jungle all was silence. They went more and more slowly, and made long halts in the peat-cuts. But if the heather itself was silent, the breeze brought distant night-sounds across the open common. A cock crowed. A dog ran barking and a man shouted at it. A little owl called

'Kee-wik, kee-wik' and something – a vole or a shrew – gave a sudden squeal. There was not a noise but seemed to tell of danger.

Late in the night, towards moonset, Hazel was looking up from a cut where they were crouching to a little bank above. As he was wondering whether to climb up to it, to see whether he could get a clear view ahead, he heard a movement behind him and turned to find Hawkbit at his shoulder. There was something furtive and hesitant about him and Hazel glanced at him sharply, wondering for a moment whether he could have sickness or poison on him.

'Er – Hazel,' said Hawkbit, looking past him into the face of the dreary, black cliff. 'I – er – that is to say we – er – feel that we – well, that we can't go on like this. We've had enough of it.'

He stopped. Hazel now saw that Speedwell and Acorn were behind him, listening expectantly. There was a pause.

'Go on, Hawkbit,' said Speedwell. 'Or shall I?'

'More than enough,' said Hawkbit, with a kind of foolish importance.

'Well, so have I,' answered Hazel, 'and I hope there won't be much more. Then we can all have a rest.'

'We want to stop now,' said Speedwell. 'We think it was stupid to come so far.'

'It gets worse and worse the further we go,' said Acorn. 'Where are we going and how long will it be before some of us stop running for good and all?'

'It's the place that worries you,' said Hazel. 'I don't like it myself, but it won't go on for ever.'

Hawkbit looked sly and shifty. 'We don't believe you know where we *are* going,' he said. 'You didn't know about the road, did you? And you don't know what there is in front of us.'

'Look here,' said Hazel, 'suppose you tell me what you want to do and I'll tell you what I think about it.'

'We want to go back,' said Acorn. 'We think Fiver was wrong.'

'How can you go back through all we've come through?' replied Hazel. 'And probably get killed for wounding an Owsla officer, if you ever do get back? Talk sense, for Frith's sake.'

'It wasn't we who wounded Holly,' said Speedwell.

'You were there and Blackberry brought you there. Do you think they won't remember that? Besides –'

Hazel stopped as Fiver approached, followed by Bigwig.

'Hazel,' said Fiver, 'could you come up on the bank with me for a few moments? It's important.'

'And while you're there,' said Bigwig, scowling round at the others from under the great sheaf of fur on his head, 'I'll just have a few words with these three. Why don't you get washed, Hawkbit? You look like the end of a rat's tail left in a trap. And as for you, Speedwell –'

Hazel did not wait to hear what Speedwell looked like. Following Fiver, he scrambled up the lumps and shelves of peat to the overhang of gravelly earth and thin grass that topped them. As soon as Fiver had found a place to clamber out, he led the way along the edge to the bank which Hazel had been looking at before Hawkbit spoke to him. It stood a few feet above the nodding, windy heather and was open and grassy at the top. They climbed it and squatted down. To their right the moon, smoky and yellow in thin night cloud, stood over a clump of distant pine trees. They looked southward across the dismal waste. Hazel waited for Fiver to speak, but he remained silent.

'What was it you wanted to say to me?' asked Hazel at last.

Fiver made no reply and Hazel paused in perplexity. From below, Bigwig was just audible.

'And you, Acorn, you dog-eared, dung-faced disgrace to a gamekeeper's gibbet; if I only had time to tell you –'

The moon sailed free of the cloud and lit the heather more brightly, but neither Hazel nor Fiver moved from the top of the bank. Fiver was looking far out beyond the edge of the common. Four miles away, along the southern skyline, rose the seven hundred and fifty-foot ridge of the downs. On the highest point, the beech trees of Cottington's Clump were moving in a stronger wind than that which blew across the heather.

'Look!' said Fiver suddenly. 'That's the place for us, Hazel. High, lonely hills, where the wind and the sound carry and the ground's as dry as straw in a barn. That's where we ought to be. That's where we have to get to.'

Hazel looked at the dim, far-off hills. Obviously, the idea of trying to reach them was out of the question. It might well prove to be all they could do to find their way across the heather to some quiet field or copse-bank like those they had been used to. It was lucky that Fiver had not come out with this foolish notion in front of any of the others, especially as there was trouble enough already. If only he could be persuaded to drop it here and now, there would be no harm done – unless indeed he had already said anything to Pipkin.

'No, I think that's altogether too far, Fiver,' he said. 'Think of the miles of danger. Everyone's frightened and tired as it is. What we need is to find a safe place soon, and I'd rather succeed in doing what we can than fail to do what we can't.'

Fiver gave no sign of having heard him. He seemed to be lost in his own thoughts. When he spoke again, it was as though he were talking to himself. 'There's a thick mist between the hills and us. I can't see through it, but through it we shall have to go. Or into it, anyway.'

'A mist?' said Hazel. 'What do you mean?'

'We're in for some mysterious trouble,' whispered Fiver, 'and it's not elil. It feels more like – like mist. Like being deceived and losing our way.'

There was no mist around them. The May night was clear and fresh. Hazel waited in silence and after a time Fiver said, slowly and expressionlessly, 'But we must go on, until we reach the hills.' His voice sank and became that of a sleep-talker. 'Until we reach the hills. The rabbit that goes back through the gap will run his head into trouble. That running – not wise. That running – not safe. Running – not –' He trembled violently, kicked once or twice and became quiet.

In the hollow below, Bigwig seemed to be drawing to a close. 'And now, you bunch of mole-snouted, muck-raking, hutch-hearted sheep-ticks, get out of my sight sharp. Otherwise I'll –' He became inaudible again.

Hazel looked once more at the faint line of the hills. Then, as Fiver stirred and muttered beside him, he pushed him gently with one fore-paw and nuzzled his shoulder.

Fiver started. 'What was I saying, Hazel?' he asked. 'I'm afraid I can't remember. I meant to tell you –'

'Never mind,' answered Hazel. 'We'll go down now. It's time we were getting them on again. If you have any more queer feelings like that, keep close to me. I'll look after you.'

11. Hard Going

Then Sir Beaumains ... rode all that ever he might ride
through marshes and fields and great dales, that many
times ... he plunged over the head in deep mires, for he
knew not the way, but took the gainest way in that
woodness ... And at the last him happened to come to a fair
green way.

Malory, *Le Morte d'Arthur*

WHEN Hazel and Fiver reached the floor of the hollow
they found Blackberry waiting for them, crouching on
the peat and nibbling at a few brown stalks of sedge-grass.

'Hullo,' said Hazel. 'What's happened? Where are the
others?'

'Over there,' answered Blackberry. 'There's been a fearful
row. Bigwig told Hawkbit and Speedwell that he'd scratch
them to pieces if they didn't obey him. And when Hawkbit
said he wanted to know who was Chief Rabbit, Bigwig
bit him. It seems a nasty business. Who *is* Chief Rabbit,
anyway – you or Bigwig?'

'I don't know,' answered Hazel, 'but Bigwig's certainly the strongest. There was no need to go biting Hawkbit: he couldn't have gone back if he'd tried. He and his friends would have seen that if they'd been allowed to talk for a bit. Now Bigwig's put their backs up, and they'll think they've got to go on because he makes them. I want them to go on because they can see it's the only thing to do. There are too few of us for giving orders and biting people. Frith in a fog! Isn't there enough trouble and danger already?'

They went over to the far end of the pit. Bigwig and Silver were talking with Buckthorn under an overhanging broom. Near-by, Pipkin and Dandelion were pretending to feed on a patch of scrub. Some way away, Acorn was making a great business of licking Hawkbit's throat, while Speedwell watched.

'Keep still if you can, poor old chap,' said Acorn, who obviously wanted to be overheard. 'Just let me clean the blood out. Steady, now!' Hawkbit winced in an exaggerated manner and backed away. As Hazel came up, all the rabbits turned and stared at him expectantly.

'Look,' said Hazel, 'I know there's been some trouble, but the best thing will be to try to forget it. This is a bad place, but we'll soon get out of it.'

'Do you really think we will?' asked Dandelion.

'If you'll follow me now,' replied Hazel desperately, 'I'll have you out of it by sunrise.'

'If I don't,' he thought, 'they'll very likely tear me to bits: and much good may it do them.'

For the second time he made his way out of the pit, and the others followed. The weary, frightening journey began again, broken only by alarms. Once a white owl swept silently overhead, so low that Hazel saw its dark eyes looking into his own. But either it was not hunting or he was too big to tackle, for it disappeared over the heather; and although he waited motionless for some time, it did not return. Once Dandelion struck the smell of a stoat and they all joined him, whispering and sniffing over the ground. But the scent was old and after a time they went on again. In this low undergrowth their disorganized progress and uneven, differing rhythms of movement delayed them still more than in the wood. There were continual stampings of alarm, pausing, freezing to the spot at the sound of movement real or imagined. It was so dark that Hazel seldom knew for certain whether he was leading or whether Bigwig or Silver might not be ahead. Once, hearing an unaccountable noise in front of him, which ceased on the instant, he kept still for a long time; and when at last he moved cautiously forward, found Silver crouching behind a tussock of cock's-foot for fear of the sound of his own approach. All was confusion, ignorance, clambering and exhaustion. Throughout the bad dream of the night's journey, Pipkin seemed to be always close beside him. Though each of the others vanished and reappeared like fragments floating round a pool, Pipkin never left him; and his need for encouragement became at last Hazel's only support against his own weariness.

'Not far now, Hlao-roo, not far now,' he kept muttering, until he realized that what he said had become meaningless, a mere refrain. He was not speaking to Pipkin or even to himself. He was talking in his sleep, or something very near it.

At last he saw the first of the dawn, like light faintly perceived round a corner at the far end of an unknown burrow; and in the same moment a yellow-hammer sang. Hazel's feelings were like those which might pass through the mind of a defeated general. Where were his followers exactly? He hoped, not far away. But were they? All of them? Where had he led them? What was he going to do now? What if an enemy appeared at this moment? He had answers to none of these questions and no spirit left to force himself to think about them. Behind him, Pipkin shivered in the damp and he turned and nuzzled him; much as the general, with nothing left to do, might fall to considering the welfare of his servant, simply because the servant happened to be there.

The light grew stronger and soon he could see that a little way ahead there was an open track of bare gravel. He limped out of the heather, sat on the stones and shook the wet from his fur. He could see Fiver's hills plainly now, greenish-grey and seeming close in the rain-laden air. He could even pick out the dots of furze bushes and stunted yew trees on the steep slopes. As he gazed at them, he heard an excited voice farther down the track.

'He's done it! Didn't I tell you he'd do it?'

Hazel turned his head and saw Blackberry on the path. He was bedraggled and exhausted, but it was he who was speaking. Out of the heather behind him came Acorn, Speedwell and Buckthorn. All four rabbits were now staring straight at him. He wondered why. Then, as they approached, he realized that they were looking not at him, but past him at something farther off. He turned round.

The gravel track led downhill into a narrow belt of silver birch and rowan. Beyond was a thin hedge; and beyond that, a green field between two copses. They had reached the other side of the common.

'Oh, Hazel,' said Blackberry, coming up to him round a puddle in the gravel. 'I was so tired and confused, I actually began to wonder whether you knew where you were going. I could hear you in the heather, saying "Not far now" and it was annoying me. I thought you were making it up. I should have known better. Frithrah, you're what I call a Chief Rabbit!'

'Well done, Hazel-rah!' said Buckthorn. 'Well done!'

Hazel did not know what to reply. He looked at them in silence and it was Acorn who spoke next.

'Come on!' he said. 'Who's going to be first into that field? I can still run.' He was off, slowly enough, down the slope, but when Hazel stamped for him to stop he did so at once.

'Where are the others?' said Hazel. 'Dandelion? Bigwig?'

At that moment Dandelion appeared out of the heather and sat on the path, looking at the field. He was followed first by Hawkbit and then by Fiver. Hazel was watching Fiver as he took in the sight of the field, when Buckthorn drew his attention back to the foot of the slope.

'Look, Hazel-rah,' he said, 'Silver and Bigwig are down there. They're waiting for us.'

Silver's light-grey fur showed up plainly against a low spray of gorse, but Hazel could not see Bigwig until he sat up and ran towards them.

'Is everybody here, Hazel?' he asked.

'Of course they are,' answered Blackberry. 'I tell you, he's what I call a Chief Rabbit. Hazel-rah, shall we –'

'Hazel-*rah*?' interrupted Bigwig. '*Chief Rabbit*? Frith in a wasps' nest! The day I call you Chief Rabbit, Hazel, that'll be the day, that will! I'll stop fighting that day.'

It did indeed prove a momentous day – and a momentous speech as well: but it lay in a future that none could foresee, and for the moment all that poor Hazel could do was to turn aside with the disappointed feeling that after all, his part in the crossing of the heather had not really been a very important one.

'Come on, then, Acorn,' he said. 'You want to run – I'll run with you.'

A few moments later they were under the silver birches and as the sun rose, striking flashes of red and green from the drops on ferns and twigs, they scrambled through the hedge, across a shallow ditch and into the thick grass of the meadow.

12. The Stranger in the Field

Nevertheless, even in a crowded warren, visitors in the form of young rabbits seeking desirable dry quarters may be tolerated ... and if powerful enough they may obtain and hold a place.

R. M. Lockley, *The Private Life of the Rabbit*

TO COME to the end of a time of anxiety and fear! To feel the cloud that hung over us lift and disperse – the cloud that dulled the heart and made happiness no more than a memory! This at least is one joy that must have been known by almost every living creature.

Here is a boy who was waiting to be punished. But then, unexpectedly, he finds that his fault has been overlooked or forgiven and at once the world reappears in brilliant colours, full of delightful prospects. Here is a soldier who was waiting, with a heavy heart, to suffer and die in battle. But suddenly the luck has changed. There is news! The war is over and everyone bursts out singing! He will go home after all! The sparrows in the ploughland were crouching in terror of the kestrel. But she has gone; and they fly pell-mell up the hedgerow, frisking, chattering and perching where they will. The bitter winter had all the country in its grip. The hares on the down, stupid and torpid with cold, were resigned to sinking further and further into the freezing heart of snow and silence. But now – who would have dreamt it? – the thaw is trickling, the great tit is ringing his bell from the top of a bare lime tree, the earth is scented; and the hares bound and skip in the warm wind. Hopelessness and reluctance are blown away like a fog and the dumb solitude where they crept, a place desolate as a crack in the ground, opens like a rose and stretches to the hills and the sky.

The tired rabbits fed and basked in the sunny meadow as though they had come no further than from the bank at the edge of the near-by copse. The heather and the stumbling darkness were forgotten as though the sunrise had melted them. Bigwig and Hawkbit chased each other through the long grass. Speedwell jumped over the little brook that ran down the middle of the field and when Acorn tried to follow him and fell short, Silver joked with him as he scrambled out and rolled him in a patch of dead oak leaves until he was dry. As the sun rose higher, shortening the shadows and drawing the dew from the grass, most of the rabbits came wandering back to the sun-flecked shade among the cow-parsley along the edge of the ditch. Here, Hazel and Fiver were sitting with Dandelion under a flowering wild cherry. The white petals spun down around them, covering the grass and speckling their fur, while thirty feet above a thrush sang 'Cherry dew, cherry dew. Knee deep, knee deep, knee deep.'

'Well, this is the place all right, isn't it, Hazel?' said Dandelion lazily. 'I suppose we'd better start having a look along the banks soon, although I must say I'm in no particular hurry. But I've got an idea it may be going to rain before much longer.'

Fiver looked as though he were about to speak, but then shook his ears and turned to nibbling at a dandelion.

'That looks a good bank, along the edge of the trees up there,' answered Hazel. 'What do you, say, Fiver? Shall we go up there now or shall we wait a bit longer?'

Fiver hesitated and then replied, 'Just as you think, Hazel.'

'Well, there's no need to do any serious digging, is there?' said Bigwig. 'That sort of thing's all right for does, but not for us.'

'Still, we'd better make one or two scrapes, don't you think?' said Hazel. 'Something to give us shelter at a pinch. Let's go up to the copse and look round. We might as well take our time and make quite sure where we'd like to have them. We don't want to have to do the work twice.'

'Yes, that's the style,' said Bigwig. 'And while you're doing that, I'll take Silver and Buckthorn here and have a run down the fields beyond, just to get the lie of the land and make sure there isn't anything dangerous.'

The three explorers set off beside the brook, while Hazel led the other rabbits across the field and up to the edge of the woodland. They went slowly along the foot of the bank, pushing in and out of the clumps of red campion and ragged robin. From time to time one or another would begin to scrape in the gravelly bank, or venture a little way in among the trees and nut-bushes to scuffle in the leaf-mould. After they had been searching and moving on quietly for some time, they reached a place from which they could see that the field below them broadened out. Both on their own side and opposite, the wood-edges curved outwards, away from the brook. They also noticed the roofs of a farm, but some distance off. Hazel stopped and they gathered round him.

'I don't think it makes much difference where we do a bit of scratching,' he said. 'It's all good, so far as I can see. Not the slightest trace of elil – no scent or tracks or droppings. That seems unusual, but it may be just that the home warren attracted more elil than other places. Anyway, we ought to do well here. Now I'll tell you what seems the right thing to me. Let's go back a little way, between the woods, and have a scratch near that oak tree there – just by that white patch of stitchwort. I know the farm's a long way off, but there's no point in being nearer to it than we need. And if we're fairly close to the wood opposite, the trees will help to break the wind a bit in winter.'

'Splendid,' said Blackberry. 'It's going to cloud over, do you see? Rain before sunset and we'll be in shelter. Well, let's make a start. Oh, look! There's Bigwig coming back along the bottom, and the other two with him.'

The three rabbits were returning down the bank of the stream and had not yet seen Hazel and the others. They passed below them, into the narrower part of the field between the two copses, and it was not until Acorn had been sent half-way down the slope to attract their attention that they turned and came up to the ditch.

'I don't think there's going to be much to trouble us here, Hazel,' said Bigwig. 'The farm's a good way away and the fields between don't show any signs of elil at all. There's a man-track – in fact, there are several – and they look as though they were used a good deal. Scent's fresh and there are the ends of those little white sticks that they burn in their mouths. But that's all for the best, I reckon. We keep away from the men and the men frighten the elil away.'

'Why do the men come, do you suppose?' asked Fiver.

'Who knows why men do anything? They may drive cows or sheep in the fields, or cut wood in the copses. What does it matter? I'd rather dodge a man than a stoat or a fox.'

'Well, that's fine,' said Hazel. 'You've found out a lot, Bigwig, and all to the good. We were just going to make some scrapes along the bank there. We'd better start. The rain won't be long now, if I know anything about it.'

Buck rabbits on their own seldom or never go in for serious digging. This is the natural job of a doe making a home for her litter before they are born, and then her buck helps her. All the same, solitary bucks – if they can find no existing holes to make use of – will sometimes scratch out short tunnels for shelter, although it is not work that they tackle at all seriously. During the morning the digging proceeded in a light-hearted and intermittent way. The bank on each side of the oak tree was bare and consisted of a light, gravelly soil. There were several false starts and fresh choices, but by ni-Frith they had three scrapes of a sort. Hazel, watching, lent help here and there and encouraged the others. Every so often he slipped back to look out over the field and make sure that all was safe. Only Fiver remained solitary. He took no part in the digging but squatted on the edge of the ditch, fidgeting backwards and forwards, sometimes nibbling and then starting up suddenly as though he could hear some sound in the wood. After speaking to him once or twice and receiving no reply, Hazel thought it best to let him alone. The next time he left the digging he kept away from Fiver and sat looking at the bank, as though entirely concerned with the work.

A little while after ni-Frith the sky clouded over thickly. The light grew dull and they could smell rain approaching from the west. The blue-tit that had been swinging on a bramble, singing 'Heigh, ho, go-and-get-another-bit-of-moss,' stopped his acrobatics and flew into the wood. Hazel was just wondering whether it would be worth while starting a side-passage to link Bigwig's hole to Dandelion's, when he felt a stamp of warning from somewhere close by. He turned quickly. It was Fiver who had stamped and he was now staring intently across the field.

Beside a tussock of grass a little way outside the opposite copse, a rabbit was sitting and gazing at them. Its ears were erect and it was evidently giving them the full attention of sight, smell and hearing. Hazel rose on his hind legs, paused, and then sat back on his haunches, in full view. The other rabbit remained motionless. Hazel, never taking his eyes off it, heard three or four of the others coming up behind him. After a moment he said,

'Blackberry?'

'He's down the hole,' replied Pipkin.

'Go and get him.'

Still the strange rabbit made no move. The wind rose and the long grass began to flutter and ripple in the dip between them. From behind, Blackberry said,

'You wanted me, Hazel?'

'I'm going over to speak to that rabbit,' said Hazel. 'I want you to come with me.'

'Can I come?' asked Pipkin.

'No, Hlao-roo. We don't want to frighten him. Three's too many.'

'Be careful,' said Buckthorn, as Hazel and Blackberry set off down the slope. 'He may not be the only one.'

At several points the brook was narrow – not much wider than a rabbit-run. They jumped it and went up the opposite slope.

'Just behave as if we were back at home,' said Hazel. 'I don't see how it can be a trap and anyway we can always run.'

As they approached, the other rabbit kept still and watched them intently. They could see now that he was a big fellow, sleek and handsome. His fur shone and his claws and teeth were in perfect condition. Nevertheless, he did not seem aggressive. On the contrary, there was a curious, rather unnatural gentleness about the way in which he waited for them to come nearer. They stopped and looked at him from a little distance.

'I don't think he's dangerous,' whispered Blackberry. 'I'll go up to him first if you like.'

'We'll both go,' replied Hazel. But at this moment the other rabbit came towards them of his own accord. He and

Hazel touched their noses together, sniffing and questioning silently. The stranger had an unusual smell, but it was certainly not unpleasant. It gave Hazel an impression of good feeding, of health and of a certain indolence, as though the other came from some rich, prosperous country where he himself had never been. He had the air of an aristocrat and as he turned to gaze at Blackberry from his great, brown eyes, Hazel began to see himself as a ragged wanderer, leader of a gang of vagabonds. He had not meant to be the first to speak, but something in the other's silence compelled him.

'We've come over the heather,' he said.

The other rabbit made no reply, but his look was not that of an enemy. His demeanour had a kind of melancholy which was perplexing.

'Do you live here?' asked Hazel, after a pause.

'Yes,' replied the other rabbit; and then added, 'We saw you come.'

'We mean to live here too,' said Hazel firmly.

The other rabbit showed no concern. He paused and then answered, 'Why not? We supposed you would. But I don't think there are enough of you, are there, to live very comfortably on your own?'

Hazel felt puzzled. Apparently the stranger was not worried by the news that they meant to stay. How big was his warren? Where was it? How many rabbits were concealed in the copse and watching them now? Were they likely to be attacked? The stranger's manner told nothing. He seemed detached, almost bored, but perfectly friendly. His lassitude, his great size and beautiful, well-groomed appearance, his unhurried air of having all he wanted and of being unaffected by the newcomers one way or the other – all these presented Hazel with a problem unlike anything he had had to deal with before. If there was some kind of trick, he had no idea what it might be. He decided that he himself, at any rate, would be perfectly candid and plain.

'There are enough of us to protect ourselves,' he said. 'We don't want to make enemies, but if we meet with any kind of interference –'

The other interrupted smoothly. 'Don't get upset – you're all very welcome. If you're going back now, I'll come over with you: that is, unless you have any objection.'

He set off down the slope. Hazel and Blackberry, after looking at each other for a moment, caught him up and went beside him. He moved easily, without haste and showed less caution than they in crossing the field. Hazel felt more mystified than ever. The other rabbit evidently had no fear that they might set upon him, hrair to one, and kill him. He was ready to go alone among a crowd of suspicious strangers, but what he stood to gain from this risk it was impossible to guess. Perhaps, thought Hazel wryly, teeth and claws would make no impression on that great, firm body and shining pelt.

When they reached the ditch, all the other rabbits were squatting together, watching their approach. Hazel stopped in front of them but did not know what to say. If the stranger had not been there, he would have given them an account of what had happened. If Blackberry and he had driven the stranger across the field by force, he could have handed him over for safe-keeping to Bigwig or Silver. But to have him sitting beside him, looking his followers over in silence and courteously waiting for someone else to speak first – this was a situation beyond Hazel's experience. It was Bigwig, straightforward and blunt as always, who broke the tension.

'Who is this, Hazel?' he said. 'Why has he come back with you?'

'I don't know,' answered Hazel, trying to look frank and feeling foolish. 'He came of his own accord.'

'Well, we'd better ask *him*, then,' said Bigwig, with something like a sneer. He came close to the stranger and sniffed, as Hazel had done. He, too, was evidently affected by the peculiar smell of prosperity, for he paused as though in uncertainty. Then, with a rough, abrupt air, he said, 'Who are you and what do you want?'

'My name is Cowslip,' said the other. 'I don't want anything. I hear you've come a long way.'

'Perhaps we have,' said Bigwig. 'We know how to defend ourselves, too.'

'I'm sure you do,' said Cowslip, looking round at the mudstained, bedraggled rabbits with an air of being too polite to comment. 'But it can be hard to defend oneself against the weather. There's going to be rain and I don't think your scrapes are finished.' He looked at Bigwig, as though waiting for him to ask another question. Bigwig seemed confused. Clearly, he could make no more of the situation than Hazel. There was silence except for the sound of the rising wind. Above them, the branches of the oak tree were beginning to creak and sway. Suddenly, Fiver came forward.

'We don't understand you,' he said. 'It's best to say so and try to get things clear. Can we trust you? Are there many other rabbits here? Those are the things we want to know.'

Cowslip showed no more concern at Fiver's tense manner than he had at anything that had gone before. He drew a fore-paw down the back of one ear and then replied,

'I think you're puzzling yourselves unnecessarily. But if you want the answers to your questions, then I'd say yes, you can trust us: we don't want to drive you away. And there is a warren here, but not as big a one as we should like. Why should we want to hurt you? There's plenty of grass, surely?'

In spite of his strange, clouded manner, he spoke so reasonably that Hazel felt rather ashamed.

'We've been through a lot of danger,' he said. 'Everything new seems like danger to us. After all, you might be afraid that we were coming to take your does or turn you out of your holes.'

Cowslip listened gravely. Then he answered,

'Well, as to the holes, that was something I thought I might mention. These scrapes aren't very deep or comfortable, are they? And although they're facing out of the wind now, you ought to know that this isn't the usual wind we get here. It's blowing up this rain from the south. We usually have a west wind and it'll go straight into these holes. There are plenty of empty burrows in our warren and if you want to come across you'll be welcome. And now if you'll excuse me, I won't stay any longer. I hate the rain. The warren is round the corner of the wood opposite.'

He ran down the slope and over the brook. They watched him leap the bank of the further copse and disappear through the green bracken. The first scatters of rain were beginning to fall, pattering into the oak leaves and pricking the bare, pink skin inside their ears.

'Fine, big fellow, isn't he?' said Buckthorn. 'He doesn't look as though he had much to bother about, living here.'

'What should we do, Hazel, do you think?' asked Silver. 'It's true what he said, isn't it? These scrapes – well, we can crouch in them out of the weather, but no more than that. And as we can't all get into one, we shall have to split up.'

'We'll join them together,' said Hazel, 'and while we're doing that I'd like to talk about what he said. Fiver, Bigwig and Blackberry, can you come with me? The rest of you split how you like.'

The new hole was short, narrow and rough. There was no room for two rabbits to pass. Four were like beans in a pod. For the first time, Hazel began to realize how much they had left behind. The holes and tunnels of an old warren become smooth, reassuring and comfortable with use. There are no snags or rough corners. Every length smells of rabbits – of that great, indestructible flood of Rabbitry in which each one is carried along, sure-footed and safe. The heavy work has all been done by countless great-grandmothers and their mates. All the faults have been put right and everything in use is of proved value. The rain drains easily and even the wind of mid-winter cannot penetrate the deeper burrows. Not one of Hazel's rabbits had ever played any part in real digging. The work they had done that morning was trifling and all they had to show for it was rough shelter and little comfort.

There is nothing like bad weather to reveal the shortcomings of a dwelling, particularly if it is too small.

You are, as they say, stuck with it and have leisure to feel all its peculiar irritations and discomforts. Bigwig, with his usual brisk energy, set to work. Hazel, however, returned and sat pensive at the lip of the hole, looking out at the silent, rippling veils of rain that drifted across and across the little valley between the two copses. Closer, before his nose, every blade of grass, every bracken frond was bent, dripping and glistening. The smell of last year's oak leaves filled the air. It had turned chilly. Across the field the bloom of the cherry tree, under which they had sat that morning, hung sodden and spoiled. While Hazel gazed, the wind slowly veered round into the west, as Cowslip had said it would, and brought the rain driving into the mouth of the hole. He backed down and rejoined the others. The pattering and whispering of the rain sounded softly but distinctly outside. The fields and woods were shut in under it, emptied and subdued. The insect life of the leaves and grass was stilled. The thrush should have been singing, but Hazel could hear no thrush. He and his companions were a muddy handful of scratchers, crouching in a narrow, draughty pit in lonely country. They were not out of the weather. They were waiting, uncomfortably, for the weather to change.

'Blackberry,' said Hazel, 'what did you think of our visitor and how would you like to go to his warren?'

'Well,' replied Blackberry, 'what I think is this. There's no way of finding out whether he's to be trusted except to try it. He seemed friendly. But then, if a lot of rabbits were afraid of some newcomers and wanted to deceive them – get them down a hole and attack them – they'd start – wouldn't they? – by sending someone who was plausible.

They might want to kill us. But then again, as he said, there's plenty of grass and as for turning them out or taking their does, if they're all up to his size and weight they've nothing to fear from a crowd like us. They must have seen us come. We were tired. Surely that was the time to attack us? Or while we were separated, before we began digging? But they didn't. I reckon they're more likely to be friendly than otherwise. There's only one thing beats me. What do they stand to get from asking us to join their warren?'

'Fools attract elil by being easy prey,' said Bigwig, cleaning the mud out of his whiskers and blowing through his long front teeth. 'And *we're* fools until we've learnt to live here. Safer to teach us, perhaps. I don't know – give it up. But I'm not afraid to go and find out. If they *do* try any tricks, they'll find I know a few as well. I wouldn't mind taking a chance, to sleep somewhere more comfortable than this. We haven't slept since yesterday afternoon.'

'Fiver?'

'I think we ought to have nothing to do with that rabbit or his warren. We ought to leave this place at once. But what's the good of talking?'

Cold and damp, Hazel felt impatient. He had always been accustomed to rely on Fiver and now, when he really needed him, he was letting them down. Blackberry's reasoning had been first-rate and Bigwig had at least shown which way any sound-hearted rabbit would be likely to lean. Apparently the only contribution Fiver could make was this beetle-spirited vapouring. He tried to remember that Fiver was under-sized and that they had had an anxious time and were all weary. At this moment the soil at the far end of the burrow began to crumble inwards: then it fell away and Silver's head and front paws appeared.

'Here we are,' said Silver cheerfully. 'We've done what you wanted, Hazel; and Buckthorn's through next door. But what I'd like to know is, how about What's-His-Name? Cowpat – no – Cowslip? Are we going to his warren or not? Surely we're not going to sit cowering in this place because we're frightened to go and see him. Whatever will he think of us?'

'I'll tell you,' said Dandelion, from over his shoulder. 'If he's not honest, he'll know we're afraid to come: and if he *is*, he'll think we're suspicious, cowardly skulkers. If we're going to live in these fields, we'll have to get on terms with his lot sooner or later, and it goes against the grain to hang about and admit we daren't visit them.'

'I don't know how many of them there are,' said Silver, 'but *we're* quite a crowd. Anyhow, I hate the idea of just keeping away. How long have rabbits been elil? Old Cowslip wasn't afraid to come into the middle of us, was he?'

'Very well,' said Hazel. 'That's how I feel myself. I just wanted to know whether you did. Would you like Bigwig and me to go over there first, by ourselves, and report back?'

'No,' said Silver. 'Let's all go. If we're going at all, for Frith's sake let's do it as though we weren't afraid. What do you say, Dandelion?'

'I think you're right.'

'Then we'll go now,' said Hazel. 'Get the others and follow me.'

Outside, in the thickening light of the late afternoon, with the rain trickling into his eyes and under his scut, he watched them as they joined him. Blackberry, alert and intelligent, looking first up and then down the ditch before he crossed it. Bigwig, cheerful at the prospect of action. The steady, reliable Silver. Dandelion, the dashing story-teller, so eager to be off that he jumped the ditch and ran a little way into the field before stopping to wait for the rest. Buckthorn, perhaps the most sensible and staunch of them all. Pipkin, who looked round for Hazel and then came over to wait beside him. Acorn, Hawkbit and Speedwell, decent enough rank-and-filers as long as they were not pushed beyond their limits. Last of all came Fiver, dejected and reluctant as a sparrow in the frost. As Hazel turned from the hole, the clouds in the west broke slightly and there was a sudden dazzle of watery, pale-gold light.

'El-ahrairah!' thought Hazel. 'These are rabbits we're going to meet. You know them as well as you know us. Let it be the right thing that I'm doing.'

'Now, brace up, Fiver!' he said aloud. 'We're waiting for you, and getting wetter every moment.'

A soaking bumble-bee crawled over a thistle-bloom, vibrated its wings for a few seconds and then flew away down the field. Hazel followed, leaving a dark track behind him over the silvered grass.

13. Hospitality

In the afternoon they came unto a land
In which it seemed always afternoon.
All round the coast the languid air did swoon,
Breathing like one that hath a weary dream.
                    Tennyson, 'The Lotus-Eaters'

THE corner of the opposite wood turned out to be an acute point. Beyond it, the ditch and trees curved back again in a re-entrant, so that the field formed a bay with a bank running all the way round. It was evident now why Cowslip, when he left them, had gone among the trees. He had simply run in a direct line from their holes to his own, passing on his way through the narrow strip of woodland that lay between. Indeed, as Hazel turned the point and stopped to look about him, he could see the place where Cowslip must have come out. A clear rabbit-track led from the bracken, under the fence and into the field. In the bank on the further side of the bay the rabbit-holes were plain to see, showing dark and distinct in the bare ground. It was as conspicuous a warren as could well be imagined.

'Sky above us!' said Bigwig. 'Every living creature for miles must know that's there! Look at all the tracks in the grass, too! Do you think they sing in the morning, like the thrushes?'

'Perhaps they're too secure to bother about concealing themselves,' said Blackberry. 'After all, the home warren was fairly plain to be seen.'

'Yes, but not like that! A couple of hrududil could go down some of those holes.'

'So could I,' said Dandelion. 'I'm getting dreadfully wet.'

As they approached, a big rabbit appeared over the edge of the ditch, looked at them quickly and vanished into the bank. A few moments later two others came out and waited for them. They, too, were sleek and unusually large.

'A rabbit called Cowslip offered us shelter here,' said Hazel. 'Perhaps you know that he came to see us?'

Both rabbits together made a curious, dancing movement of the head and front paws. Apart from sniffing, as Hazel and Cowslip had done when they met, formal gestures – except between mating rabbits – were unknown to Hazel and his companions. They felt mystified and slightly ill-at-ease. The dancers paused, evidently waiting for some acknowledgement or reciprocal gesture, but there was none.

'Cowslip is in the great burrow,' said one of them at length. 'Would you like to follow us there?'

'How many of us?' asked Hazel.

'Why, all of you,' answered the other, surprised. 'You don't want to stay out in the rain, do you?'

Hazel had supposed that he and one or two of his comrades would be taken to see the Chief Rabbit – who would probably not be Cowslip, since Cowslip had come to see them unattended – in his burrow, after which they would all be given different places to go to. It was this separation of which he had been afraid. He now realized with astonishment that there was apparently a part of the warren underground which was big enough to contain them all together. He felt so curious to visit it that he did not stop to make any detailed arrangements about the order in which they should go down. However, he put Pipkin immediately behind him. 'It'll warm his little heart for once,' he thought, 'and if the leaders *do* get attacked, I suppose we can spare him easier than some.' Bigwig he asked to bring up the rear. 'If there's any trouble, get out of it,' he said, 'and take as many as you can with you.' Then he followed their guides into one of the holes in the bank.

The run was broad, smooth and dry. It was obviously a highway, for the other runs branched off it in all directions. The rabbits in front went fast and Hazel had little time to sniff about as he followed. Suddenly he checked. He had come into an open place. His whiskers could feel no earth in front and none was near his sides. There was a good deal of air ahead of him – he could feel it moving – and there was a considerable space above his head. Also, there were several rabbits near him. It had not occurred to him that there would be a place underground where he would be exposed on three sides. He backed quickly and felt Pipkin at his tail. 'What a fool I was!' he thought. 'Why didn't I put Silver there?' At this moment he heard Cowslip speaking. He jumped, for he could tell that he was some way away. The size of the place must be immense.

'Is that you, Hazel?' said Cowslip. 'You're welcome, and so are your friends. We're glad you've come.'

No human beings, except the courageous and experienced blind, are able to sense much in a strange place where they cannot see, but with rabbits it is otherwise. They spend half their lives underground in darkness or near-darkness and touch, smell and hearing convey as much or more to them than sight. Hazel now had the clearest knowledge of where he was. He would have recognized the place if he had left at once and come back six months later. He was at one end of the largest burrow he had ever been in: sandy, warm and dry, with a hard, bare floor. There were several tree-roots running across the roof and it was these that supported the unusual span. There was a great number of rabbits in the place – many more than he was bringing. All had the same rich, opulent smell as Cowslip.

Cowslip himself was at the other end of the hall and Hazel realized that he was waiting for him to reply. His own companions were still coming out of the entrance burrow one by one and there was a good deal of scrabbling and shuffling. He wondered if he ought to be very formal. Whether or not he could call himself a Chief Rabbit, he had no experience of this sort of thing. The Threarah would no doubt have risen to the occasion perfectly. He did not want to appear at a loss or to let his followers down. He decided that it would be best to be plain and friendly. After all, there would be plenty of time, as they settled down in the warren, to show these strangers that they were as good as themselves, without risking trouble by putting on airs at the start.

'We're glad to be out of the bad weather,' he said. 'We're like all rabbits – happiest in a crowd. When you came over to see us in the field, Cowslip, you said your warren wasn't large, but judging by the holes we saw along the bank, it must be what we'd reckon a fine, big one.'

As he finished he sensed that Bigwig had just entered the hall, and knew that they were all together again. The stranger rabbits seemed slightly disconcerted by his little speech and he felt that for some reason or other he had not struck the right note in complimenting them on their numbers. Perhaps there were not very many of them after all? Had there been disease? There was no smell or sign of it. These were the biggest and healthiest rabbits he had ever met. Perhaps their fidgeting and silence had nothing to do with what he had said? Perhaps it was simply that he had not spoken very well, being new to it, and they felt that he was not up to their fine ways? 'Never mind,' he thought. 'After last night I'm sure of my own lot. We wouldn't be here at all if we weren't handy in a pinch. These other fellows will just have to get to know us. They don't seem to dislike us, anyway.'

There were no more speeches. Rabbits have their own conventions and formalities, but these are few and short by human standards. If Hazel had been a human being he would have been expected to introduce his companions one by one and no doubt each would have been taken in charge as a guest by one of their hosts. In the great burrow, however, things happened differently. The rabbits mingled naturally. They did not talk for talking's sake, in the artificial manner that human beings – and sometimes even their dogs and cats – do. But this did not mean that they were not communicating; merely that they were not communicating by talking. All over the burrow, both the newcomers and those who were at home were accustoming themselves to each other in their own way and their own time: getting to know what the strangers smelt like, how they moved, how they breathed, how they scratched, the feel of their rhythms and pulses. These were their topics and subjects of discussion, carried on without the need of speech. To a greater extent than a human in a similar gathering each rabbit, as he pursued his own fragment, was sensitive to the trend of the whole. After a time, all knew that the concourse was not going to turn sour or break up in a fight. Just as a battle begins in a state of equilibrium between the two sides, which gradually alters one way or the other, until it is clear that the balance has tilted so far that the issue can no longer be in doubt – so this gathering of rabbits in the dark, beginning with hesitant approaches, silences, pauses, movements, crouchings side-by-side and all manner of tentative appraisals, slowly moved, like a hemisphere of the world into summer, to a warmer, brighter region of mutual liking and approval, until all felt sure that they had nothing to fear. Pipkin, some way away from Hazel, crouched at his ease between two huge rabbits who could have broken his back in a second, while Buckthorn and Cowslip started a playful scuffle, nipping each other like kittens and then breaking off to comb their ears in a comical pretence of sudden gravity. Only Fiver sat alone and apart. He seemed either ill or very much depressed, and the strangers avoided him instinctively.

The knowledge that the gathering was safely round the corner came to Hazel in the form of a recollection of Silver's head and paws breaking through gravel. At once he felt warm and relaxed. He had already crossed the whole length of the hall and was pressed close to two rabbits, a buck and doe, each of whom was fully as large as Cowslip. When both together took a few slow hops down one of the runs near-by, Hazel followed and little by little they all three moved out of the hall. They came to a smaller burrow, deeper underground. Evidently this belonged to the couple, for they settled down as though at home and made no objection when Hazel did the same. Here, while the mood of the great hall slowly passed from them, all three were silent for a time.

'Is Cowslip the Chief Rabbit?' asked Hazel at length.

The other replied with a question. 'Are you called Chief Rabbit?'

Hazel found this awkward to answer. If he replied that he was, his new friends might address him so for the future, and he could imagine what Bigwig and Silver would have to say about that. As usual, he fell back on plain honesty.

'We're only a few,' he said. 'We left our warren in a hurry to escape from bad things. Most stayed behind and the Chief Rabbit was one of them. I've been trying to lead my friends, but I don't know whether they'd care to hear me called Chief Rabbit.'

'That'll make him ask a few questions,' he thought. '"Why did you leave? Why didn't the rest come? What were you afraid of?" And whatever am I going to say?'

When the other rabbit spoke, however, it was clear that either he had no interest in what Hazel had said, or else he had some other reason for not questioning him.

'We don't call anyone Chief Rabbit,' he said. 'It was Cowslip's idea to go and see you this afternoon, so he was the one who went.'

'But who decides what to do about elil? And digging and sending out scouting parties and so on?'

'Oh, we never do anything like *that*. Elil keep away from here. There was a *homba* last winter, but the man who comes through the fields, he shot it with his gun.'

Hazel stared. 'But men won't shoot a homba.'

'Well, *he* killed *this* one, anyway. He kills owls too. We never need to dig. No one's dug in my lifetime. A lot of the burrows are lying empty, you know: rats live in one part, but the man kills them as well, when he can. We don't need expeditions. There's better food here than anywhere else. Your friends will be happy living here.'

But he himself did not sound particularly happy and once again Hazel felt oddly perplexed. 'Where does the man –' he began. But he was interrupted.

'I'm called Strawberry. This is my doe, Nildro-hain.* Some of the best empty burrows are quite close. I'll show you, in case your friends want to settle into them. The great burrow is a splendid place, don't you think? I'm

---

* 'Song of the Blackbird'.

sure there can't be many warrens where all the rabbits can meet together underground. The roof's all tree-roots, you know, and of course the tree outside keeps the rain from coming through. It's a wonder the tree's alive, but it is.'

Hazel suspected that Strawberry's talking had the real purpose of preventing his own questions. He was partly irritated and partly mystified.

'Never mind,' he thought. 'If we all get as big as these chaps we shall do pretty well. There must be some good food round here somewhere. His doe's a beautiful creature, too. Perhaps there are some more like her in the warren.'

Strawberry moved out of the burrow and Hazel followed him into another run, leading deeper down below the wood. It was certainly a warren to admire. Sometimes, when they crossed a run that led upwards to a hole, he could hear the rain outside, still falling in the night. But although it had now been raining for several hours, there was not the least damp or cold either in the deep runs or in the many burrows that they passed. Both the drainage and the ventilation were better than he had been accustomed to. Here and there other rabbits were on the move. Once they came upon Acorn, who was evidently being taken on a tour of the same kind. 'Very friendly, aren't they?' he said to Hazel as they passed one another. 'I never dreamt we'd reach a place like this. You've got wonderful judgement, Hazel.' Strawberry waited politely for him to finish speaking and Hazel could not help feeling pleased that he must have heard.

At last, after skirting carefully round some openings from which there was a distinct smell of rats, they halted in a kind of pit. A steep tunnel led up into the air. Rabbit-runs tend to be bow-shaped; but this was straight, so that above them, through the mouth of the hole, Hazel could see leaves against the night sky. He realized that one wall of the pit was convex and made of some hard substance. He sniffed at it uncertainly.

'Don't you know what those are?' said Strawberry. 'They're bricks; the stones that men make their houses and barns out of. There used to be a well here long ago, but it's filled up now – the men don't use it any more. That's the outer side of the well-shaft. And this earth-wall here is completely flat because of some man-thing fixed behind it in the ground, but I'm not sure what.'

'There's something stuck on it,' said Hazel. 'Why, they're stones, pushed into the surface! But what for?'

'Do you like it?' asked Strawberry.

Hazel puzzled over the stones. They were all the same size, and pushed at regular intervals into the soil. He could make nothing of them.

'What are they for?' he asked again.

'It's El-ahrairah,' said Strawberry. 'A rabbit called Laburnum did it, some time ago now. We have others, but this is the best. Worth a visit, don't you think?'

Hazel was more at a loss than ever. He had never seen a laburnum and was puzzled by the name, which in Lapine is 'Poison-tree'. How could a rabbit be called Poison? And how could stones be El-ahrairah? What, exactly, was it that Strawberry was saying was El-ahrairah? In confusion he said, 'I don't understand.'

'It's what we call a Shape,' explained Strawberry. 'Haven't you seen one before? The stones make the shape of El-ahrairah on the wall. Stealing the King's lettuce. *You know?*'

Hazel had not felt so much bewildered since Blackberry had talked about the raft beside the Enborne. Obviously, the stones could not possibly be anything to do with El-ahrairah. It seemed to him that Strawberry might as well have said that his tail was an oak tree. He sniffed again and then put a paw up to the wall.

'Steady, steady,' said Strawberry. 'You might damage it and that wouldn't do. Never mind. We'll come again some other time.'

'But where are –' Hazel was beginning, when Strawberry once more interrupted him.

'I expect you'll be hungry now. I know I am. It's going on raining all night, I'm certain of that, but we can feed underground here, you know. And then you can sleep in the great burrow, or in my place if you prefer. We can go back more quickly than we came. There's a run that goes almost straight. Actually, it passes across –'

He chatted on relentlessly, as they made their way back. It suddenly occurred to Hazel that these desperate interruptions seemed to follow any question beginning 'Where?' He thought he would put this to the proof. After a while Strawberry ended by saying, 'We're nearly at the great burrow now, but we're coming in by a different way.'

'And where –' said Hazel. Instantly Strawberry turned into a side run and called, 'Kingcup? Are you coming down to the great burrow?' There was silence. 'That's odd!' said Strawberry, returning and once more leading the way. 'He's generally there about this time. I often call for him, you know.'

Hazel, hanging back, made a quick search with nose and whiskers. The threshold of the burrow was covered with a day-old fall of soft soil from the roof above. Strawberry's prints had marked it plainly and there were no others whatsoever.

14. 'Like Trees in November'

Courts and camps are the only places to learn the world
in . . . Take the tone of the company that you are in.
The Earl of Chesterfield, *Letters to his Son*

THE great burrow was less crowded than when they
had left it. Nildro-hain was the first rabbit they met.
She was among a group of three or four fine does who were
talking quietly together and seemed to be feeding as well.
There was a smell of green-stuff. Evidently some kind
of food was available underground, like the Threarah's
lettuce. Hazel stopped to speak to Nildro-hain. She asked
whether he had gone as far as the well-pit and the El-
ahrairah of Laburnum.

'Yes, we did,' said Hazel. 'It's something quite strange to
me, I'm afraid. But I'd rather admire you and your friends
than stones on a wall.'

As he said this, he noticed that Cowslip had joined them
and that Strawberry was talking to him quietly. He caught
the words – 'Never been near a Shape' – and a moment

later Cowslip replied, 'Well, it makes no difference from our point of view.'

Hazel suddenly felt tired and depressed. He heard Blackberry behind Cowslip's sleek, heavy shoulder and went across to him.

'Come out into the grass,' he said quietly. 'Bring anyone else who'll come.'

At that moment Cowslip turned to him and said, 'You'll be glad of something to eat now. I'll show you what we've got down here.'

'One or two of us are just going to *silflay*,'* said Hazel.

'Oh, it's still raining much too hard for that,' said Cowslip, as though there could be no two ways about it. 'We'll feed you here.'

'I should be sorry to quarrel over it,' said Hazel firmly, 'but some of us need to silflay. We're used to it, and rain doesn't bother us.'

Cowslip seemed taken aback for a moment. Then he laughed.

The phenomenon of laughter is unknown to animals; though it is possible that dogs and elephants may have some inkling of it. The effect on Hazel and Blackberry was overwhelming. Hazel's first idea was that Cowslip was showing the symptom of some kind of disease. Blackberry clearly thought that he might be going to attack them and backed away. Cowslip said nothing, but his eerie laughter continued. Hazel and Blackberry turned and scuttled up the nearest run as though he had been a ferret. Half-way

* Go above ground to feed.

up they met Pipkin, who was small enough first to let them pass and then to turn round and follow them.

The rain was still falling steadily. The night was dark and for May, cold. They all three hunched themselves in the grass and nibbled, while the rain ran off their fur in streams.

'My goodness, Hazel,' said Blackberry, 'did you really want to silflay? This is terrible! I was just going to eat whatever it is they have and then go to sleep. What's the idea?'

'I don't know,' replied Hazel. 'I suddenly felt I had to get out and I wanted your company. I can see what's troubling Fiver; though he'll get over it, I dare say. There *is* something strange about these rabbits. Do you know they push stones into the wall?'

'They do what?'

Hazel explained. Blackberry was as much at a loss as he had been himself. 'But I'll tell you another thing,' he said. 'Bigwig wasn't so far wrong. They *do* sing like the birds. I was in a burrow belonging to a rabbit called Betony. His doe has a litter and she was making a noise over them rather like a robin in autumn. To send them to sleep, she said. It made me feel queer, I can tell you.'

'And what do *you* think of them, Hlao-roo?' asked Hazel.

'They're very nice and kind,' answered Pipkin, 'but I'll tell you how they strike me. They all seem terribly sad. I can't think why, when they're so big and strong and have this beautiful warren. But they put me in mind of trees in November. I expect I'm being silly though, Hazel. You brought us here and I'm sure it must be a fine, safe place.'

'No, you're not being silly. I hadn't realized it, but you're perfectly right. They all seem to have something on their minds.'

'But after all,' said Blackberry, 'we don't know why they're so few. They don't fill the warren, anything like. Perhaps they've had some sort of trouble that's left them sad.'

'We don't know because they don't tell us. But if we're going to stay here we've got to learn to get on with them. We can't fight them: they're too big. And we don't want them fighting us.'

'I don't believe they *can* fight, Hazel,' said Pipkin. 'Although they're so big, they don't seem like fighters to me. Not like Bigwig and Silver.'

'You notice a lot, don't you, Hlao-roo?' said Hazel. 'Do you notice it's raining harder than ever? I've got enough grass in my stomach for a bit. We'll go down again now, but let's keep to ourselves for a while.'

'Why not sleep?' said Blackberry. 'It's over a night and a day now and I'm dropping.'

They returned down a different hole and soon found a dry, empty burrow, where they curled up together and slept in the warmth of their own tired bodies.

When Hazel woke he perceived at once that it was morning – some time after sunrise, by the smell of it. The scent of apple blossom was plain enough. Then he picked up the fainter smells of buttercups and horses. Mingled with these came another. Although it made him uneasy, he could not tell for some moments what it was. A dangerous smell, an unpleasant smell, a totally unnatural smell – quite close outside: a smoke smell – something was burning. Then he remembered how Bigwig, after his reconnaissance on the previous day, had spoken of the little white sticks in the grass. That was it. A man had been walking over the ground outside. That must have been what had awakened him.

Hazel lay in the warm, dark burrow with a delightful sense of security. He could smell the man. The man could not smell him. All the man could smell was the nasty smoke he was making. He fell to thinking of the shape in the well-pit, and then dropped into a drowsy half-dream, in which El-ahrairah said that it was all a trick of his to disguise himself as Poison-tree and put the stones in the wall, to engage Strawberry's attention while he himself was getting acquainted with Nildro-hain.

Pipkin stirred and turned in his sleep, murmuring, '*Sayn lay narn, marli?*' ('Is groundsel nice, mother?') and Hazel, touched to think that he must be dreaming of old days, rolled over on his side to give him room to settle again. At that moment, however, he heard a rabbit approaching down some run close by. Whoever it was, he was calling – and stamping as well, Hazel noticed – in an unnatural way. The sound, as Blackberry had said, was not unlike bird-song. As he came closer, Hazel could distinguish the word.

'*Flayrah! Flayrah!*'

The voice was Strawberry's. Pipkin and Blackberry were waking, more at the stamping than the voice, which was thin and novel, not striking through their sleep to any deep instinct. Hazel slipped out of the burrow into the run and at once came upon Strawberry busily thumping a hind leg on the hard earth floor.

'My mother used to say, "If you were a horse the ceiling would fall down",' said Hazel. 'Why do you stamp underground?'

'To wake everyone,' answered Strawberry. 'The rain went on nearly all night, you know. We generally sleep right through the early morning if it's rough weather. But it's turned fine now.'

'Why actually wake everybody, though?'

'Well, the man's gone by and Cowslip and I thought the flayrah ought not to lie about for long. If we don't go and get it the rats and rooks come and I don't like fighting rats. I expect it's all in a day's work to an adventurous lot like you.'

'I don't understand.'

'Well, come along with me. I'm just going back along this run for Nildro-hain. We haven't got a litter at present, you see, so she'll come out with the rest of us.'

Other rabbits were making their way along the run and Strawberry spoke to several of them, more than once remarking that he would enjoy taking their new friends across the field. Hazel began to realize that he liked Strawberry. On the previous day he had been too tired and bewildered to size him up. But now that he had had a good sleep, he could see that Strawberry was really a harmless, decent sort of fellow. He was touchingly devoted to the beautiful Nildro-hain; and he evidently had moods of gaiety and a great capacity for enjoyment. As they came up into the May morning he hopped over the ditch and skipped into the long grass as blithe as a squirrel. He seemed quite to have lost the preoccupied air that had troubled Hazel the night before. Hazel himself paused in the mouth of the hole, as he always had behind the bramble curtain at home, and looked out across the valley.

The sun, risen behind the copse, threw long shadows from the trees south-westwards across the field. The wet grass glittered and near-by a nut-tree sparkled iridescent, winking and gleaming as its branches moved in the light wind. The brook was swollen and Hazel's ears could distinguish the deeper, smoother sound, changed since the day before. Between the copse and the brook, the slope was covered with pale lilac lady's smocks, each standing separately in the grass, a frail stalk of bloom above a spread of cressy leaves. The breeze dropped and the little valley lay completely still, held in long beams of light and enclosed on either side by the lines of the woods. Upon this clear stillness, like feathers on the surface of a pool, fell the calling of a cuckoo.

'It's quite safe, Hazel,' said Cowslip behind him in the hole. 'I know you're used to taking a good look round when you silflay, but here we generally go straight out.'

Hazel did not mean to alter his ways or take instructions from Cowslip. However, no one had pushed him and there was no point in bickering over trifles. He hopped across the ditch to the farther bank and looked round him again. Several rabbits were already running down the field towards a distant hedge dappled white with great patches of may-bloom. He saw Bigwig and Silver and went to join them, flicking the wet off his front paws step by step, like a cat.

'I hope your friends have been looking after you as well as these fellows have looked after us, Hazel,' said Bigwig.

'Silver and I really feel at home again. If you ask me, I reckon we've all made a big change for the better. Even if Fiver's wrong and nothing terrible *has* happened back at the old warren, I'd still say we're better off here. Are you coming along to feed?'

'What is this business about going to feed, do you know?' asked Hazel.

'Haven't they told you? Apparently there's flayrah to be had down the fields. Most of them go every day.'

(Rabbits usually eat grass, as everyone knows. But more appetizing food, e.g. lettuce or carrots, for which they will make an expedition or rob a garden, is *flayrah*.)

'Flayrah? But isn't it rather late in the morning to raid a garden?' said Hazel, glancing at the distant roofs of the farm behind the trees.

'No, no,' said one of the warren rabbits, who had overheard him. 'The flayrah's left in the field, usually near the place where the brook rises. We either eat it there or bring it back – or both. But we'll have to bring some back today. The rain was so bad last night that no one went out and we ate almost everything in the warren.'

The brook ran through the hedgerow, and there was a cattle-wade in the gap. After the rain the edges were a swamp, with water standing in every hoof-print. The rabbits gave them a wide berth and came through by another gap farther up, close to the gnarled trunk of an old crab-apple tree. Beyond, surrounding a thicket of rushes, stood an enclosure of posts and rails half as high as a man. Inside it, the king-cups bloomed and the brook whelmed up from its source.

On the pasture near-by Hazel could see scattered, russet-and-orange-coloured fragments, some with feathery, light-green foliage showing up against the darker grass. They gave off a pungent, horsey smell, as if freshly cut. It attracted him. He began to salivate and stopped to pass *hraka*. Cowslip, coming up near-by, turned towards him with his unnatural smile. But now Hazel, in his eagerness, paid no attention. Powerfully drawn, he ran out of the hedgerow towards the scattered ground. He came to one of the fragments, sniffed it and tasted it. It was carrot.

Hazel had eaten various roots in his life, but only once before had he tasted carrot, when a cart-horse had spilt a nose-bag near the home warren. These were old carrots, some half-eaten already by mice or fly. But to the rabbits they were redolent with luxury, a feast to drive all other feelings out of mind. Hazel sat nibbling and biting, the rich, full taste of the cultivated roots filling him with a wave of pleasure. He hopped about the grass, gnawing one piece after another, eating the green tops along with the slices. No one interrupted him. There seemed to be plenty for all. From time to time, instinctively, he looked up and sniffed the wind, but his caution was half-hearted. 'If elil come, let them,' he thought. 'I'll fight the lot. I couldn't run, anyway. What a country! What a warren! No wonder they're all as big as hares and smell like princes!' 'Hullo, Pipkin! Fill yourself up to the ears! No more shivering on the banks of streams for you, old chap!'

'He won't know how to shiver in a week or two,' said Hawkbit, with his mouth full. 'I feel so much better for this! I'd follow you anywhere, Hazel. I wasn't myself in the heather that night. It's bad when you know you can't get underground. I hope you understand.'

'It's all forgotten,' answered Hazel. 'I'd better ask Cowslip what we're supposed to do about taking some of this stuff back to the warren.'

He found Cowslip near the spring. He had evidently finished feeding and was washing his face with his front paws.

'Are there roots here every day?' asked Hazel. 'Where –' He checked himself just in time. 'I'm learning,' he thought.

'Not always roots,' replied Cowslip. 'These are last year's, as you'll have noticed. I suppose the remains are being cleared out. It may be anything – roots, green stuff, old apples: it all depends. Sometimes there's nothing at all, especially in good summer weather. But in hard weather, in winter, there's nearly always something. Big roots, usually, or kale, or sometimes corn. We eat that too, you know.'

'Food's no problem, then. The whole place ought to be full of rabbits. I suppose –'

'If you really have finished,' interrupted Cowslip, 'and there's no hurry; do take your time – you could try carrying. It's easy with these roots – easier than anything except lettuce. You simply bite on one, take it back to the warren and put it in the great burrow. I generally take two at a time, but then I've had a lot of practice. Rabbits don't usually carry food, I know, but you'll learn. It's useful to have a store. The does need some for their young when they're getting bigger; and it's particularly convenient for all of us in bad weather. Come back with me and I'll help if you find the carrying difficult at first.'

It took Hazel some trouble to learn to grip half a carrot in his mouth and carry it, like a dog, across the field and back to the warren. He had to put it down several times. But Cowslip was encouraging and he was determined to keep up his position as the resourceful leader of the newcomers. At his suggestion they both waited at the mouth of one of the larger holes to see how his companions were shaping. They all seemed to be making an effort and doing their best, although the smaller rabbits – especially Pipkin – clearly found the task an awkward one.

'Cheer up, Pipkin,' said Hazel. 'Think how much you'll enjoy eating it tonight. Anyway, I'm sure Fiver must find it as hard as you: he's just as small.'

'I don't know where he is,' said Pipkin. 'Have you seen him?'

Now that Hazel thought about it, he had not. He became a little anxious, and, as he returned across the field with Cowslip, did his best to explain something of Fiver's peculiar temperament. 'I do hope he's all right,' he said. 'I think perhaps I'll go and look for him when we've carried this next lot. Have you any idea where he might be?'

He waited for Cowslip to reply but he was disappointed. After a few moments Cowslip said, 'Look, do you see those jackdaws hanging round the carrots? They've been a nuisance for several days now. I must get someone to try to keep them off until we've finished carrying. But they're really too big for a rabbit to tackle. Now sparrows –'

'What's that got to do with Fiver?' asked Hazel sharply.

'In fact,' said Cowslip, breaking into a run, 'I'll go myself.'

But he did not engage the jackdaws and Hazel saw him pick up another carrot and start back with it. Annoyed, he joined Buckthorn and Dandelion and the three of them returned together. As they came up to the warren bank he suddenly caught sight of Fiver. He was sitting half-concealed under the low spread of a yew tree on the edge of the copse, some way from the holes of the warren. Putting down his carrot, Hazel ran across, scrambled up the bank and joined him on the bare ground under the low, close boughs. Fiver said nothing and continued to stare over the field.

'Aren't you coming to learn to carry, Fiver?' asked Hazel at length. 'It's not too difficult once you get the hang of it.'

'I'll have nothing to do with it,' answered Fiver in a low voice. 'Dogs – you're like dogs carrying sticks.'

'Fiver! Are you trying to make me angry? I'm not going to get angry because you call me stupid names. But you're letting the others do all the work.'

'I'm the one who ought to get angry,' said Fiver. 'But I'm no good at it, that's the trouble. Why should they listen to me? Half of them think I'm mad. You're to blame, Hazel, because you know I'm not and still you won't listen.'

'So you don't like this warren any better even now? Well, I think you're wrong. Everyone makes mistakes sometimes. Why shouldn't you make a mistake, like everybody else? Hawkbit was wrong in the heather and you're wrong now.'

'Those are rabbits down there, trotting along like a lot of squirrels with nuts. How can that be right?'

'Well, I'd say they've copied a good idea from the squirrels and that makes them better rabbits.'

'Do you suppose the man, whoever he is, puts the roots out there because he has a kind heart? What's he up to?'

'He's just throwing away rubbish. How many rabbits have had a good meal off men's rubbish heaps? Shot lettuces, old turnips? You know we all do, when we can. It's not poisoned, Fiver, I can tell you that. And if he wanted to shoot rabbits he's had plenty of chances this morning. But he hasn't done it.'

Fiver seemed to grow even smaller as he flattened himself on the hard earth. 'I'm a fool to try to argue,' he said miserably. 'Hazel – dear old Hazel – it's simply that I *know* there's something unnatural and evil twisted all round this place. I don't know what it is, so no wonder I can't talk about it. I keep getting near it, though. You know how you poke your nose against wire netting and push it up against an apple tree, but you still can't bite the bark because of the wire. I'm close to this – whatever it is – but I can't grip it. If I sit here alone I may reach it yet.'

'Fiver, why not do as I say? Have a meal on those roots and then go underground and sleep. You'll feel all the better for it.'

'I tell you I'll have nothing to do with the place,' said Fiver. 'As for going underground, I'd rather go back over the heather. The roof of that hall is made of bones.'

'No, no – tree roots. But after all, you were underground all night.'

'I wasn't,' said Fiver.

'What? Where were you then?'

'Here.'

'All night?'

'Yes. A yew tree gives good shelter, you know.'

Hazel was now seriously worried. If Fiver's horrors had kept him above ground all night in the rain, oblivious of cold and prowling elil, then clearly it was not going to be easy to talk him out of them. He was silent for some time. At last he said, 'What a shame! I still think you'd do better to come and join us. But I'll let you alone now and come and see how you're feeling later. Don't go eating the yew tree, either.'

Fiver made no reply and Hazel went back to the field.

The day was certainly not one to encourage foreboding. By ni-Frith it was so hot that the lower part of the field was humid. The air was heavy with thick, herbal smells, as though it were already late June; the water-mint and marjoram, not yet flowering, gave off scent from their leaves and here and there an early meadow-sweet stood in bloom. The chiff-chaff was busy all morning, high in a silver birch near the abandoned holes across the dip; and from deep in the copse, somewhere by the disused well, came the beautiful song of the blackcap. By early afternoon there was a stillness of heat, and a herd of cows from the higher fields slowly grazed their way down into the shade. Only a few of the rabbits remained above ground. Almost all were asleep in the burrows. But still Fiver sat alone under the yew tree.

In the early evening Hazel sought out Bigwig and together they ventured into the copse behind the warren. At first they moved cautiously, but before long they grew confident at finding no trace of any creature larger than a mouse.

'There's nothing to smell,' said Bigwig, 'and no tracks. I think Cowslip's told us no more than the truth. There really aren't any elil here. Different from that wood where we crossed the river. I don't mind telling you, Hazel, I was scared stiff that night, but I wasn't going to show it.'

'So was I,' answered Hazel. 'But I agree with you about this place. It seems completely clear. If we –'

'This is odd, though,' interrupted Bigwig. He was in a clump of brambles, in the middle of which was a rabbit-hole that led up from one of the warren passages below. The ground was soft and damp, with old leaves thick in the mould. Where Bigwig had stopped there were signs of commotion. The rotten leaves had been thrown up in showers. Some were hanging on the brambles and a few flat, wet clots were lying well out in open ground beyond the clump. In the centre the earth had been laid bare and was scored with long scratches and furrows, and there was a narrow, regular hole, about the same size as one of the carrots they had carried that morning. The two rabbits sniffed and stared, but could make nothing of it.

'The funny thing is there's no smell,' said Bigwig.

'No – only rabbit, and that's everywhere, of course. And man – that's everywhere too. But that smell might very well have nothing to do with it. All it tells us is that a man walked through the wood and threw a white stick down. It wasn't a man that tore up this ground.'

'Well, these mad rabbits probably dance in the moonlight or something.'

'I wouldn't be surprised,' said Hazel. 'It would be just like them. Let's ask Cowslip.'

'That's the only silly thing you've said so far. Tell me, since we came here has Cowslip answered any question you've asked him?'

'Well, no – not many.'

'Try asking him where he dances in the moonlight. Say "Cowslip, where –"'

'Oh, you've noticed that too, have you? He won't answer "Where" anything. Neither will Strawberry. I think they may be nervous of us. Pipkin was right when he said they weren't fighters. So they're keeping up a mystery to stay even with us. It's best just to put up with it. We don't want to upset them and it's bound to smooth itself out in time.'

'There's more rain coming tonight,' said Bigwig. 'Soon, too, I think. Let's go underground and see if we can get them to talk a bit more freely.'

'I think that's something we can only wait for. But I agree about going underground now. And for goodness' sake let's get Fiver to come with us. He troubles me. Do you know he was out all night in the rain?'

As they went back through the copse Hazel recounted his talk with Fiver that morning. They found him under the yew tree and after a rather stormy scene, during which Bigwig grew rough and impatient, he was bullied rather than persuaded into going down with them into the great burrow.

It was crowded, and as the rain began to fall more rabbits came down the runs. They pushed about, cheerful and chattering. The carrots which had been brought in were eaten between friends or carried away to does and families in burrows all over the warren. But when they were finished the hall remained full. It was pleasantly warm with the heat of so many bodies. Gradually the talkative groups settled into a contented silence, but no one seemed disposed to go to sleep. Rabbits are lively at nightfall, and when evening rain drives them underground they still feel gregarious. Hazel noticed that almost all his companions seemed to have become friendly with the warren rabbits. Also, he found that whenever he moved into one group or another, the warren rabbits evidently knew who he was and treated him as the leader of the newcomers. He could not find Strawberry, but after a time Cowslip came up to him from the other end of the hall.

'I'm glad you're here, Hazel,' he said. 'Some of our lot are suggesting a story from somebody. We're hoping one of your people would like to tell one, but we can begin ourselves, if you'd prefer.'

There is a rabbit saying, 'In the warren, more stories than passages'; and a rabbit can no more refuse to tell a story than an Irishman can refuse to fight. Hazel and his friends conferred. After a short time Blackberry announced, 'We've asked Hazel to tell you about our adventures: how we made our journey here and had the good luck to join you.'

There was an uncomfortable silence, broken only by shuffling and whispering. Blackberry, dismayed, turned back to Hazel and Bigwig.

'What's the matter?' he asked in a low voice. 'Surely there's no harm in that?'

'Wait,' replied Hazel quietly. 'Let them tell us if they don't like it. They have their own ways here.'

However, the silence continued for some time, as though the other rabbits did not care to mention what they thought was wrong.

'It's no good,' said Blackberry at last. 'You'll have to say something yourself, Hazel. No, why should you? I'll do it.' He spoke up again. 'On second thoughts, Hazel remembers that we have a good story-teller among us. Dandelion will tell you a story of El-ahrairah. That can't go wrong, anyway,' he whispered.

'Which one, though?' said Dandelion.

Hazel remembered the stones by the well-pit. 'The King's Lettuce,' he answered. 'They think a lot of that, I believe.'

Dandelion took up his cue with the same plucky readiness that he had shown in the wood. 'I'll tell the story of the King's Lettuce,' he said aloud.

'We shall enjoy that,' replied Cowslip immediately.

'He'd better,' muttered Bigwig.

Dandelion began.

15. The Story of the King's Lettuce

Don Alfonso: 'Eccovi il medico, signore belle.'
Ferrando and Guglielmo: 'Despina in maschera, che triste pelle!'
                                 Lorenzo da Ponte, *Cosi fan tutte*

'THEY say that there was a time when El-ahrairah and his followers lost all their luck. Their enemies drove them out and they were forced to live down in the marshes of Kelfazin. Now where the marshes of Kelfazin may be I do not know, but at the time when El-ahrairah and his followers were living there, of all the dreary places in the world they were the dreariest. There was no food but coarse grass and even the grass was mixed with bitter rushes and docks. The ground was too wet for digging: the water stood in any hole that was made. But all the other animals had grown so suspicious of El-ahrairah and his tricks that they would not let him out of that wretched country and every day Prince Rainbow used to come walking through the marshes to make sure that El-ahrairah was still there. Prince Rainbow had the power of the sky and the power of the hills and Frith had told him to order the world as he thought best.

'One day, when Prince Rainbow was coming through the marshes, El-ahrairah went up to him and said, "Prince Rainbow, my people are cold and cannot get underground because of the wet. Their food is so dull and poor that they will be ill when the bad weather comes. Why do you keep us here against our will? We do no harm."

'"El-ahrairah," replied Prince Rainbow, "all the animals know that you are a thief and a trickster. Now your tricks have caught up with you and you have to live here until you can persuade us that you will be an honest rabbit."

'"Then we shall never get out," said El-ahrairah, "for I would be ashamed to tell my people to stop living on their wits. Will you let us out if I can swim across a lake full of pike?"

'"No," said Prince Rainbow, "for I have heard of that trick of yours, El-ahrairah, and I know how it is done."

'"Will you let us go if I can steal the lettuces from King Darzin's garden?" asked El-ahrairah.

'Now King Darzin ruled over the biggest and richest of the animal cities in the world at that time. His soldiers were very fierce and his lettuce garden was surrounded by a deep ditch and guarded by a thousand sentries day and night. It was near his palace, on the edge of the city where all his followers lived. So when El-ahrairah talked of stealing King Darzin's lettuces, Prince Rainbow laughed and said,

'"You can try, El-ahrairah, and if you succeed I will multiply your people everywhere and no one will be able to keep them out of a vegetable garden from now till the end of the world. But what will really happen is that you will be killed by the soldiers and the world will be rid of a smooth, plausible rascal."

'"Very well," said El-ahrairah. "We shall see."

'Now Yona the hedgehog was near-by, looking for slugs and snails in the marshes, and he heard what passed between Prince Rainbow and El-ahrairah. He slipped away to the great palace of King Darzin and begged to be rewarded for warning him against his enemies.

'"King Darzin," he sniffled, "that wicked thief, El-ahrairah, has said he will steal your lettuces and he is coming to trick you and get into the garden."

'King Darzin hurried down to the lettuce garden and sent for the captain of the guard.

'"You see these lettuces?" he said. "Not one of them has been stolen since the seed was sown. Very soon now they will be ready and then I mean to hold a great feast for all my people. But I have heard that that scoundrel El-ahrairah means to come and steal them if he can. You are to double the guards: and all the gardeners and weeders are to be examined every day. Not one leaf is to go out of the garden until either I or my chief taster gives the order."

'The captain of the guard did as he was told. That night El-ahrairah came out of the marshes of Kelfazin and went secretly up to the great ditch. With him was his trusty Captain of Owsla, Rabscuttle. They squatted in the bushes and watched the doubled guards patrolling up and down. When the morning came they saw all the gardeners and weeders coming up to the wall and every one was looked at by three guards. One was new and had come instead of his uncle who was ill, but the guards would not let him in because they did not know him by sight and they nearly threw him into the ditch before they would even let him go home. El-ahrairah and Rabscuttle came away in perplexity and that day, when Prince Rainbow came walking through the marshes, he said, "Well, well, Prince with the Thousand Enemies, where are the lettuces?"

'"I am having them delivered," answered El-ahrairah. "There will be rather too many to carry." Then he and Rabscuttle went secretly down one of their few holes where there was no water, put a sentry outside and thought and talked for a day and a night.

'On the top of the hill near King Darzin's palace there was a garden and here his many children and his chief followers' children used to be taken to play by their mothers and nursemaids. There was no wall round the garden. It was guarded only when the children were there: at night it was empty, because there was nothing to steal and no one to be hunted. The next night Rabscuttle, who had been told by El-ahrairah what he had to do, went to the garden and dug a scrape. He hid in the scrape all night; and the next morning, when the children were brought to play, he slipped out and joined them. There were so many children that each one of the mothers and nursemaids thought that he must belong to somebody else, but as he was about the same size as the children and not much different to look at, he was able to make friends with some of them. Rabscuttle was full of tricks and games and quite soon he was running and playing just as if he had been one of the children himself. When the time came for the children to go home, Rabscuttle went too. They came up to the gate of the city and the guards saw Rabscuttle with King Darzin's son. They stopped him and asked which was his mother, but the king's son said, "You let him alone. He's my friend," and Rabscuttle went in with all the others.

'Now as soon as Rabscuttle got inside the king's palace, he scurried off and went into one of the dark burrows; and here he hid all day. But in the evening he came out and made his way to the royal store-rooms, where the food was being got ready for the king and his chief followers and wives. There were grasses and fruits and roots and even nuts and berries, for King Darzin's people went everywhere in those days, through the woods and fields. There were no soldiers in the store-rooms and Rabscuttle hid there in the dark. And he did all he could to make the food bad, except what he ate himself.

'That evening King Darzin sent for the chief taster and asked him whether the lettuces were ready. The chief taster said that several of them were excellent and that he had already had some brought into the stores.

'"Good," said the king. "We will have two or three tonight."

'But the next morning the king and several of his people were taken ill with bad stomachs. Whatever they ate they kept on getting ill, because Rabscuttle was hiding in the store-rooms and spoiling the food as fast as it was brought in. The king ate several more lettuces but he got no better. In fact, he got worse.

'After five days Rabscuttle slipped out again with the children and came back to El-ahrairah. When he heard that the king was ill and that Rabscuttle had done all he wanted, El-ahrairah set to work to disguise himself. He clipped his white tail and made Rabscuttle nibble his fur short and stain it with mud and blackberries. Then he covered himself all over with trailing strands of goose-grass and big burdocks and he even found ways to alter his smell. At last even his own wives could not recognize him, and El-ahrairah told Rabscuttle to follow some way behind and off he went to King Darzin's palace. But Rabscuttle waited outside, on the top of the hill.

'When he got to the palace, El-ahrairah demanded to see the captain of the guard. "You are to take me to the king," he said. "Prince Rainbow has sent me. He has heard that the king is ill and he has sent for me, from the distant land beyond Kelfazin, to find the cause of his sickness. Be quick! I am not accustomed to be kept waiting."

'"How do I know this is true?" asked the captain of the guard.

'"It is all one to me," replied El-ahrairah. "What is the sickness of a little king to the chief physician of the land beyond the golden river of Frith? I will return and tell Prince Rainbow that the king's guard were foolish and gave me such treatment as one might expect from a crowd of flea-bitten louts."

'He turned and began to go away, but the captain of the guard became frightened and called him back. El-ahrairah allowed himself to be persuaded and the soldiers took him to the king.

'After five days of bad food and bad stomach, the king was not inclined to be suspicious of someone who said that

Prince Rainbow had sent him to make him better. He begged El-ahrairah to examine him and promised to do all he said.

'El-ahrairah made a great business of examining the king. He looked at his eyes and his ears and his teeth and his droppings and the ends of his claws and he inquired what he had been eating. Then he demanded to see the royal store-rooms and the lettuce-garden. When he came back he looked very grave and said, "Great king, I know well what sorry news it will be to you, but the cause of your sickness is those very lettuces by which you set such store."

'"The lettuces?" cried King Darzin. "Impossible! They are all grown from good, healthy seed and guarded day and night."

'"Alas!" said El-ahrairah, "I know it well! But they have been infected by the dreaded Lousepedoodle, that flies in ever-decreasing circles through the Gunpat of the Cludge – a deadly virus – dear me, yes! – isolated by the purple Avvago and maturing in the grey-green forests of the Okey Pokey. This, you understand, is to put the matter for you in simple terms, insofar as I can. Medically speaking, there are certain complexities with which I will not weary you."

'"I cannot believe it," said the king.

'"The simplest course," said El-ahrairah, "will be to prove it to you. But we need not make one of your subjects ill. Tell the soldiers to go out and take a prisoner."

'The soldiers went out and the first creature they found was Rabscuttle, grazing on the hill-top. They dragged him through the gates and into the king's presence.

'"Ah, a rabbit," said El-ahrairah. "Nasty creature! So much the better. Disgusting rabbit, eat that lettuce!"

'Rabscuttle did so and soon afterwards he began to moan and thrash about. He kicked in convulsions and rolled his eyes. He gnawed at the floor and frothed at the mouth.

'"He is very ill," said El-ahrairah. "He must have got an exceptionally bad one. Or else, which is more probable, the infection is particularly deadly to rabbits. But in any event, let us be thankful it was not Your Majesty. Well, he has served our purpose. Throw him out! I would strongly advise Your Majesty," went on El-ahrairah, "not to leave the lettuces where they are, for they will shoot and flower and seed. The infection will spread. I know it is disappointing, but you must get rid of them."

'At that moment, as luck would have it, in came the captain of the guard, with Yona the hedgehog.

'"Your Majesty," he cried, "this creature returns from the marshes of Kelfazin. The people of El-ahrairah are mustering for war. They say they are coming to attack Your Majesty's garden and steal the royal lettuces. May I have Your Majesty's order to take out the soldiers and destroy them?"

'"Aha!" said the king, "I have thought of a trick worth two of that. 'Particularly deadly to rabbits.' Well! Well! Let them have all the lettuces they want. In fact, you are to take a thousand down to the marshes of Kelfazin and leave them there. Ho! Ho! What a joke! I feel all the better for it!"

'"Ah, what deadly cunning!" said El-ahrairah. "No wonder Your Majesty is ruler of a great people. I believe you are already recovering. As with many illnesses, the cure is simple, once perceived. No, no, I will accept no reward. In any case, there is nothing here that would be thought of value in the shining land beyond the golden river of Frith. I have done as Prince Rainbow required. It is sufficient. Perhaps you will be so good as to tell your guards to accompany me to the foot of the hill?" He bowed, and left the palace.

'Later that evening, as El-ahrairah was urging his rabbits to growl more fiercely and run up and down in the marshes of Kelfazin, Prince Rainbow came over the river.

'"El-ahrairah," he called, "am I bewitched?"

'"It is quite possible," said El-ahrairah. "The dreaded Lousepedoodle –"

'"There are a thousand lettuces in a pile at the top of the marsh. Who put them there?"

'"I told you they were being delivered," said El-ahrairah. "You could hardly expect my people, weak and hungry as they are, to carry them all the way from King Darzin's garden. However, they will soon recover now, under the treatment that I shall prescribe. I am a physician, I may say, and if you have not heard as much, Prince Rainbow, you may take it that you soon will, from another quarter. Rabscuttle, go out and collect the lettuces."

'Then Prince Rainbow saw that El-ahrairah had been as good as his word, and that he himself must keep his promise too. He let the rabbits out of the marshes of Kelfazin and they multiplied everywhere. And from that day to this, no power on earth can keep a rabbit out of a vegetable garden, for El-ahrairah prompts them with a thousand tricks, the best in the world.'

16. Silverweed

He said, 'Dance for me' and he said,
'You are too beautiful for the wind
To pick at, or the sun to burn.' He said,
'I'm a poor tattered thing, but not unkind
To the sad dancer and the dancing dead.'

Sidney Keyes, *Four Postures of Death*

'WELL done,' said Hazel, as Dandelion ended.

'He's very good, isn't he?' said Silver. 'We're lucky to have him with us. It raises your spirits just to hear him.'

'That's put their ears flat for them,' whispered Bigwig. 'Let's just see them find a story-teller to beat him.'

They were all in no doubt that Dandelion had done them credit. Ever since their arrival most of them had felt out of their depth among these magnificent, well-fed strangers, with their detached manners, their shapes on the wall, their elegance, their adroit evasion of almost all questions – above all, their fits of un-rabbit-like melancholy.

Now, their own story-teller had shown that they were no mere bunch of tramps. Certainly, no reasonable rabbit could withhold admiration. They waited to be told as much, but after a few moments realized with surprise that their hosts were evidently less enthusiastic.

'Very nice,' said Cowslip. He seemed to be searching for something more to say, but then repeated, 'Yes, very nice. An unusual tale.'

'But he must know it, surely?' muttered Blackberry to Hazel.

'I always think these traditional stories retain a lot of charm,' said another of the rabbits, 'especially when they're told in the real, old-fashioned spirit.'

'Yes,' said Strawberry. 'Conviction, that's what it needs. You really have to *believe* in El-ahrairah and Prince Rainbow, don't you? Then all the rest follows.'

'Don't say anything, Bigwig,' whispered Hazel: for Bigwig was scuffling his paws indignantly. 'You can't force them to like it if they don't. Let's wait and see what they can do themselves.' Aloud, he said, 'Our stories haven't changed in generations, you know. After all, we haven't changed ourselves. Our lives have been the same as our fathers' and their fathers' before them. Things are different here. We realize that, and we think your new ideas and ways are very exciting. We're all wondering what kind of things *you* tell stories about.'

'Well, we don't tell the old stories very much,' said Cowslip. 'Our stories and poems are mostly about our own lives here. Of course, that Shape of Laburnum that you saw – that's old-fashioned now. El-ahrairah doesn't really mean much to us. Not that your friend's story wasn't very charming,' he added hastily.

'El-ahrairah is a trickster,' said Buckthorn, 'and rabbits will always need tricks.'

'No,' said a new voice from the further end of the hall, beyond Cowslip. 'Rabbits need dignity and above all, the will to accept their fate.'

'We think Silverweed is one of the best poets we've had for many months,' said Cowslip. 'His ideas have a great following. Would you like to hear him now?'

'Yes, yes,' said voices from all sides. 'Silverweed!'

'Hazel,' said Fiver suddenly, 'I want to get a clear idea of this Silverweed, but I daren't go closer by myself. Will you come with me?'

'Why, Fiver, whatever do you mean? What is there to be afraid of?'

'Oh, Frith help me!' said Fiver, trembling, 'I can smell him from here. He terrifies me.'

'Oh, Fiver, don't be absurd! He just smells the same as the rest of them.'

'He smells like barley rained down and left to rot in the fields. He smells like a wounded mole that can't get underground.'

'He smells like a big, fat rabbit to me, with a lot of carrots inside. But I'll come with you.'

When they had edged their way through the crowd to the far end of the burrow, Hazel was surprised to realize that Silverweed was a mere youngster. In the Sandleford warren no rabbit of his age would have been asked to tell a story, except perhaps to a few friends alone. He had a wild, desperate air and his ears twitched continually. As he began to speak, he seemed to grow less and less aware of his audience and continually turned his head, as though listening to some sound, audible only to himself, from the entrance tunnel behind him. But there was an arresting fascination in his voice, like the movement of wind and light on a meadow, and as its rhythm entered into his hearers the whole burrow became silent.

'The wind is blowing, blowing over the grass.
It shakes the willow catkins; the leaves shine silver.
Where are you going, wind? Far, far away
Over the hills, over the edge of the world.
Take me with you, wind, high over the sky.
I will go with you, I will be rabbit-of-the-wind,
Into the sky, the feathery sky and the rabbit.
The stream is running, running over the gravel,
Through the brooklime, the kingcups, the blue and gold of
    spring.
Where are you going, stream? Far, far away
Beyond the heather, sliding away all night.
Take me with you, stream, away in the starlight.
I will go with you, I will be rabbit-of-the-stream,
Down through the water, the green water and the rabbit.

'In autumn the leaves come blowing, yellow and brown.
They rustle in the ditches, they tug and hang on the hedge.
Where are you going, leaves? Far, far away
Into the earth we go, with the rain and the berries.

Take me, leaves, O take me on your dark journey.
I will go with you, I will be rabbit-of-the-leaves,
In the deep places of the earth, the earth and the rabbit.

'Frith lies in the evening sky. The clouds are red about him.
I am here, Lord Frith, I am running through the long grass.
O take me with you, dropping behind the woods,
Far away, to the heart of light, the silence.
For I am ready to give you my breath, my life,
The shining circle of the sun, the sun and the rabbit.'

Fiver, as he listened, had shown a mixture of intense absorption and incredulous horror. At one and the same time he seemed to accept every word and yet to be stricken with fear. Once he drew in his breath, as though startled to recognize his own half-known thoughts: and when the poem was ended he seemed to be struggling to come to himself. He bared his teeth and licked his lips, as Blackberry had done before the dead hedgehog on the road.

A rabbit in fear of an enemy will sometimes crouch stock-still, either fascinated or else trusting to its natural inconspicuousness to remain unnoticed. But then, unless the fascination is too powerful, there comes the point when keeping still is discarded and the rabbit, as though breaking a spell, turns in an instant to its other resource – flight. So it seemed to be with Fiver now. Suddenly he leapt up and began to push his way violently across the great burrow. Several rabbits were jostled and turned angrily on him, but he took no notice. Then he came to a place where he could not push between two heavy warren bucks. He became hysterical, kicking and scuffling, and Hazel, who was behind him, had difficulty in preventing a fight.

'My brother's a sort of poet too, you know,' he said to the bristling strangers. 'Things affect him very strongly sometimes and he doesn't always know why.'

One of the rabbits seemed to accept what Hazel had said, but the other replied, 'Oh, another poet? Let's hear him, then. That'll be some return for my shoulder, anyway. He's scratched a great tuft of fur out.'

Fiver was already beyond them and thrusting towards the farther entrance tunnel. Hazel felt that he must follow him. But after all the trouble that he himself had taken to be friendly, he felt so cross at the way in which Fiver had antagonized their new friends that as he passed Bigwig, he said, 'Come and help me to get some sense into him. The last thing we want is a fight now.' He felt that Fiver really deserved a short touch of Bigwig.

They followed Fiver up the run and overtook him at the entrance. Before either of them could say a word, he turned and began to speak as though they had asked him a question.

'You felt it, then? And you want to know whether I did? Of course I did. That's the worst part of it. There isn't any trick. He speaks the truth. So long as he speaks the truth it can't be folly – that's what you're going to say, isn't it? I'm not blaming you, Hazel. I felt myself moving towards him like one cloud drifting into another. But then at the last moment I drifted wide. Who knows why? It wasn't my own will; it was an accident. There was just some little part of me that carried me wide of him. Did I say the roof of that hall was made of bones? No! It's like a great mist of folly that covers the whole sky: and we shall never see to go by Frith's light any more. Oh, what will become of us? A thing can be true and still be desperate folly, Hazel.'

'What on earth's all this?' said Hazel to Bigwig in perplexity.

'He's talking about that lop-eared nitwit of a poet down there,' answered Bigwig. 'I know that much. But why he seems to think we should want to have anything to do with him and his fancy talk – that's more than I can imagine. You can save your breath, Fiver. The only thing that's bothering us is the row you've started. As for Silverweed, all I can say is, I'll keep Silver and he can be just plain Weed.'

Fiver gazed back at him with eyes that, like a fly's, seemed larger than his head. 'You think that,' he said. 'You believe that. But each of you, in his own way, is thick in that mist. Where is the –'

Hazel interrupted him and as he did so Fiver started. 'Fiver, I won't pretend that I didn't follow you up here to speak angrily. You've endangered our good start in this warren –'

'Endangered?' cried Fiver. 'Endangered? Why, the whole place –'

'Be quiet. I was going to be angry, but you're obviously so much upset that it would be pointless. But what you *are* going to do now is to come underground with the two of us and sleep. Come on! And don't say any more for the moment.'

One respect in which rabbits' lives are less complicated than those of humans is that they are not ashamed to use force. Having no alternative, Fiver accompanied Hazel and Bigwig to the burrow where Hazel had spent the previous night. There was no one there and they lay down and slept.

17. The Shining Wire

When the green field comes off like a lid
Revealing what was much better hid,
    Unpleasant;
And look! Behind, without a sound
The woods have come up and are standing round
    In deadly crescent.
And the bolt is sliding in its groove,
Outside the window is the black remover's van,
And now with sudden, swift emergence
Come the women in dark glasses, the hump-backed
surgeons
    And the scissor-man.

                W. H. Auden, 'The Witnesses'

IT WAS cold, it was cold and the roof was made of bones. The roof was made of the interlaced sprays of the yew tree, stiff twigs twisted in and out, over and under, hard as ice and set with dull-red berries. 'Come on, Hazel,' said Cowslip. 'We're going to carry the yew berries home in our mouths and eat them in the great burrow. Your friends must learn to do that if they want to go our way.' 'No! No!' cried Fiver, 'Hazel, no!' But then came Bigwig, twisting in and out of the branches, his mouth full of berries. 'Look!' said Bigwig, 'I can do it. I'm running another way. Ask me where, Hazel! Ask me where! Ask me where!' Then they were running another way, running, not to the warren but over the fields in the cold, and Bigwig dropped the berries – blood-red drops, red droppings hard as wire. 'It's no good,' he said. 'No good biting them. They're cold.'

Hazel woke. He was in the burrow. He shivered. Why was there no warmth of rabbit bodies lying close together? Where was Fiver? He sat up. Near by, Bigwig was stirring and twitching in his sleep, searching for warmth, trying to press against another rabbit's body no longer there. The shallow hollow in the sandy floor where Fiver had lain was not quite cold: but Fiver was gone.

'Fiver!' said Hazel in the dark.

As soon as he had spoken he knew there would be no reply. He pushed Bigwig with his nose, butting urgently. 'Bigwig! Fiver's gone! Bigwig!'

Bigwig was wide awake on the instant and Hazel had never felt so glad of his sturdy readiness.

'What did you say? What's wrong?'

'Fiver's gone.'

'Where's he gone?'

'Silf – outside. It can only be silf. You know he wouldn't go wandering about in the warren. He hates it.'

'He's a nuisance, isn't he? He's left this burrow cold, too. You think he's in danger, don't you? You want to go and look for him?'

'Yes, I must. He's upset and over-wrought and it's not light yet. There may be elil, whatever Strawberry says.'

Bigwig listened and sniffed for a few moments.

'It's very nearly light,' he said. 'There'll be light enough to find him by. Well, I'd better come with you, I suppose. Don't worry – he can't have gone far. But by the King's Lettuce! I won't half give him a piece of my mind when we catch him.'

'I'll hold him down while you kick him, if only we can find him. Come on!'

They went up the run to the mouth of the hole and paused together. 'Since our friends aren't here to push us,' said Bigwig, 'we may as well make sure the place isn't crawling with stoats and owls before we go out.'

At that moment a brown owl's call sounded from the opposite wood. It was the first call, and by instinct they both crouched motionless, counting four heart-beats until the second followed.

'It's moving away,' said Hazel.

'How many field-mice say that every night, I wonder! You know the call's deceptive. It's meant to be.'

'Well, I can't help it,' said Hazel. 'Fiver's somewhere out there and I'm going after him. You were right, anyway. It *is* light – just.'

'Shall we look under the yew tree first?'

But Fiver was not under the yew tree. The light, as it grew, began to show the upper field, while the distant hedge and brook remained dark, linear shapes below. Bigwig jumped down from the bank into the field and ran in a long curve across the wet grass. He stopped almost opposite the hole by which they had come up, and Hazel joined him.

'Here's his line all right,' said Bigwig. 'Fresh, too. From the hole straight down towards the brook. He won't be far away.'

When raindrops are lying it is easy to see where grass has recently been crossed. They followed the line down the field and reached the hedge beside the carrot-ground and the source of the brook. Bigwig had been right when he said the line was fresh. As soon as they had come through the hedge they saw Fiver. He was feeding, alone. A few fragments of carrot were still lying about near the spring, but he had left these untouched and was eating the grass not far from the gnarled crab-apple tree. They approached and he looked up.

Hazel said nothing and began to feed beside him. He was now regretting that he had brought Bigwig. In the darkness before morning and the first shock of discovering that Fiver was gone, Bigwig had been a comfort and a stand-by. But now, as he saw Fiver, small and familiar, incapable of hurting anyone or of concealing what he felt, trembling in the wet grass, either from fear or from cold, his anger melted away. He felt only sorry for him and sure that, if they could stay alone together for a while, Fiver would come round to an easier state of mind. But it was probably too late to persuade Bigwig to be gentle: he could only hope for the best.

Contrary to his fears, however, Bigwig remained as silent as himself. Evidently he had been expecting Hazel to speak first and was somewhat at a loss. For some time all three moved on quietly over the grass, while the shadows grew stronger and the wood-pigeons clattered among the distant trees. Hazel was beginning to feel that all would be well and that Bigwig had more sense than he had given him credit for, when Fiver sat up on his hind legs, cleaned his face with his paws and then, for the first time, looked directly at him.

'I'm going now,' he said. 'I feel very sad. I'd like to wish you well, Hazel, but there's no good to wish you in this place. So just good-bye.'

'But where are you going, Fiver?'

'Away. To the hills, if I can get there.'

'By yourself, alone? You can't. You'd die.'

'You wouldn't have a hope, old chap,' said Bigwig. 'Something would get you before ni-Frith.'

'No,' said Fiver very quietly. 'You are closer to death than I.'

'Are you trying to frighten me, you miserable little lump of chattering chickweed?' cried Bigwig. 'I've a good mind –'

'Wait, Bigwig,' said Hazel. 'Don't speak roughly to him.'

'Why, you said yourself –' began Bigwig.

'I know. But I feel differently now. I'm sorry, Bigwig. I was going to ask you to help me to make him come back to the warren. But now – well, I've always found that there was something in what Fiver had to say. For the last two days I've refused to listen to him and I still think he's out of his senses. But I haven't the heart to drive him back to the warren. I really believe that for some reason or other the place is frightening him out of his wits. I'll go with him a little way and perhaps we can talk. I can't ask you to risk it too. Anyway, the others ought to know what we're doing and they won't unless you go and tell them. I'll be back before ni-Frith. I hope we both shall.'

Bigwig stared. Then he turned furiously on Fiver. 'You wretched little black beetle,' he said. 'You've never learnt to obey orders, have you? It's me, me, me all the time. "Oh, I've got a funny feeling in my toe, so we must all go and stand on our heads!" And now we've found a fine warren and got into it without even having to fight, *you've* got to do your best to upset everyone! And then you risk the life of one of the best rabbits we've got, just to play nursey while you go wandering about like a moon-struck field-mouse. Well, *I'm* finished with you, I'll tell you plain. And now I'm going back to the warren to make sure everyone else is finished with you as well. *And* they will be – don't make any mistake about that.'

He turned and dashed back through the nearest gap in the hedge. On the instant, a fearful commotion began on the farther side. There were sounds of kicking and plunging. A stick flew into the air. Then a flat, wet clot of dead leaves shot clean through the gap and landed clear of the hedge, close to Hazel. The brambles thrashed up and down. Hazel and Fiver stared at each other, both fighting against the impulse to run. What enemy was at work on the other side of the hedge? There were no cries – no spitting of a cat, no squealing of a rabbit – only the crackling of twigs and the tearing of the grass in violence.

By an effort of courage against all instinct, Hazel forced himself forward into the gap, with Fiver following. A terrible sight lay before them. The rotten leaves had been thrown up in showers. The earth had been laid bare and was scored with long scratches and furrows. Bigwig was lying on his side, his back legs kicking and struggling. A length of twisted copper wire, gleaming dully in the first sunlight, was looped round his neck and ran taut across one fore-paw to the head of a stout peg driven into the ground. The running knot had pulled tight and was buried in the fur behind his ear. The projecting point of one strand had lacerated his neck and drops of blood, dark and red as yew berries, welled one by one down his shoulder. For a few moments he lay panting, his side heaving in exhaustion. Then again began the struggling and fighting, backwards and forwards, jerking and falling, until he choked and lay quiet.

Frenzied with distress, Hazel leapt out of the gap and squatted beside him. Bigwig's eyes were closed and his lips pulled back from the long front teeth in a fixed snarl. He had bitten his lower lip and from this, too, the blood was running. Froth covered his jaws and chest.

'Thlayli!' said Hazel, stamping. 'Thlayli! Listen! You're in a snare – a snare! What did they say in the Owsla? Come on – think. How can we help you?'

There was a pause. Then Bigwig's back legs began to kick once more, but feebly. His ears drooped. His eyes opened unseeing and the whites showed blood-shot as the brown irises rolled one way and the other. After a moment his voice came thick and low, bubbling out of the bloody spume in his mouth.

'Owsla – no good – biting wire. Peg – got to – dig out.'

A convulsion shook him and he scrabbled at the ground, covering himself in a mask of wet earth and blood. Then he was still again.

'Run, Fiver, run to the warren,' cried Hazel. 'Get the others – Blackberry, Silver. Be quick! He'll die.'

Fiver was off up the field like a hare. Hazel, left alone, tried to understand what was needed. What was the peg? How was he to dig it out? He looked down at the foul mess before him. Bigwig was lying across the wire, which came out under his belly and seemed to disappear into the ground. Hazel struggled with his own incomprehension. Bigwig had said, 'Dig.' That at least he understood. He began to scratch into the soft earth beside the body, until after a time his claws scraped against something smooth and firm. As he paused, perplexed, he found Blackberry at his shoulder.

'Bigwig just spoke,' he said to him, 'but I don't think he can now. He said, "Dig out the peg." What does that mean? What have we got to do?'

'Wait a moment,' said Blackberry. 'Let me think, and try not to be impatient.'

Hazel turned his head and looked down the course of the brook. Far away, between the two copses, he could see the cherry tree where two days before he had sat with Blackberry and Fiver in the sunrise. He remembered how Bigwig had chased Hawkbit through the long grass, forgetting the quarrel of the previous night in the joy of their arrival. He could see Hawkbit running towards him now and two or three of the others – Silver, Dandelion and

Pipkin. Dandelion, well in front, dashed up to the gap and checked, twitching and staring.

'What is it, Hazel? What's happened? Fiver said –'

'Bigwig's in a wire. Let him alone till Blackberry tells us. Stop the others crowding round.'

Dandelion turned and raced back as Pipkin came up.

'Is Cowslip coming?' said Hazel. 'Perhaps *he* knows –'

'He wouldn't come,' replied Pipkin. 'He told Fiver to stop talking about it.'

'Told him *what*?' asked Hazel incredulously. But at that moment Blackberry spoke and Hazel was beside him in a flash.

'This is it,' said Blackberry. 'The wire's on a peg and the peg's in the ground – there, look. We've got to dig it out. Come on – dig beside it.'

Hazel dug once more, his fore-paws throwing up the soft, wet soil and slipping against the hard sides of the peg. Dimly, he was aware of the others waiting near-by. After a time he was forced to stop, panting. Silver took his place, and was followed by Buckthorn. The nasty, smooth, clean, man-smelling peg was laid bare to the length of a rabbit's ear, but still it did not come loose. Bigwig had not moved. He lay across the wire, torn and bloody, with closed eyes. Buckthorn drew his head and paws out of the hole and rubbed the mud off his face.

'The peg's narrower down there,' he said. 'It tapers. I think it could be bitten through, but I can't get my teeth to it.'

'Send Pipkin in,' said Blackberry. 'He's smaller.'

Pipkin plunged into the hole. They could hear the wood splintering under his teeth – a sound like a mouse in a shed wainscot at midnight. He came out with his nose bleeding.

'The splinters prick you and it's hard to breathe, but the peg's nearly through.'

'Fiver, go in,' said Hazel.

Fiver was not long in the hole. He, too, came out bleeding.

'It's broken in two. It's free.'

Blackberry pressed his nose against Bigwig's head. As he nuzzled him gently the head rolled sideways and back again.

'Bigwig,' said Blackberry in his ear, 'the peg's out.'

There was no response. Bigwig lay still as before. A great fly settled on one of his ears. Blackberry thrust at it angrily and it flew up, buzzing, into the sunshine.

'I think he's gone,' said Blackberry. 'I can't feel his breathing.'

Hazel crouched down by Blackberry and laid his nostrils close to Bigwig's, but a light breeze was blowing and he could not tell whether there was breath or not. The legs were loose, the belly flaccid and limp. He tried to think of what little he had heard of snares. A strong rabbit could break his neck in a snare. Or had the point of a sharp wire pierced the wind-pipe?

'Bigwig,' he whispered, 'we've got you out. You're free.'

Bigwig did not stir. Suddenly it came to Hazel that if Bigwig was dead – and what else could hold *him* silent in the mud? – then he himself must get the others away before the dreadful loss could drain their courage and break their spirit – as it would if they stayed by the body. Besides, the man would come soon. Perhaps he was already coming, with his gun, to take poor Bigwig away. They must go; and he must do his best to see that all of them – even he himself – put what had happened out of mind, for ever.

'My heart has joined the Thousand, for my friend stopped running today,' he said to Blackberry, quoting a rabbit proverb.

'If only it were not Bigwig,' said Blackberry. 'What shall we do without him?'

'The others are waiting,' said Hazel. 'We have to stay alive. There has to be something for them to think about. Help me, or it will be more than I can do.'

He turned away from the body and looked for Fiver among the rabbits behind him. But Fiver was nowhere to be seen and Hazel was afraid to ask for him, in case to do so should seem like weakness and a need for comfort.

'Pipkin,' he snapped, 'why don't you clean up your face and stop the bleeding? The smell of blood attracts elil. You know that, don't you?'

'Yes, Hazel. I'm sorry. Will Bigwig –'

'And another thing,' said Hazel desperately. 'What was it you were telling me about Cowslip? Did you say he told Fiver to be quiet?'

'Yes, Hazel. Fiver came into the warren and told us about the snare, and that poor Bigwig –'

'Yes, all right. And then Cowslip –?'

'Cowslip and Strawberry and the others pretended not to hear. It was ridiculous, because Fiver was calling out to everybody. And then as we were running out Silver said to Cowslip, "Surely you're coming?" And Cowslip simply turned his back. So then Fiver went up and spoke to him very quietly, but I heard what Cowslip answered. He said, "Hills or Inlé, it's all one to me where you go. You hold your tongue." And then he struck at Fiver and scratched his ear.'

'I'll kill him,' gasped a low, choking voice behind them. They all leapt round. Bigwig had raised his head and was supporting himself on his fore-paws alone. His body was twisted and his hind-parts and back legs still lay along the ground. His eyes were open, but his face was such a fearful mask of blood, foam, vomit and earth that he looked more like some demon-creature than a rabbit. The immediate sight of him, which should have filled them with relief and joy, brought only terror. They cringed away and none said a word.

'I'll kill him,' repeated Bigwig, spluttering through his fouled whiskers and clotted fur. 'Help me, rot you! Can't anyone get this stinking wire off me?' He struggled, dragging his hind-legs. Then he fell again and crawled forward, trailing the wire through the grass with the broken peg snickering behind it.

'Let him alone!' cried Hazel, for now they were all pressing forward to help him. 'Do you want to kill him? Let him rest! Let him breathe!'

'No, not rest,' panted Bigwig. 'I'm all right.' As he spoke he fell again and immediately struggled up on his fore-paws as before. 'It's my back legs. 'Won't move. That Cowslip! I'll kill him!'

'Why do we let them stay in that warren?' cried Silver. 'What sort of rabbits are they? They left Bigwig to die. You all heard Cowslip in the burrow. They're cowards. Let's drive them out – kill them! Take the warren and live there ourselves!'

'Yes! Yes!' they all answered. 'Come on! Back to the warren! Down with Cowslip! Down with Silverweed! Kill them!'

'O *embleer Frith!*' cried a squealing voice in the long grass.

At this shocking impiety, the tumult died away. They looked about them, wondering who could have spoken. There was silence. Then, from between two great tussocks of hair-grass came Fiver, his eyes blazing with a frantic urgency. He growled and gibbered at them like a witch-hare and those nearest to him fell back in fear. Even Hazel could not have said a word for his life. They realized that he was speaking.

'The warren? You're going to the warren? You fools! That warren's nothing but a death-hole! The whole place is one foul elil's larder! It's snared – everywhere, every day! That explains everything: everything that's happened since we came here.'

He sat still and his words seemed to come crawling up the sunlight, over the grass.

'Listen, Dandelion. You're fond of stories, aren't you? I'll tell you one – yes, one for El-ahrairah to cry at. Once there was a fine warren on the edge of a wood, overlooking the meadows of a farm. It was big, full of rabbits. Then one day the white blindness came and the rabbits fell sick and died. But a few survived, as they always do. The warren became almost empty. One day the farmer thought, "I could increase those rabbits: make them part of my farm – their meat, their skins. Why should I bother to keep rabbits in hutches? They'll do very well where they are." He began to shoot all elil – lendri, homba, stoat, owl. He put out food for the rabbits, but not too near the warren. For his purpose they had to become accustomed to going about in the fields and the wood. And then he snared them – not too many: as many as he wanted and not as many as would frighten them all away or destroy the warren. They grew big and strong and healthy, for he saw to it that they had all of the best, particularly in winter, and nothing to fear – except the running knot in the hedge-gap and the wood-path. So they lived as he wanted them to live and all the time there were a few who disappeared. The rabbits became strange in many ways, different from other rabbits. They knew well enough what was happening. But even to themselves they pretended that all was well, for the food was good, they were protected, they had nothing to fear but the one fear; and that struck here and there, never enough at a time to drive them away. They forgot the ways of wild rabbits. They forgot El-ahrairah, for what use had they for tricks and cunning, living in the enemy's warren and paying his price? They found out other marvellous arts to take the place of tricks and old stories. They danced in ceremonious greeting. They sang songs like the birds and made shapes on the walls; and though these could help them not at all, yet they passed the time and enabled them to tell themselves that they were splendid fellows, the very flower of Rabbitry, cleverer than magpies. They had no Chief Rabbit – no, how could they? – for a Chief Rabbit must be El-ahrairah to his warren and keep them from death: and here there was no death but one, and what Chief Rabbit could have an answer to that? Instead, Frith sent them strange singers, beautiful and sick like oak-apples, like robins' pin-cushions on the wild rose. And since they could not bear the truth, these singers, who might in some other place have been wise, were squeezed under the terrible weight of the warren's secret until they gulped out fine folly – about dignity and acquiescence, and anything else that could make believe that the rabbit loved the shining wire. But one strict rule they had; oh yes, the strictest. No one must ever ask where another rabbit was and anyone who asked, "Where?" – except in a song or a poem – must be silenced. To say "Where?" was bad enough, but to speak openly of the wires – that was intolerable. For that they would scratch and kill.'

He stopped. No one moved. Then, in the silence, Bigwig lurched to his feet, swayed a moment, tottered a few steps towards Fiver and fell again. Fiver paid him no heed but looked from one to another among the rabbits. Then he began speaking again.

'And then *we* came, over the heather in the night. Wild rabbits, making scrapes across the valley. The warren rabbits didn't show themselves at once. They needed to think what was best to be done. But they hit on it quite soon. To bring us into the warren and tell us nothing. Don't you see? The farmer only sets so many snares at a time and if one rabbit dies, the others will live that much longer. You suggested that Hazel should tell them our adventures, Blackberry, but it didn't go down well, did it? Who wants to hear about brave deeds when he's ashamed of his own, and who likes an open, honest tale from someone he's deceiving? Do you want me to go on? I tell you, every single thing that's happened fits like a bee in a foxglove. And kill them, you say, and help ourselves to the great burrow? We shall help ourselves to a roof of bones, hung with shining wires! Help ourselves to misery and death!'

Fiver sank down into the grass. Bigwig, still trailing his horrible, smooth peg, staggered up to him and touched his nose with his own.

'I'm still alive, Fiver,' he said. 'So are all of us. You've bitten through a bigger peg than this one I'm dragging. Tell us what to do.'

'Do?' replied Fiver. 'Why, go – now. I told Cowslip we were going before I left the burrow.'

'Where?' said Bigwig. But it was Hazel who answered.

'To the hills,' he said.

South of them, the ground rose gently away from the brook. Along the crest was the line of a cart-track and beyond, a copse. Hazel turned towards it and the rest began to follow him up the slope in ones and twos.

'What about the wire, Bigwig?' said Silver. 'The peg will catch and tighten it again.'

'No, it's loose now,' said Bigwig. 'I could shake it off if I hadn't hurt my neck.'

'Try,' said Silver. 'You won't get far otherwise.'

'Hazel,' said Speedwell suddenly, 'there's a rabbit coming down from the warren. Look!'

'Only one?' said Bigwig. 'What a pity! You take him, Silver. I won't deprive you. Make a good job of it while you're at it.'

They stopped and waited, dotted here and there about the slope. The rabbit who was coming was running in a curious, headlong manner. Once he ran straight into a thick-stemmed thistle, knocking himself sideways and rolling over and over. But he got up and came blundering on towards them.

'Is it the white blindness?' said Buckthorn. 'He's not looking where he's going.'

'Frith forbid!' said Blackberry. 'Shall we run away?'

'No, he couldn't run like that with the white blindness,' said Hazel. 'Whatever ails him, it isn't that.'

'It's Strawberry!' cried Dandelion.

Strawberry came through the hedge by the crab-apple tree, looked about him and made his way to Hazel. All his urbane self-possession had vanished. He was staring and trembling and his great size seemed only to add to his air of stricken misery. He cringed before them in the grass as Hazel waited, stern and motionless, with Silver at his side.

'Hazel,' said Strawberry, 'are you going away?'

Hazel made no answer, but Silver said sharply, 'What's that to you?'

'Take me with you.' There was no reply and he repeated, 'Take me with you.'

'We don't care for creatures who deceive us,' said Silver. 'Better go back to Nildro-hain. No doubt she's less particular.'

Strawberry gave a kind of choking squeal, as though he had been wounded. He looked from Silver to Hazel and then to Fiver. At last, in a pitiful whisper, he said,

'The wires.'

Silver was about to answer, but Hazel spoke first.

'You can come with us,' he said. 'Don't say any more. Poor fellow.'

A few minutes later the rabbits had crossed the cart-track and vanished into the copse beyond. A magpie, seeing some light-coloured object conspicuous on the empty slope, flew closer to look. But all that lay there was a splintered peg and a twisted length of wire.

PART TWO

On Watership Down

18. Watership Down

What is now proved was once only imagin'd.
William Blake, 'The Marriage of Heaven and Hell'

IT WAS evening of the following day. The north-facing escarpment of Watership Down, in shadow since early morning, now caught the western sun for an hour before twilight. Three hundred feet the down rose vertically in a stretch of no more than six hundred – a precipitous wall, from the thin belt of trees at the foot to the ridge where the steep flattened out. The light, full and smooth, lay like a gold rind over the turf, the furze and yew bushes, the few wind-stunted thorn trees. From the ridge, the light seemed to cover all the slope below, drowsy and still. But down in the grass itself, between the bushes, in that thick forest trodden by the beetle, the spider and the hunting shrew, the moving light was like a wind that danced among them to set them scurrying and weaving. The red rays flickered in and out of the grass stems, flashing minutely on membranous wings, casting long shadows behind the thinnest of filamentary legs, breaking each patch of bare soil into a myriad individual grains. The insects buzzed, whined, hummed, stridulated and droned as the air grew warmer in the sunset. Louder yet calmer than they, among the trees, sounded the yellow-hammer, the linnet and greenfinch. The larks went up, twittering in the scented air above the down. From the summit, the apparent immobility of the vast, blue distance was broken, here and there, by wisps of smoke and tiny, momentary flashes of glass. Far below lay the fields green with wheat, the flat pastures grazed by horses, the darker greens of the woods. They too, like the hillside jungle, were tumultuous with evening, but from the remote height turned to stillness, their fierceness tempered by the air that lay between.

At the foot of the turf cliff, Hazel and his companions were crouching under the low branches of two or three spindle-trees. Since the previous morning they had journeyed nearly three miles. Their luck had been good, for everyone who had left the warren was still alive. They had splashed through two brooks and wandered fearfully in the deep woodlands west of Ecchinswell. They had rested in the straw of a Starveall, or lonely barn, and woken to find themselves attacked by rats. Silver and Buckthorn, with Bigwig helping them, had covered the retreat until, once all were together outside, they had taken to flight. Buckthorn had been bitten in the foreleg and the wound, in the manner of a rat-bite, was irritant and painful. Skirting a small lake, they had stared to see a great, grey fisher-bird that stabbed and paddled in the sedge, until a flight of wild duck had frightened them away with their clamour. They had crossed more than half a mile of open pasture without a trace of cover, expecting every moment some attack that did not come. They had heard the unnatural humming of a pylon in the summer air; and had actually gone beneath it, on Fiver's assurance that it could do them no harm. Now they lay under the spindle-trees and sniffed in weariness and doubt at the strange, bare country round them.

Since leaving the warren of the snares they had become warier, shrewder, a tenacious band who understood each other and worked together. There was no more quarrelling. The truth about the warren had been a grim shock. They had come closer together, relying on and valuing each other's capacities. They knew now that it was on these and on nothing else that their lives depended, and they were not going to waste anything they possessed between them. In spite of Hazel's efforts beside the snare, there was not one of them who had not turned sick at heart to think that Bigwig was dead and wondered, like Blackberry, what would become of them now. Without Hazel, without Blackberry, Buckthorn and Pipkin – Bigwig would have died. Without himself he would have died, for which else, of them all, would not have stopped running after such punishment? There was no more questioning of Bigwig's strength, Fiver's insight, Blackberry's wits or Hazel's authority. When the rats came, Buckthorn and Silver had obeyed Bigwig and stood their ground. The rest had followed Hazel when he roused them and, without explanation, told them to go quickly outside the barn. Later, Hazel had said that there was nothing for it but to cross the open pasture and under Silver's direction they had crossed it, with Dandelion running ahead to reconnoitre. When Fiver said the iron tree was harmless they believed him.

Strawberry had had a bad time. His misery made him slow-witted and careless and he was ashamed of the part he had played at the warren. He was soft and more used than he dared admit to indolence and good food. But he made no complaint and it was plain that he was determined to show what he could do and not to be left behind. He had proved useful in the woodland, being better accustomed to thick woods than any of the others. 'He'll be all right, you know, if we give him a chance,' said Hazel to Bigwig by the lake. 'So he darned well ought to be,' replied Bigwig, 'the great dandy' – for by their standards, Strawberry was scrupulously clean and fastidious. 'Well, I won't have him brow-beaten, Bigwig, mind. That won't help him.' This Bigwig had accepted, though rather sulkily. Yet he himself had become less overbearing. The snare had left him weak and overwrought. It was he who had given the alarm in the barn, for he could not sleep and at the sound of scratching had started up at once. He would not let Silver and Buckthorn fight alone, but he had felt obliged to leave the worst of it to them. For the first time in his life, Bigwig had found himself driven to moderation and prudence.

As the sun sank lower and touched the edge of the cloud-belt on the horizon, Hazel came out from under the branches and looked carefully round the lower slope. Then he stared upwards over the ant-hills, to the open down rising above. Fiver and Acorn followed him out and fell to nibbling at a patch of sainfoin. It was new to them, but they did not need to be told that it was good and it raised their spirits. Hazel turned back and joined them among the big, rosy-veined, magenta flower-spikes.

'Fiver,' he said, 'let me get this right. You want us to climb up this place, however far it is, and find shelter on the top. Is that it?'

'Yes, Hazel.'

'But the top must be very high. I can't even see it from here. It'll be open and cold.'

'Not in the ground: and the soil's so light that we shall be able to scratch some shelter easily when we find the right place.'

Hazel considered again. 'It's getting started that bothers me. Here we are, all tired out. I'm sure it's dangerous to stay here. We've nowhere to run to. We don't know the country and we can't get underground. But it seems out of the question for everybody to climb up there tonight. We should be even less safe.'

'We shall be forced to dig, shan't we?' said Acorn. 'This place is almost as open as that heather we crossed, and the trees won't hide us from anything hunting on four feet.'

'It would have been the same any time we came,' said Fiver.

'I'm not saying anything against it, Fiver,' replied Acorn, 'but we need holes. It's a bad place not to be able to get underground.'

'Before everyone goes up to the top,' said Hazel, 'we ought to find out what it's like. I'm going up myself to have a look round. I'll be as quick as I can and you'll have to hope for the best until I get back. You can rest and feed anyway.'

'You're not going alone,' said Fiver firmly.

Since each one of them was ready to go with him in spite of their fatigue, Hazel gave in and chose Dandelion and Hawkbit, who seemed less weary than the others. They set out up the hillside, going slowly, picking their way from one bush and tussock to another and pausing continually to sniff and stare along the great expanse of grass, which stretched on either side as far as they could see.

A man walks upright. For him it is strenuous to climb a steep hill, because he has to keep pushing his own vertical mass upwards and cannot gain any momentum. The rabbit is better off. His forelegs support his horizontal body and the great back legs do the work. They are more than equal to thrusting uphill the light mass in front of them. Rabbits can go fast uphill. In fact, they have so much power behind that they find going downhill awkward, and sometimes, in flight down a steep place, they may actually go head over heels. On the other hand the man is five or six feet above the hillside and can see all round. To him the ground may be steep and rough but on the whole it is even; and he can pick his direction easily from the top of his moving, six-foot tower. The rabbits' anxieties and strain in climbing the down were different, therefore, from those which you, reader, will experience if you go there. Their main trouble was not bodily fatigue. When Hazel had said that they were all tired out, he had meant that they were feeling the strain of prolonged insecurity and fear.

Rabbits above ground, unless they are in proved, familiar surroundings close to their holes, live in continual fear. If it grows intense enough they can become glazed and

paralysed by it – *tharn*, to use their own word. Hazel and
his companions had been on the jump for nearly two days.
Indeed, ever since they had left their home warren, five
days before, they had faced one danger after another. They
were all on edge, sometimes starting at nothing and again,
lying down in any patch of long grass that offered. Bigwig
and Buckthorn smelt of blood and everyone else knew they
did. What bothered Hazel, Dandelion and Hawkbit was
the openness and strangeness of the down and their
inability to see very far ahead. They climbed not over but
through the sun-red grass, among the awakened insect
movement and the light ablaze. The grass undulated about
them. They peered over ant-hills and looked cautiously
round clumps of teazle. They could not tell how far away
the ridge might be. They topped each short slope only to
find another above it. To Hazel, it seemed a likely place for
a weasel: or the white owl, perhaps, might fly along the
escarpment at twilight, looking inwards with its stony eyes,
ready to turn a few feet sideways and pick off the shelf
anything that moved. Some elil wait for their prey, but the
white owl is a seeker and he comes in silence.

As Hazel still went up, the south wind began to blow
and the June sunset reddened the sky to the zenith. Hazel,
like nearly all wild animals, was unaccustomed to look up
at the sky. What he thought of as the sky was the horizon,
usually broken by trees and hedges. Now, with his head
pointing upwards, he found himself gazing at the ridge, as
over the sky-line came the silent, moving, red-tinged
cumuli. Their movement was disturbing, unlike that of
trees or grass or rabbits. These great masses moved steadily,

noiselessly and always in the same direction. They were not of his world.

'O Frith,' thought Hazel, turning his head for a moment to the bright glow in the west, 'are you sending us to live among the clouds? If you spoke truly to Fiver, help me to trust him.' At this moment he saw Dandelion, who had run well ahead, squatting on an ant-hill clear against the sky. Alarmed, he dashed forward.

'Dandelion, get down!' he said.' Why are you sitting up there?'

'Because I can see,' replied Dandelion, with a kind of excited joy. 'Come and look! You can see the whole world.'

Hazel came up to him. There was another ant-hill nearby and he copied Dandelion, sitting upright on his hind legs and looking about him. He realized now that they were almost on level ground. Indeed, the slope was no more than gentle for some way back along the line by which they had come; but he had been preoccupied with the idea of danger in the open and had not noticed the change. They were on top of the down. Perched above the grass, they could see far in every direction. Their surroundings were empty. If anything had been moving they would have seen it immediately: and where the turf ended, the sky began. A man, a fox – even a rabbit – coming over the down would be conspicuous. Fiver had been right. Up here, they would have clear warning of any approach.

The wind ruffled their fur and tugged at the grass, which smelt of thyme and self-heal. The solitude seemed like a release and a blessing. The height, the sky and the distance went to their heads and they skipped in the sunset. 'O Frith on the hills!' cried Dandelion. 'He must have made it for us!'

'He may have made it, but Fiver thought of it for us,' answered Hazel. 'Wait till we get him up here! Fiver-rah!'

'Where's Hawkbit?' said Dandelion suddenly.

Although the light was still clear, Hawkbit was not to be seen anywhere on the upland. After staring about for some time, they ran across to a little mound some way away and looked again. But they saw nothing except a field-mouse, which came out of its hole and began furricking in a patch of seeded grasses.

'He must have gone down,' said Dandelion.

'Well, whether he has or not,' said Hazel, 'we can't go on looking for him. The others are waiting and they may be in danger. We must go down ourselves.'

'What a shame to lose him, though,' said Dandelion, 'just when we'd reached Fiver's hills without losing anyone. He's such a duffer; we shouldn't have brought him up. But how could anything have got hold of him here, without our seeing?'

'No, he's gone back for sure,' said Hazel. 'I wonder what Bigwig will say to him? I hope he won't bite him again. We'd better get on.'

'Are you going to bring them up tonight?' asked Dandelion.

'I don't know,' said Hazel. 'It's a problem. Where's the shelter to be found?'

They made for the steep edge. The light was beginning to fail. They picked their direction by a clump of stunted trees which they had passed on their way up. These formed a kind of dry oasis – a little feature common on the downs. Half a dozen thorns and two or three elders grew together above and below a bank. Between them the ground was bare and the naked chalk showed a pallid, dirty white under the cream-coloured elder bloom. As they approached, they suddenly saw Hawkbit sitting among the thorn trunks, cleaning his face with his paws.

'We've been looking for you,' said Hazel. 'Where in the world have you been?'

'I'm sorry, Hazel,' replied Hawkbit meekly. 'I've been looking at these holes. I thought they might be some good to us.'

In the low bank behind him were three rabbit holes. There were two more flat on the ground, between the thick, gnarled roots. They could see no foot-marks and no droppings. The holes were clearly deserted.

'Have you been down?' asked Hazel, sniffing round.

'Yes, I have,' said Hawkbit. 'Three of them, anyway. They're shallow and rather rough, but there's no smell of death or disease and they're perfectly sound. I thought they might do for us – just for the moment, anyway.'

In the twilight a swift flew screaming overhead and Hazel turned to Dandelion.

'News! News!' he said. 'Go and get them up here.'

Thus it fell to one of the rank-and-file to make a lucky find that brought them at last to the downs: and probably saved a life or two; for they could hardly have spent the night in the open, either on or under the hill, without being attacked by some enemy or other.

19. Fear in the Dark

'Who's in the next room? – who?
    A figure wan
With a message to one in there of something due?
    Shall I know him anon?'
'Yea, he; and he brought such; and you'll know him anon.'

Thomas Hardy, 'Who's in the Next Room?'

THE HOLES certainly were rough – 'Just right for a lot of vagabonds* like us,' said Bigwig – but the exhausted and those who wander in strange country are not particular about their quarters. At least there was room for twelve rabbits and the burrows were dry. Two of the

---

* Bigwig's word was *hlessil,* which I have rendered in various places in the story as wanderers, scratchers, vagabonds. A *hlessi* is a rabbit living in the open, without a hole. Solitary bucks and unmated rabbits who are wandering do this for quite long periods, especially in summer. Bucks do not usually dig much in any case, although they will scratch shallow shelters or make use of existing holes where these are available. Real digging is done for the most part by does preparing for litters.

runs – the ones among the thorn trees – led straight down to burrows scooped out of the top of the chalk subsoil. Rabbits do not line their sleeping-places and a hard, almost rocky floor is uncomfortable for those not accustomed to it. The holes in the bank, however, had runs of the usual bow-shape, leading down to the chalk and then curving up again to burrows with floors of trampled earth. There were no connecting passages, but the rabbits were too weary to care. They slept four to a burrow, snug and secure. Hazel remained awake for some time, licking Buckthorn's leg, which was stiff and tender. He was reassured to find no smell of infection, but all that he had ever heard about rats decided him to see that Buckthorn got a good deal of rest and was kept out of the dirt until the wound was better. 'That's the third one of us to get hurt: still, all in all, things could have been far worse,' he thought, as he fell asleep.

The short June darkness slipped by in a few hours. The light returned early to the high down but the rabbits did not stir. Well after dawn they were still sleeping, undisturbed in a silence deeper than they had ever known. Nowadays, among fields and woods, the noise level by day is high – too high for some kinds of animal to tolerate. Few places are far from human noise – cars, buses, motor-cycles, tractors, lorries. The sound of a housing estate in the morning is audible a long way off. People who record bird-song generally do it very early – before six o'clock – if they can. Soon after that, the invasion of distant noise in most woodland becomes too constant and too loud. During the last fifty years the silence of much of the country has been destroyed. But here, on Watership Down, there floated up only faint traces of the daylight noise below.

The sun was well up, though not yet as high as the down, when Hazel woke. With him in the burrow were Buckthorn, Fiver and Pipkin. He was nearest to the mouth of the hole and did not wake them as he slipped up the run. Outside, he stopped to pass hraka and then hopped through the thorn patch to the open grass. Below, the country was covered with early morning mist which was beginning to clear. Here and there, far off, were the shapes of trees and roofs, from which streamers of mist trailed down like broken waves pouring from rocks. The sky was cloudless and deep blue, darkening to mauve along the whole rim of the horizon. The wind had dropped and the spiders had already gone well down into the grass. It was going to be a hot day.

Hazel rambled about in the usual way of a rabbit feeding – five or six slow, rocking hops through the grass; a pause to look round, sitting up with ears erect; then busy nibbling for a short time, followed by another move of a few yards. For the first time for many days he felt relaxed and safe. He began to wonder whether they had much to learn about their new home.

'Fiver was right,' he thought. 'This is the place for us. But we shall need to get used to it and the fewer mistakes we make the better. I wonder what became of the rabbits who made these holes? Did they stop running or did they just move away? If we could only find them they could tell us a lot.'

At this moment he saw a rabbit come rather hesitantly out of the hole farthest from himself. It was Blackberry. He, too, passed hraka, scratched himself and then hopped into the full sunlight and combed his ears. As he began to feed Hazel came up and fell in with him, nibbling among the grass tussocks and wandering on wherever his friend pleased. They came to a patch of milkwort – a blue as deep as that of the sky – with long stems creeping through the grass and each minute flower spreading its two upper petals like wings. Blackberry sniffed at it, but the leaves were tough and unappetizing.

'What is this stuff, do you know?' he asked.

'No, I don't,' said Hazel, 'I've never seen it before.'

'There's a lot we don't know,' said Blackberry. 'About this place, I mean. The plants are new, the smells are new. We're going to need some new ideas ourselves.'

'Well, you're the fellow for ideas,' said Hazel. 'I never know anything until you tell me.'

'But you go in front and take the risks first,' answered Blackberry. 'We've all seen that. And now our journey's over, isn't it? This place is as safe as Fiver said it would be. Nothing can get near us without our knowing: that is, as long as we can smell and see and hear.'

'We can all do that.'

'Not when we're asleep: and we can't see in the dark.'

'It's bound to be dark at night,' said Hazel, 'and rabbits have got to sleep.'

'In the open?'

'Well, we can go on using these holes if we want to, but I expect a good many will lie out. After all, you can't expect a bunch of bucks to dig. They might make a scrape or two – like that day after we came over the heather – but they won't do more than that.'

'That's what I've been thinking about,' said Blackberry. 'Those rabbits we left – Cowslip and the rest – a lot of the things they did weren't natural to rabbits – pushing stones into the earth and carrying food underground and Frith knows what.'

'The Threarah's lettuce was carried underground, if it comes to that.'

'Exactly. Don't you see, they'd altered what rabbits do naturally because they thought they could do better? And if they altered their ways, so can we if we like. You say buck rabbits don't dig. Nor they do. But they could, if they wanted to. Suppose we had deep, comfortable burrows to sleep in? To be out of bad weather and underground at night? Then we *would* be safe. And there's nothing to stop us having them, except that buck rabbits won't dig. Not can't – won't.'

'What's your idea, then?' asked Hazel, half-interested and half-reluctant. 'Do you want us to try to turn these holes into a regular warren?'

'No, these holes won't do. It's easy to see why they've been deserted. Only a little way down and you come to this hard, white stuff that no one can dig. They must be bitterly cold in winter. But there's a wood just over the top of the hill. I got a glimpse of it last night when we came. Suppose we go up higher now, just you and I, and have a look at it?'

They ran uphill to the summit. The beech hanger lay some little way off to the south-east, on the far side of a grassy track that ran along the ridge.

'There are some big trees there,' said Blackberry. 'The roots must have broken up the ground pretty deep. We could dig holes and be as well off as ever we were in the old warren. But if Bigwig and the others won't dig or say they can't – well, it's bare and bleak here. That's why it's lonely and safe, of course; but when bad weather comes we shall be driven off the hills for sure.'

'It never entered my head to try to make a lot of bucks dig regular holes,' said Hazel doubtfully, as they returned down the slope. 'Rabbit kittens need holes, of course; but do we?'

'We were all born in a warren that was dug before our mothers were born,' said Blackberry. 'We're used to holes and not one of us has ever helped to dig one. And if ever there was a new one, who dug it? A doe. I'm quite sure, myself, that if we don't change our natural ways we shan't be able to stay here very long. Somewhere else, perhaps; but not here.'

'It'll mean a lot of work.'

'Look, there's Bigwig come up now and some of the others with him. Why not put it to them and see what they say?'

During silflay, however, Hazel mentioned Blackberry's idea to no one but Fiver. Later on, when most of the rabbits had finished feeding and were either playing in the grass or lying in the sunshine, he suggested that they might go across to the hanger – 'just to see what sort of a wood it is'. Bigwig and Silver agreed at once and in the end no one stayed behind.

It was different from the meadow copses they had left: a narrow belt of trees, four or five hundred yards long but barely fifty wide; a kind of wind-break common on the downs. It consisted almost entirely of well-grown beeches. The great, smooth trunks stood motionless in their green shade, the branches spreading flat, one above another in crisp, light-dappled tiers. Between the trees the ground was open and offered hardly any cover. The rabbits were perplexed. They could not make out why the wood was so light and still and why they could see so far between the trees. The continuous, gentle rustling of the beech leaves was unlike the sounds to be heard in a copse of nut-bushes, oak and silver birch.

Moving uncertainly in and out along the edge of the hanger, they came to the north-east corner. Here there was a bank from which they looked out over the empty stretches of grass beyond. Fiver, absurdly small beside the hulking Bigwig, turned to Hazel with an air of happy confidence.

'I'm sure Blackberry's right, Hazel,' he said. 'We ought to do our best to make some holes here. I'm ready to try, anyway.'

The others were taken aback. Pipkin, however, readily joined Hazel at the foot of the bank and soon two or three more began scratching at the light soil. The digging was easy and although they often broke off to feed or merely to sit in the sun, before midday Hazel was out of sight and tunnelling between the tree-roots.

The hanger might have little or no undergrowth but at least the branches gave cover from the sky: and kestrels, they soon realized, were common in this solitude. Although kestrels seldom prey on anything bigger than a rat, they will sometimes attack young rabbits. No doubt this is why most grown rabbits will not remain under a hovering kestrel. Before long, Acorn spotted one as it flew up from the south. He stamped and bolted into the trees, followed by the other rabbits who were in the open. They had not long come out and resumed digging when they saw another – or perhaps the same one – hovering some way off, high over the very fields that they had crossed the previous morning. Hazel placed Buckthorn as a sentry while the day's haphazard work went on, and twice more during the afternoon the alarm was given. In the early evening they were disturbed by a horseman cantering along the ridge-track that passed the north end of the wood. Otherwise they saw nothing larger than a pigeon all day.

After the horseman had turned south near the summit of Watership and disappeared in the distance, Hazel returned to the edge of the wood and looked out northwards towards the bright, still fields and the dim pylon-line stalking away into the distance north of Kingsclere. The air was cooler and the sun was beginning once more to reach the north escarpment.

'I think we've done enough,' he said, 'for today, anyway. I should like to go down to the bottom of the hill and find some really good grass. This stuff's all right in its way but it's rather thin and dry. Does anyone feel like coming with me?'

Bigwig, Dandelion and Speedwell were ready, but the others preferred to graze their way back to the thorn-trees and go underground with the sun. Bigwig and Hazel picked the line that offered most cover and, with the others following, set out on the four or five hundred yards to the foot of the hill. They met no trouble and were soon feeding in the grass at the edge of the wheat-field, the very picture of rabbits in an evening landscape. Hazel, tired though he was, did not forget to look for somewhere to bolt if there should be an alarm. He was lucky enough to come upon a short length of old, overgrown ditch, partly fallen in and so heavily overhung with cow-parsley and nettles that it was almost as sheltered as a tunnel; and all four of them made sure that they could reach it quickly from the open.

'That'll be good enough at a pinch,' said Bigwig, munching clover and sniffing at the fallen bloom from a wayfaring tree. 'My goodness, we've learnt a few things since we left the old warren, haven't we? More than we'd have learnt in a life-time back there. And digging! It'll be flying next, I suppose. Have you noticed that this soil's quite different from the soil in the old warren? It smells differently and it slides and falls quite differently too.'

'That reminds me,' said Hazel. 'I meant to ask you. There was one thing at that terrible warren of Cowslip's that I admired very much – the great burrow. I'd like to copy it. It's a wonderful idea to have a place underground where everybody can be together – talk and tell stories and so on. What do you think? Could it be done?'

Bigwig considered. 'I know this,' he said. 'If you make a burrow too big the roof starts falling in. So if you want a place like that you'll need something to hold the roof up. What did Cowslip have?'

'Tree roots.'

'Well, there are those where we're digging. But are they the right sort?'

'We'd better get Strawberry to tell us what he knows about the great burrow; but it may not be much. I'm sure he wasn't alive when it was dug.'

'He may not be dead when it falls in either. That warren's tharn as an owl in daylight. He was wise to leave when he did.'

Twilight had fallen over the cornfield, for although long, red rays still lit the upper down, the sun had set below. The uneven shadow of the hedge had faded and disappeared. There was a cool smell of moisture and approaching darkness. A cockchafer droned past. The grasshoppers had fallen silent.

'Owls'll be out,' said Bigwig. 'Let's go up again.'

At this moment, from out in the darkening field, there came the sound of a stamp on the ground. It was followed by another, closer to them, and they caught a glimpse of a white tail. They both immediately ran to the ditch. Now that they had to use it in earnest, they found it even narrower than they had thought. There was just room to turn round at the far end and as they did so Speedwell and Dandelion tumbled in behind them.

'What is it?' asked Hazel. 'What did you hear?'

'There's something coming up the line of the hedge,' replied Speedwell. 'An animal. Making a lot of noise, too.'

'Did you see it?'

'No, and I couldn't smell it either. It's down-wind. But I heard it plainly enough.'

'I heard it too,' said Dandelion. 'Something fairly big – as big as a rabbit, anyway – moving clumsily but trying to keep concealed, or so it seemed to me.'

'Homba?'

'No, that we *should* have smelt,' said Bigwig, 'wind or no wind. From what you say, it sounds like a cat. I hope it's not a stoat. *Hoi, hoi, u embleer hrair!* What a nuisance! We'd better sit tight for a bit. But get ready to bolt if it spots us.'

They waited. Soon it grew dark. Only the faintest light came through the tangled summer growth above them. The far end of the ditch was so much overgrown that they could not see out of it, but the place where they had come in showed as a patch of sky – an arc of very dark blue. As the time passed, a star crept out from among the overhanging grasses. It seemed to pulsate in a rhythm as faint and uneven as that of the wind. At length Hazel turned his eyes away from watching it.

'Well, we can snatch some sleep here,' he said. 'The night's not cold. Whatever it was you heard, we'd better not risk going out.'

'Listen,' said Dandelion. 'What's that?'

For a moment Hazel could hear nothing. Then he caught a distant but clear sound – a kind of wailing or crying, wavering and intermittent. Although it did not sound like any sort of hunting call, it was so unnatural that it filled him with fear. As he listened, it ceased.

'What in Frith's name makes a noise like that?' said Bigwig, his great fur cap hackling between his ears.

'A cat?' said Speedwell, wide-eyed.

'That's no cat!' said Bigwig, his lips drawn back in a stiffened, unnatural grimace. 'That's no cat! Don't you know what it is? Your mother –' He broke off. Then he said, very low, 'Your mother told you, didn't she?'

'No!' cried Dandelion, 'No! It's some bird – some rat – wounded –'

Bigwig stood up. His back was arched and his head nodded on his stiffened neck.

'The Black Rabbit of Inlé,' he whispered. 'What else – in a place like this?'

'Don't talk like that!' said Hazel. He could feel himself trembling, and braced his legs against the sides of the narrow cut.

Suddenly the noise sounded again, nearer: and now there could be no mistake. What they heard was the voice of a rabbit, but changed out of all recognition. It might have come from the cold spaces of the dark sky outside, so unearthly and desolate was the sound. At first there was only a wailing. Then, distinct and beyond mistaking, they heard – they all heard – words.

'*Zorn! Zorn!*'* cried the dreadful, squealing voice. 'All dead! O *zorn!*'

Dandelion whimpered. Bigwig was scuffling into the ground.

'Be quiet!' said Hazel. 'And stop kicking that earth over me! I want to listen.'

At that moment, quite distinctly, the voice cried, 'Thlayli! O Thlayli!'

At this, all four rabbits felt the trance of utter panic. They grew rigid. Then Bigwig, his eyes set in a fixed, glazed stare, began to jerk his way up the ditch towards the opening. 'You have to go,' he muttered, so thickly that Hazel could hardly catch the words. 'You have to go when he calls you.'

---

* *Zorn* means 'finished' or 'destroyed', in the sense of some terrible catastrophe.

Hazel felt so much frightened that he could no longer collect his wits. As on the river bank, his surroundings became unreal and dream-like. Who – or what – was calling Bigwig by name? How could any living creature in this place know his name? Only one idea remained to him – Bigwig must be prevented from going out, for he was helpless. He scrambled past him, pressing him against the side of the ditch.

'Stay where you are,' he said, panting. 'Whatever sort of rabbit it is, I'm going to see for myself.' Then, his legs almost giving way beneath him, he pulled himself out into the open.

For a few moments he could see little or nothing; but the smells of dew and elder-bloom were unchanged and his nose brushed against cool grass-blades. He sat up and looked about him. There was no creature near-by.

'Who's there?' he said.

There was silence, and he was about to speak again when the voice replied, 'Zorn! O zorn!'

It came from the hedge along the side of the field. Hazel turned towards the sound and in a few moments made out, under a clump of hemlock, the hunched shape of a rabbit. He approached it and said, 'Who are you?' but there was no reply. As he hesitated, he heard a movement behind him.

'I'm here, Hazel,' said Dandelion, in a kind of choking gasp.

Together they went closer. The figure did not move as they came up. In the faint starlight they both saw a rabbit as real as themselves: a rabbit in the last stages of exhaustion, its back legs trailing behind its flattened rump as though paralysed: a rabbit that stared, white-eyed, from one side to the other, seeing nothing, yet finding no respite from its fear, and then fell to licking wretchedly at one ripped and bloody ear that drooped across its face: a rabbit that suddenly cried and wailed as though entreating the Thousand to come from every quarter to rid it of a misery too terrible to be borne.

It was Captain Holly of the Sandleford Owsla.

20. A Honeycomb and a Mouse

His face was that of one who has undergone a long journey.

The Epic of Gilgamesh

IN THE Sandleford warren, Holly had been a rabbit of consequence. He was greatly relied upon by the Threarah and had more than once carried out difficult orders with a good deal of courage. During the early spring, when a fox had moved into a neighbouring copse, Holly, with two or three volunteers, had kept it steadily under observation for several days and reported all its movements, until one evening it left as suddenly as it had come. Although he had decided on his own initiative to arrest Bigwig, he had not the reputation of being vindictive. He was, rather, a stander of no nonsense who knew when duty was done and did it himself. Sound, unassuming, conscientious, a bit lacking in the rabbit sense of mischief, he was something of the born second-in-command. There could have been no question of trying to persuade him to leave the warren with Hazel and Fiver. To find him under Watership Down at all, therefore, was astonishing enough. But to find him in such a condition was all but incredible.

In the first moments after they had recognized the poor creature under the hemlock, Hazel and Dandelion felt completely stupefied, as though they had come upon a squirrel underground or a stream that flowed uphill. They could not trust their senses. The voice in the dark had proved not to be supernatural, but the reality was frightening enough. How could Captain Holly be here, at the foot of the down? And what could have reduced him – of all rabbits – to this state?

Hazel pulled himself together. Whatever the explanation might be, the immediate need was to take first things first. They were in open country, at night, away from any refuge but an overgrown ditch, with a rabbit who smelt of blood, was crying uncontrollably and looked as though he could not move. There might very well be a stoat on his trail at this moment. If they were going to help him they had better be quick.

'Go and tell Bigwig who it is,' he said to Dandelion, 'and come back with him. Send Speedwell up the hill to the others and tell him to make it clear that no one is to come down. They couldn't help and it would only add to the risk.'

Dandelion had no sooner gone than Hazel became aware that something else was moving in the hedge. But he had no time to wonder what it might be, for almost immediately another rabbit appeared and limped to where Holly was lying.

'You must help us if you can,' he said to Hazel. 'We've had a very bad time and my master's ill. Can we get underground here?'

Hazel recognized him as one of the rabbits who had come to arrest Bigwig, but he did not know his name.

'Why did you stay in the hedge and leave him to crawl about in the open?' he asked.

'I ran away when I heard you coming,' replied the other rabbit. 'I couldn't get the captain to move. I thought you were elil and there was no point in staying to be killed. I don't think I could fight a field-mouse.'

'Do you know me?' said Hazel. But before the other could answer, Dandelion and Bigwig came out of the darkness. Bigwig stared at Holly for a moment and then crouched before him and touched noses.

'Holly, this is Thlayli,' he said. 'You were calling me.'

Holly did not answer, but only stared fixedly back at him. Bigwig looked up. 'Who's that who came with him?' he said. 'Oh, it's you, Bluebell. How many more of you?'

'No more,' said Bluebell. He was about to go on when Holly spoke.

'Thlayli,' he said. 'So we *have* found you.'

He sat up with difficulty and looked round at them.

'You're Hazel, aren't you?' he asked. 'And that's – oh, I should know, but I'm in very poor shape, I'm afraid.'

'It's Dandelion,' said Hazel. 'Listen – I can see that you're exhausted, but we can't stay here. We're in danger. Can you come with us to our holes?'

'Captain,' said Bluebell, 'do you know what the first blade of grass said to the second blade of grass?'

Hazel looked at him sharply, but Holly replied, 'Well?'

'It said, "Look, there's a rabbit! We're in danger!" '

'This is no time –' began Hazel.

'Don't silence him,' said Holly. 'We wouldn't be here at all without his blue-tit's chatter. Yes, I can go now. Is it far?'

'Not too far,' said Hazel, thinking it all too likely that Holly would never get there.

It took a long time to climb the hill. Hazel made them separate, himself remaining with Holly and Bluebell, while Bigwig and Dandelion went out to either side. Holly was forced to stop several times and Hazel, full of fear, had hard work to suppress his impatience. Only when the moon began to rise – the edge of its great disc growing brighter and brighter on the skyline below and behind them – did he at last beg Holly to hurry. As he spoke he saw, in the white light, Pipkin coming down to meet them.

'What are you doing?' he said sternly. 'I told Speedwell no one was to come down.'

'It isn't Speedwell's fault,' said Pipkin. 'You stood by me at the river, so I thought I'd come and look for you, Hazel. Anyway, the holes are just here. Is it really Captain Holly you've found?'

Bigwig and Dandelion approached.

'I'll tell you what,' said Bigwig. 'These two will need to rest for a good long time. Suppose Pipkin here and Dandelion take them to an empty burrow and stay with them as long as they want? The rest of us had better keep away until they feel better.'

'Yes, that's best,' said Hazel. 'I'll go up with you now.'

They ran the short distance to the thorn-trees. All the other rabbits were above ground, waiting and whispering together.

'Shut up,' said Bigwig, before anyone had asked a question. 'Yes, it is Holly, and Bluebell is with him – no one else. They're in a bad way and they're not to be troubled. We'll leave this hole empty for them. Now I'm going underground myself and so will you if you've got any sense.'

But before he went, Bigwig turned to Hazel and said, 'You got yourself out of that ditch down there instead of me, didn't you, Hazel? I shan't forget that.'

Hazel remembered Buckthorn's leg and took him down with him. Speedwell and Silver followed them.

'I say, what's happened, Hazel?' asked Silver. 'It must be something very bad. Holly would never leave the Threarah.'

'I don't know,' replied Hazel, 'and neither does anyone else yet. We'll have to wait until tomorrow. Holly may stop running but I don't think Bluebell will. Now let me alone to do this leg of Buckthorn's.'

The wound was a great deal better and soon Hazel fell asleep.

The next day was as hot and cloudless as the last. Neither Pipkin nor Dandelion were at morning silflay; and Hazel relentlessly took the others up to the beech hanger to go on with the digging. He questioned Strawberry about the great burrow and learned that its ceiling, as well as being vaulted with a tangle of fibres, was strengthened by roots going vertically down into the floor. He remarked that he had not noticed these.

'There aren't many, but they're important,' said Strawberry. 'They take a lot of the load. If it weren't for those roots the ceiling would fall after heavy rain. On stormy nights you could sense the extra weight in the earth above, but there was no danger.'

Hazel and Bigwig went underground with him. The beginnings of the new warren had been hollowed out among the roots of one of the beech trees. It was still no more than a small, irregular cave with one entrance. They set to work to enlarge it, digging between the roots and tunnelling upwards to make a second run that would emerge inside the wood. After a time Strawberry stopped digging and began moving about between the roots, sniffing, biting and scuffling in the soil with his front paws. Hazel supposed that he was tired and pretending to be busy while he had a rest, but at length he came back to them and said that he had some suggestions.

'It's this way,' he explained. 'There isn't a big spread of fine roots above here. That was a lucky chance in the great burrow and I don't think we can expect to find it again. But all the same, we can do pretty well with what we've got.'

'And what *have* we got?' asked Blackberry, who had come down the run while he was talking.

'Well, we've got several thick roots that go straight down – more than there were in the great burrow. The best thing will be to dig round them and leave them. They shouldn't be gnawed through and taken out. We shall need them if we're going to have a hall of any size.'

'Then our hall will be full of these thick, vertical roots?' asked Hazel. He felt disappointed.

'Yes, it will,' said Strawberry, 'but I can't see that it's going to be any the worse for that. We can go in and out among them and they won't hinder anyone who's talking or telling a story. They'll make the place warmer and they'll help to conduct sound from above, which might be useful some time or other.'

The excavation of the hall (which came to be known among them as the Honeycomb) turned out to be something of a triumph for Strawberry. Hazel contented himself with organizing the diggers and left it to Strawberry to say what was actually to be done. The work went on in shifts and the rabbits took it in turns to feed, play and lie in the sun above ground. Throughout the day the solitude remained unbroken by noise, men, tractors or even cattle, and they began to feel still more deeply what they owed to Fiver's insight. By the late afternoon the big burrow was beginning to take shape. At the north end, the beech roots formed a kind of irregular colonnade. This gave way to a more open, central space: and beyond, where there were no supporting roots, Strawberry left blocks of the earth untouched, so that the south end consisted of three or four separate bays. These narrowed into low-roofed runs that led away into sleeping burrows.

Hazel, much better pleased now that he could see for himself how the business was going to turn out, was sitting with Silver in the mouth of the run, when suddenly there was a stamping of 'Hawk! Hawk!' and a dash for cover by the rabbits outside. Hazel, safe where he was, remained looking out past the shadow of the wood to the open, sunlit grass beyond. The kestrel sailed into view and took up station, the black-edged flange of its tail bent down and its pointed wings beating rapidly as it searched the down below.

'But do you think it *would* attack us?' asked Hazel, watching it drop lower and recommence its poised fluttering. 'Surely it's too small?'

'You're probably right,' replied Silver. 'All the same, would you care to go out there and start feeding?'

'I'd like to try standing up to some of these elil,' said Bigwig, who had come up the run behind them. 'We're afraid of too many. But a bird from the air would be awkward, especially if it came fast. It might get the better of even a big rabbit if it took him by surprise.'

'See the mouse?' said Silver suddenly. 'There, look. Poor little beast.'

They could all see the field-mouse, which was exposed in a patch of smooth grass. It had evidently strayed too far from its hole and now could not tell what to do. The kestrel's shadow had not passed over it, but the rabbits' sudden disappearance had made it uneasy and it was pressed to the ground, looking uncertainly this way and that. The kestrel had not yet seen it, but could hardly fail to do so as soon as it moved.

'Any moment now,' said Bigwig callously.

On an impulse, Hazel hopped down the bank and went a little way into the open grass. Mice do not speak Lapine, but there is a very simple, limited *lingua franca* of the hedgerow and woodland. Hazel used it now.

'Run,' he said. 'Here; quick.'

The mouse looked at him but did not move. Hazel spoke again and the mouse began suddenly to run towards him as the kestrel turned and slid sideways and downwards. Hazel hastened back to the hole. Looking out, he saw the mouse following him. When it had almost reached the foot of the bank it scuttered over a fallen twig with two or three green leaves. The twig turned, one of the leaves caught the sunlight slanting through the trees and Hazel saw it flash for an instant. Immediately the kestrel came lower in an oblique glide, closed its wings and dropped.

Before Hazel could spring back from the mouth of the hole, the mouse had dashed between his front paws and was pressed to the ground between his back legs. At the same moment the kestrel, all beak and talons, hit the loose earth immediately outside like a missile thrown from the tree above. It scuffled savagely and for an instant the three rabbits saw its round, dark eyes looking straight down the run. Then it was gone. The speed and force of the pounce, not a length away, were terrifying and Hazel leapt backwards, knocking Silver off his balance. They picked themselves up in silence.

'Like to try standing up to that one?' said Silver, looking round at Bigwig. 'Let me know when. I'll come and watch.'

'Hazel,' said Bigwig. 'I know you're not stupid, but what did we get out of that? Are you going in for protecting every mole and shrew that can't get underground?'

The mouse had not moved. It was still crouching a little inside the run, on a level with their heads and outlined against the light. Hazel could see it watching him.

'Perhaps hawk not gone,' he said. 'You stay now. Go later.'

Bigwig was about to speak again when Dandelion appeared in the mouth of the hole. He looked at the mouse, pushed it gently aside and came down the run.

'Hazel,' he said, 'I thought I ought to come and tell you about Holly. He's much better this evening, but he had a very bad night and so did we. Every time he seemed to be going to sleep, he kept starting up and crying. I thought he was going out of his mind. Pipkin kept talking to him – he was first-rate – and he seems to set a lot of store by Bluebell. Bluebell kept on making jokes. He was worn out before the morning and so were the lot of us – we've been sleeping all day. Holly's been more or less himself since he woke up this afternoon, and he's been up to silflay. He asked where you and the others would be tonight and as I didn't know I came to ask.'

'Is he fit to talk to us, then?' asked Bigwig.

'I think so. It would be the best thing for him, if I'm any judge: and if he was with all of us together he'd be less likely to have another bad night.'

'Well, where *are* we going to sleep?' said Silver.

Hazel considered. The Honeycomb was still rough-dug and half-finished, but it would probably be as comfortable as the holes under the thorn-trees. Besides, if it proved otherwise, they would have all the more inducement to improve it. To know that they were actually making use of their day's hard work would please everybody and they were likely to prefer this to a third night in the chalk holes.

'I should think here,' he said. 'But we'll see how the others feel.'

'What's this mouse doing in here?' asked Dandelion.

Hazel explained. Dandelion was as puzzled as Bigwig had been.

'Well, I'll admit I hadn't any particular idea when I went out to help it,' said Hazel. 'I have now, though, and I'll explain later what it is. But first of all, Bigwig and I ought to go and talk to Holly. And Dandelion, you go and tell the rest what you told me, will you, and see what they want to do tonight?'

They found Holly with Bluebell and Pipkin, on the turf by the ant-hill where Dandelion had first looked over the down. Holly was sniffing at a purple orchis. The head of mauve blooms rocked gently on its stem as he pushed his nose against it.

'Don't frighten it, master,' said Bluebell. 'It might fly away. After all, it's got a lot of spots to choose from. Look at them all over the leaves.'

'Oh, get along with you, Bluebell,' answered Holly good-humouredly. 'We need to learn about the ground here. Half the plants are strange to me. This isn't one to eat, but at least there's plenty of burnet and that's always good.' A fly settled on his wounded ear and he winced and shook his head.

Hazel was glad to see that Holly was evidently in better spirits. He began to say that he hoped he felt well enough to join the others, but Holly soon interrupted him with questions.

'Are there many of you?' he asked.

'Hrair,' said Bigwig.

'All that left the warren with you?'

'Every one,' replied Hazel proudly.

'No one hurt?'

'Oh, several have been hurt, one way and another.'

'Never a dull moment, really,' said Bigwig.

'Who's this coming? I don't know him.'

Strawberry came running down from the hanger and as he joined them began to make the same curious, dancing gesture of head and fore-paws which they had first seen in the rainy meadow before they entered the great burrow. He checked himself in some confusion and, to forestall Bigwig's rebuke, spoke to Hazel at once.

'Hazel-rah,' he said (Holly looked startled but said nothing), 'everyone wants to stay in the new warren tonight: and they're all hoping that Captain Holly will feel able to tell them what's happened and how he came here.'

'Well, naturally, we all want to know,' said Hazel to Holly. 'This is Strawberry. He joined us on our journey and we've been glad to have him. But do you think you can manage it?'

'I can manage it,' said Holly. 'But I must warn you that it will strike the frost into the heart of every rabbit that hears it.'

He himself looked so sad and dark as he spoke that no one made any reply, and after a few moments all six rabbits made their way up the slope in silence. When they reached the corner of the wood, they found the others feeding or basking in the evening sun on the north side of the beech trees. After a glance round among them Holly went up to Silver, who was feeding with Fiver in a patch of yellow trefoil.

'I'm glad to see you here, Silver,' he said. 'I hear you've had a rough time.'

'It hasn't been easy,' answered Silver. 'Hazel's done wonders and we owe a lot to Fiver here as well.'

'I've heard of you,' said Holly, turning to Fiver. 'You're the rabbit who saw it all coming. You talked to the Threarah, didn't you?'

'He talked to me,' said Fiver.

'If only he'd listened to you! Well, it can't be changed now, till acorns grow on thistles. Silver, there's something I want to say and I can say it more easily to you than to Hazel or Bigwig. I'm not out to make any trouble here – trouble for Hazel, I mean. He's your Chief Rabbit now, that's plain. I hardly know him, but he must be good or you'd all be dead; and this is no time to be squabbling. If any of the other rabbits are wondering whether I might want to alter things, will you let them know that I shan't?'

'Yes, I will,' said Silver.

Bigwig came up. 'I know it's not owl-time yet,' he said, 'but everyone's so eager to hear you, Holly, that they want to go underground at once. Will that suit you?'

'Underground?' replied Holly. 'But how can you all hear me underground? I was expecting to talk here.'

'Come and see,' said Bigwig.

Holly and Bluebell were impressed by the Honeycomb.

'This is something quite new,' said Holly. 'What keeps the roof up?'

'It doesn't need to be kept up,' said Bluebell. 'It's right up the hill already.'

'An idea we found on the way,' said Bigwig.

'Lying in a field,' said Bluebell. 'It's all right, master, I'll be quiet while you're speaking.'

'Yes, you must,' said Holly. 'Soon no one will want jokes.'

Almost all the rabbits had followed them down. The Honeycomb, though big enough for everybody, was not so

airy as the great burrow and on this June evening it seemed
somewhat close.

'We can easily make it cooler, you know,' said Strawberry
to Hazel. 'In the great burrow they used to open tunnels for
the summer and close them for the winter. We can dig
another run on the evening side tomorrow and pick up the
breeze.'

Hazel was just going to ask Holly to begin when
Speedwell came down the eastern run. 'Hazel,' he said,
'your – er – visitor – your mouse. He wants to speak to
you.'

'Oh, I'd forgotten him,' said Hazel. 'Where is he?'

'Up the run.'

Hazel went up. The mouse was waiting at the top.

'You go now?' said Hazel. 'You think safe?'

'Go now,' said the mouse. 'No wait owl. But a what I
like a say. You 'elp a mouse. One time a mouse 'elp a you.
You want 'im, 'e come.'

'Frith in a pond!' muttered Bigwig, farther down the
run. 'And so will all his brothers and sisters. I dare say the
place'll be crawling. Why don't you ask them to dig us a
burrow or two, Hazel?'

Hazel watched the mouse make off into the long grass.
Then he returned to the Honeycomb and settled down
near Holly, who had just begun to speak.

21. 'For El-Ahrairah to Cry'

Love the animals. God has given them the rudiments of thought and joy untroubled. Don't trouble it, don't harass them, don't deprive them of their happiness, don't work against God's intent.

Dostoevsky, *The Brothers Karamazov*

> Acts of injustice done
> Between the setting and the rising sun
> In history lie like bones, each one.
>
> W. H. Auden, 'The Ascent of F.6'

'THE NIGHT you left the warren, the Owsla were turned out to look for you. How long ago it seems now! We followed your scent down to the brook, but when we told the Threarah that you appeared to have set off downstream, he said there was no point in risking lives by following you. If you were gone, you were gone. But anyone who came back was to be arrested. So then I called off the search.

'Nothing unusual happened the next day. There was a certain amount of talk about Fiver and the rabbits who'd gone with him. Everyone knew that Fiver had said that something bad was going to happen and all sorts of rumours started. A lot of rabbits said there was nothing in it, but some thought that Fiver might have foreseen men with guns and ferrets. That was the worst thing anyone could think of – that or the white blindness.

'Willow and I talked things over with the Threarah. "These rabbits," he said, "who claim to have the second sight – I've known one or two in my time. But it's not usually advisable to take much notice of them. For one thing, many are just plain mischievous. A weak rabbit who can't hope to get far by fighting sometimes tries to make himself important by other means and prophecy is a favourite. The curious thing is that when he turns out to be wrong, his friends seldom seem to notice, as long as he puts on a good act and keeps talking. But then again, you may get a rabbit who really has this odd power, for it does exist. He foretells a flood perhaps, or ferrets and guns. All right; so a certain number of rabbits will stop running. What's the alternative? To evacuate a warren is a tremendous business. Some refuse to go. The Chief Rabbit leaves with as many as will come. His authority is likely to be put to the most severe test and if he loses it he won't get it back in a hurry. At the best, you've got a big bunch of hlessil trailing round in the open, probably with does and kittens tacked on. Elil appear in hordes. The remedy's worse than the disease. Almost always, it's better for the warren as a whole if rabbits sit tight and do their best to dodge their dangers underground."'

'Of course, I never sat down and thought,' said Fiver. 'It would take the Threarah to think all that out. I simply had the screaming horrors. Great golden Frith, I hope I never have them like that again! I shall never forget it – that and the night I spent under the yew-tree. There's terrible evil in the world.'

'It comes from men' (said Holly). 'All other elil do what they have to do and Frith moves them as he moves us. They live on the earth and they need food. Men will never rest till they've spoiled the earth and destroyed the animals. But I'd better go on with this tale of mine.

'The next day in the afternoon, it began to rain.

('Those scrapes we dug in the bank,' whispered Buckthorn to Dandelion.)

'Everyone was underground, just chewing pellets or sleeping. I'd gone up for a few minutes to pass hraka. I was on the edge of the wood, quite near the ditch, when I saw some men come through the gate at the top of the opposite slope, up by that board thing. I don't know how many there were – three or four, I suppose. They had long, black legs and they were burning white sticks in their mouths. They didn't seem to be going anywhere. They began walking slowly about in the rain, looking at the hedges and the brook. After a time they crossed the brook and came clumping up towards the warren. Whenever they came to a rabbit-hole, one of them would prod at it; and they kept talking all the time. I remember the smell of the elder bloom in the rain and the smell of the white sticks. Later, when they came closer, I slipped underground again. I could hear them for some time, thumping about and talking. I kept thinking, "Well, they've got no guns and no ferrets." But somehow I didn't like it.'

'What did the Threarah say?' asked Silver.

'I've no idea. I didn't ask him and neither did anyone else as far as I know. I went to sleep and when I woke there was no sound up above. It was evening and I decided to silflay. The rain had settled in, but I pottered round and fed for a while all the same. I couldn't see that anything was altered, except that here and there the mouth of a hole had been poked in.

'The next morning was clear and fine. Everyone was out for silflay as usual. I remember Nightshade told the Threarah that he ought to be careful not to tire himself now that he was getting on in years: and the Threarah said he'd show him who was getting on in years and cuffed him and pushed him down the bank. It was all quite good-humoured, you know, but he did it just to show Nightshade that the Chief Rabbit was still a match for him. I was going out for lettuces that morning and for some reason or other I'd decided to go alone.'

'Three's the usual number for a lettuce-party,' said Bigwig.

'Yes, I know three used to be the usual number, but there was some special reason why I went alone that day. Oh yes, I remember – I wanted to see if there were any early carrots – I thought they might just be ready – and I reckoned that if I was going hunting about in a strange part of the garden I'd be better off by myself. I was out most of the morning and it can't have been long before ni-Frith when I came back through the wood. I was coming down Silent

Bank – I know most rabbits preferred the Green Loose, but I nearly always went by Silent Bank. I'd got into the open part of the wood, where it comes down towards the old fence, when I noticed a hrududu in the lane at the top of the opposite slope. It was standing at the gate by the board and a lot of men were getting out. There was a boy with them and he had a gun. They took down some big, long things – I don't know how to describe them to you – they were made of the same sort of stuff as a hrududu and they must have been heavy, because it took two men to carry one of them. The men carried these things into the field and the few rabbits who were above ground went down. I didn't. I'd seen the gun and I thought they were probably going to use ferrets and perhaps nets. So I stayed where I was and watched. I thought, "As soon as I'm sure what they're up to, I'll go and warn the Threarah."

'There was more talking and more white sticks. Men never hurry, do they? Then one of them got a spade and began filling in the mouths of all the holes he could find. Every hole he came to, he cut out the turf above and pushed it into the hole. That puzzled me, because with ferrets they want to drive the rabbits out. But I was expecting that they'd leave a few holes open and net them: although that would have been a foolish way to ferret, because a rabbit that went up a blocked run would be killed underground and then the man wouldn't get his ferret back very easily, you know.'

'Don't make it too grim, Holly,' said Hazel, for Pipkin was shuddering at the thought of the blocked run and the pursuing ferret.

'Too grim?' replied Holly bitterly. 'I've hardly started yet. Would anyone like to go away?' No one moved and after a few moments he continued.

'Then another of the men fetched some long, thin, bending things. I haven't got words for all these men-things, but they were something like lengths of very thick bramble. Each of the men took one and put it on one of the heavy things. There was a kind of hissing noise and – and – well, I know you must find this difficult to understand, but the air began to turn bad. For some reason I got a strong scent of this stuff that came out of the bramble-things, even though I was some way off: and I couldn't see or think. I seemed to be falling. I tried to jump up and run, but I didn't know where I was and I found I'd run down to the edge of the wood, towards the men. I stopped just in time. I was bewildered and I'd lost all idea of warning the Threarah. After that I just sat where I was.

'The men put a bramble into each hole they'd left open and after that nothing happened for a while. And then I saw Scabious – you remember Scabious? He came out of a hole along the hedge – one they hadn't noticed. I could see at once that he'd smelt this stuff. He didn't know what he was doing. The men didn't see him for a few moments and then one of them stuck out his arm to show where he was and the boy shot him. He didn't kill him – Scabious began to scream – and one of the men went over and picked him up and hit him. I really believe he may not have suffered very much, because the bad air had turned him silly; but I wish I hadn't seen it. After that, the man stopped up the hole that Scabious had come out of.

'By this time the poisoned air must have been spreading through the runs and burrows underground. I can imagine what it must have been like –'

'You can't,' said Bluebell. Holly stopped and after a pause Bluebell went on.

'I heard the commotion beginning before I smelt the stuff myself. The does seemed to get it first and some of them began trying to get out. But the ones who had litters wouldn't leave the kittens and they were attacking any rabbit who came near them. They wanted to fight – to protect the kittens, you know. Very soon the runs were crammed with rabbits clawing and clambering over each other. They went up the runs they were accustomed to use and found them blocked. Some managed to turn round, but they couldn't get back because of the rabbits coming up. And then the runs began to be blocked lower down with dead rabbits and the live rabbits tore them to pieces.

'I shall never know how I got away with what I did. It was a chance in a thousand. I was in a burrow near one of the holes that the men were using. They made a lot of noise putting the bramble thing in and I've got an idea it wasn't working properly. As soon as I picked up the smell of the stuff I jumped out of the burrow, but I was still fairly clearheaded. I came up the run just as the men were taking the bramble out again. They were all looking at it and talking and they didn't see me. I turned round, actually in the mouth of the hole, and went down again.

'Do you remember the Slack Run? I suppose hardly a rabbit went down there in our lifetime – it was so very deep and it didn't lead anywhere in particular. No one knows even who made it. Frith must have guided me, for I went straight down into the Slack Run and began creeping along it. I was actually digging at times. It was all loose earth and fallen stones. There were all sorts of forgotten shafts and drops that led in from above, and down those were coming the most terrible sounds – cries for help, kittens squealing for their mothers, Owsla trying to give orders, rabbits cursing and fighting each other. Once a rabbit came tumbling down one of the shafts and his claws just scratched me, like a horse-chestnut burr falling in autumn. It was Celandine and he was dead. I had to tear at him before I could get over him – the place was so low and narrow – and then I went on. I could smell the bad air, but I was so deep down that I must have been beyond the worst of it.

'Suddenly I found there was another rabbit with me. He was the only one I met in the whole length of the Slack Run. It was Pimpernel and I could tell at once that he was in a bad way. He was spluttering and gasping, but he was able to keep going. He asked if I was all right, but all I said was, "Where do we get out?" "I can show you that," he said, "if you can help me along." So I followed him and every time he stopped – he kept forgetting where we were – I shoved him hard. I even bit him once. I was terrified that he was going to die and block the run. At last we began to come up and I could smell fresh air. We found we'd got into one of those runs that led out into the wood.'

'The men had done their work badly' (resumed Holly). 'Either they didn't know about the wood holes or they couldn't be bothered to come and block them. Almost every rabbit that came up in the field was shot, but I saw two get away. One was Nose-in-the-Air, but I don't remember who the other was. The noise was very frightening and I would have run myself, but I kept waiting to see whether the Threarah would come. After a while I began to realize that there were a few other rabbits in the wood. Pine-needles was there, I remember, and Butterbur and Ash. I got hold of all I could and told them to sit tight under cover.

'After a long time the men finished. They took the bramble things out of the holes and the boy put the bodies on a stick –'

Holly stopped and pressed his nose under Bigwig's flank.

'Well, never mind about that bit,' said Hazel in a steady voice. 'Tell us how you came away.'

'Before that happened' (said Holly), 'a great hrududu came into the field from the lane. It wasn't the one the men came in. It was very noisy and it was yellow – as yellow as charlock: and in front there was a great silver, shining thing that it held in its huge front paws. I don't know how to describe it to you. It looked like Inlé, but it was broad and not so bright. And this thing – how can I tell you? – it tore the field to bits. It destroyed the field.'

He stopped again.

'Captain,' said Silver, 'we all know you've seen things bad beyond telling. But surely that's not quite what you mean?'

'Upon my life' (said Holly, trembling), 'it buried itself in the ground and pushed great masses of earth in front of it until the field was destroyed. The whole place became like a cattle-wade in winter, and you could no longer tell where any part of the field had been, between the wood and the brook. Earth and roots and grass and bushes it pushed before it and – and other things as well, from underground.

'After a long time I went back through the wood. I'd forgotten any idea of collecting other rabbits, but there were three who joined me all the same – Bluebell here and Pimpernel and young Toadflax. Toadflax was the only member of the Owsla I'd seen and I asked him about the Threarah, but he couldn't talk any kind of sense. I never found out what happened to the Threarah. I hope he died quickly.

'Pimpernel was light-headed – chattering nonsense – and Bluebell and I weren't much better. For some reason all I could think of was Bigwig. I remembered how I'd gone to arrest him – to kill him, really – and I felt I had to find him and tell him I'd been wrong: and this idea was all the sense I had left. The four of us went wandering away and we must have gone almost in a half-circle, because after a long time we came to the brook, below what had been our field. We followed it down into a big wood; and that night, while we were still in the wood, Toadflax died. He was clear-headed for a short time before and I remember something he said. Bluebell had been saying that he knew the men hated us for raiding their crops and gardens and Toadflax answered, "That wasn't why they destroyed the warren. It was just because we were in their way. They killed us to suit themselves." Soon after that he went to sleep and a little later, when we were alarmed by some noise or other, we tried to wake him and realized he was dead.

'We left him lying where he was and went on until we reached the river. I needn't describe it because I know you were all there. It was morning by this time. We thought you might be somewhere near and we began to go along the bank, upstream, looking for you. It wasn't long before we found the place where you must have crossed. There were tracks – a great many – in the sand under a steep bank, and hraka about three days old. The tracks didn't go upstream or downstream so I knew you must have gone over. I swam across and found more tracks on the other side: so then the others came over too. The river was high. I suppose you must have had it easier, before all the rain.

'I didn't like the fields on the other side of the river. There was a man with a gun who kept walking everywhere. I took the other two on, across a road, and soon we came to a bad place – all heather and soft, black earth. We had a hard time there, but again I came upon hraka about three days old and no sign of holes or rabbits, so I thought there was a chance that they were yours. Bluebell was all right, but Pimpernel was feverish and I was afraid he was going to die too.

'Then we had a bit of luck – or so we thought at the time. That night we fell in with a hlessi on the edge of the heather – an old, tough rabbit with his nose all scratched and scarred – and he told us that there was a warren not far off and showed us which way to go. We came to woods and fields again, but we were so much exhausted that we couldn't start looking for the warren. We crept into a ditch and I hadn't the heart to tell one of the others to keep awake. I tried to keep awake myself, but I couldn't.'

'When was this?' asked Hazel.

'The day before yesterday' (said Holly), 'early in the morning. When I woke it was still some time before ni-Frith. Everything was quiet and all I could smell was rabbit, but I felt at once that something was wrong. I woke Bluebell and I was just going to wake Pimpernel when I realized that there was a whole bunch of rabbits all round us. They were great, big fellows and they had a very odd smell. It was like – well, like –'

'We know what it was like,' said Fiver.

'I thought you probably did. Then one of them said, "My name's Cowslip. Who are you and what are you doing here?" I didn't like the way he spoke, but I couldn't see that they had any reason to wish us harm, so I told him that we'd had a bad time and come a long way and that we were looking for some rabbits from our warren – Hazel, Fiver and Bigwig. As soon as I said those names this rabbit turned to the others and cried, "I knew it! Tear them to pieces!" And they all set on us. One of them got me by the ear and ripped it up before Bluebell could pull him off. We were fighting the lot of them. I was so much taken by surprise that I couldn't do a great deal at first. But the funny thing was that although they were so big and yelling for our blood, they couldn't fight at all: they obviously didn't know the first thing about fighting. Bluebell knocked down a couple twice his size and although my ear was pouring with blood I was never really in danger. All the same they were too many for us, and we had to run. Bluebell and I had just got clear of the ditch when we realized that Pimpernel was still there. He was ill, as I told you, and he didn't wake in time. So after all he'd been through, poor Pimpernel was killed by rabbits. What do you think of that?'

'I think it was a damned shame,' said Strawberry, before anyone else could speak.

'We were running down the fields, beside a little stream' (Holly went on). 'Some of these rabbits were still chasing us and suddenly I thought. "Well, I'll have one of them anyway." I didn't care for the idea of doing nothing more than just run away to save our skins – not after Pimpernel. I saw that this Cowslip was ahead of the others and out on his own, so I let him catch me up and then I suddenly turned and went for him. I had him down and I was just going to rip him up when he squealed out, "I can tell you where your friends have gone." "Hurry up, then," I said, with my back legs braced in his stomach. "They've gone to the hills," he panted. "The high hills you can see away over there. They went yesterday morning." I pretended not to believe him and acted as though I was going to kill him. But he didn't alter his story, so I scratched him and let him go and away we came. It was clear weather and we could see the hills plainly enough.

'After that we had the worst time of all. If it hadn't been for Bluebell's jokes and chatter we'd have stopped running for certain.'

'Hraka one end, jokes the other,' said Bluebell. 'I used to roll a joke along the ground and we both followed it. That was how we kept going.'

'I can't really tell you much about the rest of it' (said Holly). 'My ear was terribly painful and all the time I kept thinking that Pimpernel's death was my fault. If I hadn't gone to sleep he wouldn't have died. Once we tried to sleep again, but my dreams were more than I could bear. I was out of my mind, really. I had only this one idea – to find Bigwig and tell him that he'd been right to leave the warren.

'At last we reached the hills, just at nightfall of the next day. We were past caring – we came over the flat, open land at owl-time. I don't know what I'd been expecting. You know how you let yourself think that everything will be all right if you can only get to a certain place or do a certain thing. But when you get there you find it's not that simple. I suppose I'd had some sort of foolish notion that Bigwig would be waiting to meet us. We found the hills were enormous – bigger than anything we'd ever seen. No woods, no cover, no rabbits: and night setting in. And then everything seemed to go to pieces. I saw Scabious, as plain as grass – and heard him crying too; and I saw the Threarah and Toadflax and Pimpernel. I tried to talk to them. I was calling Bigwig, but I didn't really expect him to hear because I was sure he wasn't there. I can remember coming out from a hedge into the open and I know I was really hoping that the elil would come and make an end of me. But when I came to my senses, there was Bigwig. My first thought was that I must be dead, but then I began to wonder whether he was real or not. Well, you know the rest. It's a pity I frightened you so much. But if I wasn't the – the Black Rabbit, there's hardly a living creature that can ever have been closer to him than we have.'

After a silence, he added, 'You can imagine what it means to Bluebell and me to find ourselves underground, among friends. It wasn't I who tried to arrest you, Bigwig – that was another rabbit, long, long ago.'

22. The Story of the Trial of El-Ahrairah

Has he not a rogue's face? ... Has a damn'd Tyburn-face,
without the benefit of the clergy.

Congreve, *Love for Love*

RABBITS (says Mr Lockley) are like human beings in
many ways. One of these is certainly their staunch
ability to withstand disaster and to let the stream of their
life carry them along, past reaches of terror and loss. They
have a certain quality which it would not be accurate to
describe as callousness or indifference. It is, rather, a
blessedly circumscribed imagination and an intuitive
feeling that Life is Now. A foraging wild creature, intent
above all upon survival, is as strong as the grass. Collectively,
rabbits rest secure upon Frith's promise to El-ahrairah.
Hardly a full day had elapsed since Holly had come
crawling in delirium to the foot of Watership Down. Yet
already he was near recovery, while the more light-hearted

Bluebell seemed even less the worse for the dreadful catastrophe that he had survived. Hazel and his companions had suffered extremes of grief and horror during the telling of Holly's tale. Pipkin had cried and trembled piteously at the death of Scabious, and Acorn and Speedwell had been seized with convulsive choking as Bluebell told of the poisonous gas that murdered underground. Yet, as with primitive humans, the very strength and vividness of their sympathy brought with it a true release. Their feelings were not false or assumed. While the story was being told, they heard it without any of the reserve or detachment that the kindest of civilized humans retains as he reads his newspaper. To themselves, they seemed to struggle in the poisoned runs and to blaze with rage for poor Pimpernel in the ditch. This was their way of honouring the dead. The story over, the demands of their own hard, rough lives began to reassert themselves in their hearts, in their nerves, their blood and appetites. Would that the dead were not dead! But there is grass that must be eaten, pellets that must be chewed, hraka that must be passed, holes that must be dug, sleep that must be slept. Odysseus brings not one man to shore with him. Yet he sleeps sound beside Calypso and when he wakes thinks only of Penelope.

Even before Holly had finished his story, Hazel had fallen to sniffing at his wounded ear. He had not previously been able to get a good look at it, but now that he did, he realized that terror and fatigue had probably not been the principal causes of Holly's collapse. He was badly wounded – worse than Buckthorn. He must have lost a lot of blood. His ear was in ribbons and there was any amount of dirt in it. Hazel felt annoyed with Dandelion. As several of the rabbits began to silflay, attracted by the mild June night and the full moon, he asked Blackberry to wait. Silver, who had been about to leave by the other run, returned and joined them.

'Dandelion and the other two seem to have cheered you up all right,' said Hazel to Holly. 'It's a pity they didn't *clean* you up as well. That dirt's dangerous.'

'Well, you see –' began Bluebell, who had remained beside Holly.

'Don't make a joke,' said Hazel. 'You seem to think –'

'I wasn't going to,' said Bluebell. 'I was only going to say that I wanted to clean the captain's ear, but it's too tender to be touched.'

'He's quite right,' said Holly. 'I'm afraid I made them neglect it, but do as you think best, Hazel. I'm feeling much better now.'

Hazel began on the ear himself. The blood had caked black and the task needed patience. After a while the long, jagged wounds bled again as they slowly became clean. Silver took over. Holly, bearing it as well as he could, growled and scuffled and Silver cast about for something to occupy his attention.

'Hazel,' he asked, 'what was this idea you had – about the mouse? You said you'd explain it later. How about trying it out on us now?'

'Well,' said Hazel, 'the idea is simply that in our situation, we can't afford to waste anything that might do us good. We're in a strange place we don't know much about and we need friends. Now elil can't do us good, obviously, but there are many creatures that aren't elil – birds, mice, yonil and so on. Rabbits don't usually have much to do with them, but their enemies are our enemies for the most part. I think we ought to do all we can to make these creatures friendly. It might turn out to be well worth the trouble.'

'I can't say I fancy the idea myself,' said Silver, wiping Holly's blood out of his nose. 'These small animals are more to be despised than relied upon, I reckon. What good can they do us? They can't dig for us, they can't get food for us, they can't fight for us. They'd *say* they were friendly, no doubt, as long as we were helping them; but that's where it would stop. I heard that mouse tonight – "You want 'im, 'e come." You bet he will, as long as there's any grub or warmth going, but surely we're not going to have the warren over-run with mice and – and stag-beetles, are we?'

'No, I didn't mean quite that,' said Hazel. 'I'm not suggesting we should go about looking for field-mice and inviting them to join us. They wouldn't thank us for that, anyway. But that mouse tonight – we saved his life –'

'*You* saved his life,' said Blackberry.

'Well, his life was saved. He'll remember that.'

'But how's it going to help us?' asked Bluebell.

'To start with, he can tell us what he knows about the place –'

'What mice know. Not what rabbits need to know.'

'Well, I admit a mouse might or might not come in handy,' said Hazel. 'But I'm sure a bird would, if we could only do enough for it. We can't fly, but some of them know the country for a long way round. They know a lot about the weather, too. All I'm saying is this. If anyone finds an animal or bird, that isn't an enemy, in need of help, for goodness' sake don't miss the opportunity. That would be like leaving carrots to rot in the ground.'

'What do you think?' said Silver to Blackberry.

'I think it's a good idea, but real opportunities of the kind Hazel has in mind aren't likely to come very often.'

'I think that's about right,' said Holly, wincing as Silver resumed licking. 'The idea's all right as far as it goes, but it won't come to a great deal in practice.'

'I'm ready to give it a try,' said Silver. 'I reckon it'll be worth it, just to see Bigwig telling bed-time stories to a mole.'

'El-ahrairah did it once,' said Bluebell, *'and* it worked. Do you remember?'

'No,' said Hazel, 'I don't know that story. Let's have it.'

'Let's silflay first,' said Holly. 'This ear's had all I can stand for the time being.'

'Well, at least it's clean now,' said Hazel. 'But I'm afraid it'll never be as good as the other, you know. You'll have a ragged ear.'

'Never mind,' said Holly. 'I'm still one of the lucky ones.'

The full moon, well risen in a cloudless eastern sky, covered the high solitude with its light. We are not conscious of daylight as that which displaces darkness. Daylight, even when the sun is clear of clouds, seems to us simply the natural condition of the earth and air. When we think of the downs, we think of the downs in daylight, as we think of a rabbit with its fur on. Stubbs may have envisaged the skeleton inside the horse, but most of us do not: and we do not usually envisage the downs without daylight, even though the light is not a part of the down itself as the hide is part of the horse itself. We take daylight for granted. But moonlight is another matter. It is inconstant. The full moon wanes and returns again. Clouds may obscure it to an extent to which they cannot obscure daylight. Water is necessary to us, but a waterfall is not. Where it is to be found it is something extra, a beautiful ornament. We need daylight and to that extent it is utilitarian, but moonlight we do not need. When it comes, it serves no necessity. It transforms. It falls upon the banks and the grass, separating one long blade from another; turning a drift of brown, frosted leaves from a single heap to innumerable, flashing fragments; or glimmering lengthways along wet twigs as though light itself were ductile. Its long beams pour, white and sharp, between the trunks of trees, their clarity fading as they recede into the powdery, misty distance of beech-woods at night. In moonlight, two acres of coarse bent-grass, undulant and ankle-deep, tumbled and rough as a horse's mane, appear like a bay of waves, all shadowy troughs and hollows. The growth is so thick and matted that even the wind does not move it, but it is the moonlight that seems to confer stillness upon it. We do not take moonlight for granted. It is like snow, or like the dew on a July morning. It does not reveal but changes what it covers. And its low intensity – so much lower than that of daylight – makes us conscious that it is something added to the down, to give it, for only a little time, a singular and marvellous quality that we should admire while we can, for soon it will be gone again.

As the rabbits came up by the hole inside the beech-wood, a swift gust of wind passed through the leaves, checkering and dappling the ground beneath, stealing and giving light under the branches. They listened, but beyond the rustle of the leaves, there came from the open down outside no sound except the monotonous tremolo of a grasshopper warbler, far off in the grass.

'What a moon!' said Silver. 'Let's enjoy it while it's here.'

As they went over the bank they met Speedwell and Hawkbit returning.

'Oh, Hazel,' said Hawkbit, 'we've been talking to another mouse. He'd heard about the kestrel this evening and was very friendly. He told us about a place just the other side of the wood where the grass has been cut short – something to do with horses, he said. "You like a nice a grass? 'E very fine grass." So we went there. It's first rate.'

The gallop turned out to be a good forty yards wide, mown to less than six inches. Hazel, with a delightful sense of having been proved right by events, set to work on a patch of clover. They all munched for some time in silence.

'You're a clever chap, Hazel,' said Holly at last. 'You and your mouse. Mind you, we'd have found the place ourselves sooner or later, but not as soon as this.'

Hazel could have pressed his chin-glands for satisfaction, but he replied merely, 'We shan't need to go down the hill so much after all.' Then he added, 'But Holly, you smell of blood, you know. It may be dangerous, even here. Let's go back to the wood. It's such a beautiful night that we can sit near the holes to chew pellets and Bluebell can tell us his story.'

They found Strawberry and Buckthorn on the bank; and when everyone was comfortably chewing, with ears laid flat, Bluebell began.

'Dandelion was telling me last night about Cowslip's warren and how he told the story of the King's Lettuce. That's what put me in mind of this tale, even before Hazel explained his idea. I used to hear it from my grandfather and he always said that it happened after El-ahrairah had got his people out of the marshes of Kelfazin. They went to the meadows of Fenlo and there they dug their holes. But Prince Rainbow had his eye on El-ahrairah; and he was determined to see that he didn't get up to any more of his tricks.

'Now one evening, when El-ahrairah and Rabscuttle were sitting on a sunny bank, Prince Rainbow came through the meadows and with him was a rabbit that El-ahrairah had never seen before.

'"Good evening, El-ahrairah," said Prince Rainbow. "This is a great improvement on the marshes of Kelfazin. I see all your does are busy digging holes along the bank. Have they dug a hole for you?"

'"Yes," said El-ahrairah. "This hole here belongs to Rabscuttle and myself. We liked the look of this bank as soon as we saw it."

'"A very nice bank," said Prince Rainbow. "But I am afraid I have to tell you, El-ahrairah, that I have strict orders from Lord Frith himself not to allow you to share a hole with Rabscuttle."

'"Not share a hole with Rabscuttle?" said El-ahrairah. "Why ever not?"

'"El-ahrairah," said Prince Rainbow, "we know you and your tricks: and Rabscuttle is nearly as slippery as you are. Both of you in one hole would be altogether too much of a good thing. You would be stealing the clouds out of the sky before the moon had changed twice. No – Rabscuttle must go and look after the holes at the other end of the warren. Let me introduce you. This is Hufsa. I want you to be his friend and look after him."

'"Where does he come from?" asked El-ahrairah. "I certainly haven't seen him before."

'"He comes from another country," said Prince Rainbow, "but he is no different from any other rabbit. I hope you will help him to settle down here. And while he is getting to know the place, I'm sure you will be glad to let him share your hole."

'El-ahrairah and Rabscuttle felt desperately annoyed that they were not to be allowed to live together in their hole. But it was one of El-ahrairah's rules never to let anyone see when he was angry and besides, he felt sorry for Hufsa because he supposed that he was feeling lonely and awkward, being far away from his own people. So he welcomed him and promised to help him settle down. Hufsa was perfectly friendly and seemed anxious to please everyone; and Rabscuttle moved down to the other end of the warren.

'After a time, however, El-ahrairah began to find that something was always going wrong with his plans. One night, in the spring, when he had taken some of his people to a cornfield to eat the green shoots, they found a man with a gun walking about in the moonlight and were lucky to get away without trouble. Another time, after El-ahrairah had reconnoitred the way to a cabbage garden and scratched a hole under the fence, he arrived the next morning to find it blocked with wire, and he began to suspect that his plans were leaking out to people who were not intended to learn them.

'One day he determined to set a trap for Hufsa, to find out whether it was he who was at the bottom of the trouble. He showed him a path across the fields and told him that it led to a lonely barn full of swedes and turnips: and he went on to say that he and Rabscuttle meant to go there the next morning. In fact El-ahrairah had no such plans and took care not to say anything about the path or the barn to anyone else. But next day, when he went cautiously along the path, he found a wire set in the grass.

'This made El-ahrairah really angry, for any of his people might have been snared and killed. Of course he did not suppose that Hufsa was setting wires himself, or even that he had known that a wire was going to be set. But evidently Hufsa was in touch with somebody who did not stick at setting a wire. In the end, El-ahrairah decided that probably Prince Rainbow was passing on Hufsa's information to a farmer or a gamekeeper and not bothering himself about what happened as a result. His rabbits' lives were in danger because of Hufsa – to say nothing of all the lettuces and cabbages they were missing. After this, El-ahrairah tried not to tell Hufsa anything at all. But it was difficult to prevent him from hearing things because, as you all know, rabbits are very good at keeping secrets from other animals, but no good at keeping secrets from each other. Warren life doesn't make for secrecy. He considered killing Hufsa. But he knew that if he did, Prince Rainbow would come and they would end in more trouble. He felt decidedly uneasy even about keeping things from Hufsa, because he thought that if Hufsa realized that they knew he was a spy, he would tell Prince Rainbow and Prince Rainbow would probably take him away and think of something worse.

'El-ahrairah thought and thought. He was still thinking the next evening, when Prince Rainbow paid one of his visits to the warren.

'"You are quite a reformed character these days, El-ahrairah," said Prince Rainbow. "If you are not careful, people will begin to trust you. Since I was passing by, I thought I would just stop to thank you for your kindness in looking after Hufsa. He seems quite at home with you."

'"Yes, he does, doesn't he?" said El-ahrairah. "We grow in beauty side by side; we fill one hole with glee. But I always say to my people, 'Put not your trust in princes, nor in any –'"

'"Well, El-ahrairah," said Prince Rainbow, interrupting him, "I am sure I can trust *you*. And to prove it, I have decided that I will grow a nice crop of carrots in the field behind the hill. It is an excellent bit of ground and I am sure they will do well. Especially as no one would dream of stealing them. In fact, you can come and watch me plant them, if you like."

'"I will," said El-ahrairah. "That will be delightful."

'El-ahrairah, Rabscuttle, Hufsa and several other rabbits accompanied Prince Rainbow to the field behind the hill; and they helped him to sow it with long rows of carrot seed. It was a light, dry sort of soil – just the thing for carrots – and the whole business infuriated El-ahrairah, because he was certain that Prince Rainbow was doing it to tease him and to show that he felt sure that he had clipped his claws at last.

'"That will do splendidly," said Prince Rainbow when they had finished. "Of course, I know that no one would dream of stealing my carrots. But if they did – if they *did* steal them, El-ahrairah – I should be very angry indeed. If King Darzin stole them, for instance, I feel sure that Lord Frith would take away his kingdom and give it to someone else."

'El-ahrairah knew that Prince Rainbow meant that if he caught him stealing the carrots he would either kill him or else banish him and put some other rabbit over his people: and the thought that the other rabbit would probably be Hufsa made him grind his teeth. But he said, "Of course, of course. Very right and proper." And Prince Rainbow went away.

'One night, in the second moon after the planting, El-ahrairah and Rabscuttle went to look at the carrots. No one had thinned them out and the tops were thick and green. El-ahrairah judged that most of the roots would be a little thinner than a fore-paw. And it was while he was looking at them in the moonlight that his plan came to him. He had become so cautious about Hufsa – and indeed no one ever knew where Hufsa would be next – that on the way back he and Rabscuttle made for a hole in a lonely bank and went down it to talk together. And there El-ahrairah promised Rabscuttle not only that he would steal Prince Rainbow's carrots, but also that between them they would see the back of Hufsa into the bargain. They came out of the hole and Rabscuttle went to the farm to steal some seed corn. El-ahrairah spent the rest of the night gathering slugs; and a nasty business it was.

'The next evening El-ahrairah went out early and after a little while found Yona the hedgehog pottering along the hedge.

'"Yona," he said, "would you like a whole lot of nice, fat slugs?"

'"Yes, I would, El-ahrairah," said Yona, "but they're not so easily found. You'd know that if you were a hedgehog."

'"Well, here are some nice ones," said El-ahrairah, "and you can have them all. But I can give you a great many more if you will do what I say and ask no questions. Can you sing?"

'"Sing, El-ahrairah? No hedgehog can sing."

'"Good," said El-ahrairah. "Excellent. But you will have to try if you want those slugs. Ah! There is an old, empty box, I see, that the farmer has left in the ditch. Better and better. Now you listen to me."

'Meanwhile, in the wood, Rabscuttle was talking to Hawock the pheasant.

'"Hawock," he said, "can you swim?"

'"I never go near water if I can avoid it, Rabscuttle," said Hawock. "I dislike it very much. But I suppose if I had to, I could make shift to keep afloat for a little while."

'"Splendid," said Rabscuttle. "Now attend. I have a whole lot of corn – and you know how scarce it is at this time of year – and you can have it all, if only you will do a little swimming in the pond on the edge of the wood. Just let me explain as we go down there." And off they went through the wood.

'Fu Inlé, El-ahrairah strolled into his hole and found Hufsa chewing pellets. "Ah, Hufsa, you're here," he said. "That's fine. I can't trust anyone else, but you'll come with me, won't you? Just you and I – no one else must know."

'"Why, what's to be done, El-ahrairah?" asked Hufsa.

'"I've been looking at those carrots of Prince Rainbow's," replied El-ahrairah. "I can't stand it any longer. They're the best I've ever seen. I'm determined to steal them – or most of them, anyway. Of course, if I took a lot of rabbits on an expedition of this kind we'd soon be in trouble. Things would leak out and Prince Rainbow would be sure to get to hear. But if you and I go alone, no one will ever know who did it."

'"I'll come," said Hufsa. "Let's go tomorrow night." For he thought that that would give him time to tell Prince Rainbow.

'"No," said El-ahrairah, "I'm going now. At once."

'He wondered whether Hufsa would try to turn him against this idea, but when he looked at him he could see that Hufsa was thinking that this would be the end of El-ahrairah and that he himself would be made king of the rabbits.

'They set out together in the moonlight.

'They had gone a good way along the hedge when they came upon an old box lying in the ditch. Sitting on top of the box was Yona the hedgehog. His prickles were stuck all over with dog-rose petals and he was making an extraordinary squeaking, grunting noise and waving his black paws. They stopped and looked at him.

'"Whatever are you doing, Yona?" asked Hufsa in astonishment.

'"Singing to the moon," answered Yona. "All hedgehogs have to sing to the moon to make the slugs come. Surely you know that?

'"O Slug-a-Moon, O Slug-a-Moon,
O grant thy faithful hedgehog's boon!"

'"What a frightful noise!" said El-ahrairah and indeed it was. "Let's get on quickly before he brings all the elil round us." And on they went.

'After a time they drew near the pond on the edge of the wood. As they approached it they heard a squawking and splashing and then they saw Hawock the pheasant scuttering about in the water, with his long tail feathers floating out behind him.

'"Whatever has happened?" said Hufsa. "Hawock, have you been shot?"

'"No, no," replied Hawock. "I always go swimming in the full moon. It makes my tail grow longer and besides, my head wouldn't stay red, white and green without swimming. But you must know that, Hufsa, surely? Everyone knows that."

'"The truth is, he doesn't like other animals to catch him at it," whispered El-ahrairah. "Let's go on."

'A little farther on they came to an old well by a big oak tree. The farmer had filled it up long ago, but the mouth looked very deep and black in the moonlight.

'"Let's have a rest," said El-ahrairah, "just for a short time."

'As he spoke, a most curious-looking creature came out of the grass. It looked something like a rabbit, but even in the moonlight they could see that it had a red tail and long green ears. In its mouth it was carrying the end of one of the white sticks that men burn. It was Rabscuttle, but not even Hufsa could recognize him. He had found some sheep-dip powder at the farm and sat in it to make his tail red. His ears were festooned with trails of bryony and the white stick was making him feel ill.

'"Frith preserve us!" said El-ahrairah. "What can it be? Let's only hope it isn't one of the Thousand!" He leapt up, ready to run. "Who are you?" he asked, trembling.

'Rabscuttle spat out the white stick.

'"So!" he said commandingly. "So you have seen me, El-ahrairah! Many rabbits live out their lives and die, but few see me. Few or none! I am one of the rabbit messengers of Lord Frith, who go about the earth secretly by day and return nightly to his golden palace! He is even now awaiting me on the other side of the world and I must go to him swiftly, through the heart of the earth! Farewell, El-ahrairah!"

'The strange rabbit leapt over the edge of the well and disappeared into the darkness below.

'"We have seen what we should not!" said El-ahrairah in an awe-stricken voice. "How dreadful is this place! Let us go quickly!"

'They hurried on and presently they came to Prince Rainbow's field of carrots. How many they stole I cannot say; but of course, as you know, El-ahrairah is a great prince and no doubt he used powers unknown to you and me. But my grandfather always said that before morning the field was stripped bare. The carrots were hidden down a deep hole in the bank beside the wood and El-ahrairah and Hufsa made their way home. El-ahrairah collected two or three followers and stayed underground with them all day, but Hufsa went out in the afternoon without saying where he was going.

'That evening, as El-ahrairah and his people began to silflay under a fine red sky, Prince Rainbow came over the fields. Behind him were two great, black dogs.

'"El-ahrairah," he said, "you are under arrest."

'"What for?" asked El-ahrairah.

'"You know very well what for," said Prince Rainbow. "Let me have no more of your tricks and insolence, El-ahrairah. Where are the carrots?"

'"If I am under arrest," said El-ahrairah, "may I be told what for? It is not fair to tell me I am under arrest and then to ask me questions."

'"Come, come, El-ahrairah," said Prince Rainbow, "you are merely wasting time. Tell me where the carrots are and I will only send you to the great North and not kill you."

'"Prince Rainbow," said El-ahrairah, "for the third time, may I know for what I am under arrest?"

'"Very well," said Prince Rainbow, "if this is the way you want to die, El-ahrairah, you shall have the full process of law. You are under arrest for stealing my carrots. Are you seriously asking for a trial? I warn you that I have direct evidence and it will go ill with you."

'By this time all El-ahrairah's people were crowding round, as near as they dared for the dogs. Only Rabscuttle was nowhere to be seen. He had spent the whole day moving the carrots to another, secret hole and he was now hiding, because he could not get his tail white again.

'"Yes, I would like a trial," said El-ahrairah, "and I would like to be judged by a jury of animals. For it is not right, Prince Rainbow, that you should both accuse me and be the judge as well."

'"A jury of animals you shall have," said Prince Rainbow. "A jury of elil, El-ahrairah. For a jury of rabbits would refuse to convict you, in spite of the evidence."

'To everyone's surprise El-ahrairah immediately replied that he would be content with a jury of elil: and Prince Rainbow said that he would bring them that night. El-ahrairah was sent down his hole and the dogs were put on guard outside. None of his people was allowed to see him, although many tried.

'Up and down the hedges and copses the news spread that El-ahrairah was on trial for his life and that Prince Rainbow was going to bring him before a jury of elil. Animals came crowding in. Fu Inlé, Prince Rainbow returned with the elil – two badgers, two foxes, two stoats, an owl and a cat. El-ahrairah was brought up and placed between the dogs. The elil sat staring at him and their eyes glittered in the moon. They licked their lips; and the dogs muttered that they had been promised the task of carrying out the sentence. There were a great many animals – rabbits and others – and every one of them felt sure that this time it was all up with El-ahrairah.

'"Now," said Prince Rainbow, "let us begin. It will not take long. Where is Hufsa?"

'Then Hufsa came out, bowing and bobbing his head, and he told the elil that El-ahrairah had come the night before, when he was quietly chewing pellets, and terrified him into going with him to steal Prince Rainbow's carrots. He had wanted to refuse but he had been too much frightened. The carrots were hidden in a hole that he could show them. He had been forced to do what he did, but the next day he had gone as quickly as possible to tell Prince Rainbow, whose loyal servant he was.

'"We will recover the carrots later," said Prince Rainbow. "Now, El-ahrairah, have you any evidence to call or anything to say? Make haste."

'"I would like to ask the witness some questions," said El-ahrairah; and the elil agreed that this was only fair.

'"Now, Hufsa," said El-ahrairah, "can we hear a little more about this journey that you and I are supposed to have made? For really I can remember nothing about it at all. You say we went out of the hole and set off in the night. What happened then?"

'"Why, El-ahrairah," said Hufsa, "you can't possibly have forgotten. We came along the ditch, and don't you remember that we saw a hedgehog sitting on a box singing a song to the moon?"

'"A hedgehog doing *what*?" said one of the badgers.

'"Singing a song to the moon," said Hufsa eagerly. "They do that, you know, to make the slugs come. He had rose petals stuck all over him and he was waving his paws and –"

'"Now steady, steady," said El-ahrairah kindly, "I wouldn't like you to say anything you don't mean. Poor fellow," he added to the jury," he really believes these things he says, you know. He doesn't mean any harm, but –"

'"But he *was*," shouted Hufea. "He was singing 'O Slug-a-moon! O Slug-a-moon! O grant –' "

'"What the hedgehog sang is not evidence," said El-ahrairah. "Really, one is inclined to wonder what is. Well, all right. We saw a hedgehog covered with roses, singing a song on a box. What happened then?"

'"Well," said Hufsa, "then we went on and came to the pond, where we saw a pheasant."

'"Pheasant, eh?" said one of the foxes. "I wish I'd seen it. What was it doing?"

'"It was swimming round and round in the water –" said Hufsa.

'"Wounded, eh?" said the fox.

"No, no," said Hufsa. "They all do that, to make their tails grow longer. I'm surprised you don't know."

'"To make *what*?" said the fox.

'"To make their tails grow longer," said Hufsa sulkily. "He said so himself."

'"You've only had this stuff for a very short time," said El-ahrairah to the elil. "It takes a bit of getting used to. Look at me. I've been forced to live with it for the last two months, day in and day out. I've been as kind and understanding as I can, but apparently just to my own harm."

'A silence fell. El-ahrairah, with an air of fatherly patience, turned back to the witness.

'"My memory is so bad," he said. "Do go on."

'"Well, El-ahrairah," said Hufsa, "you're pretending very cleverly, but even you won't be able to say you've forgotten what happened next. A huge, terrifying rabbit, with a red tail and green ears, came out of the grass. He had a white stick in his mouth and he plunged into the ground down a great hole. He told us he was going through the middle of the earth to see Lord Frith on the other side."

'This time not one of the elil said a word. They were staring at Hufsa and shaking their heads.

'"They're all mad, you know," whispered one of the stoats, "nasty little beasts. They'll say anything when they're cornered. But this one is the worst I've ever heard. How much longer have we got to stay here? I'm hungry."

'Now El-ahrairah had known beforehand that while elil detest all rabbits, they would dislike most the one who looked the biggest fool. That was why he had agreed to a jury of elil. A jury of rabbits might have tried to get to the bottom of Hufsa's story; but not the elil, for they hated and despised the witness and wanted to be off hunting as soon as they could.

'"So it comes to this," said El-ahrairah. "We saw a hedgehog covered with roses, singing a song: and then we saw a perfectly healthy pheasant swimming round and round the pond: and then we saw a rabbit with a red tail, green ears and a white stick, and he jumped straight down a deep well. Is that right?"

'"Yes," said Hufsa.

'"And then we stole the carrots?"

'"Yes."

'"Were they purple with green spots?"

'"Were what purple with green spots?"

'"The carrots."

'"Well, you know they weren't, El-ahrairah. They were the ordinary colour. They're down the hole!" shouted Hufsa desperately. "Down the hole! Go and look!"

'The court adjourned while Hufsa led Prince Rainbow to the hole. They found no carrots and returned.

'"I've been underground all day," said El-ahrairah, "and I can prove it. I ought to have been asleep, but it's very difficult when m'learned friend – well, never mind. I simply mean that obviously I couldn't have been out moving carrots or anything else. If there ever *were* any carrots," he added. "But I've nothing more to say."

'"Prince Rainbow," said the cat, "I hate all rabbits. But I don't see how we can possibly say that it's been proved that that rabbit took your carrots. The witness is obviously out of his mind – mad as the mist and snow – and the prisoner will have to be released." They all agreed.

'"You had better go quickly," said Prince Rainbow to El-ahrairah. "Go down your hole, El-ahrairah, before I hurt you myself."

'"I will, my lord," said El-ahrairah. "But may I beg you to remove that rabbit you sent among us, for he troubles us with his foolishness?"

'So Hufsa went away with Prince Rainbow and El-ahrairah's people were left in peace, apart from indigestion brought on by eating too many carrots. But it was a long time before Rabscuttle could get his tail white again, so my grandfather always said.'

23. Kehaar

The wing trails like a banner in defeat,
No more to use the sky for ever but live with famine and pain a
    few days.
He is strong and pain is worse to the strong incapacity is worse.
No one but death the redeemer will humble that head,
The intrepid readiness, the terrible eyes.

Robinson Jeffers, Hurt Hawks

HUMAN beings say, 'It never rains but it pours.' This is not very apt, for it frequently does rain without pouring. The rabbits' proverb is better expressed. They say, 'One cloud feels lonely': and indeed it is true that the appearance of a single cloud often means that the sky will soon be overcast. However that may be, the very next day provided a dramatic second opportunity to put Hazel's idea into practice.

It was early morning and the rabbits were beginning to silflay, coming up into clear, grey silence. The air was still chilly. There was a good deal of dew and no wind. Five or six wild duck flew overhead in a swiftly moving V, intent on some far-off destination. The sound made by their wings came down distinctly, diminishing as they went away southwards. The silence returned. With the melting of the last of the twilight there grew a kind of expectancy and tension, as though it were thawing snow about to slide from a sloping roof. Then the whole down and all below it, earth and air, gave way to the sunrise. As a bull, with a slight but irresistible movement, tosses its head from the grasp of a man who is leaning over the stall and idly holding its horn, so the sun entered the world in smooth, gigantic power. Nothing interrupted or obscured its coming. Without a sound, the leaves shone and the grass coruscated along the miles of the escarpment.

Outside the wood, Bigwig and Silver combed their ears, sniffed the air and hopped away, following their own long shadows to the grass of the gallop. As they moved over the short turf – nibbling, sitting up and looking round them – they approached a little hollow, no more than three feet across. Before they reached the edge Bigwig, who was ahead of Silver, checked and crouched, staring. Although he could not see into the hollow, he knew that there was some creature in it – something fairly big. Peering through the blades of grass round his head, he could see the curve of a white back. Whatever the creature was, it was nearly as big as himself. He waited, stock-still, for some little time, but it did not move.

'What has a white back, Silver?' whispered Bigwig.

Silver considered. 'A cat?'

'No cats here.'

'How do you know?'

At that moment they both heard a low, breathy hissing from the hollow. It lasted for a few moments. Then there was silence once more.

Bigwig and Silver had a good opinion of themselves. Apart from Holly, they were the only survivors of the Sandleford Owsla and they knew that their comrades looked up to them. The encounter with the rats in the barn had been no joke and had proved their worth. Bigwig, who was generous and honest, had never for a moment resented Hazel's courage on the night when his own superstitious fear had got the better of him. But the idea of going back to the Honeycomb and reporting that he had glimpsed an unknown creature in the grass and left it alone was more than he could swallow. He turned his head and looked at Silver. Seeing that he was game, he took a final look at the strange, white back and then went straight up to the edge of the hollow. Silver followed.

It was no cat. The creature in the hollow was a bird – a big bird, nearly a foot long. Neither of them had ever seen a bird like it before. The white part of its back, which they had glimpsed through the grass, was in fact only the shoulders and neck. The lower back was light grey and so were the wings, which tapered to long, black-tipped primaries folded together over the tail. The head was very dark brown – almost black – in such sharp contrast to the white neck that the bird looked as though it were wearing a kind of hood. The one dark-red leg that they could see ended in a webbed foot and three powerful, taloned toes. The beak, hooked slightly downwards at the end, was strong and sharp. As they stared it opened, disclosing a red mouth and throat. The bird hissed savagely and tried to strike, but still it did not move.

'It's hurt,' said Bigwig.

'Yes, you can tell that,' replied Silver. 'But it's not wounded anywhere that I can see. I'll go round –'

'Look out!' said Bigwig. 'He'll have you!'

Silver, as he started to move round the hollow, had come closer to the bird's head. He jumped back just in time to avoid a quick, darting blow of the beak.

'That would have broken your foot,' said Bigwig.

As they squatted, looking at the bird – for they both sensed intuitively that it would not rise – it suddenly burst into loud, raucous cries – 'Yark! Yark! Yark!' – a tremendous sound at close quarters – that split the morning and carried far across the down. Bigwig and Silver turned and ran.

They collected themselves sufficiently to pull up short of the wood and make a more dignified approach to the bank. Hazel came to meet them in the grass. There was no mistaking their wide eyes and dilated nostrils.

'Elil?' asked Hazel.

'Well, I'm blest if I know, to tell you the truth,' replied Bigwig. 'There's a great bird out there, like nothing I've ever seen.'

'How big? As big as a pheasant?'

'Not quite so big,' admitted Bigwig, 'but bigger than a wood-pigeon: and a lot fiercer.'

'Is that what cried?'

'Yes. It startled me all right. We were actually beside it. But for some reason or other it can't move.'

'Dying?'

'I don't think so.'

'I'll go and have a look at it,' said Hazel.

'It's savage. For goodness' sake be careful.'

Bigwig and Silver returned with Hazel. The three of them squatted outside the bird's reach as it looked sharply and desperately from one to the other. Hazel spoke in the hedgerow patois.

'You hurt? You no fly?'

The answer was a harsh gabbling which they all felt immediately to be exotic. Wherever the bird came from, it was somewhere far away. The accent was strange and guttural, the speech distorted. They could catch only a word here and there.

'Come keel – kah! kah! – you come keel – yark! – t'ink me finish – me no finish – 'urt you dam' plenty –' The dark brown head flickered from side to side. Then, unexpectedly, the bird began to drive its beak into the ground. They noticed for the first time that the grass in front of it was torn and scored with lines. For some moments it stabbed here and there; then gave up, lifted its head and watched them again.

'I believe it's starving,' said Hazel. 'We'd better feed it. Bigwig, go and get some worms or something, there's a good fellow.'

'Er – what did you say, Hazel?'

'Worms.'

'Me dig for worms?'

'Didn't the Owsla teach – oh, all right, I'll do it,' said Hazel. 'You and Silver wait here.'

After a few moments, however, Bigwig followed Hazel back to the ditch and began to join him in scratching at the dry ground. Worms are not plentiful on the downs and there had been no rain for days. After a time Bigwig looked up.

'What about beetles? Woodlice? Something like that?'

They found some rotten sticks and carried them back. Hazel pushed one forward cautiously.

'Insects.'

The bird split the stick three ways in as many seconds and snapped up the few insects inside. Soon there was a small pile of debris in the hollow as the rabbits brought anything from which it could get food. Bigwig found some horse-dung along the track, dug the worms out of it, overcame his disgust and carried them one by one. When Hazel praised him, he muttered something about 'the first time any rabbit's done this and don't tell the blackbirds'. At last, long after they had all grown weary, the bird stopped feeding and looked at Hazel.

'Finish eat.' It paused. 'Vat for you do?'

'You hurt?' said Hazel.

The bird looked crafty. 'No hurt. Plenty fight. Stay small time, den go.'

'You stay there you finish,' said Hazel. 'Bad place. Come homba, come kestrel.'

'Damn de lot. Fight plenty.'

'I bet it would, too,' said Bigwig, looking with admiration at the two-inch beak and thick neck.

'We no want you finish,' said Hazel. 'You stay here you finish. We help you maybe.'

'Piss off!'

'Come on,' said Hazel immediately to the others. 'Let it alone.' He began to lollop back to the wood. 'Let it try keeping the kestrels off for a bit.'

'What's the idea, Hazel?' said Silver. 'That's a savage brute. You can't make a friend out of that.'

'You may be right,' said Hazel. 'But what's the good of a blue-tit or a robin to us? They don't fly any distance. We need a big bird.'

'But why do you want a bird so particularly?'

'I'll explain later,' said Hazel 'I'd like Blackberry and Fiver to hear as well. But let's go underground now. If you don't want to chew pellets, I do.'

During the afternoon Hazel organized more work on the warren. The Honeycomb was as good as finished – though rabbits are not methodical and are never really certain when anything is finished – and the surrounding burrows and runs were taking shape. Quite early in the evening, however, he made his way once more to the hollow. The bird was still there. It looked weaker and less alert, but snapped feebly as Hazel came up.

'Still here?' said Hazel. 'You fight hawk?'

'No fight,' answered the bird. 'No fight, but vatch, vatch, alvays vatch. Ees no good.'

'Hungry?'

The bird made no reply.

'Listen,' said Hazel. 'Rabbits not eat birds. Rabbits eat grass. We help you.'

'Vat for 'elp me?'

'Never mind. We make you safe. Big hole. Food too.'

The bird considered. 'Legs fine. Ving no good. 'E bad.'

'Well, walk then.'

'You 'urt me, I 'urt you like dam'.'

Hazel turned away. The bird spoke again.

'Ees long vay?'

'No, not far.'

'Come den.'

It got up with a good deal of difficulty, staggering on its strong, blood-red legs. Then it opened its wings high above its body and Hazel jumped back, startled by the great, arching span. But at once it closed them again, grimacing with pain.

'Ving no good. I come.'

It followed Hazel docilely enough across the grass, but he was careful to keep out of its reach. Their arrival outside the wood caused something of a sensation, which Hazel cut short with a peremptory sharpness quite unlike his usual manner.

'Come on, get busy,' he said to Dandelion and Buckthorn. 'This bird's hurt and we're going to shelter it until it's better. Ask Bigwig to show you how to get it some food. It eats worms and insects. Try grasshoppers, spiders – anything. Hawkbit! Acorn! Yes, and you too, Fiver – come out of that rapt trance, or whatever you're in. We need an open, wide hole, broader than it's deep, with a flat floor a little below the level of the entrance; by nightfall.'

'We've been digging all the afternoon, Hazel –'

'I know. I'll come and help you,' said Hazel, 'in just a little while. Only get started. The night's coming.'

The astonished rabbits obeyed him, grumbling. Hazel's authority was put to something of a test, but held firm with the support of Bigwig. Although he had no idea what Hazel had in mind, Bigwig was fascinated by the strength and courage of the bird and had already accepted the idea of taking it in, without troubling himself about the reason. He led the digging while Hazel explained to the bird, as well as he could, how they lived, their ways of protecting themselves from their enemies and the kind of shelter they could provide. The amount of food the rabbits produced was not very large, but once inside the wood the bird clearly felt safer and was able to hobble about and do some foraging for itself.

By owl-time Bigwig and his helpers had scratched out a kind of lobby inside the entrance to one of the runs leading down from the wood. They lined the floor with beech twigs and leaves. As darkness began to fall the bird was installed. It was still suspicious, but seemed to be in a good deal of pain. Evidently, since it could not think of any better plan for itself, it was ready to try a rabbit hole to save its life. From outside, they could see its dark head alert in the gloom, the black eyes still watchful. It was not asleep when they themselves finished a late silflay and went underground.

Black-headed gulls are gregarious. They live in colonies where they forage and feed, chatter and fight all day long. Solitude and reticence are unnatural to them. They move southwards in the breeding-season and at such times a wounded one is only too likely to find itself deserted. The gull's savagery and suspicion had been due partly to pain and partly to the unnerving knowledge that it had no companions and could not fly. By the following morning its natural instincts to mix with a flock and to talk were beginning to return. Bigwig made himself its companion. He would not hear of the gull going out to forage. Before ni-Frith the rabbits had managed to produce as much as it could eat – for a time at all events – and were able to sleep through the heat of the day. Bigwig, however, remained with the gull, making no secret of his admiration, talking and listening to it for several hours. At the evening feed he joined Hazel and Holly near the bank where Bluebell had told his story of El-ahrairah.

'How's the bird now?' asked Hazel.

'A good deal better, I think,' replied Bigwig. 'He's very tough, you know. My goodness, what a life he's had! You don't know what you're missing! I could sit and listen to him all day.'

'How was it hurt?'

'A cat jumped on him in a farmyard. He never heard it until the last moment. It tore the muscle of one of his wings, but apparently he gave it something to remember before he made off. Then he got himself up here somehow or other and just collapsed. Think of standing up to a cat! I can see now that I haven't really started yet. Why shouldn't a rabbit stand up to a cat? Let's just suppose that –'

'But what is this bird?' interrupted Holly.

'Well, I can't quite make out,' answered Bigwig. 'But if I understand him properly – and I'm not at all sure that I do – he says that where he comes from there are thousands of his kind – more than we can possibly imagine. Their flocks make the whole air white and in the breeding season their nests are like leaves in a wood – so he says.'

'But where? I've never seen *one*, even.'

'He says,' said Bigwig, looking very straight at Holly, 'he says that a long way from here the earth stops and there isn't any more.'

'Well, obviously it stops somewhere. What is there beyond?'

'Water.'

'A river, you mean?'

'No,' said Bigwig, 'not a river. He says there's a vast place of water, going on and on. You can't see to the other side. There isn't another side. At least there is, because he's been there. Oh, I don't know – I must admit I can't altogether understand it.'

'Was it telling you that it's been outside the world and come back again? That must be untrue.'

'I don't know,' said Bigwig, 'but I'm sure he's not lying. This water, apparently, moves all the time and keeps breaking against the earth: and when he can't hear that, he misses it. That's his name – Kehaar. It's the noise the water makes.'

The others were impressed in spite of themselves.

'Well, why's it here?' asked Hazel.

'He shouldn't be. He ought to have been off to this Big Water place a long time ago, to breed. Apparently a lot of them come away in winter, because it gets so cold and wild. Then they go back in summer. But he's been hurt once already this spring. It was nothing much, but it held him up. He rested and hung around a rookery for a bit. Then he got stronger and left them, and he was coming along when he stopped in the farmyard and met this foul cat.'

'So when it's better it'll go on again?' said Hazel.

'Yes.'

'We've been wasting our time, then.'

'Why, Hazel, what is it you have in mind?'

'Go and get Blackberry and Fiver: we'd better have Silver too. Then I'll explain.'

The quiet of the evening silflay, when the western sun shone straight along the ridge, the grass tussocks threw shadows twice as long as themselves and the cool air smelt of thyme and dog roses, was something which they had all come to enjoy even more than former evenings in the meadows of Sandleford. Although they could not know it, the down was more lonely than it had been for hundreds of years. There were no sheep, and villagers from Kingsclere and Sydmonton no longer had any occasion to walk over the hills, either for business or for pleasure. In the fields of Sandleford the rabbits had seen men almost every day. Here, since their arrival, they had seen one and him on a horse. Looking round the little group that gathered on the grass, Hazel saw that all of them – even Holly – were looking stronger, sleeker and in better shape than when they had first come to the down. Whatever might lie ahead, at least he could feel that he had not failed them so far.

'We're doing well here,' he began, 'Or so it seems to me. We're certainly not a bunch of hlessil any more. But all the same, there's something on my mind. I'm surprised, as a matter of fact, that I should be the first one of us to start thinking about it. Unless we can find the answer, then this warren's as good as finished, in spite of all we've done.'

'Why, how can that be, Hazel?' said Bigwig.

'Do you remember Nildro-hain?' asked Hazel.

'She stopped running. Poor Strawberry.'

'I know. And we have no does – not one – and no does means no kittens and in a few years no warren.'

It may seem incredible that the rabbits had given no thought to so vital a matter. But men have made the same mistake more than once – left the whole business out of account, or been content to trust to luck and the fortune of war. Rabbits live close to death and when death comes closer than usual, thinking about survival leaves little room for anything else. But now, in the evening sunshine on the friendly, empty down, with a good burrow at his back and the grass turning to pellets in his belly, Hazel knew that he was lonely for a doe. The others were silent and he could tell that his words had sunk in.

The rabbits grazed or lay basking in the sun. A lark went twittering up into the brighter sunshine above, soared and sang and came slowly down, ending with a sideways, spread-wing glide and a wagtail's run through the grass. The sun dipped lower. At last Blackberry said, 'What's to be done? Set out again?'

'I hope not,' said Hazel. 'It all depends. What I'd like to do is get hold of some does and bring them here.'

'Where from?'

'Another warren.'

'But are there any on these hills? How do we find out? The wind never brings the least smell of rabbits.'

'I'll tell you how,' said Hazel. 'The bird. The bird will go and search for us.'

'Hazel-rah,' cried Blackberry, 'what a marvellous idea! That bird could find out in a day what we couldn't discover for ourselves in a thousand! But are you certain it can be persuaded to do it? Surely as soon as it gets better, it'll simply fly away and leave us?'

'I can't tell,' answered Hazel. 'All we can do is feed it and hope for the best. But Bigwig, since you seem to be getting on with it so well, perhaps you can explain to it how much this means to us. It has only to fly over the downs and let us know what it sees.'

'You leave him to me,' said Bigwig. 'I think I know how to do it.'

Hazel's anxiety and the reason for it were soon known to all the rabbits and there was not one who did not realize what they were up against. There was nothing very startling in what he had said. He was simply the one – as a Chief Rabbit ought to be – through whom a strong feeling, latent throughout the warren, had come to the surface. But his plan to make use of the gull excited everyone and was seen as something that not even Blackberry could have hit upon. Reconnaissance is familiar to all rabbits – indeed it is second nature – but the idea of making use of a bird, and one so strange and savage, convinced them that Hazel, if he could really do it, must be as clever as El-ahrairah himself.

For the next few days a lot of hard work went into feeding Kehaar. Acorn and Pipkin, boasting that they were the best insect-catchers in the warren, brought in great numbers of beetles and grasshoppers. At first the gull's principal hardship was lack of water. He suffered a good deal and was reduced to tearing at the stems of the long grasses for moisture. However, during his third night in the warren it rained for three or four hours and puddles formed on the track. A cluttery spell set in, as it often does in Hampshire when hay-time approaches. High winds from the south laid the grass flat all day, turning it to a dull, damascene silver. The great branches of the beeches moved little but spoke loudly. There were squalls of rain on the wind. The weather made Kehaar restless. He walked about a good deal, watched the flying clouds and snapped up everything the foragers brought. Searching became harder, for in the wet the insects burrowed into the deep grass and had to be scratched out.

One afternoon Hazel, who now shared a burrow with Fiver as in the old days, was woken by Bigwig to be told that Kehaar had something to say to him. He made his way to Kehaar's lobby without coming above ground. The first thing he noticed was that the gull's head was moulting and turning white, though a dark-brown patch remained behind each eye. Hazel greeted him and was surprised to be answered in a few words of halting, broken Lapine. Evidently Kehaar had prepared a short speech.

'Meester 'Azel, ees rabbits vork 'ard,' said Kehaar. 'I no finish now. Soon I go fine.'

'That's good news,' said Hazel. 'I'm glad.'

Kehaar relapsed into hedgerow vernacular.

'Meester Pigvig, 'e plenty good fella.'

'Yes, he is.'

'E say you no getting mudders. Ees finish mudders. Plenty trouble for you.'

'Yes, that's true. We don't know what to do. No mothers anywhere.'

'Listen. I get peeg, fine plan. I go fine now. Ving, 'e better. Vind finish, den I fly. Fly for you. Find plenty mudders, tell you vere dey are, ya?'

'Why, what a splendid idea, Kehaar! How clever of you to think of it! You very fine bird.'

'Ees finish mudders for me dis year. Ees too late. All mudders sitting on nest now. Eggs come.'

'I'm sorry.'

'Nudder time I get mudder. Now I fly for you.'

'We'll do everything we possibly can to help you.'

The next day the wind dropped and Kehaar made one or two short flights. However, it was not until three days later that he felt able to set out on his search. It was a perfect June morning. He was snapping up numbers of the little white-shelled, downland snails from the wet grass and cracking them in his great beak, when he suddenly turned to Bigwig and said,

'Now I fly for you.'

He opened his wings. The two-foot span arched above Bigwig, who sat perfectly still while the white feathers beat the air round his head in a kind of ceremonious farewell. Laying his ears flat in the fanned draught, he stared up at Kehaar as the gull rose, rather heavily, into the air. When he flew his body, so long and graceful on the ground, took on the appearance of a thick, stumpy cylinder, from the front of which his red beak projected between his round, black eyes. For a few moments he hovered, his body rising and falling between his wings. Then he began to climb, sailed sideways over the grass and disappeared northwards below the edge of the escarpment. Bigwig returned to the hanger with the news that Kehaar had set out.

The gull was away several days – longer than the rabbits had expected. Hazel could not help wondering whether he really would return, for he knew that Kehaar, like themselves, felt the mating urge and he thought it quite likely that after all he would be off to the Big Water and the raucous, teeming gull-colonies of which he had spoken with such feeling to Bigwig. As far as he was able he kept his anxiety to himself, but one day when they were alone, he asked Fiver whether he thought Kehaar would return.

'He will return,' said Fiver unhesitatingly.

'And what will he bring with him?'

'How can I tell?' replied Fiver. But later, when they were underground, silent and drowsy, he said suddenly, 'The gifts of El-ahrairah. Trickery; great danger; and blessing for the warren.' When Hazel questioned him again, he seemed to be unaware that he had spoken and could add nothing more.

Bigwig spent most of the hours of daylight watching for Kehaar's return. He was inclined to be surly and short and once, when Bluebell remarked that he thought Meester Pigvig's fur cap was moulting in sympathy for absent friends, he showed a flash of his old sergeant-major spirit and cuffed and abused him twice round the Honeycomb, until Holly intervened to save his faithful jester from further trouble.

It was late one afternoon, with a light north wind blowing and the smell of hay drifting up from the fields of Sydmonton, when Bigwig came hurtling down into the Honeycomb to announce that Kehaar was back. Hazel suppressed his excitement and told everyone to keep out of the way while he went to see him alone. On second thoughts, however, he took Fiver and Bigwig with him.

The three of them found Kehaar back in his lobby. It was full of droppings, messy and malodorous. Rabbits will not excrete underground and Kehaar's habit of fouling his own nest had always disgusted Hazel. Now, in his eagerness to hear his news, the guano smell seemed almost welcome.

'Glad to see you back, Kehaar,' he said. 'Are you tired?'

'Ving 'e still go tired. Fly liddle bit, stop liddle bit, everyt'ing go fine.'

'Are you hungry? Shall we get you some insects?'

'Fine. Fine. Good fellas. Plenty beetle.' (All insects were 'beetle' to Kehaar.)

Clearly, he had missed their attentions and was ready to enjoy being back. Although he no longer needed to have food brought to the lobby, he evidently felt that he deserved it. Bigwig went to get his foragers and Kehaar kept them busy until sunset. At last he looked shrewdly at Fiver and said,

'Eh, Meester Liddle Von, you know vat I pring, ya?'

'I've no idea,' replied Fiver, rather shortly.

'Den I tell. All dis peeg ill, I go along 'im, dis vay, dat vay, vere sun come up, vere sun go down. Ees no rabbits. Ees nodings, nodings.'

He stopped. Hazel looked at Fiver apprehensively.

'Den I go down, go down in bottom. Ees farm vid peeg trees all round, on liddle hill. You know?'

'No, we don't know it. But go on.'

'I show you. 'E not far. You see 'im. Und here ees rabbits. Ees rabbits live in box; live vid men. You know?'

'Live with men? Did you say "Live with men?"'

'Ya, ya, live vid men. In shed; rabbits live in box in shed. Men pring food. You know?'

'I know this happens,' said Hazel. 'I've heard of it. That's fine, Kehaar. You've been very thorough. But it can't help us, can it?'

'I t'ink ees mudders. In peeg box. But else ees no rabbits; not in fields, not in voods. No rabbits. Anyvays I no see em.'

'That sounds bad.'

'Vait. I tell more. Now you 'ear. I go flying, oder vay, vere sun go middle of day. You know, dis vay ees Peeg Vater.'

'Did you go to the Big Water, then?' asked Bigwig.

'Na, na, not near so far. But out dis vay ees river, you know?'

'No, we haven't been so far.'

'Ees river,' repeated Kehaar. 'Und here ees town of rabbits.'

'On the other side of the river?'

'Na, na. You go dat vay, ees peeg fields all de vay. Den after long vay ees come to town of rabbits, ver' big. Und after dat ees iron road und den river.'

'Iron road?' asked Fiver.

'Ya, ya, iron road. You not seen heem – iron road? Men make heem.'

Kehaar's speech was so outlandish and distorted at the best of times that it was only too common for the rabbits to be unsure what he meant. The vernacular words which he used now for 'iron' and 'road' (familiar enough to seagulls), his listeners had scarcely ever heard. Kehaar was quick to impatience and now, as often, they felt at a disadvantage in the face of his familiarity with a wider world than their own. Hazel thought quickly. Two things were clear. Kehaar had evidently found a big warren some way off to the south: and whatever the iron road was, the warren was on this side both of it and of a river. If he had understood rightly, it seemed to follow that the iron road and the river could be ignored for their purposes.

'Kehaar,' he said, 'I want to be certain. Can we get to the rabbits' town without bothering about the iron road and the river?'

'Ya, ya. Not go to iron road. Rabbit's town in bushes for peeg, lonely fields. Plenty mudders.'

'How long would it take to go from here to the – to the town?'

'I t'ink two days. Ees long vay.'

'Good for you, Kehaar. You've done everything we hoped. You rest now. We'll feed you as long as you want.'

'Sleep now. Tomorrow plenty beetle, ya, ya.'

The rabbits made their way back to the Honeycomb. Hazel told Kehaar's news and a long, disorderly, intermittent discussion began. This was their way of reaching a conclusion. The fact that there was a warren two or three days' journey to the south flickered and oscillated down among them as a penny wavers down through deep water, moving one way and the other, shifting, vanishing, reappearing, but always sinking towards the firm bottom. Hazel let the talk run on as long as it would, until at last they dispersed and slept.

The next morning they went about their lives as usual, feeding Kehaar and themselves, playing and digging. But all this time, just as a drop of water slowly swells until it is heavy enough to fall from a twig, the idea of what they meant to do was becoming clear and unanimous. By the following day Hazel saw it plain. It so happened that the time for speaking came when he was sitting on the bank at sunrise, with Fiver and three or four others. There was no need to summon a general gathering. The thing was settled. When it reached them, those who were not there would accept what he had said without having heard him at all.

'This warren that Kehaar found,' said Hazel, 'he said it was big.'

'So we can't take it by force,' said Bigwig.

'I don't think I want to go and join it,' said Hazel. 'Do you?'

'And leave here?' replied Dandelion. 'After all our work? Besides, I reckon we'd have a thin time. No, I'm sure none of us wants to do that.'

'What we want is to get some does and bring them back here,' said Hazel. 'Will that be difficult, do you think?'

'I should have thought not,' said Holly. 'Big warrens are often overcrowded and some of the rabbits can't get enough to eat. The young does get edgy and nervous and some of them don't have any kittens on that account. At least, the kittens begin to grow inside them and then they melt away again into their bodies. You know this?'

'I didn't know,' said Strawberry.

'That's because you've never been overcrowded. But our warren – the Threarah's warren – was overcrowded a year or two back and a lot of the younger does were re-absorbing their litters before they were born. The Threarah told me that long ago, El-ahrairah made a bargain with Frith. Frith promised him that rabbits were not to be born dead or unwanted. If there's little chance of a decent life for them, it's a doe's privilege to take them back into her body unborn.'

'Yes, I remember the bargain story,' said Hazel. 'So you think there may be discontented does? That's hopeful. We're agreed, then, that we ought to send an expedition to this warren and that there's a good chance of being successful without fighting. Do you want everyone to go?'

'I'd say not,' said Blackberry. 'Two or three days' journey; and we're all in danger, both going and coming. It would be less dangerous for three or four rabbits than for hrair. Three or four can travel quickly and aren't conspicuous: and the Chief Rabbit of this warren would be less likely to object to a few strangers coming with a civil request.'

'I'm sure that's right,' said Hazel. 'We'll send four rabbits: and they can explain how we come to be in this difficulty and ask to be allowed to persuade some does to come back with them. I don't see that any Chief Rabbit can object to that. I wonder which of us would be the best to send?'

'Hazel-rah, you mustn't go,' said Dandelion. 'You're needed here and we don't want to risk you. Everyone's agreed on that.'

Hazel had known already that they would not let him lead the embassy. It was a disappointment, but nevertheless he felt that they were right. The other warren would have little opinion of a Chief Rabbit who ran his own errands. Besides, he was not particularly impressive in appearance or as a speaker. This was a job for someone else.

'All right,' he said. 'I knew you wouldn't let me go. I'm not the right fellow anyway – Holly is. He knows everything about moving in the open and he'll be able to talk well when he gets there.'

No one contradicted this. Holly was the obvious choice, but to select his companions was less easy. Everyone was ready to go, but the business was so important that at last they considered each rabbit in turn, discussing who would be the most likely to survive the long journey, to arrive in good shape and to go down well in a strange warren. Bigwig, rejected on the grounds that he might quarrel in strange company, was inclined to be sulky at first, but came round when he remembered that he could go on looking after Kehaar. Holly himself wanted to take Bluebell but as Blackberry said, one funny joke at the expense of the Chief Rabbit might ruin everything. Finally they chose Silver, Buckthorn and Strawberry. Strawberry said little but was obviously very much pleased. He had suffered a good deal to show that he was no coward and now he had the satisfaction of knowing that he was worth something to his new friends.

They started early in the morning, in the grey light. Kehaar had undertaken to fly out later in the day, to make sure they were going in the right direction and bring back news of their progress. Hazel and Bigwig went with them to the southern end of the hanger and watched as they slipped away, heading to the west of the distant farm. Holly seemed confident and the other three were in high spirits. Soon they were lost to sight in the grass and Hazel and Bigwig turned back into the wood.

'Well, we've done the best we can,' said Hazel. 'The rest's up to them and to El-ahrairah, now. But surely it ought to be all right?'

'Not a doubt of it,' said Bigwig. 'Let's hope they're back soon. I'm looking forward to a nice doe and a litter of kittens in my burrow. Lots of little Bigwigs, Hazel! Think of that, and tremble!'

24. Nuthanger Farm

When Robyn came to Notyngham,
  Sertenly withouten layn,
He prayed to God and myld Mary
  To bryng hym out save agayn.

Beside him stod a gret-hedid munke,
  I pray to God woo he be!
Fful sone he knew gode Robyn,
  As sone as he hym se.

Child, No. 119, *Robin Hood and the Monk*

HAZEL sat on the bank in the midsummer night. There had been no more than five hours' darkness and that of a pallid, twilit quality which kept him wakeful and restless. Everything was going well. Kehaar had found Holly during the afternoon and corrected his line a little to the west. He had left him in the shelter of a thick hedge, sure of his course for the big warren. It seemed certain now that two days would be enough for the journey. Bigwig and some

257

of the other rabbits had already begun enlarging their burrows in preparation for Holly's return. Kehaar had had a violent quarrel with a kestrel, screaming insults in a voice fit to startle a Cornish harbour: and although it had ended inconclusively, the kestrel seemed likely to regard the neighbourhood of the hanger with healthy respect for the future. Things had not looked better since they had first set out from Sandleford.

A spirit of happy mischief entered into Hazel. He felt as he had on the morning when they crossed the Enborne and he had set out alone and found the beanfield. He was confident and ready for adventure. But what adventure? Something worth telling to Holly and Silver on their return. Something to – well, not to diminish what they were going to do. No, of course not – but just to show them that their Chief Rabbit was up to anything that they were up to. He thought it over as he hopped down the bank and sniffed out a patch of salad burnet in the grass. What, now, would be likely to give them just a little, not unpleasant shock? Suddenly he thought, 'Suppose, when they got back, that there were one or two does here already?' And in the same moment he remembered what Kehaar had said about a box full of rabbits at the farm. What sort of rabbits could they be? Did they ever come out of their box? Had they ever seen a wild rabbit? Kehaar had said that the farm was not far from the foot of the down, on a little hill. So it could easily be reached in the early morning, before its men were about. Any dogs would probably be chained, but the cats would be loose. A rabbit could outrun a cat as long as he kept in the open and saw it coming first. The important thing was not to be stalked unawares. He should be able to move along the hedgerows without attracting elil, unless he was very unlucky.

But what did he intend to do exactly? Why was he going to the farm? Hazel finished the last of the burnet and answered himself in the starlight. 'I'll just have a look round,' he said, 'and if I can find those box rabbits I'll try to talk to them; nothing more than that. I'm not going to take any risks – well, not real risks – not until I see whether it's worth it, anyway.'

Should he go alone? It would be safer and more pleasant to take a companion; but not more than one. They must not attract attention. Who would be best? Bigwig? Dandelion? Hazel rejected them. He needed someone who would do as he was told and not start having ideas of his own. At once he thought of Pipkin. Pipkin would follow him without question and do anything he asked. At this moment he was probably asleep in the burrow which he shared with Bluebell and Acorn, down a short run leading off the Honeycomb.

Hazel was lucky. He found Pipkin close to the mouth of the burrow and already awake. He brought him out without disturbing the other two rabbits and led him up by the run that gave on the bank. Pipkin looked about him uncertainly, bewildered and half-expecting some danger.

'It's all right, Hlao-roo,' said Hazel. 'There's nothing to be afraid of. I want you to come down the hill and help me to find a farm I've heard about. We're just going to have a look round it.'

'Round a farm, Hazel-rah? What for? Won't it be dangerous? Cats and dogs and –'

'No, you'll be quite all right with me. Just you and me – I don't want anyone else. I've got a secret plan; you mustn't tell the others – for the time being anyway. I particularly want you to come and no one else will do.'

This had exactly the effect that Hazel intended. Pipkin needed no further persuasion and they set off together, over the grass track, across the turf beyond and down the escarpment. They went through the narrow belt of trees and came into the field where Holly had called Bigwig in the dark. Here Hazel paused, sniffing and listening. It was the time before dawn when owls return, usually hunting as they go. Although a full-grown rabbit is not really in danger from owls, there are few who take no account of them. Stoats and foxes might be abroad also, but the night was still and damp and Hazel, secure in his mood of gay confidence, felt sure that he would either smell or hear any hunter on four feet.

Wherever the farm might be, it must lie beyond the road that ran along the opposite edge of the field. He set off at an easy pace, with Pipkin close behind. Moving quietly in and out of the hedgerow up which Holly and Bluebell had come and passing, on their way, under the cables humming faintly in the darkness above, they took only a few minutes to reach the road.

There are times when we know for a certainty that all is well. A batsman who has played a fine innings will say afterwards that he felt he could not miss the ball and a speaker or an actor, on his lucky day, can sense his audience carrying him as though he were swimming in miraculous, buoyant water. Hazel had this feeling now. All round him was the quiet, summer night, luminous with starlight but paling to dawn on one side. There was nothing to fear and he felt ready to skip through a thousand farmyards one after the other. As he sat with Pipkin on the bank above the tar-smelling road, it did not strike him as particularly lucky when he saw a young rat scuttle across from the opposite hedge and disappear into a clump of fading stitchwort below them. He had known that some guide or other would turn up. He scrambled quickly down the bank and found the rat nosing in the ditch.

'The farm,' said Hazel, 'where's the farm – near here, on a little hill?'

The rat stared at him with twitching whiskers. It had no particular reason to be friendly, but there was something in Hazel's look that made a civil answer natural.

'Over road. Up lane.'

The sky was growing lighter each moment. Hazel crossed the road without waiting for Pipkin, who caught him up under the hedge bordering the near side of the little lane. From here, after another listening pause, they began to make their way up the slope towards the northern skyline.

Nuthanger is like a farm in an old tale. Between Ecchinswell and the foot of Watership Down and about half a mile from each, there is a broad knoll, steeper on the north side but falling gently on the south – like the down ridge itself. Narrow lanes climb both slopes and come together in a great ring of elm trees which encircles the flat summit. Any wind – even the lightest – draws from the height of the elms a rushing sound, multifoliate and powerful. Within this ring stands the farmhouse, with its barns and out-buildings. The house may be two hundred years old or it may be older, built of brick, with a stone-faced front looking south towards the down. On the east side, in front of the house, a barn stands clear of the ground on staddle-stones; and opposite is the cow-byre.

As Hazel and Pipkin reached the top of the slope, the first light showed clearly the farmyard and buildings. The birds singing all about them were those to which they had been accustomed in former days. A robin on a low branch twittered a phrase and listened for another that answered him from beyond the farmhouse. A chaffinch gave its little falling song and farther off, high in an elm, a chiff-chaff began to call. Hazel stopped and then sat up, the better to scent the air. Powerful smells of straw and cow-dung mingled with those of elm-leaves, ashes and cattle-feed. Fainter traces came to his nose as the overtones of a bell sound in a trained ear. Tobacco, naturally; a good deal of cat and rather less dog and then, suddenly and beyond doubt, rabbit. He looked at Pipkin and saw that he too had caught it.

While these scents reached them they were also listening. But beyond the light movements of birds and the first buzzing of the flies immediately around them, they could hear nothing but the continual susurration of the trees. Under the northern steep of the down the air had been still, but here the southerly breeze was magnified by the elms, with their myriads of small, fluttering leaves, just as the effect of sunlight on a garden is magnified by dew. The sound, coming from the topmost branches, disturbed Hazel because it suggested some huge approach – an approach that was never completed: and he and Pipkin remained still for some time, listening tensely to this loud yet meaningless vehemence high overhead.

They saw no cat but near the house stood a flat-roofed dog-kennel. They could just glimpse the dog asleep inside – a large, smooth-haired, black dog, with head on paws. Hazel could not see a chain; but then, after a moment, he noticed the line of a thin rope that came out through the kennel door and ended in some sort of fastening on the roof. 'Why a rope?' he wondered and then thought, 'Because a restless dog cannot rattle it in the night.'

The two rabbits began to wander among the outbuildings. At first they took care to remain in cover and continually on the watch for cats. But they saw none and soon grew bolder, crossing open spaces and even stopping to nibble at dandelions in the patches of weeds and rough grass. Guided by scent, Hazel made his way to a low-roofed shed. The door was half open and he went through it with scarcely a pause at the brick threshold. Immediately opposite the door, on a broad wooden shelf – a kind of platform – stood a wire-fronted hutch. Through the mesh he could see a brown bowl, some greenstuff and the ears of two or three rabbits. As he stared, one of the rabbits came close to the wire, looked out and saw him.

Beside the platform, on the near side, was an up-ended bale of straw. Hazel jumped lightly on it and from there to the thick planks, which were old and soft-surfaced, dusty and covered with chaff. Then he turned back to Pipkin, waiting just inside the door.

'Hlao-roo,' he said, 'there's only one way out of this place. You'll have to keep watching for cats or we may be trapped. Stay at the door and if you see a cat outside, tell me at once.'

'Right, Hazel-rah,' said Pipkin. 'It's all clear at the moment.'

Hazel went up to the side of the hutch. The wired front projected over the edge of the shelf so that he could neither reach it nor look in, but there was a knot-hole in one of the boards facing him and on the far side he could see a twitching nose.

'I am Hazel-rah,' he said. 'I have come to talk to you. Can you understand me?'

The answer was in slightly strange but perfectly intelligible Lapine.

'Yes, we understand you. My name is Boxwood. Where do you come from?'

'From the hills. My friends and I live as we please, without men. We eat the grass, lie in the sun and sleep underground. How many are you?'

'Four. Bucks and does.'

'Do you ever come out?'

'Yes, sometimes. A child takes us out and puts us in a pen on the grass.'

'I have come to tell you about my warren. We need more rabbits. We want you to run away from the farm and join us.'

'There's a wire door at the back of this hutch,' said Boxwood. 'Come down there: we can talk more easily.'

The door was made of wire netting on a wooden frame, with two leather hinges nailed to the uprights and a hasp and staple fastened with a twist of wire. Four rabbits were crowded against the wire, pressing their noses through the mesh. Two – Laurel and Clover – were short-haired black Angoras. The others, Boxwood and his doe Haystack, were black and white Himalayans.

Hazel began to speak about the life of the downs and the excitement and freedom enjoyed by wild rabbits. In his usual straightforward way he told about the predicament of his warren in having no does and how he had come to look for some. 'But,' he said, 'we don't want to steal your does. All four of you are welcome to join us, bucks and does alike. There's plenty for everyone on the hills.' He went on to talk of the evening feed in the sunset and of early morning in the long grass.

The hutch rabbits seemed at once bewildered and fascinated. Clover, the Angora doe – a strong, active rabbit – was clearly excited by Hazel's description and asked several questions about the warren and the downs. It became plain that they thought of their life in the hutch as dull but safe. They had learned a good deal about elil from some source or other and seemed sure that few wild rabbits survived for long. Hazel realized that although they were glad to talk to him and welcomed his visit because it brought a little excitement and change into their monotonous life, it was not within their capacity to take a decision and act on it. They did not know how to make up their minds. To him and his companions, sensing and acting were second nature; but these rabbits had never had to act to save their lives or even to find a meal. If he was going to get any of them as far as the down they would have to be urged. He sat quiet for a little, nibbling a patch of bran spilt on the boards outside the hutch. Then he said,

'I must go back now to my friends in the hills: but we shall return. We shall come one night and when we do, believe me, we shall open your hutch as easily as the farmer does: and then, any of you who wish will be free to come with us.'

Boxwood was about to reply when suddenly Pipkin spoke from the floor. 'Hazel, there's a cat in the yard outside!'

'We're not afraid of cats,' said Hazel to Boxwood, 'as long as we're in the open.' Trying to appear unhurried, he went back to the floor by way of the straw-bale and crossed over to the door. Pipkin was looking through the hinge. He was plainly frightened.

'I think it's smelt us, Hazel,' he said. 'I'm afraid it knows where we are.'

'Don't stay there, then,' said Hazel. 'Follow me close and run when I do.' Without waiting to look out through the hinge, he went round the half-open door of the shed and stopped on the threshold.

The cat, a tabby with white chest and paws, was at the farther end of the little yard, walking slowly and deliberately along the side of a pile of logs. When Hazel appeared in the doorway it saw him at once and stood stock-still, with staring eyes and twitching tail. Hazel hopped slowly across the threshold and stopped again. Already sunlight was slanting across the yard and in the stillness the flies buzzed about a patch of dung a few feet away. There was a smell of straw and dust and hawthorn.

'You look hungry,' said Hazel to the cat. 'Rats getting too clever, I suppose?'

The cat made no reply. Hazel sat blinking in the sunshine. The cat crouched almost flat on the ground, thrusting its head forward between its front paws. Close behind, Pipkin fidgeted and Hazel, never taking his eyes from the cat, could sense that he was trembling.

'Don't be frightened, Hlao-roo,' he whispered. 'I'll get you away, but you must wait till it comes for us. Keep still.'

The cat began to lash its tail. Its hindquarters lifted and wagged from side to side in mounting excitement.

'Can you run?' said Hazel. 'I think not. Why, you pop-eyed, back-door saucer-scraper –'

The cat flung itself across the yard and the two rabbits leapt into flight with great thrusts of their hind legs. The cat came very fast indeed and although both of them had been braced ready to move on the instant, they were barely out of the yard in time. Racing up the side of the long barn, they heard the Labrador barking in excitement as it ran to the full extent of its rope. A man's voice shouted to it. From the cover of the hedge beside the lane they turned and looked back. The cat had stopped short and was licking one paw with a pretence of nonchalance.

'They hate to look silly,' said Hazel. 'It won't give us any more trouble. If it hadn't charged at us like that it would have followed us much farther and probably called up another as well. And somehow you can't make a dash unless they do it first. It's a good thing you saw it coming, Hlao-roo.'

'I'm glad if I helped, Hazel. But what were we up to, and why did you talk to the rabbits in the box?'

'I'll tell you all about it later on. Let's go into the field now, and feed; then we can make our way home as slowly as you like.'

25. The Raid

He went consenting, or else he was no king ... It was no
one's place to say to him, 'It is time to make the offering.'

Mary Renault, *The King Must Die*

AS THINGS turned out, Hazel and Pipkin did not
come back to the Honeycomb until the evening. They
were still feeding in the field when it came on to rain, with
a cold wind, and they took shelter first in the near-by ditch
and then – since the ditch was on a slope and had a fair
flow of rainwater in about ten minutes – among some
sheds half-way down the lane. They burrowed into a thick
pile of straw and for some time remained listening for rats.
But all was quiet and they grew drowsy and fell asleep,
while outside the rain settled in for the morning. When
they woke it was mid-afternoon and still drizzling. It
seemed to Hazel that there was no particular hurry. The
going would be troublesome in the wet and anyway no
self-respecting rabbit could leave without a forage round
the sheds. A pile of mangels and swedes occupied them for

some time and they set out only when the light was beginning to fade. They took their time and reached the hanger a little before dark, with nothing worse to trouble them than the discomfort of soaking wet fur. Only two or three of the rabbits were out to a rather subdued silflay in the wet. No one remarked on their absence and Hazel went underground at once, telling Pipkin to say nothing about their adventure for the time being. He found his burrow empty, lay down and fell asleep.

Waking, he found Fiver beside him as usual. It was some time before dawn. The earth floor felt pleasantly dry and snug and he was about to go back to sleep when Fiver spoke.

'You've been wet through, Hazel.'

'Well, what about it? The grass is wet, you know.'

'You didn't get so wet on silflay. You were soaked. You weren't here at all yesterday, were you?'

'Oh, I went foraging down the hill.'

'Eating swedes: and your feet smell of farmyard – hens' droppings and bran. But there's some other funny thing besides – something I *can't* smell. What happened?'

'Well, I had a bit of a brush with a cat, but why worry?'

'Because you're concealing something, Hazel. Something dangerous.'

'It's Holly that's in danger, not I. Why bother about me?'

'Holly?' replied Fiver in surprise. 'But Holly and the others reached the big warren early yesterday evening. Kehaar told us. Do you mean to say you didn't know?'

Hazel felt fairly caught out. 'Well, I know now,' he replied. 'I'm glad to hear it.'

'So it comes to this,' said Fiver. 'You went to a farm yesterday and escaped from a cat. And whatever you were up to, it was so much on your mind that you forgot to ask about Holly last night.'

'Well, all right, Fiver – I'll tell you all about it. I took Pipkin and went to that farm that Kehaar told us about, where there are rabbits in a hutch. I found the rabbits and talked to them and I've taken a notion to go back one night and get them out, to come and join us here.'

'What for?'

'Well, two of them are does, that's what for.'

'But if Holly's successful we shall soon have plenty of does: and from all I've ever heard of hutch rabbits, they don't take easily to wild life. The truth is, you're just trying to be clever.'

'Trying to be clever?' said Hazel. 'Well, we'll just see whether Bigwig and Blackberry think so.'

'Risking your life and other rabbits' lives for something that's of little or no value to us,' said Fiver. 'Oh yes, of course the others will go with you. You're their Chief Rabbit. You're supposed to decide what's sensible and they trust you. Persuading them will prove nothing, but three or four dead rabbits will prove you're a fool, when it's too late.'

'Oh, be quiet,' answered Hazel. 'I'm going to sleep.'

During silflay next morning, with Pipkin for a respectful chorus, he told the others about his visit to the farm. As he had expected, Bigwig jumped at the idea of a raid to free the hutch rabbits.

'It can't go wrong,' he said. 'It's a splendid idea, Hazel! I don't know how you open a hutch, but Blackberry will see to that. What annoys me is to think you ran from that cat. A good rabbit's a match for a cat, any day. My mother went for one once and she fairly gave it something to remember, I can tell you: scratched its fur out like willow-herb in autumn! Just leave the farm cats to me and one or two of the others!'

Blackberry took a little more convincing: but he, like Bigwig and Hazel himself, was secretly disappointed not to have gone on the expedition with Holly: and when the other two pointed out that they were relying on him to tell them how to get the hutch open, he agreed to come.

'Do we need to take everyone?' he asked. 'You say the dog's tied up and I suppose there can't be more than three cats. Too many rabbits will only be a nuisance in the dark: someone will get lost and we shall have to spend time looking for him.'

'Well, Dandelion, Speedwell and Hawkbit then,' said Bigwig, 'and leave the others behind. Do you mean to go tonight, Hazel-rah?'

'Yes, the sooner the better,' said Hazel. 'Get hold of those three and tell them. Pity it's going to be dark – we could have taken Kehaar: he'd have enjoyed it.'

However, their hopes for that night were disappointed, for the rain returned before dusk, settling in on a northwest wind and carrying up the hill the sweet-sour smell of flowering privet from cottage hedges below. Hazel sat on the bank until the light had quite faded. At last, when it was clear that the rain was going to stay for the night, he joined the others in the Honeycomb. They had persuaded Kehaar to come down out of the wind and wet, and one of

Dandelion's tales of El-ahrairah was followed by an extraordinary story, that left everyone mystified but fascinated, about a time when Frith had to go away on a journey, leaving the whole world to be covered with rain. But a man built a great, floating hutch that held all the animals and birds until Frith returned and let them out.

'It won't happen tonight, will it, Hazel-rah?' asked Pipkin, listening to the rain in the beech leaves outside. 'There's no hutch here.'

'Kehaar'll fly you up to the moon, Hlao-roo,' said Bluebell, 'and you can come down on Bigwig's head like a birch branch in the frost. But there's time to go to sleep first.'

Before Fiver slept, however, he talked again to Hazel about the raid.

'I suppose it's no good asking you not to go?' he said.

'Look here,' answered Hazel, 'have you got one of your bad turns about the farm? If you have, why not say so straight out? Then we'd all know where we were.'

'I've no feelings about the farm one way or the other,' said Fiver. 'But that doesn't necessarily mean it's all right. The feelings come when they will – they don't always come. Not for the lendri, not for the crow. If it comes to that, I've no idea what's happening to Holly and the others. It might be good or bad. But there's something that frightens me about you yourself, Hazel: just you, not any of the others. You're all alone, sharp and clear, like a dead branch against the sky.'

'Well, if you mean you can see trouble for me and not for any of the others, tell them and I'll leave it to them to decide whether I ought to keep out of it. But that's giving up a lot, Fiver, you know. Even with your word for it, someone's bound to think I'm afraid.'

'Well, I say it's not worth the risk, Hazel. Why not wait for Holly to come back? That's all we have to do.'

'I'll be snared if I wait for Holly. Can't you see that the very thing I want is to have these does here when he comes back? But look, Fiver, I'll tell you what. I've come to trust you so much that I'll take the greatest care. In fact, I won't even go into the farmyard myself. I'll stay outside, at the top of the lane: and if that's not meeting your fears halfway, then I don't know what is.'

Fiver said no more and Hazel turned his thoughts to the raid and the difficulty he foresaw of getting the hutch rabbits to go the distance back to the warren.

The next day was bright and dry, with a fresh wind that cleared up what remained of the wet. The clouds came racing over the ridge from the south as they had on the May evening when Hazel first climbed the down. But now they were higher and smaller, settling at last into a mackerel sky like a beach at low tide. Hazel took Bigwig and Blackberry to the edge of the escarpment, whence they could look across to Nuthanger on its little hill. He described the approach and went on to explain how the rabbit-hutch was to be found. Bigwig was in high spirits. The wind and the prospect of action excited him and he spent some time with Dandelion, Hawkbit and Speedwell, pretending to be a cat and encouraging them to attack him as realistically as they could. Hazel, whose talk with Fiver had somewhat clouded him, recovered as he watched them tussling over the grass and ended by joining in himself, first as an attacker and then as the cat, staring and quivering for all the world like the Nuthanger tabby.

'I shall be disappointed if we don't meet a cat after all this,' said Dandelion, as he waited for his turn to run at a fallen beech branch from one side, claw it twice and dash out again. 'I feel a really dangerous animal.'

'You vatch heem, Meester Dando,' said Kehaar, who was hunting for snails in the grass near-by. 'Meester Pigvig, 'e vant you t'ink all vun peeg yoke; make you prave. Cat 'e no yoke. You no see 'im, you no 'ear 'im. Den yomp! 'E come.'

'But we're not going there to eat, Kehaar,' said Bigwig. 'That makes all the difference. We shan't stop watching for cats the whole time.'

'Why not eat the cat?' said Bluebell. 'Or bring one back here for breeding? That ought to improve the warren stock no end.'

Hazel and Bigwig had decided that the raid should be carried out as soon after dark as the farm was quiet. This meant that they would cover the half mile to the outlying sheds at sunset, instead of risking the confusion of a night journey over ground that only Hazel knew. They could steal a meal among the swedes, halt till darkness and cover the short distance to the farm after a good rest. Then – provided they could cope with the cats – there would be plenty of time to tackle the hutch; whereas if they were to arrive at dawn they would be working against time before men came on the scene. Finally, the hutch rabbits would not be missed until the following morning.

'And remember,' said Hazel, 'it'll probably take these rabbits a long time to get to the down. We shall have to be patient with them. I'd rather do that in darkness, elil or no elil. We don't want to be messing about in broad daylight.'

'If it comes to the worst,' said Bigwig, 'we can leave the hutch rabbits and bolt. Elil take the hindmost, don't they? I know it's tough, but if there's real trouble we ought to save our own rabbits first. Let's hope that doesn't happen, though.'

When they came to set out, Fiver was nowhere to be seen. Hazel felt relieved, for he had been afraid that Fiver might say something that would lower their spirits. But there was nothing worse to contend with than Pipkin's disappointment at being left behind; and this was dispelled when Hazel assured him that the only reason was that he had already done his bit. Bluebell, Acorn and Pipkin came with them to the foot of the hill and watched them down the hedgerow.

They reached the sheds in the twilight after sunset. The summer nightfall was unbroken by owls and so quiet that they could plainly hear the intermittent, monotonous 'Chug chug chug' of a nightingale in the distant woods. Two rats among the swedes showed their teeth, thought better of it and left them alone. When they had foraged, they rested comfortably in the straw until the western light was quite gone.

Rabbits do not name the stars, but nevertheless Hazel was familiar with the sight of Capella rising; and he watched it now until it stood gold and bright in the dark north-eastern horizon to the right of the farm. When it reached a certain point which he had fixed, beside a bare branch, he roused the others and led them up the slope towards the elms. Near the top he slipped through the hedge and brought them down into the lane.

Hazel had already told Bigwig of his promise to Fiver to keep out of danger; and Bigwig, who had changed much since the early days, had no fault to find.

'If that's what Fiver says, you'd better do it, Hazel,' he said. 'Anyhow, it'll suit us. You stay outside the farm in a safe place and we'll bring the rabbits out to you: then you can take over and get us all away.' What Hazel had not said was that the idea that he should remain in the lane was his own suggestion, and that Fiver had acquiesced only because he could not persuade him to give up the idea of the raid altogether.

Crouching under a fallen branch on the verge of the lane, Hazel watched the others as they followed Bigwig down towards the farmyard. They went slowly, rabbit-fashion, hop, step and pause. The night was dark and they were soon out of sight, though he could hear them moving down the side of the long barn. He settled down to wait.

Bigwig's hopes of action were fulfilled almost at once. The cat that he met as he reached the far end of the barn was not Hazel's tabby, but another; ginger, black and white (and therefore a female); one of those slim, trotting, quick-moving, tail-twitching cats that sit on farm window-sills in the rain or keep watch from the tops of sacks on sunny afternoons. It came briskly round the corner of the barn, saw the rabbits and stopped dead.

Without an instant's hesitation Bigwig went straight for it, as though it had been the beech branch on the down. But quicker even than he Dandelion ran forward, scratched it and leapt clear. As it turned, Bigwig threw his full weight upon it from the other side. The cat closed with him, biting and scratching, and Bigwig rolled over on the ground. The others could hear him swearing like a cat himself and struggling for a hold. Then he sank one back leg into the cat's side and kicked backwards rapidly, several times.

Anyone who is familiar with cats knows that they do not care for a determined assailant. A dog that tries to make itself pleasant to a cat may very well get scratched for its pains. But let that same dog rush in to the attack and many a cat will not wait to meet it. The farm cat was bewildered by the speed and fury of Bigwig's charge. It was no weakling and a good ratter, but it had the bad luck to be up against a dedicated fighter who was spoiling for action. As it scrabbled out of Bigwig's reach, Speedwell cuffed it across the face. This was the last blow struck, for the wounded cat made off across the yard and disappeared under the fence of the cow-byre.

Bigwig was bleeding from three deep, parallel scratches on the inside of one hind leg. The others gathered round, praising him, but he cut them short, looking round the dark yard as he tried to get his bearings.

'Come on,' he said. 'Quickly too, while the dog's still quiet. The shed: the hutch – where do we go?'

It was Hawkbit who found the little yard. Hazel had been anxious in case the shed door might be shut; but it stood just ajar and the five of them slipped in one after the other. In the thick gloom they could not make out the hutch, but they could both smell and hear the rabbits.

'Blackberry,' said Bigwig quickly, 'you come with me and get the hutch open. You other three, keep watching. If another cat comes, you'll have to take it on yourselves.'

'Fine,' said Dandelion. 'Just leave it to us.'

Bigwig and Blackberry found the straw bale and climbed on the planks. As they did so, Boxwood spoke from the hutch.

'Who's that? Hazel-rah, have you come back?'

'Hazel-rah has sent us,' answered Blackberry. 'We've come to let you out. Will you come with us?'

There was a pause and some movement in the hay and then Clover replied, 'Yes, let us out.'

Blackberry sniffed his way round to the wire door and sat up, nosing over the frame, the hasp and the staple. It took him some time to realize that the leather hinges were soft enough to bite. Then he found that they lay so smooth and flush with the frame that he could not get his teeth to them. Several times he tried to find a grip and at last sat back on his haunches, at a loss.

'I don't think this door's going to be any good,' he said. 'I wonder whether there's some other way?'

At that moment it happened that Boxwood stood on his hind legs and put his front paws high on the wire. Beneath his weight the top of the door was pressed slightly outwards and the upper of the two leather hinges gave slightly where the outer nail held it to the body of the hutch itself. As Boxwood dropped back on all fours, Blackberry saw that the hinge had buckled and risen just clear of the wood.

'Try it now,' he said to Bigwig.

Bigwig got his teeth to the hinge and pulled. It tore a very little.

'By Frith, that'll do,' said Blackberry, for all the world like the Duke of Wellington at Salamanca. 'We just need time, that's all.'

The hinge had been well made and did not give way until they had put it to a great deal more tugging and biting. Dandelion grew nervous and twice gave a false alarm. Bigwig, realizing that the sentries were on the jump from watching and waiting with nothing to do, changed places with him and sent Speedwell up to take over from Blackberry. When at last Dandelion and Speedwell had pulled the leather strip off the nail, Bigwig came back to the hutch himself. But they did not seem much nearer to success. Whenever one of the rabbits inside stood up and rested its fore-paws on the upper part of the wire, the door pivoted lightly on the axis of the staple and the lower hinge. But the lower hinge did not tear. Blowing through his whiskers with impatience, Bigwig brought Blackberry back from the threshold. 'What's to be done?' he said. 'We need some magic, like that lump of wood you shoved into the river.'

Blackberry looked at the door as Boxwood, inside, pushed it again. The upright of the frame pressed tight against the lower strip of leather, but it held smooth and firm, offering no purchase for teeth.

'Push it the other way – push from this side,' he said. 'You push, Bigwig. Tell that rabbit inside to get down.'

When Bigwig stood up and pushed the top of the door inwards, the frame immediately pivoted much farther than before, because there was no sill along the bottom of the outer side to stop it. The leather hinge twisted and Bigwig nearly lost his balance. If it had not been for the metal water staple arresting the pivoting, he might actually have fallen inside the hutch. Startled, he jumped back, growling.

'Well, you said magic, didn't you?' said Blackberry with satisfaction. 'Do it again.'

No strip of leather, held by only one broad-headed nail at each end, can stand up for long to repeated twisting. Soon one of the nail-heads was almost out of sight under the frayed edges.

'Careful now,' said Blackberry. 'If it gives way suddenly you'll go flying. Just pull it off with your teeth.'

Two minutes later the door hung sagging on the staple alone. Clover pushed the hinge side open and came out, followed by Boxwood.

When several creatures – men or animals – have worked together to overcome something offering resistance and have at last succeeded there follows often a pause – as though they felt the propriety of paying respect to the adversary who has put up so good a fight. The great tree falls, splitting, cracking, rushing down in leaves to the final, shuddering blow along the ground. Then the foresters are silent, and do not at once sit down. After hours, the deep snowdrift has been cleared and the lorry is ready to take the men home out of the cold. But they stand a while, leaning on their spades and only nodding unsmilingly as the car-drivers go through, waving their thanks. The cunning hutch door had become nothing but a piece of wire netting, tacked to a frame made from four strips of half-by-half; and the rabbits sat on the planks, sniffing and nosing it without talking. After a little while the other two occupants of the hutch, Laurel and Haystack, came hesitantly out and looked about them.

'Where is Hazel-rah?' asked Laurel.

'Not far away,' said Blackberry. 'He's waiting in the lane.'

'What is the lane?'

'The lane?' said Blackberry in surprise. 'Surely –'

He stopped as it came over him that these rabbits knew neither lane nor farmyard. They had not the least idea of their most immediate surroundings. He was reflecting on what this meant when Bigwig spoke.

'We mustn't wait about now,' he said. 'Follow me, all of you.'

'But where?' said Boxwood.

'Well, out of here, of course,' said Bigwig impatiently.

Boxwood looked about him. 'I don't know –' he began.

'Well, I do,' said Bigwig. 'Just come with us. Never mind anything else.'

The hutch rabbits looked at each other in bewilderment. It was plain that they were afraid of the great, bristling buck, with his strange shock of fur and his smell of fresh blood. They did not know what to do or understand what was expected of them. They remembered Hazel; they had been excited by the forcing of the door and curious to come through it once it was open. Otherwise, they had no purpose whatever and no means of forming one. They had no more idea of what was involved than a small child who says he will accompany the climbers up the fell.

Blackberry's heart sank. What was to be done with them? Left to themselves, they would hop slowly about the shed and the yard until the cats got them. Of their own accord they could no more run to the hills than fly to the moon. Was there no simple, plain idea that might get them – or some of them – on the move? He turned to Clover.

'I don't suppose you've ever eaten grass by night,' he said. 'It tastes much better than by day. Let's all go and have some, shall we?'

'Oh yes,' said Clover, 'I'd like that. But will it be safe? We're all very much afraid of the cats, you know. They come and stare at us sometimes through the wire and it makes us shiver.'

This showed at least the beginnings of sense, thought Blackberry.

'The big rabbit is a match for any cat,' he replied. 'He nearly killed one on the way here tonight.'

'And he doesn't want to fight another if he can help it,' said Bigwig briskly. 'So if you *do* want to eat grass by moonlight, let's go to where Hazel's waiting for us.'

As Bigwig led the way into the yard, he could make out the shape of the cat that he had beaten, watching from the woodpile. Cat-like, it was fascinated by the rabbits and could not leave them alone, but it evidently had no stomach for another fight and as they crossed the yard it stayed where it was.

The pace was frighteningly slow. Boxwood and Clover seemed to have grasped that there was some sort of urgency and were clearly doing their best to keep up, but the other two rabbits, once they had hopped into the yard, sat up and looked about them in a foolish manner, completely at a loss. After a good deal of delay, during which the cat left the wood-pile and began to move stealthily round towards the side of the shed, Blackberry managed to get them out into the farmyard. But here, finding themselves in an even more open place, they settled into a kind of static panic, like that which sometimes comes upon inexperienced climbers exposed on a sheer face. They could not move, but sat blinking and staring about them in the darkness, taking no notice of Blackberry's coaxing or Bigwig's orders. At this moment a second cat – Hazel's tabby – came round the farther end of the farmhouse and made towards them. As it passed the kennel the Labrador woke and sat up, thrusting out its head and shoulders and looking first to one side and then the other. It saw the rabbits, ran to the length of its rope and began to bark.

'Come on!' said Bigwig. 'We can't stay here. Up the lane, everybody, and quickly too.' Blackberry, Speedwell and Hawkbit ran at once, taking Boxwood and Clover with them into the darkness under the barn. Dandelion remained beside Haystack, begging her to move and expecting every moment to feel the cat's claws in his back. Bigwig leapt across to him.

'Dandelion,' he said in his ear, 'get out of it, unless you want to be killed!'

'But the –' began Dandelion.

'Do as I say!' said Bigwig. The noise of barking was fearful and he himself was close to panic. Dandelion hesitated a moment longer. Then he left Haystack and shot up the lane, with Bigwig beside him.

They found the others gathered round Hazel, under the bank. Boxwood and Clover were trembling and seemed exhausted. Hazel was talking to them reassuringly, but broke off as Bigwig appeared out of the dark. The dog stopped barking and there was quiet.

'We're all here,' said Bigwig. 'Shall we go, Hazel?'

'But there were four hutch-rabbits,' said Hazel. 'Where are the other two?'

'In the farmyard,' said Blackberry. 'We couldn't do anything with them: and then the dog began to bark.'

'Yes, I heard it. You mean they're loose?'

'They'll be a lot looser soon,' said Bigwig angrily. 'The cats are there.'

'Why did you leave them, then?'

'Because they wouldn't move. It was bad enough before the dog started.'

'Is the dog tied?' asked Hazel.

'Yes, it's tied. But do you expect any rabbit to stand his ground a few feet from an angry dog?'

'No, of course not,' replied Hazel. 'You've done wonders, Bigwig. They were just telling me, before you came, that you gave one of the cats such a beating that it was afraid to come back for more. Now look, do you think you and Blackberry, with Speedwell here and Hawkbit, can get these two rabbits back to the warren? I'm afraid you may need most of the night. They can't go very fast and you'll have to be patient with them. Dandelion, you come with me, will you?'

'Where, Hazel-rah?'

'To fetch the other two,' said Hazel. 'You're the fastest, so it won't be so dangerous for you, will it? Now, don't hang about, Bigwig, there's a good fellow. I'll see you tomorrow.'

Before Bigwig could reply he had disappeared under the elms. Dandelion remained where he was, looking at Bigwig uncertainly.

'Are you going to do what he says?' asked Bigwig.

'Well, are you?' said Dandelion.

It took Bigwig no more than a moment to realize that if he said he was not, complete disorganization would follow. He could not take all the others back into the farm, and he could not leave them alone. He muttered something about Hazel being too embleer clever by half, cuffed Hawkbit off a sow-thistle he was nibbling and led his five rabbits over the bank into the field. Dandelion, left alone, set off after Hazel into the farmyard.

As he went down the side of the barn, he could hear Hazel out in the open, near the doe Haystack. Neither of the hutch rabbits had moved from where he and Bigwig had left them. The dog had returned to its kennel; but although it was not to be seen, he felt that it was awake and watchful. He came cautiously out of the shadow and approached Hazel.

'I'm just having a chat with Haystack here,' said Hazel. 'I've been explaining that we've got a little way to go. Do you think you could hop across to Laurel and get him to join us?'

He spoke almost gaily, but Dandelion could see his dilated eyes and the slight trembling of his front paws. He himself was now sensing something peculiar – a kind of luminosity – in the air. There seemed to be a curious vibration somewhere in the distance. He looked round for the cats and saw that, as he feared, both were crouching in front of the farmhouse a little way off. Their reluctance to come closer could be attributed to Bigwig: but they would not go away. Looking across the yard at them, Dandelion felt a sudden clutch of horror.

'Hazel!' he whispered. 'The cats! Dear Frith, why are their eyes glittering green like that? Look!'

Hazel sat up quickly and as he did so Dandelion leapt back in real terror, for Hazel's eyes were shining a deep, glowing red in the dark. At that moment the humming vibration grew louder, quenching the rushing of the night breeze in the elms. Then all four rabbits sat as though transfixed by the sudden, blinding light that poured over them like a cloud-burst. Their very instinct was numbed in this terrible glare. The dog barked and then became silent once more. Dandelion tried to move but could not. The awful brightness seemed to cut into his brain.

The car, which had driven up the lane and over the brow under the elms, came on a few more yards and stopped.

'Lucy's rabbits is out, look!'

'Ah! Best get 'un in quick. Leave loights on!'

The sound of men's voices, from somewhere beyond the fierce light, brought Hazel to his senses. He could not see, but nothing, he realized, had happened to his hearing or his nose. He shut his eyes and at once knew where he was.

'Dandelion! Haystack! Shut your eyes and run,' he said. A moment later he smelt the lichen and cool moisture of one of the staddle-stones. He was under the barn. Dandelion was near him and a little farther away was Haystack. Outside the men's boots scraped and grated over the stones.

'That's it! Get round be'ind 'un.'

''E won't go far!'

'Pick 'n up then!'

Hazel moved across to Haystack. 'I'm afraid we'll have to leave Laurel,' he said. 'Just follow me.'

Keeping under the raised floor of the barn, they all three scuttled back towards the elm trees. The men's voices were left behind. Coming out into the grass near the lane, they found the darkness behind the headlights full of the fumes of exhaust – a hostile, choking smell that added to their confusion. Haystack sat down once more and could not be persuaded to move.

'Shouldn't we leave her, Hazel-rah?' asked Dandelion. 'After all, the men won't hurt her – they've caught Laurel and taken him back to the hutch.'

'If it was a buck, I'd say yes,' said Hazel. 'But we need this doe. That's what we came for.'

At this moment they caught the smell of burning white sticks and heard the men returning up the farmyard. There was a metallic bumping as they rummaged in the car. The sound seemed to rouse Haystack. She looked round at Dandelion.

'I don't want to go back to the hutch,' she said.

'You're sure?' asked Dandelion.

'Yes. I'll go with you.'

Dandelion immediately turned for the hedgerow. It was only when he crossed it and reached the ditch beyond that he realized that he was on the opposite side of the lane from that on which they had first approached. He was in a strange ditch. However, there seemed to be nothing to worry about – the ditch led down the slope and that was the way home. He moved slowly along it, waiting for Hazel to join them.

Hazel had crossed the lane a few moments after Dandelion and Haystack. Behind him, he heard the men moving away from the hrududu. As he topped the bank, the beam of a torch shone up the lane and picked out his red eyes and white tail disappearing into the hedge.

'There's ol' woild rabbit, look!'

'Ah! Reckon rest of ours ain't s' far off. Got up there with 'un, see? Best go'n 'ave a look.'

In the ditch, Hazel overtook Haystack and Dandelion under a clump of brambles.

'Get on quickly if you can,' he said to Haystack. 'The men are just behind.'

'We can't get on, Hazel,' said Dandelion, 'without leaving the ditch. It's blocked.'

Hazel sniffed ahead. Immediately beyond the brambles, the ditch was closed by a pile of earth, weeds and rubbish. They would have to come into the open. Already the men were over the bank and the torch-light was flickering up and down the hedgerow and through the brambles above their very heads. Then, only a few yards away, footfalls vibrated along the edge of the ditch. Hazel turned to Dandelion.

'Listen,' he said, 'I'm going to run across the corner of the field, from this ditch to the other one, so that they see me. They'll try to shine that light on me for sure. While they're doing that, you and Haystack climb the bank, get into the lane and run down to the swede-shed. You can hide there and I'll join you. Ready?'

There was no time to argue. A moment later Hazel broke almost under the men's feet and ran across the field.

'There 'e goes!'

'Keep torch on 'un, then. Noice and steady!'

Dandelion and Haystack scrambled over the bank and dropped into the lane. Hazel, with the torch-beam behind him, had almost reached the other ditch when he felt a sharp blow on one of his hind legs and a hot, stinging pain along his side. The report of the cartridge sounded an instant later. As he somersaulted into a clump of nettles in the ditch-bottom, he remembered vividly the scent of bean-flowers at sunset. He had not known that the men had a gun.

Hazel crawled through the nettles, dragging his injured leg. In a few moments the men would shine their torch on him and pick him up. He stumbled along the inner wall of the ditch, feeling the blood flowing over his foot. Suddenly he was aware of a draught against one side of his nose, a smell of damp, rotten matter and a hollow, echoing sound at his very ear. He was beside the mouth of a land-drain which emptied into the ditch – a smooth, cold tunnel, narrower than a rabbit-hole, but wide enough. With flattened ears and belly pressed to the wet floor he crawled up it, pushing a little pile of thin mud in front of him, and lay still as he felt the thud of boots coming nearer.

'I don' roightly know, John, whether you 'it 'e er not.'

'Ah, I 'it 'un all roight. That's blood down there, see?'

'Ah well, but that don't signify. 'E might be a long ways off be now. I reckon you've lost 'e.'

'I reckon 'e's in them nettles.'

''Ave a look then.'

'No 'e ain't.'

'Well, us can't go beggarin' up and down 'ere 'alf bloody night. We got to catch them as got out th'utch. Didn't ought 'ave fired be roights, John. Froightened they off, see? You c'n 'ave a look for 'im tomorrow, if 'e's 'ere.'

The silence returned, but still Hazel lay motionless in the whispering chill of the tunnel. A cold lassitude came over him and he passed into a dreaming, inert stupor, full of cramp and pain. After a time, a thread of blood began to trickle over the lip of the drain into the trampled, deserted ditch.

Bigwig, crouched close to Blackberry in the straw of the cattle-shed, leapt to flight at the sound of the shot two hundred yards up the lane. He checked himself and turned to the others.

'Don't run!' he said quickly. 'Where do you want to run to, anyway? No holes here.'

'Farther away from the gun,' replied Blackberry, white-eyed.

'Wait!' said Bigwig, listening. 'They're running down the lane. Can't you hear them?'

'I can hear only two rabbits,' answered Blackberry, after a pause, 'and one of them sounds exhausted.'

They looked at each other and waited. Then Bigwig got up again.

'Stay here, all of you,' he said. 'I'll go and bring them in.'

Out on the verge he found Dandelion urging Haystack, who was lamed and spent.

'Come in here quickly,' said Bigwig. 'For Frith's sake, where's Hazel?'

'The men have shot him,' replied Dandelion.

They reached the other five rabbits in the straw. Dandelion did not wait for their questions.

'They've shot Hazel,' he said. 'They'd caught that Laurel and put him back in the hutch. Then they came after us. The three of us were at the end of a blocked ditch. Hazel went out of his own accord, to distract their attention while we got away. But we didn't know they had a gun.'

'Are you sure they killed him?' said Speedwell.

'I didn't actually see him hit, but they were very close to him.'

'We'd better wait,' said Bigwig.

They waited a long time. At last Blackberry and Bigwig went cautiously back up the lane. They found the bottom of the ditch trampled by boots and streaked with blood, and returned to tell the others.

The journey back, with the three limping hutch rabbits, lasted more than two weary hours. All were dejected and wretched. When at last they reached the foot of the down Bigwig told Blackberry, Speedwell and Hawkbit to leave them and go on to the warren. They approached the wood just at first light and a rabbit ran to meet them through the wet grass. It was Fiver. Blackberry stopped and waited beside him while the other two went on in silence.

'Fiver,' he said, 'there's bad news. Hazel –'

'I know,' replied Fiver. 'I know now.'

'How do you know?' asked Blackberry, startled.

'As you came through the grass just now,' said Fiver, very low, 'there was a fourth rabbit behind you, limping and covered with blood. I ran to see who it was, and then there were only three of you, side by side.'

He paused and looked across the down, as though still seeking the bleeding rabbit who had vanished in the half-light. Then, as Blackberry said nothing more, he asked, 'Do you know what happened?'

When Blackberry had told his news, Fiver returned to the warren and went underground to his empty burrow. A little later, Bigwig brought the hutch rabbits up the hill and at once called everyone to meet in the Honeycomb. Fiver did not appear.

It was a dismal welcome for the strangers. Not even Bluebell could find a cheerful word. Dandelion was inconsolable to think that he might have stopped Hazel breaking from the ditch. The meeting came to an end in a dreary silence and a half-hearted silflay.

Later that morning Holly came limping into the warren. Of his three companions, only Silver was alert and unharmed. Buckthorn was wounded in the face and Strawberry was shivering and evidently ill from exhaustion. There were no other rabbits with them.

26. Fiver Beyond

On his dreadful journey, after the shaman has wandered
through dark forests and over great ranges of mountains . . .
he reaches an opening in the ground. The most difficult
stage of the adventure now begins. The depths of the
underworld open before him.

Uno Harva, quoted by Joseph Campbell
in *The Hero with a Thousand Facts*

FIVER lay on the earth floor of the burrow. Outside, the
downs were still in the intense, bright heat of noon.
The dew and gossamer had dried early from the grass and
by mid-morning the finches had fallen silent. Now, along
the lonely expanses of wiry turf, the air wavered. On the
footpath that led past the warren, bright threads of light –
watery, a mirage – trickled and glittered across the shortest,
smoothest grass. From a distance the trees along the edge
of the beech hanger appeared full of great, dense shadows,
impenetrable to the dazzled eye. The only sound was the

'Zip, zip' of the grasshoppers, the only scent that of the warm thyme.

In the burrow, Fiver slept and woke uneasily through the heat of the day, fidgeting and scratching as the last traces of moisture dried out of the earth above him. Once, when a trickle of powdery soil fell from the roof, he leapt out of sleep and was in the mouth of the run before he came to himself and returned to where he had been lying. Each time he woke, he remembered the loss of Hazel and suffered once more the knowledge that had pierced him as the shadowy, limping rabbit disappeared in the first light of morning on the down. Where was that rabbit now? Where had it gone? He began to follow it among the tangled paths of his own thoughts, over the cold, dew-wet ridge and down into the dawn-mist of the fields below.

The mist swirled round Fiver as he crept through thistles and nettles. Now he could no longer see the limping rabbit ahead. He was alone and afraid, yet perceiving old, familiar sounds and smells – those of the field where he was born. The thick weeds of summer were gone. He was under the bare ash boughs and the flowering blackthorn of March. He was crossing the brook, going up the slope towards the lane, towards the place where Hazel and he had come upon the notice board. Would the board still be there? He looked timidly up the slope. The view was blotted with mist, but as he neared the top he saw a man busy over a pile of tools – a spade, a rope and other, smaller implements, the use of which he did not know. The notice board lay flat on the ground. It was smaller than he remembered and fixed to a single, long, square post, sharpened at the farther end to put into the earth. The surface of the board was white, just as he had seen it before, and covered with the sharp, black lines like sticks. Fiver came hesitantly up the slope and stopped close to the man, who stood looking down into a deep, narrow hole sunk in the ground at his feet. The man turned to Fiver with the kind of amiability that an ogre might show to a victim whom they both know that he will kill and eat as soon as it suits him to do so.

'Ah! An' what am I doin', eh?' asked the man.

'What *are* you doing?' answered Fiver, staring and twitching with fear.

'I'm just putt'n up this 'ere ol' board,' said the man. 'And I s'pose you wants t'know what for, eh?'

'Yes,' whispered Fiver.

'It's fer that there old 'Azel,' said the man. 'On'y where t'is, see, we got t' put up a bit of a notice, like, on 'is account. And what d'you reckon it says, eh?'

'I don't know,' said Fiver. 'How – how can a board say anything?'

'Ah, but it do, see?' replied the man. 'That's where we knows what you don't. That's why we kills you when we 'as a mind to. Now you wants take a good look at that there board and then very likely you'll know more 'n what you knows now.'

In the livid, foggy twilight, Fiver stared at the board. As he stared, the black sticks flickered on the white surface. They raised their sharp, wedge-shaped little heads and chattered together like a nestful of young weasels. The sound, mocking and cruel, came faintly to his ears, as though muffled by sand or sacking. 'In memory of Hazel-rah!

In memory of Hazel-rah! In memory of Hazel-rah! Ha ha ha ha ha ha!'

'Well, that's where 't'is, see?' said the man. 'And I've got t'ang 'im up on this 'ere board. That's t' say, soon's I gets it stood up proper. Same as you'd 'ang up jay, like, or old stoat. Ah! Gon' 'ang 'im up.'

'No!' cried Fiver. 'No, you shan't!'

'On'y I ain't got 'im, see?' went on the man. 'That's why I can't get done. I can't 'ang 'im up, 'cos 'e've gone down th' bloody 'ole, that's where 'e've gone. E've gone down th' bloody 'ole, just when I'd got 'n lined an' all, and I can't get 'n out.'

Fiver crept up to the man's boots and peered into the hole. It was circular, a cylinder of baked earthenware that disappeared vertically into the ground. He called, 'Hazel! Hazel!' Far down in the hole, something moved and he was about to call again. Then the man bent down and hit him between the ears.

Fiver was struggling in a thick cloud of earth, soft and powdery. Someone was saying, 'Steady, Fiver, steady!' He sat up. There was soil in his eyes, his ears and nostrils. He could not smell. He shook himself and said, 'Who is it?'

'It's Blackberry. I came to see how you were. It's all right; a bit of the roof's fallen, that's all. There've been falls all over the warren today – it's the heat. Anyway, it woke you from a nightmare, if I know anything. You were thrashing about and calling out for Hazel. Poor Fiver! What a miserable thing it is to have happened! We must try to bear it as best we can. We've all got to stop running one day, you know. They say Frith knows all the rabbits, every one.'

'Is it evening?' asked Fiver.

'Not yet, no. But it's a fair time after ni-Frith. Holly and the others have come back. Strawberry's very ill and they haven't any does with them – not one. Everything's as bad as it could be. Holly's still asleep – he was completely exhausted. He said he'd tell us what happened this evening. When we told him about poor Hazel, he said – Fiver, you're not listening. I expect you'd rather I kept quiet.'

'Blackberry,' said Fiver, 'do you know the place where Hazel was shot?'

'Yes, Bigwig and I went and looked at the ditch before we came away. But you mustn't –'

'Could you go there with me now?'

'Go back there? Oh no. It's a long way, Fiver, and what would be the good? The risk, and this fearful heat, and you'd only make yourself wretched.'

'Hazel isn't dead,' said Fiver.

'Yes, the men took him away. Fiver, I saw the blood.'

'Yes, but you didn't see Hazel, because he isn't dead. Blackberry, you must do what I ask.'

'You're asking too much.'

'Then I shall have to go alone. But what I'm asking you to do is to come and save Hazel's life.'

When at last Blackberry had reluctantly given in and they had set out down the hill, Fiver went almost as fast as though he were running for cover. Again and again he urged Blackberry to make haste. The fields were empty in the glare. Every creature bigger than a blue-bottle was sheltering from the heat. When they reached the outlying sheds beside the lane, Blackberry began to explain how he and Bigwig had gone back to search; but Fiver cut him short.

'We have to go up the slope, I know that; but you must show me the ditch.'

The elms were still. There was not the least sound in the leaves. The ditch was thick with cow-parsley, hemlock and long trails of green-flowering bryony. Blackberry led the way to the trampled patch of nettles and Fiver sat still among them, sniffing and looking about him in the silence. Blackberry watched him disconsolately. A faint breath of wind stole across the fields and a blackbird began to sing from somewhere beyond the elms. At last Fiver began to move along the bottom of the ditch. The insects buzzed round his ears and suddenly a little cloud of flies flew up, disturbed from a projecting stone. No, not a stone. It was smooth and regular – a circular lip of earthenware. The brown mouth of a drain, stained black at the lower edge by a thin, dried thread of blood: of rabbit's blood.

'The bloody hole!' whispered Fiver. 'The bloody hole!'

He peered into the dark opening. It was blocked. Blocked by a rabbit. That was plain to be smelt. A rabbit whose faint pulse could just be heard, magnified in the confined tunnel.

'Hazel?' said Fiver.

Blackberry was beside him at once. 'What is it, Fiver?'

'Hazel's in that hole,' said Fiver, 'and he's alive.'

27. 'You Can't Imagine it Unless You've been There'

My Godda bless, never I see sucha people.
Signor Piozzi, quoted by Cecilia Thrale

IN THE Honeycomb, Bigwig and Holly were waiting to begin the second meeting since the loss of Hazel. As the air began to cool, the rabbits woke and first one and then another came down the runs that led from the smaller burrows. All were subdued and doubtful at heart. Like the pain of a bad wound, the effect of a deep shock takes some while to be felt. When a child is told, for the first time in his life, that a person he has known is dead, although he does not disbelieve it, he may well fail to comprehend it and later ask – perhaps more than once – where the dead person is and when he is coming back. When Pipkin had planted in himself, like some sombre tree, the knowledge that Hazel would never return, his bewilderment exceeded his grief: and this bewilderment he saw on every side among his companions. Faced with no crisis of action and with nothing to prevent them from continuing their life in the warren as before, the rabbits were nevertheless overcome by the conviction that their luck was gone. Hazel was dead and Holly's expedition had totally failed. What would follow?

Holly, gaunt, his staring pelt full of goose-grass and fragments of burdock, was talking with the three hutch rabbits and reassuring them as best he could. No one could say now that Hazel had thrown away his life in a foolhardy prank. The two does were the only gain that anyone had made; the warren's only asset. But they were plainly so ill-at-ease in their new surroundings that Holly was already contending against his own belief that there was little to be hoped for from them. Does who are upset and on edge tend to be infertile; and how were these does to make themselves at home in strange conditions and a place where everyone was lost so poorly in his thoughts? They would die, perhaps, or wander away. He buckled once more to the task of explaining that he was sure better times lay ahead; and as he did so, felt himself the least convinced of any.

Bigwig had sent Acorn to see whether there was anyone still to come. Acorn returned to say that Strawberry felt too ill and that he could find neither Blackberry nor Fiver.

'Well, leave Fiver,' said Bigwig. 'Poor fellow, he'll feel better by himself for a time, I dare say.'

'He's not in his burrow, though,' said Acorn.

'Never mind,' said Bigwig. But the thought came to him, 'Fiver and Blackberry? Could they have left the warren without telling anyone? If they have, what will happen when the others get to know?' Should he ask Kehaar to go and look for them while there was still light? But if Kehaar found them, what then? They could not be compelled to return. Or if they were, what good would that do, if they wanted to be gone? At that moment Holly began to speak and everyone became quiet.

'We all know we're in a mess,' said Holly, 'and I suppose before long we shall have to talk about what's best to be done. But I thought that first of all I ought to tell you how it is that we four – Silver, Buckthorn, Strawberry and I – have come back without any does. You don't have to remind me that when we set out, everyone thought it was going to be straightforward. And here we are, one rabbit sick, one wounded and nothing to show for it. You're all wondering why.'

'No one's blaming you, Holly,' said Bigwig.

'I don't know whether I'm to blame or not,' replied Holly. 'But you'll tell me that when you've heard the story.'

'That morning when we left, it was good weather for hlessil on the move and we all felt there was no hurry. It was cool, I remember, and looked as if it would be some time before the day got really bright and cloudless. There's a farm not far away from the other end of this wood, and although there were no men about so early, I didn't fancy going that way, so we kept up on high ground on the evening side. We were all expecting to come to the edge of the down, but there isn't any steep edge as there is on the north. The upland just goes on and on, open, dry and lonely. There's plenty of cover for rabbits – standing corn, hedges and banks – but no real woodland: just great, open fields of light soil with big, white flintstones. I was hoping that we might find ourselves in the sort of country we used to know – meadows and woods – but we didn't. Anyhow, we found a track with a good, thick hedge along one side and we decided to follow that. We took it easy and stopped a good deal, because I was taking care to avoid running into elil. I'm sure it's bad country for stoats as well as foxes, and I hadn't much idea what we were going to do if we met one.'

'I'm pretty certain we did pass close to a weasel,' said Silver. 'I could smell it. But you know how it is with elil – if they're not actually hunting they often take no notice of you. We left very little scent, and buried our hraka as though we were cats.'

'Well, before ni-Frith,' went on Holly, 'the track brought us to a long, thin wood running right across the way we were going. These downland woods are queer, aren't they? This was no thicker than the one above us now, but it stretched as far as we could see either way, in a dead straight line. I don't like straight lines: men make them. And sure enough, we found a road beside this wood. It was a very lonely, empty road, but all the same, I didn't want to hang about there, so we went straight through the wood and out the other side. Kehaar spotted us in the fields beyond and told us to alter our direction. I asked him how we were getting on and he said we were about half-way, so I thought we might as well start looking for somewhere to lie up for the night. I didn't fancy the open and in the end we made scrapes in the bottom of a kind of little pit we found. Then we had a good feed and passed the night very well.

'I don't think we need tell you everything about the journey. It came on to rain just after the morning feed and there was a nasty, cold wind with it, so we stayed where we were until after ni-Frith. It brightened up then and we went on. The going wasn't very nice because of the wet, but by early evening I reckoned we ought to be near the place. I was looking round when a hare came through the grass and I asked him whether he knew of a big warren close by.

'"*Efrafa?*" he asked. "Are you going to Efrafa?"*

'"If that's what it's called," I answered.

'"Do you know it?"

'"No," I said, "we don't. We want to know where it is."

'"Well," he said, "my advice to you is to run, and quickly."

'I was just wondering what to make of that, when suddenly three big rabbits come over the bank, just the way I did that night when I came to arrest you, Bigwig: and one of them said, "Can I see your marks?"

'"Marks?" I said. "What marks? I don't understand."

'"You're not from Efrafa?"

'"No," I said, "we're going there. We're strangers."

'"Will you come with me?" No "Have you come far?" or "Are you wet through?" or anything like that.

'So then these three rabbits took us off down the bank and that was how we came to Efrafa, as they call it. And I'd better try and tell you something about it, so that you'll know what a dirty little bunch of snivelling hedge-scrapers we are here.

---

* The first syllable is stressed and not the second, as in the word 'Majesty'.

'Efrafa is a big warren – a good deal bigger than the one we came from – the Threarah's, I mean. And the one fear of every rabbit in it is that men are going to find them and infect them with the white blindness. The whole warren is organized to conceal its existence. The holes are all hidden and the Owsla have every rabbit in the place under orders. You can't call your life your own: and in return you have safety – if it's worth having at the price you pay.

'As well as the Owsla, they have what they call a Council, and each of the Council rabbits has some special thing he looks after. One looks after feeding; another's responsible for the ways in which they keep hidden; another looks after breeding, and so on. As far as the ordinary rabbits are concerned, only a certain number can be above ground at one time. Every rabbit is marked when he's a kitten: they bite them, deep, under the chin or in a haunch or fore-paw. Then they can be told by the scar for the rest of their lives. You mustn't be found above ground unless it's the right time of day for your Mark.'

'Who's to stop you?' growled Bigwig.

'That's the really frightening part. The Owsla – well, you can't imagine it unless you've been there. The Chief is a rabbit named Woundwort: General Woundwort, they call him. I'll tell you more about him in a minute. Then under him there are captains – each one in charge of a Mark – and each captain has his own officers and sentries. There's a Mark captain with his band on duty at every time of the day and night. If a man happens to come anywhere near, which isn't often, the sentries give warning long before he comes close enough to see anything. They give warning of elil too. They prevent anyone dropping hraka except in special places in the ditches, where it's buried. And if they see any rabbit above ground whom they don't recognize as having the right to be there, they ask to see his mark. Frith knows what happens if he can't explain himself – but I can guess pretty well. Rabbits in Efrafa quite often go days at a time without the sight of Frith. If their Mark's on night silflay then they feed by night, wet or fine, warm or cold. They're all used to talking, playing and mating in the burrows underground. If a Mark can't silflay at their appointed time for some reason or other – say there was a man working somewhere near – that's just too bad. They miss their turn till next day.'

'But surely it alters them very much, living like that?' asked Dandelion.

'Very much indeed,' replied Holly. 'Most of them can't do anything but what they're told. They've never been out of Efrafa and never smelt an enemy. The one aim of every rabbit in Efrafa is to get into the Owsla, because of the privileges: and the one aim of everyone in the Owsla is to get into the Council. The Council have the best of everything. But the Owsla have to keep very strong and tough. They take it in turn to do what they call Wide Patrol. They go out over the country – all round the place – living in the open for days at a time. It's partly to find out anything they can, and partly to train them and make them tough and cunning. Any hlessil they find they pick up and bring back to Efrafa. If they won't come, they kill them. They reckon hlessil a danger, because they may attract the attention of men. The Wide Patrols report back to General

Woundwort and the Council decide what to do about anything new that they think may be dangerous.'

'They missed you on the way in, then?' said Bluebell.

'Oh no, they didn't. We learned later that some time after we'd been brought in by this rabbit – Captain Campion – a runner arrived from a Wide Patrol to say that they'd picked up the track of three or four rabbits coming towards Efrafa from the north; and were there any orders? He was sent back to say that we were safely under control.

'Anyway, this Captain Campion took us down to a hole in the ditch. The mouth of the hole was a bit of old earthenware pipe and if a man had pulled it out, the opening would have fallen in and showed no trace of the run inside. And there he handed us over to another captain – because he had to go back above ground for the rest of his spell of duty, you see. We were taken to a big burrow and told to make ourselves at home.

'There were other rabbits in the burrow and it was by listening to them and asking questions that I learnt most of what I've been telling you. We got talking to some of the does and I made friends with one called Hyzenthlay.* I told her about our problem here and why we'd come, and then she told us about Efrafa. When she'd finished I said, "It sounds terrible. Has it always been like this?" She said no, her mother had told her that in years gone by the warren had been elsewhere and much smaller: but when General Woundwort came, he had made them move to Efrafa and then he'd worked out this whole system of concealment

* Hyzenthlay: 'Shine-Dew-Fur' – Fur shining like dew.

and perfected it until rabbits in Efrafa were as safe as stars in the sky. "Most rabbits here die of old age, unless the Owsla kill them off," she said. "But the trouble is, there are more rabbits now than the warren can hold. Any fresh digging that's allowed has to be done under Owsla supervision and they do it terribly slowly and carefully. It all has to be hidden, you see. We're overcrowded and a lot of rabbits don't get above ground as much as they need to. And for some reason there are not enough bucks and too many does. A lot of us have found we can't produce litters, because of the overcrowding, but no one is ever allowed to leave. Only a few days ago, several of us does went to the Council and asked whether we could form an expedition to start a new warren somewhere else. We said we'd go far, far away – as far away as they liked. But they wouldn't hear of it – not on any account. Things can't go on like this – the system's breaking down. But it doesn't do to be heard talking about it."

'Well, I thought, this sounds hopeful. Surely they won't object to our proposals? We only want to take a few does and no bucks. They've got more does than there's room for and we want to take them farther away than anyone here can ever have been.

'A little later another captain came and said we were to come with him to the Council meeting.

'The Council meet in a kind of big burrow. It's long and rather narrow – not as good as this Honeycomb of ours, because they've got no tree-roots to make a wide roof. We had to wait outside while they were talking about all sorts of other things. We were just one piece of daily Council business: "Strangers apprehended." There was another rabbit waiting and he was under special guard – Owslafa, they call them: the Council police. I've never been near anyone so frightened in my life – I thought he'd go mad with fear. I asked one of these Owslafa what was the matter and he said that this rabbit, Blackavar, had been caught trying to run away from the warren. Well, they took him inside and first of all we heard the poor fellow trying to explain himself, and then he was crying and begging for mercy; and when he came out they'd ripped both his ears to shreds, worse than this one of mine. We were all sniffing at him, absolutely horror-stricken; but one of the Owslafa said, "You needn't make such a fuss. He's lucky to be alive." So while we were chewing on that, someone came out and said the Council were ready for us.

'As soon as we got in, we were put up in front of this General Woundwort: and he really is a grim customer. I don't think even you'd match up to him, Bigwig. He's almost as big as a hare and there's something about his mere presence that frightens you, as if blood and fighting and killing were all just part of the day's work to him. I thought he'd begin by asking us some questions about who we were and what we wanted, but he didn't do anything like that. He said, "I'm going to explain the rules of the warren and the conditions on which you'll live here. You must listen carefully, because the rules are to be kept and any breaking of them will be punished." So then I spoke up at once and said that there was a misunderstanding. We were an embassy, I said, come from another warren to ask for Efrafa's goodwill and help. And I went on to explain that all we wanted was their agreement to our persuading a few does to come back with us. When I'd finished, General Woundwort said that it was out of the question: there was nothing to discuss. I replied that we'd like to stay with them for a day or two and try to persuade them to change their mind.

'"Oh yes," he said, "you'll stay. But there'll be no further occasion for you to take up the Council's time – for the next few days at any rate."

'I said that seemed very hard. Our request was surely a reasonable one. And I was just going to ask them to consider one or two things from our point of view, when another of the councillors – a very old rabbit – said, "You seem to think you're here to argue with us and drive a bargain. But we're the ones to say what you're going to do."

'I said they should remember that we were representing another warren, even if it was smaller than theirs. We thought of ourselves as their guests. And it was only when I'd said that, that I realized with a horrible shock that they thought of us as their prisoners: or as good as prisoners, whatever *they* might call it.

'Well, I'd rather say no more about the end of that meeting. Strawberry tried all he could to help me. He spoke very well about the decency and comradeship natural to animals. "Animals don't behave like men," he said. "If they have to fight, they fight; and if they have to kill, they kill. But they don't sit down and set their wits to work to devise ways of spoiling other creatures' lives and hurting them. They have dignity and animality."

'But it was all no use. At last we fell silent and General Woundwort said, "The Council can't spare any more time for you now, and I shall have to leave it to your Mark Captain to tell you the rules. You'll join the Right Flank Mark under Captain Bugloss. Later, we shall see you again and you'll find us perfectly friendly and helpful to rabbits who understand what's expected of them."

'So then the Owsla took us out to join the Right Flank Mark. Apparently Captain Bugloss was too busy to see us and I took care to keep out of his way, because I thought he might want to start marking us then and there. But soon I began to understand what Hyzenthlay had meant when she said the system wasn't working properly any more. The burrows were overcrowded – at least by our standards. It was easy to escape attention. Even in one Mark the rabbits don't all know each other. We found places in a burrow and tried to get some sleep, but early in the night we were woken and told to silflay. I thought there might be a chance to run for it in the moonlight, but there seemed to be sentries everywhere. And besides the sentries, the Captain kept two runners with him, whose job was to rush off at once in any direction from which an alarm might be given.

'When we'd fed we went underground again. Nearly all the rabbits were very subdued and docile. We avoided them, because we meant to escape if we could and we didn't want to get known. But try as I would, I couldn't think of a plan.

'We fed again some time before ni-Frith the next day, and then it was back underground. The time dragged terribly. At last – it must have been as evening was coming on – I joined a little group of rabbits listening to a story. And do you know, it was "The King's Lettuce"? The rabbit who was telling it was nowhere near as good as Dandelion, but I listened all the same, just for something to do. And it was when he got to the bit where El-ahrairah dresses up and pretends to be the doctor at King Darzin's palace, that I suddenly had an idea. It was a very risky one, but I thought there was a chance that it might work, simply because every rabbit in Efrafa usually does what he's told without question. I'd been watching Captain Bugloss and he struck me as a nice enough fellow, conscientious and a bit weak and rather harassed by having more to do than he could really cope with.

'That night, when we were called to silflay, it was pitch dark and raining; but you don't bother about a little thing like that in Efrafa – you're only too glad to get out and get some food. All the rabbits trooped up; and we waited until the very last. Captain Bugloss was out on the bank, with two of his sentries. Silver and the others went out in front of me and then I came up to him panting as if I'd been running.

'"Captain Bugloss?"

'"Yes?" he said. "What is it?"

'"You're wanted by the Council, at once."

'"Why, what do you mean?" he asked. "What for?"

'"No doubt they'll tell you that when they see you," I answered. "I shouldn't keep them waiting if I were you."

'"Who are you?" he said. "You're not one of the Council runners. I know them all. What Mark are you?"

'"I'm not here to answer your questions," I said. "Shall I go back and tell them you won't come?"

'He looked doubtful at that and I made as if I were going. But then, all of a sudden, he said, "Very well" – he looked awfully frightened, poor fellow – "but who's to take over here while I'm gone?"

'"I am," I said. "General Woundwort's orders. But come back quickly. I don't want to hang about half the night doing your job." He scuttled off. I turned to the other two and said, "Stay here: and look alive, too. I'm going round the sentries."

'Well, then the four of us ran off into the dark and sure enough after we'd gone a little way two sentries popped up and tried to stop us. We all piled straight into them. I thought they'd run, but they didn't. They fought like mad and one of them tore Buckthorn all down the nose. But of course there were four of us; and in the end we broke past them and simply tore across the field. We had no idea which way we were going, what with the rain and the night: we just ran. I think the reason why the pursuit was a bit slow off the mark was because poor old Bugloss wasn't there to give the orders. Anyway, we had a fair start. But presently we could hear that we were being followed: and what was worse, we were being overtaken.

'The Efrafan Owsla are no joke, believe me. They're all picked for size and strength and there's nothing they don't know about moving in wet and darkness. They're all so much afraid of the Council that they're not afraid of anything else. It wasn't long before I knew we were in trouble. The patrol that was after us could actually follow us in the dark and rain faster than we could run away and before long they were close behind. I was just going to tell the others that there was nothing for it but to turn and fight when we came to a great, steep bank that seemed to slope almost straight up into the air. It was steeper than this hillside below us here, and the slope seemed to be regular, as if men had made it.

'Well, there was no time to think about it, so up we went. It was covered with rough grass and bushes. I don't know how far it was to the top exactly, but I should guess it was as high as a well-grown rowan tree – perhaps a bit higher. When we got to the top we found ourselves on small, light stones that shifted as we ran on them. That gave us away completely. Then we came upon broad, flat pieces of wood and two great, fixed bars of metal that made a noise – a kind of low, humming noise in the dark. I was just saying to myself, "This is men's work all right," when I fell over the other side. I hadn't realized that the whole top of the bank was only a very short distance across and the other side was just as steep. I went head over heels down the bank in the dark and fetched up against an elder bush: and there I lay.'

Holly stopped and fell silent, as though pondering on what he remembered. At last he said,

'It's going to be very hard to describe to you what happened next. Although all four of us were there, we don't understand it ourselves. But what I'm going to say now is the cold truth. Lord Frith sent one of his great Messengers to save us from the Efrafan Owsla. Each one of us had fallen over the edge of the bank in one place or another. Buckthorn, who was half-blinded with his own blood, went down almost to the bottom. I'd picked myself up and was looking back at the top. There was just enough light in the sky to see the Efrafans if they came over. And then – then an enormous thing – I can't give you any idea of it – as big as a thousand hrududil – bigger – came rushing out of the night. It was full of fire and smoke and light and it roared and beat on the metal lines until the ground shook beneath it. It drove in between us and the Efrafans like a thousand thunderstorms with lightning. I tell you, I was beyond being afraid. I couldn't move. The flashing and the noise – they split the whole night apart. I don't know what happened to the Efrafans: either they ran away or it cut them down. And then suddenly it was gone and we heard it disappearing, rattle and bang, rattle and bang, far away in the distance. We were completely alone.

'For a long time I couldn't move. At last I got up and found the others, one by one, in the dark. None of us said a word. At the bottom of the slope we discovered a kind of tunnel that went right through the bank from one side to the other. We crept into it and came out on the side where we'd gone up. Then we went a long way through the fields, until I reckoned we must be well clear of Efrafa. We crawled into a ditch and slept there, all four of us, until morning. There was no reason why anything shouldn't have come and killed us, and yet we knew we were safe. You may think it's a wonderful thing to be saved by Lord Frith in his power. How many rabbits has that happened to, I wonder? But I tell you, it was far more frightening than being chased by the Efrafans. Not one of us will forget lying on that bank in the rain, while the fire-creature went by above our heads. Why did it come on our account? That's more than we shall ever know.

'The next morning I cast around a bit and soon I knew which was the right direction. You know how you always do. The rain had stopped and we set out. But it was a very hard journey back. We were exhausted long before the end – all except Silver: I don't know what we'd have done without him. We went on for a day and a night without any real rest at all. We all felt that the only thing we wanted to do was to get back here as soon as we could. When I reached the wood this morning I was just limping along in a bad dream. I'm not really much better than poor old Strawberry, I'm afraid. He never complained, but he'll need a long rest and I rather think I shall too. And Buckthorn – that's the second bad wound he's had. But that's not the worst now, is it? We've lost Hazel: the worst thing that could have happened. Some of you asked me earlier this evening if I would be Chief Rabbit. I'm glad to know you trust me, but I'm completely done in and I can't possibly take it on yet. I feel as dry and empty as an autumn puff-ball – as though the wind could blow my fur away.'

28. At the Foot of the Hill

Marvellous happy it was to be
Alone, and yet not solitary.
O out of terror and dark, to come
In sight of home.

Walter de la Mare, 'The Pilgrim'

'YOU'RE not too tired to silflay, are you?' asked Dandelion. 'And at the proper time of day for a change? It's a lovely evening, if my nose says right. We ought to try not to be more miserable than we can help, you know.'

'Just before we silflay,' said Bigwig, 'can I tell you, Holly, that I don't believe anyone else could have brought himself and three other rabbits safely back out of a place like that?'

'Frith meant us to get back,' replied Holly. 'That's the real reason why we're here.'

As he turned to follow Speedwell up the run that led into the wood, he found Clover beside him. 'You and your friends must find it strange to go outside and eat grass,' he said. 'You'll get used to it, you know. And I can promise you that Hazel-rah was right when he told you it's a better life here than in a hutch. Come with me and I'll show you a patch of nice, short tail-grass, if Bigwig hasn't had it all while I've been away.'

Holly had taken to Clover. She seemed more robust and less timid than Boxwood and Haystack and was evidently doing her best to adapt herself to warren life. What her stock might be he could not tell, but she looked healthy.

'I like it underground all right,' said Clover, as they came up into the fresh air. 'The closed space is really very much like a hutch, except that it's darker. The difficult thing for us is going to be feeding in the open. We're not used to being free to go where we like and we don't know what to do. You all act so quickly and half the time I don't know why. I'd prefer not to feed very far from the hole, if you don't mind.'

They moved slowly across the sunset grass, nibbling as they went: Clover was soon absorbed in feeding, but Holly stopped continually to sit up and sniff about him at the peaceful, empty down. When he noticed Bigwig, a little way off, staring fixedly to the north, he at once followed his gaze.

'What is it?' he asked.

'It's Blackberry,' replied Bigwig. He sounded relieved.

Blackberry came hopping rather slowly down from the sky-line. He looked tired out, but as soon as he saw the other rabbits he came on faster and made his way to Bigwig.

'Where have you been?' asked Bigwig. 'And where's Fiver? Wasn't he with you?'

'Fiver's with Hazel,' said Blackberry. 'Hazel's alive. He's been wounded – it's hard to tell how badly – but he won't die.'

The other three rabbits looked at him speechlessly. Blackberry waited, enjoying the effect.

'Hazel's *alive*?' said Bigwig. 'Are you sure?'

'Quite sure,' said Blackberry. 'He's at the foot of the hill at this very moment, in that ditch where you were the night Holly and Bluebell arrived.'

'I can hardly believe it,' said Holly. 'If it's true, it's the best news I've ever heard in my life. Blackberry, you really are sure? What happened? Tell us.'

'Fiver found him,' said Blackberry. 'Fiver took me with him, nearly all the way back to the farm: then he went along the ditch and found Hazel gone to ground up a land-drain. He was very weak from loss of blood and he couldn't get out of the drain by himself. We had to drag him by his good hind leg. He couldn't turn round, you see.'

'But how on earth did Fiver know?'

'How does Fiver know what he knows? You'd better ask him. When we'd got Hazel into the ditch, Fiver looked to see how badly he was hurt. He's got a nasty wound in one hind leg, but the bone isn't broken: and he's torn all along one side. We cleaned up the places as well as we could and then we started out to bring him back. It's taken us the whole evening. Can you imagine it – daylight, dead silence and a lame rabbit reeking of fresh blood? Luckily, it's been the hottest day we've had this summer – not a mouse stirring. Time and again we had to take cover in the cow-parsley and rest. I was all on the jump, but Fiver was like a butterfly on a stone. He sat in the grass and combed his ears. "Don't get upset," he kept saying. "There's nothing to worry about. We can take our time." After what I'd seen,

I'd have believed him if he'd said we could hunt foxes. But when we got to the bottom of the hill Hazel was completely finished and he couldn't go any further. He and Fiver have taken shelter in the overgrown ditch and I came on to tell you. And here I am.'

There was silence while Bigwig and Holly took in the news. At last Bigwig said, 'Will they stay there tonight?'

'I think so,' replied Blackberry. 'I'm sure Hazel won't be able to manage the hill until he's a good deal stronger.'

'I'll go down there,' said Bigwig. 'I can help to make the ditch a bit more comfortable, and probably Fiver will be able to do with someone else to help to look after Hazel.'

'I should hurry then, if I were you,' said Blackberry. 'The sun will be down soon.'

'Hah!' said Bigwig. 'If I meet a stoat, it'd better look out, that's all. I'll bring you one back tomorrow, shall I?' He raced off and disappeared over the edge.

'Let's go and get the others together,' said Holly. 'Come on, Blackberry, you'll have to tell the whole thing, from the beginning.'

The three quarters of a mile in the blazing heat, from Nuthanger to the foot of the hill, had cost Hazel more pain and effort than anything in his life. If Fiver had not found him, he would have died in the drain. When Fiver's urging had penetrated his dark, ebbing stupor, he had at first actually tried not to respond. It was so much easier to remain where he was, on the far side of the suffering he had undergone. Later, when he found himself lying in the green gloom of the ditch, with Fiver searching his wounds and assuring him that he could stand and move, still he could not face the idea of setting out to return. His torn side throbbed and the pain in his leg seemed to have affected his senses. He felt dizzy and could not hear or smell properly. At last, when he understood that Fiver and Blackberry had risked a second journey to the farm, in the broadest of daylight, solely to find him and save his life, he forced himself to his feet and began to stumble down the slope to the road. His sight was swimming and he had to stop again and again. Without Fiver's encouragement he would have lain down once more and given up. In the road, he could not climb the bank and had to limp along the verge until he could crawl under a gate. Much later, as they came under the pylon line, he remembered the overgrown ditch at the foot of the hill and set himself to reach it. Once there, he lay down and at once returned to the sleep of total exhaustion.

When Bigwig arrived, just before dark, he found Fiver snatching a quick feed in the long grass. It was out of the question to disturb Hazel by digging and they spent the night crouched beside him on the narrow floor.

Coming out in the grey light before dawn, the first creature Bigwig saw was Kehaar, foraging between the elders. He stamped to attract his attention and Kehaar sailed across to him with one beat of his wings and a long glide.

'Meester Pigvig, you find Meester 'Azel?'

'Yes,' said Bigwig, 'he's in the ditch here.'

''E not dead?'

'No, but he's wounded and very weak. The farm men shot him with a gun, you know.'

'You get black stones out?'

'How do you mean?'

'Alvays vid gun ees coming liddle black stones. You never see?'

'No, I don't know about guns.'

'Take out black stones, 'e get better. 'E come now, ya?'

'I'll see,' said Bigwig. He went down to Hazel and found him awake and talking to Fiver. When Bigwig told him that Kehaar was outside he dragged himself up the short run and into the grass.

'Dis dam' gun,' said Kehaar. ''E put liddle stones for 'urt you. I look, ya?'

'I suppose you'd better,' said Hazel. 'My leg's still very bad, I'm afraid.'

He lay down and Kehaar's head flicked from side to side as though he were looking for snails in Hazel's brown fur. He peered closely up the length of the torn flank.

'Ees not stones 'ere,' he said. 'Go in, go out – no stop. Now I see you leg. Maybe 'urt you, not long.'

Two shot-gun pellets were buried in the muscle of the haunch. Kehaar detected them by smell and removed them exactly as he might have picked spiders out of a crack. Hazel had barely time to flinch before Bigwig was sniffing at the pellets in the grass.

'Now ees more bleed,' said Kehaar. 'You stay, vait maybe vun, two day. Den goot like before. Dose rabbits up dere, all vait, vait for Meester 'Azel. I tell dem 'e come.' He flew off before they could reply.

As things turned out, Hazel stayed three days at the foot of the hill. The hot weather continued and for much of the time he sat under the elder branches, dozing above ground like some solitary hlessi and feeling his strength returning. Fiver stayed with him, keeping the wounds clean and watching his recovery. Often, they would say nothing for hours together, lying in the rough, warm grass while the shadows moved to evening, until at last the local blackbird cocked its tail and tuck-tucked away to roost. Neither spoke of Nuthanger Farm, but Hazel showed plainly enough that for the future Fiver, when he gave advice, would have no hard task to get him to accept it.

'Hrair-roo,' said Hazel one evening, 'what would we have done without you? We'd none of us be here, would we?'

'You're sure we *are* here, then?' asked Fiver.

'That's too mysterious for me,' replied Hazel. 'What do you mean?'

'Well, there's another place – another country – isn't there? We go there when we sleep; at other times too; and when we die. El-ahrairah comes and goes between the two as he wants, I suppose, but I never could quite make that out, from the tales. Some rabbits will tell you it's all easy there, compared with the waking dangers that they understand. But I think that only shows they don't know much about it. It's a wild place, and very unsafe. And where are we really – there or here?'

'Our bodies stay here – that's good enough for me. You'd better go and talk to that Silverweed fellow – he might know more.'

'Oh, you remember him? I felt that when we were listening to him, you know. He terrified me and yet I knew that I understood him better than anyone else in that place.

322

He knew where he belonged, and it wasn't here. Poor fellow, I'm sure he's dead. They'd got him all right – the ones in that country. They don't give their secrets away for nothing, you know. But look! Here come Holly and Blackberry, so we'd better feel sure we're here just for the moment anyway.'

Holly had already come down the hill on the previous day to see Hazel and tell again the story of his escape from Efrafa. When he had spoken of his deliverance by the great apparition in the night, Fiver had listened attentively and asked one question, 'Did it make a noise?' Later, when Holly had gone back, he told Hazel that he felt sure there was some natural explanation, though he had no idea what it could be. Hazel, however, had not been greatly interested. For him, the important thing was their disappointment and the reason for it. Holly had achieved nothing and this was entirely due to the unexpected unfriendliness of the Efrafan rabbits. This evening, as soon as they had begun to feed, Hazel returned to the matter.

'Holly,' he said, 'we're hardly any nearer to solving our problem, are we? You've done wonders and got nothing to show for it, and the farm raid was only a silly lark, I'm afraid – and an expensive one for me, at that. The real hole has still got to be dug.'

'Well,' said Holly, 'you say it was only a lark, Hazel, but at least it gave us two does: and they're the only two we've got.'

'Are they any good?'

The kind of ideas that have become natural to many male human beings in thinking of females – ideas of protection, fidelity, romantic love and so on – are, of course, unknown to rabbits, although rabbits certainly do form exclusive attachments much more frequently than most people realize. However, they are not romantic and it came naturally to Hazel and Holly to consider the two Nuthanger does simply as breeding stock for the warren. This was what they had risked their lives for.

'Well, it's hard to say, yet,' replied Holly. 'They're doing their best to settle down with us – Clover particularly. She seems very sensible. But they're extraordinarily helpless, you know – I've never seen anything like it – and I'm afraid they may turn out to be delicate in bad weather. They might survive next winter and then again they might not. But you weren't to know that, when you got them out of the farm.'

'With a bit of luck, they might each have a litter before the winter,' said Hazel. 'I know the breeding season's over, but everything's so topsy-turvy with us here that there's no saying.'

'Well, you ask me what I think,' said Holly. 'I'll tell you. I think they're precious little to be the only thing between us and the end of everything we've managed to do so far. I think they may very well not have any kittens for some time, partly because this isn't the season and partly because the life's so strange to them. And when they do, the kittens will very likely have a lot of this man-bred hutch-stock in them. But what else is there to hope for? We must do the best we can with what we've got.'

'Has anyone mated with them yet?' asked Hazel.

'No, neither of them has been ready so far. But I can see some fine old fights breaking out when they are.'

'That's another problem. We can't go on with nothing but these two does.'

'But what else can we do?'

'I know *what* we've got to do,' said Hazel, 'but I still can't see *how*. We've got to go back and get some does out of Efrafa.'

'You might as well say you were going to get them out of Inlé, Hazel-rah. I'm afraid I can't have given you a very clear description of Efrafa.'

'Oh yes, you have – the whole idea scares me stiff. But we're going to do it.'

'It can't be done.'

'It can't be done by fighting or fair words, no. So it will have to be done by means of a trick.'

'There's no trick will get the better of that lot, believe me. There are far more of them than there are of us: they're very highly organized; and I'm only telling the truth when I say that they can fight, run and follow a trail every bit as well as we can and a lot of them, much better.'

'The trick,' said Hazel, turning to Blackberry, who all this time had been nibbling and listening in silence, 'the trick will have to do three things. First, it will have to get the does out of Efrafa and secondly it will have to put paid to the pursuit. For a pursuit there's bound to be and we can't expect another miracle. But that's not all. Once we're clear of the place, we've got to become impossible to find – beyond the reach of any Wide Patrol.'

'Yes,' said Blackberry doubtfully. 'Yes, I agree. To succeed we should have to manage all those things.'

'Yes. And this trick, Blackberry, is going to be devised by you.'

The sweet, carrion scent of dogwood filled the air; in the evening sunshine the insects hummed around the dense, white cymes hanging low above the grass. A pair of brown and orange beetles, disturbed by the feeding rabbits, took off from a grass-stem and flew away, still coupled together.

'They mate: we don't,' said Hazel, watching them go. 'A trick, Blackberry: a trick to put us right once and for all.'

'I can see how to do the first thing,' said Blackberry. 'At least, I think I can. But it's dangerous. The other two I can't see at all yet and I'd like to talk it over with Fiver.'

'The sooner Fiver and I get back to the warren the better,' said Hazel. 'My leg's good enough now, but all the same I think we'll leave it for tonight. Good old Holly, will you tell them that Fiver and I will come early tomorrow morning? It worries me to think that Bigwig and Silver may start fighting about Clover at any moment.'

'Hazel,' said Holly, 'listen. I don't like this idea of yours at all. I've been in Efrafa and you haven't. You're making a bad mistake and you might very well get us all killed.'

It was Fiver who replied. 'It ought to feel like that, I know,' he said, 'but somehow it doesn't: not to me. I believe we can do it. Anyway, I'm sure Hazel's right when he says it's the only chance we've got. Suppose we go on talking about it for a bit?'

'Not now,' said Hazel. 'Time for underground down here – come on. But if you two race up the hill, you'll probably be in time for some more sunshine at the top. Good night.'

29. Return and Departure

He which hath no stomach to this fight,
Let him depart, his passport shall be made
And crowns for convoy put into his purse.
We would not die in that man's company
That fears his fellowship, to die with us.

Shakespeare, *Henry V*

THE FOLLOWING morning all the rabbits were out at silflay by dawn and there was a good deal of excitement as they waited for Hazel. During the previous few days Blackberry had had to repeat several times the story of the journey to the farm and the finding of Hazel in the drain. One or two had suggested that Kehaar must have found Hazel and told Fiver secretly. But Kehaar denied this and, when pressed, replied cryptically that Fiver was one who had travelled a good deal farther than he had himself. As for Hazel, he had acquired, in everyone's eyes, a kind of magical quality. Of all the warren, Dandelion was the last rabbit to fail to do justice to a good story and he made the most of Hazel's heroic dash out of the ditch to save his friends from the farmers. No one had even suggested that Hazel might have been reckless in going to the farm. Against all odds he had got them two does; and now he was bringing their luck back to the warren.

Just before sunrise Pipkin and Speedwell saw Fiver coming through the wet grass near the summit of the down. They ran out to meet him and waited with him until Hazel came up to them. Hazel was limping and had evidently found the climb a strain, but after resting and feeding for a short time he was able to run down to the warren almost as fast as the others. The rabbits crowded round. Everyone wanted to touch him. He was sniffed and tussled with and rolled over in the grass until he felt almost as though he were being attacked. Human beings, on occasions of this kind, are usually full of questions, but the rabbits expressed their delight simply by proving to themselves through their senses that this was really Hazel-rah. It was all he could do to stand up to the rough play. 'I wonder what would happen if I lay down under it?' he thought. 'They'd kick me out, I dare say. They wouldn't have a crippled Chief Rabbit. This is a test as well as a welcome, even though they don't know it themselves. I'll test them, the rascals, before I'm done.'

He pushed Buckthorn and Speedwell off his back and broke away to the edge of the wood. Strawberry and Boxwood were on the bank and he joined them and sat washing and combing himself in the sunrise.

'We can do with a few well-behaved fellows like you,' he said to Boxwood. 'Look at that rough lot out there – they nearly finished me off! What on earth do you make of us and how are you settling down?'

'Well, of course we find it strange,' said Boxwood, 'but we're learning. Strawberry here has been helping me a great deal. We were just seeing how many smells I could tell on the wind, but that's something that'll only come slowly. The smells are awfully strong on a farm, you know, and they don't mean much when you live behind wire. As far as I can make out, you all live by smell.'

'Don't take too many risks to begin with,' said Hazel. 'Keep near the burrows – don't go out alone – all that sort of thing. And how about you, Strawberry? Are you better?'

'More or less,' answered Strawberry, 'as long as I sleep a lot and sit in the sun, Hazel-rah. I've been terrified half out of my wits – that's the bottom of it. I've had the shivers and the horrors for days. I kept thinking I was back in Efrafa.'

'What was it like in Efrafa?' asked Hazel.

'I'd rather die than go back to Efrafa,' said Strawberry, 'Or risk going anywhere near it. I don't know which was worse, the boredom or the fear. All the same,' he added after a few moments, 'there are rabbits there who'd be the same as we are if they could only live naturally, like us. Several would be glad to leave the place if they only could.'

Before they went underground Hazel talked to almost all the rabbits. As he expected, they were disappointed over the failure at Efrafa and full of indignation at the ill-treatment of Holly and his companions. More than one thought, like Holly, that the two does were likely to give rise to trouble.

'There should have been more, Hazel,' said Bigwig. 'We shall all be at each other's throats, you know – I don't see how it's to be helped.'

Late in the afternoon Hazel called everyone into the Honeycomb.

'I've been thinking things over,' he said. 'I know you must all have been really disappointed not to have got rid of me at Nuthanger Farm the other day, so I've decided to go a bit further next time.'

'Where?' asked Bluebell.

'To Efrafa,' replied Hazel, 'if I can get anyone to come with me: and we shall bring back as many does as the warren needs.'

There were murmurs of astonishment, and then Speedwell asked, 'How?'

'Blackberry and I have got a plan,' said Hazel, 'but I'm not going to explain it now, for this reason. You all know that this is going to be a dangerous business. If any of you get caught and taken into Efrafa, they'll make you talk all right. But those who don't know a plan can't give it away. I'll explain it later on, at the proper time.'

'Are you going to need many rabbits, Hazel-rah?' asked Dandelion. 'From all I hear, the whole lot of us wouldn't be enough to fight the Efrafans.'

'I hope we shan't have to fight at all,' replied Hazel, 'but there's always the possibility. Anyway, it'll be a long journey home with the does, and if by any chance we meet a Wide Patrol on the way, there have got to be enough of us to deal with them.'

'Would we have to go into Efrafa?' asked Pipkin timidly.

'No,' said Hazel, 'we shall –'

'I never thought, Hazel,' interrupted Holly, 'I never thought that the time would come when I should feel obliged to speak against you. But I can only say again that this is likely to be a complete disaster. I know what you think – you're counting on General Woundwort not having anyone as clever as Blackberry and Fiver. You're quite right – I don't think he has. But the fact remains that no one can get a bunch of does away from that place. You all know that I've spent my life patrolling and tracking in the open. Well, there are rabbits in the Efrafan Owsla who are better at it than I am – I'm admitting it: and they'll hunt you down with your does and kill you. Great Frith! We all have to meet our match some time or other! I know you want only to help us all, but do be sensible and give this scheme up. Believe me, the best thing to do with a place like Efrafa is to stay as far away from it as possible.'

Talk broke out all over the Honeycomb. 'That must be right!' 'Who wants to be torn to pieces?' 'That rabbit with the mutilated ears –' 'Well, but Hazel-rah must know what he's doing.' 'It's too far.' 'I don't want to go.'

Hazel waited patiently for quiet. At last he said, 'It's like this. We can stay here and try to make the best of things as they are: or we can put them right once and for all. Of course there's a risk: anyone knows that who's heard what happened to Holly and the others. But haven't we faced one risk after another, all the way from the warren we left? What do you mean to do? Stay here and scratch each other's eyes out over two does, when there are plenty in Efrafa that you're afraid to go and get, even though they'd be only too glad to come and join us?'

Someone called out, 'What does Fiver think?'

'I'm certainly going,' said Fiver quietly. 'Hazel's perfectly right and there's nothing the matter with his plan. But I promise you this, all of you. If I do come, later on, to feel any kind of misgiving, I shan't keep it to myself.'

'And if that happens, I shan't ignore it,' said Hazel.

There was silence. Then Bigwig spoke.

'You may as well all know that I'm going,' he said, 'and we shall have Kehaar with us, if that appeals to you at all.'

There was a buzz of surprise.

'Of course, there are some of us who ought to stay here,' said Hazel. 'The farm rabbits can't be expected to go: and I'm not asking anyone who went the first time to go back again.'

'I'll come, though,' said Silver. 'I hate General Woundwort and his Council with all my guts and if we're really going to make fools of them I want to be there, as long as I don't have to go back inside the place – that I couldn't face. But after all, you're going to need someone who knows the way.'

'I'll come,' said Pipkin. 'Hazel-rah saved my – I mean, I'm sure he knows what's –' He became confused. 'Anyway, I'll come,' he repeated, in a very nervous voice.

There was a scuffling in the run that led down from the wood and Hazel called, 'Who's that?'

'It's I, Hazel-rah – Blackberry.'

'Blackberry!' said Hazel. 'Why, I thought you'd been here all the time. Where have you been?'

'Sorry not to have come before,' said Blackberry. 'I've been talking to Kehaar, as a matter of fact, about the plan. He's improved it a good deal. If I'm not mistaken, General Woundwort's going to look remarkably silly before we've finished. I thought at first that it couldn't be done, but now I feel sure it can.'

'Come where the grass is greener,' said Bluebell,

'And the lettuces grow in rows,

'And a rabbit of free demeanour

'Is known by his well-scratched nose.

'I think I shall have to come, just to satisfy my curiosity. I've been opening and shutting my mouth like a baby bird to know about this plan and no one puts anything in. I suppose Bigwig's going to dress up as a hrududu and drive all the does across the field.'

Hazel turned on him sharply. Bluebell sat up on his hind legs and said, 'Please, General Woundwort, sir, I'm only a little hrududu and I've left all my petrol on the grass, so if you wouldn't mind eating the grass, sir, while I just give this lady a ride –'

'Bluebell,' said Hazel, 'shut up!'

'I'm sorry, Hazel-rah,' replied Bluebell in surprise. 'I didn't mean any harm. I was only trying to cheer everyone up a bit. After all, most of us feel frightened at the idea of going to this place and you can't blame us, can you? It sounds horribly dangerous.'

'Well, look here,' said Hazel, 'we'll finish this meeting now. Let's wait and see what we decide – that's the rabbits' way. No one has to go to Efrafa who doesn't want to, but it's clear enough that some of us mean to go. Now I'm off to talk to Kehaar myself.'

He found Kehaar just inside the trees, snapping and tearing with his great beak at a foul-smelling piece of flaking, brown flesh, which seemed to be hanging from a tracery of bones. He wrinkled his nose in disgust at the odour, which filled the wood around and was already attracting ants and blue-bottles.

'What on earth is that, Kehaar?' he asked. 'It smells appalling!'

'You not know? Heem feesh, feesh, come from Peeg Vater. Ees goot.'

'Come from Big Water? (Ugh!) Did you find it there?'

'Na, na. Men have heem. Down to farm ees plenty peeg rubbish place, all t'ings dere. I go for food, find heem, all smell like Peeg Vater, pick heem up, pring heem back: make me t'ink all about Peeg Vater.' He began to tear again at the half-eaten kipper. Hazel sat choking with nausea and disgust as Kehaar lifted it entire and beat it against a beech-root, so that small fragments flew round them. He collected himself and made an effort.

'Kehaar,' he said, 'Bigwig says you told him you'd come and help us to get the mothers out of the big warren.'

'Ya, ya, I come for you. Meester Pigvig, 'e need me for 'elp 'im. Ven 'e dere, 'e talk to me, I not rabbit. Ees goot, ya?'

'Yes, rather. It's the only possible way. You're a good friend to us, Kehaar.'

'Ya, ya, 'elp you for get mudders. But now ees dis, Meester 'Azel. Alvays I vant Peeg Vater now – alvays,

alvays. Ees hearing Peeg Vater, vant to fly to Peeg Vater. Now soon you go for get mudders, I 'elp you, 'ow you like. Den, ven you getting mudders, I leave you dere, fly avay, no come back. But I come back anudder time, ya? Come in autumn, in vinter I come live 'ere vid you, ya?'

'We shall miss you, Kehaar. But when you come back we'll have a fine warren here, with lots of mothers. You'll be able to feel proud of all you did to help us.'

'Ya, vill be so. But Meester 'Azel, ven you go? I vant 'elp you but I no vant vait for go Peeg Vater. Ees hard now for stay, you know? Dis vat you do, do heem queek, ya?'

Bigwig came up the run, put his head out of the hole and stopped in horror.

'Frith up a tree!' he said. 'What a fearful smell! Did you kill it, Kehaar, or did it die under a stone?'

'You like, Meester Pigvig? I pring you nice liddle pit, ya?'

'Bigwig,' said Hazel, 'can you go and tell all the others that we're setting off at day-break tomorrow? Holly will look after things here until we get back and Buckthorn, Strawberry and the farm rabbits are to stay with him. Anyone else who wants to stay will be perfectly free to do so.'

'Don't worry,' said Bigwig, from the hole. 'I'll send them all up to silflay with Kehaar. They'll go anywhere you like before a duck can dive.'

PART THREE

Efrafa

30. A New Journey

An undertaking of great advantage, but nobody to
know what it is.

         Company Prospectus of the South Sea Bubble

WITH the exception of Buckthorn and the addition
of Bluebell, the rabbits who set off from the southern
end of the beech hanger early the next morning were those
who had left Sandleford with Hazel five weeks before.
Hazel had said nothing more to persuade them, feeling that
it would be better simply to leave things to set in his favour.
He knew that they were afraid, for he was afraid himself.
Indeed, he guessed that they, like himself, could not be free
from the thought of Efrafa and its grim Owsla. But working
against this fear was their longing and need to find more
does and the knowledge that there were plenty of does in
Efrafa. Then there was their sense of mischief. All rabbits
love to trespass and steal and when it comes to the point
very few will admit that they are afraid to do so; unless
(like Buckthorn or Strawberry on this occasion) they know

that they are not fit and that their bodies may let them down in the pinch. Again, in speaking about his secret plan, Hazel had aroused their curiosity. He had hoped that, with Fiver behind him, he could lure them with hints and promises: and he had been right. The rabbits trusted him and Fiver, who had got them out of Sandleford before it was too late, crossed the Enborne and the common, taken Bigwig out of the wire, founded the warren on the downs, made an ally of Kehaar and produced two does against all odds. There was no telling what they would do next. But they were evidently up to something; and since Bigwig and Blackberry seemed to be confidently in on it, no one was ready to say that he would rather stay out; especially since Hazel had made it clear that anyone who wished could remain at home and welcome – implying that if he was so poor-spirited as to choose to miss the exploit, they could do without him. Holly, in whom loyalty was second nature, had said no more to queer the pitch. He accompanied them as far as the end of the wood with all the cheerfulness he could muster; only begging Hazel, out of hearing of the rest, not to under-rate the danger. 'Send news by Kehaar when he reaches you,' he said, 'and come back soon.'

Nevertheless, as Silver guided them southwards along higher ground to the west of the farm, almost all, now that they were actually committed to the adventure, felt dread and apprehension. They had heard enough about Efrafa to daunt the stoutest heart. But before reaching it – or wherever they were going – they had to expect two days on the open down. Foxes, stoats, weasels – any of these might be encountered, and the only recourse would be flight above ground. Their progress was straggling and broken, slower than that which Holly had made with his picked band of three. Rabbits strayed, took alarm, stopped to rest. After a time Hazel divided them into groups, led by Silver, Bigwig and himself. Yet still they moved slowly, like climbers on a rock-face, first some and then others taking their turn to cross the same piece of ground.

But at least the cover was good. June was moving towards July and high summer. Hedgerows and verges were at their rankest and thickest. The rabbits sheltered in dim-green, sun-flecked caves of grass, flowering marjoram and cow-parsley: peered round spotted hairy-stemmed clumps of viper's bugloss, blooming red and blue above their heads: pushed between towering stalks of yellow mullein. Sometimes they scuttled along open turf, coloured like a tapestry meadow with self-heal, centaury and tormentil. Because of their anxiety about elil and because they were nose-to-ground and unable to see far ahead, the way seemed long.

Had their journey been made in years gone by, they would have found the downs far more open, without standing crops, grazed close by sheep; and they could hardly have hoped to go far unobserved by enemies. But the sheep were long gone and the tractors had ploughed great expanses for wheat and barley. The smell of the green, standing corn was round them all day. The mice were numerous and so were the kestrels. The kestrels were disturbing, but Hazel had been right when he guessed that a healthy, full-grown rabbit was too large a quarry for them. At all events, no one was attacked from above.

Some time before ni-Frith, in the heat of the day, Silver paused in a little patch of thorn. There was no breeze and the air was full of the sweet, chrysanthemum-like smell of the flowering compositae of dry uplands – corn-chamomile, yarrow and tansy. As Hazel and Fiver came up and squatted beside him, he looked out across the open ground ahead.

'There, Hazel-rah,' he said, 'that's the wood that Holly didn't like.'

Two or three hundred yards away and directly across their line, a belt of trees ran straight across the down, stretching in each direction as far as they could see. They had come to the line of the Portway – only intermittently a road – which runs from north of Andover, through St Mary Bourne with its bells and streams and watercress beds, through Bradley Wood, on across the downs and so to Tadley and at last to Silchester – the Romans' Calleva Atrebatum. Where it crosses the downs, the line is marked by Caesar's Belt, a strip of woodland as straight as the road, narrow indeed but more than three miles long. In this hot noon-day the trees of the Belt were looped and netted with darkest shadow. The sun lay outside, the shadows inside the trees. All was still, save for the grasshoppers and the falling finch-song of the yellow-hammer on the thorn. Hazel looked steadily for a long time, listening with raised ears and wrinkling his nose in the unmoving air.

'I can't see anything wrong with it,' he said at last. 'Can you, Fiver?'

'No,' replied Fiver. 'Holly thought it was a strange kind of wood and so it is, but there don't seem to be any men there. All the same, someone ought to go and make sure, I suppose. Shall I?'

The third group had come up while Hazel had been gazing at the Belt, and now all the rabbits were either nibbling quietly or resting, with ears laid flat, in the light green sun-and-shade of the thorn thicket.

'Is Bigwig there?' asked Hazel.

Throughout the morning Bigwig had seemed unlike himself – silent and preoccupied, with little attention for what was going on around him. If his courage had not been beyond question, it might have been thought that he was feeling nervous. During one long halt Bluebell had overheard him talking with Hazel, Fiver and Blackberry and later had told Pipkin that it sounded for all the world as though Bigwig were being reassured. 'Fighting, yes, anywhere,' he had heard him say, 'but I still reckon that this game is more in someone else's line than mine.' 'No,' replied Hazel, 'you're the only one that can do it; and remember, this isn't sport, if the farm raid was. Everything depends on it.' Then, realizing that Bluebell could hear him, he added, 'Anyway, keep on thinking about it and try to get used to the idea. We must get on now.' Bigwig had gone moodily down the hedgerow to collect his group.

Now, he came out of a near-by clump of mugwort and flowering thistle and joined Hazel under the thorn.

'What do you want?' he asked abruptly.

'King of cats,' (*pfeffa-rah*) answered Hazel, 'would you like to go and have a look in those trees: and if you find any cats or men or anything like that, just chase them off, would you, and then come and tell us it's all right?'

When Bigwig had slipped away, Hazel said to Silver, 'Have you any idea how far the Wide Patrols go out? Are we inside their range yet?'

'I don't know, but I'd guess that we are,' said Silver. 'As I understand it, the range is up to the patrol. Under a pushing sort of captain, a patrol may go out a long way, I believe.'

'I see,' said Hazel. 'Well, I don't want to meet a patrol if it can possibly be helped, and if we do, not one of them must get back to Efrafa. That's one reason why I brought so many of us. But by way of avoiding them, I'm going to try to make use of this wood. Perhaps they don't fancy it any more than Holly did.'

'But surely it doesn't run the way we want to go?' said Silver.

'We're not going to Efrafa, though,' said Hazel. 'We're going to find somewhere to hide, as near to it as we can safely get. Any ideas?'

'Only that it's terribly dangerous, Hazel-rah,' said Silver. 'You *can't* get near Efrafa safely and I don't know how you can begin to look for somewhere to hide. And then the patrol – if there is one – they'll be cunning brutes. They might very well spot us and not show themselves at all – simply go and report.'

'Well, here comes Bigwig back again,' said Hazel. 'Is it all right, Bigwig? Good – let's get them into the wood and go down the length of it a little way. Then we must slip out on the other side and make sure that Kehaar finds us. He's coming to look for us this afternoon and at all costs we mustn't miss him.'

Less than half a mile to the west, they came upon a spinney adjoining the southern edge of Caesar's Belt. To the west again was a shallow, dry downland combe, perhaps four hundred yards across and overgrown with weeds and rough, yellowing summer tussocks. There, well before sunset, Kehaar, flying westwards down the Belt, spotted the rabbits lying up, all among the nettles and goose-grass. He sailed down and alighted near Hazel and Fiver.

'How's Holly?' asked Hazel.

''E sad,' said Kehaar. ''E say you no come back.' Then he added, 'Mees Clover, she ready for mudder.'

'That's good,' said Hazel. 'Is anyone doing anything about it?'

'Ya, ya, ees all to fight.'

'Oh well, I suppose it'll sort itself out.'

'Vat you do now, Meester 'Azel?'

'This is where you start helping, Kehaar. We need a place to hide, as near the big warren as we can safely get – somewhere where those other rabbits won't find us. If you know the country well enough, perhaps you can suggest something.'

'Meester 'Azel, 'ow close you vant?'

'Well, no further away than Nuthanger Farm is from the Honeycomb. In fact, that's really about the limit.'

'Ees only von t'ing, Meester 'Azel. You go udder side river, den dey not find you.'

'Over the river? You mean we swim across?'

'Na, na, rabbit no sveem dis river. Ees peeg, ees deep, go queek. But ees pridge, den udder side plenty place for hide. Ees close to varren, like you say.'

'And you think that's the best we can do?'

'Ees plenty trees und ees river. Udder rabbits no find you.'

'What do you think?' said Hazel to Fiver.

'It sounds better than I'd hoped for,' said Fiver. 'I hate to say it, but I think we ought to go straight there as fast as we can, even if it makes everyone exhausted. We're in danger all the time we're on the down, but once we get off it we can rest.'

'Well, I suppose we'd better go on by night, if they'll do it – we've done it before – but they must feed and rest first. Start fu Inlé? There'll be a moon.'

'Oh, how I've come to loathe those words "start" and "fu Inlé",' said Blackberry.

However, the evening feed was peaceful and cool and after a time everyone felt refreshed. As the sun was sinking, Hazel brought them all together, under close cover, to chew pellets and rest. Although he did his best to appear confident and cheerful, he could feel that they were on edge, and after parrying one or two questions about the plan, he began to wonder how he could distract their thoughts and get them to relax until they were ready to set off again. He remembered the time, on the first night of his leadership, when they had been forced to rest in the wood above the Enborne. At least it was good to see that no one was exhausted now: they were as tough a bunch of hlessil as ever raided a garden. Not a blade of grass to choose between them, thought Hazel: Pipkin and Fiver looked as fresh as Silver and Bigwig. Still, a little entertainment would be all to the good and raise their spirits. He was just going to speak up when Acorn saved him the trouble.

'Will you tell us a story, Dandelion?' he asked.

'Yes! yes!' said several others. 'Come on! Make it a stunner while you're at it!'

'All right,' said Dandelion. 'How about "El-ahrairah and the Fox in the Water"?'

'Let's have "The Hole in the Sky",' said Hawkbit.

'No, not that,' said Bigwig suddenly. He had spoken very little all the evening and everyone looked round. 'If you're going to tell a story, there's only one I want,' he went on. '"El-ahrairah and the Black Rabbit of Inlé."'

'Perhaps not that one,' said Hazel. Bigwig rounded on him, snarling.

'If there's going to be a story, don't you think I've got as good a right as anyone to choose it?' he asked.

Hazel did not reply and after a pause, during which no one else spoke, Dandelion, with a rather subdued manner, began.

31. The Story of El-Ahrairah and the Black Rabbit of Inlé

The power of the night, the press of the storm,
    The post of the foe;
Where he stands, the Arch Fear in a visible form,
    Yet the strong man must go.

                  Robert Browning, 'Prospice'

'SOONER or later, everything leaks out and animals get to hear what others think about them. Some say that it was Hufsa who told King Darzin the truth about the trick with the lettuces. Others say that Yona the hedgehog went gossiping in the copses. But however it was, King Darzin got to know that he had been made a fool when he delivered his lettuces to the marshes of Kelfazin. He did not call his soldiers out to fight – not yet. But he made up his mind that he would find an opportunity to get his own back on El-ahrairah. El-ahrairah knew this and he warned all his people to be careful, especially when they went about alone.

'Now late one afternoon in February, Rabscuttle led some of the rabbits out to a rubbish heap on the edge of a garden, some way away from the warren. The evening came on cold and misty and well before twilight a fog came down thick. They set off for home but they got lost; and then they had trouble with an owl and became confused over their direction. Anyway, Rabscuttle got separated from the others and after wandering about for some time, he strayed into the guards' quarters outside King Darzin's city; and they caught him and took him up to the king.

'King Darzin saw his chance to spite El-ahrairah. He put Rabscuttle into a special prison-hole and every day he was brought out and made to work, sometimes in the frost, digging and tunnelling. But El-ahrairah swore he would get him out somehow. And so he did, for he and two of his does spent four days digging a tunnel from the wood into the back of the bank where Rabscuttle had been set to work. And in the end this tunnel came near to the hole in the bank down which Rabscuttle had been sent. He was supposed to be digging to turn the hole into a store-room and the guards were watching outside while he worked. But El-ahrairah reached him, for he could hear him scratching in the dark; and they all slipped away down the tunnel and escaped through the wood.

'When the news reached King Darzin, he became very angry indeed: and he determined that this time he would start a war and finish El-ahrairah once and for all. His soldiers set out in the night and went to the meadows of Fenlo; but they couldn't get down the rabbit-holes. Some tried, to be sure, but they soon came out again, because they met El-ahrairah and the other rabbits. They were not used to fighting in narrow places in the dark and they got bitten and scratched until they were glad to come out tail-first.

'But they didn't go away: they sat outside and waited. Whenever any of the rabbits tried to silflay they found their enemies ready to jump on them. King Darzin and his soldiers couldn't watch all the holes – there were too many – but they were quick enough to dash off wherever they saw a rabbit show his nose. Very soon El-ahrairah's people found that it was all they could do to snatch a mouthful or two of grass – just enough to keep alive – before they had to bolt underground again. El-ahrairah tried every trick he could think of, but he couldn't be rid of King Darzin or get his own people away. The rabbits began to become thin and miserable underground and some of them fell ill.

'At last El-ahrairah felt quite desperate and one night, when he had been risking his life again and again to bring down a few mouthfuls of grass for a doe and her family whose father had been killed the day before, he called out, "Lord Frith! I would do anything to save my people! I would drive a bargain with a stoat or a fox – yes, or with the Black Rabbit of Inlé!"

'Now as soon as he had said this, El-ahrairah realized in his heart that if there was one creature anywhere who might have the will and certainly had the power to destroy his enemies, it was the Black Rabbit of Inlé. For he was a rabbit and yet more powerful than King Darzin a thousand times over. But the thought made El-ahrairah sweat and shudder, so that he had to crouch down where he was in the run. After a time he went to his own burrow and began to think of what he had said and what it meant.

'Now as you all know, the Black Rabbit of Inlé is fear and everlasting darkness. He *is* a rabbit, but he is that cold, bad dream from which we can only entreat Lord Frith to save us today and tomorrow. When the snare is set in the gap, the Black Rabbit knows where the peg is driven; and when the weasel dances, the Black Rabbit is not far off. You all know how some rabbits seem just to throw their lives away between two jokes and a theft: but the truth is that their foolishness comes from the Black Rabbit, for it is by his will that they do not smell the dog or see the gun. The Black Rabbit brings sickness too. Or again, he will come in the night and call a rabbit by name: and then that rabbit must go out to him, even though he may be young and strong to save himself from any other danger. He goes with the Black Rabbit and leaves no trace behind. Some say that the Black Rabbit hates us and wants our destruction. But the truth is – or so they taught me – that he too serves Lord Frith and does no more than his appointed task – to bring about what must be. We come into the world and we have to go: but we do not go merely to serve the turn of one enemy or another. If that were so, we would all be destroyed in a day. We go by the will of the Black Rabbit of Inlé and only by his will. And though that will seems hard and bitter to us all, yet in his way he is our protector, for he knows Frith's promise to the rabbits and he will revenge any rabbit who may chance to be destroyed without the consent of himself. Anyone who has seen a game-keeper's gibbet knows what the Black Rabbit can bring down on elil who think they will do what they will.

'El-ahrairah spent the night alone in his burrow and his thoughts were terrible. As far as he knew, no rabbit had ever tried to do what he had in mind. But the more he thought about it – as well as he could for hunger and fear and the trance that comes upon rabbits face-to-face with death – the more it seemed to him that there was at least a chance of success. He would seek out the Black Rabbit and offer him his own life in return for the safety of his people. But if, when he offered his life, he did not mean the offer to be accepted, it would be better not to go near the Black Rabbit at all. The Black Rabbit might not accept his life: yet still, perhaps, he might get a chance to try something else. Only, there could be no cheating the Black Rabbit. If his people's safety were to be had, by whatever means, the price would be his life. So unless he failed, he would not return. He would therefore need a companion to bring back whatever it was that was going to overthrow King Darzin and save the warren.

'In the morning, El-ahrairah went to find Rabscuttle and they talked far into the day. Then he called his Owsla together and told them what he meant to do.

'Later that evening, in the last of the twilight, the rabbits came out and attacked King Darzin's soldiers. They fought very bravely and some of them were killed. The enemy thought they were trying to break out of the warren and did everything they could to surround them and force them back into their holes. But the truth was that all the fighting was simply to distract King Darzin's attention and keep his soldiers busy. As darkness set in, El-ahrairah and Rabscuttle slipped out from the other end of the warren and made off down the ditch, while the Owsla fell back and King Darzin's soldiers jeered at them down the holes. As for King Darzin, he sent a message to say that he was ready to talk to El-ahrairah about terms of surrender.

'El-ahrairah and Rabscuttle set out on their dark journey. What way they went I don't know and no rabbit knows. But I always remember what old Feverfew – d'you remember him? – used to say when he told this story. "They didn't take long," he said. "They took no time at all. No. They limped and stumbled through a bad dream to that terrible place they were bound for. Where they were travelling, the sun and moon mean nothing and winter and summer less. But you will never know" – and then he used to look all round at us – "you will never know and neither do I, how far El-ahrairah went on his journey into the dark. You see the top of a great stone sticking out of the ground. How far is it to the middle? Split the stone. Then you'll know."

'At last they came to a high place where there was no grass. They scrambled upwards, over splinters of slate, among grey rocks bigger than sheep. Mist and icy rain swirled about them and there was no sound but the trickling of water and sometimes, from far above, the cry of some great, evil bird on the wing. And these sounds echoed, for they were between black cliffs of stone, taller than the tallest trees. The snow lay in patches all about, for the sun never shone to melt it. The moss was slippery and whenever they pushed out a pebble, it rattled down and down behind them in the gullies. But El-ahrairah knew the way and on he went, until the mist grew so thick that they could see nothing. Then they kept close to the cliff and little by little, as they went, it overhung them until it made a dark roof above their backs. Where the cliff ended was the mouth of a tunnel, like a huge rabbit hole. In the freezing cold and silence, El-ahrairah stamped and flashed his tail to Rabscuttle. And then, as they were about to go into the tunnel, they realized that what they had thought, in the gloom, to be a part of the rock was not rock. It was the Black Rabbit of Inlé, close beside them, still as lichen and cold as the stone.'

'Hazel,' said Pipkin, staring into the dusk and trembling, 'I don't like this story. I know I'm not brave –'

'It's all right, Hlao-roo,' said Fiver, 'you're not the only one.' In fact he himself seemed composed and even detached, which was more than could be said for any other rabbit in the audience: but Pipkin was hardly to realize this. 'Let's go out there for a bit and watch the spiders catching moths, shall we?' said Fiver. 'I think I can remember where I left a patch of vetch – it must be somewhere this way.' Still talking quietly, he led Pipkin out into the overgrown combe. Hazel turned to make sure of the direction they had taken and as he did so Dandelion hesitated, uncertain whether to resume.

'Go on,' said Bigwig, 'and don't leave anything out.'

'I think many things are left out, if only the truth could be known' (said Dandelion), 'for no one can say what happens in that country where El-ahrairah went of his own accord and we do not. But as I was told, when they first became aware of the Black Rabbit, they fled down the tunnel – as needs they must, for there was nowhere else to run. And this they did although they had come on purpose to encounter him and all depended on their doing so. They did no differently from all of us; and the end too, was no different, for when they had done slipping and tripping and falling along the tunnel, they found themselves in a vast, stone burrow. All was of stone: the Black Rabbit had dug it out of the mountain with his claws. And there they found, waiting for them, him from whom they had fled. There were others in that burrow also – shadows without sound or smell. The Black Rabbit has his Owsla too, you know. I would not care to meet them.

'The Black Rabbit spoke with the voice of water that falls into pools in echoing places in the dark.

'"El-ahrairah, why have you come here?"

'"I have come for my people," whispered El-ahrairah.

'The Black Rabbit smelt as clean as last year's bones and in the dark El-ahrairah could see his eyes, for they were red with a light that gave no light.

'"You are a stranger here, El-ahrairah," said the Black Rabbit. "You are alive."

'"My lord," replied El-ahrairah, "I have come to give you my life. My life for my people."

'The Black Rabbit drew his claws along the floor.

'"Bargains, bargains, El-ahrairah," he said. "There is not a day or a night but a doe offers her life for her kittens, or some honest captain of Owsla his life for his Chief Rabbit's. Sometimes it is taken, sometimes it is not. But there is no bargain, for here, what is, is what must be."

'El-ahrairah was silent. But he thought, "Perhaps I can trick him into taking my life. He would keep a promise, as Prince Rainbow kept his."

'"You are my guest, El-ahrairah," said the Black Rabbit. "Stay in my burrow as long as you wish. You may sleep here. And you may eat here, and they are few indeed who can do as much. Let him eat," he said to the Owsla.

'"We will not eat, my lord," said El-ahrairah, for he knew that if he ate the food which they gave him in that burrow, his secret thoughts would become plain and there would be an end of tricks.

'"Then at least we must entertain you," said the Black Rabbit. "You must feel at home, El-ahrairah, and make yourself comfortable. Come, let us play bob-stones."*

'"Very well," said El-ahrairah, "and if I win, my lord, perhaps you will be so good as to accept my life in return for my people's safety.'

'"I will," said the Black Rabbit. "But if I win, El-ahrairah, you shall give me both your tail and your whiskers."

'The stones were brought and El-ahrairah sat down in the cold and the echoes to play against the Black Rabbit of Inlé. Now as you may suppose, El-ahrairah knew how to play bob-stones. He could play as well as any rabbit that ever covered a cast. But there – in that dreadful place, with

---

* Bob-stones is a traditional game of rabbits. It is played with small stones, fragments of stick or the like. Fundamentally it is a very simple kind of gambling, on the lines of 'Odds or Evens'. A 'cast' of stones on the ground is covered by the player's front paw. The opponent must then hazard some sort of surmise about its nature, e.g. one or two, light or dark, rough or smooth.

the Black Rabbit's eyes upon him and the Owsla who made no sound – try as he would, his wits deserted him and even before he cast, he felt that the Black Rabbit knew what was down. The Black Rabbit showed never the least haste. He played as the snow falls, without sound or change, until at last El-ahrairah's spirit failed him and he knew that he could not win.

'"You can pay your stakes to the Owsla, El-ahrairah," said the Black Rabbit, "and they will show you a burrow to sleep in. I shall return tomorrow and if you are still here I will see you. But you are free to leave whenever you wish."

'Then the Owsla took El-ahrairah away and cut off his tail and pulled out his whiskers: and when he came to himself, he was alone with Rabscuttle in a hollow stone burrow, with an opening to the mountain outside.

'"Oh, master," said Rabscuttle, "what will you do now? For Frith's sake let us go away. I can feel for both of us in the dark."

'"Certainly not," said El-ahrairah. He still hoped to get what he wanted from the Black Rabbit somehow and he felt sure that they had been put into this burrow so that they would be tempted to steal away. "Certainly not. I can make do very well with some willow-herb and clematis. Go out and get some, Rabscuttle, but make sure you come back before tomorrow evening. You had better try to bring some food, too, if you can."

'Rabscuttle went out as he was told and El-ahrairah was left alone. He slept very little, partly for the pain and partly for the fear that never left him; but chiefly because he was still searching for some trick that would serve his turn. The next day Rabscuttle returned with some pieces of turnip and after El-ahrairah had eaten them, Rabscuttle helped him to patch himself up with a grey tail and whiskers, made from the winter drift of clematis and ragwort. In the evening he went to meet the Black Rabbit as though nothing had happened.

'"Well, El-ahrairah," said the Black Rabbit – and he did not wrinkle his nose up and down when he sniffed, but thrust it forward, as a dog does – "my burrow cannot be what you are used to: but perhaps you have done your best to make yourself comfortable?"

'"I have, my lord," said El-ahrairah. "I am glad that you allow me to stay."

'"Perhaps we will not play bob-stones tonight," said the Black Rabbit. "You must understand, El-ahrairah, that I have no wish to make you suffer. I am not one of the Thousand. I repeat, you may stay or leave as you please. But if you are going to remain, perhaps you would care to hear a story; and to tell one yourself, if you like."

'"Certainly, my lord," said El-ahrairah, "And if I can tell a story as good as yours, perhaps you will accept my life and grant the safety of my people."

'"I will," said the Black Rabbit. "But if not, El-ahrairah, you will have to forfeit your ears." He waited to see whether El-ahrairah would refuse the wager, but he did not.

'Then the Black Rabbit told such a tale of fear and darkness as froze the hearts of Rabscuttle and El-ahrairah where they crouched on the rock, for they knew that every word was true. Their wits turned. They seemed to be plunged in icy clouds that numbed their senses; and the

Black Rabbit's story crept into their hearts like a worm into a nut, leaving them shrivelled and empty. When at last that terrible story was ended, El-ahrairah tried to speak. But he could not collect his thoughts and he stammered and ran about the floor, like a mouse when the hawk glides low. The Black Rabbit waited silently, with no sign of impatience. At last it was clear that there would be no story from El-ahrairah, and the Owsla took him and put him into a deep sleep; and when he woke, his ears were gone and only Rabscuttle was beside him in the stone burrow, crying like a kitten.

'"Oh, master," said Rabscuttle, "what good can this suffering bring? For the sake of Lord Frith and the green grass, let me take you home."

'"Nonsense," said El-ahrairah. "Go out and get me two good, big dock-leaves. They will do very well for ears."

'"They will wither, master," said Rabscuttle, "and I am withered now."

'"They will last long enough," said El-ahrairah grimly, "for what I have to do. But I cannot find the way."

'When Rabscuttle was gone, El-ahrairah forced himself to think clearly. The Black Rabbit would not accept his life. Also, it was plain that he himself would never be able to win any sort of wager against him: he might as well try to run a race across a sheet of ice. But if the Black Rabbit did not hate him, why did he inflict these sufferings upon him? To destroy his courage and make him give up and go away. But why not simply send him away? And why wait, before hurting him, till he himself proposed a wager and lost it? The answer came to him suddenly. These shadows had no power either to send him away or to hurt him, except with his own consent. They would not help him, no. They would seek possession of his will and break it if they could. But supposing that he could find among them something that would save his people, could they stop him from taking it away?

'When Rabscuttle came back, he helped El-ahrairah to disguise his horrible, maimed head with two dock-leaves in place of ears and after a while they slept. But El-ahrairah kept dreaming of his starving rabbits waiting in the runs to push back King Darzin's soldiers and placing all their hopes on him: and at last he woke, cold and cramped, and wandered out into the runs of the stone warren. As he limped along, trailing the dock-leaves on either side of his head – for he could not raise or move them like the ears he had lost – he came to a place from which several narrow runs led down deeper into the ground: and here he found two of the ghastly, shadowy Owsla moving about some dark business of their own. They turned and stared, to make him afraid, but El-ahrairah was past being afraid and he stared back at them, wondering what they had in mind to persuade him to lose.

' "Turn back, El-ahrairah," said one at last. "You have no business here, in the pit. You are alive; and have suffered much already."

' "Not as much as my people," replied El-ahrairah.

' "There is enough suffering here for a thousand warrens," said the shadow. "Do not be stubborn, El-ahrairah. In these holes lie all the plagues and diseases that come to rabbits – fever and mange and the sickness of the bowels. And here, too, in this nearest hole, lies the white blindness, that sends creatures hobbling out to die in the fields, where even the elil will not touch their rotting bodies. This is our task, to see that all these are ready for the use of Inlé-rah. For what is, is what must be."

'Then El-ahrairah knew that he must give himself no time to think. He pretended to go back, but suddenly turned, rushed upon the shadows and plunged into the nearest hole faster than a raindrop into the ground. And there he lay, while the shadows flickered and gibbered about the entrance, for they had no power to move him, except by fear. After a time they went away and El-ahrairah was left alone, wondering whether he would be able to reach King Darzin's army in time without the use of whiskers or ears.

'At last, when he was sure that he must have stayed in the hole long enough to be infected, El-ahrairah came out and began to make his way back along the run. He did not know how soon the disease would appear or how long he would take to die, but plainly he ought to return as quickly as he could – if possible, before there was any sign of illness on him. Without going near Rabscuttle, he must tell him to hurry ahead, reach the rabbits in the warren and warn them to block all the holes and stay inside until King Darzin's army was destroyed.

'He blundered into a stone in the dark, for he was shivering and feverish and in any case he could feel little or nothing without his whiskers. At that moment a quiet voice said, "El-ahrairah, where are you going?" He had heard nothing, but he knew that the Black Rabbit was beside him.

'"I am going home, my lord," he replied. "You said that I might go when I wished."

'"You have some purpose, El-ahrairah," said the Black Rabbit. "What is it?"

'"I have been in the pit, my lord," answered El-ahrairah. "I am infected with the white blindness and I am going to save my people by destroying the enemy."

'"El-ahrairah," said the Black Rabbit, "do you know how the white blindness is carried?"

'A sudden misgiving seized upon El-ahrairah. He said nothing.

'"It is carried by the fleas in rabbits' ears," said the Black Rabbit. "They pass from the ears of a sick rabbit to those of his companions. But El-ahrairah, you have no ears and fleas will not go to dock-leaves. You can neither catch nor carry the white blindness."

'Then at last El-ahrairah felt that his strength and courage were gone. He fell to the ground. He tried to move, but his back legs dragged along the rock and he could not get up. He scuffled and then lay still in the silence.

'"El-ahrairah," said the Black Rabbit at last, "this is a cold warren: a bad place for the living and no place at all for warm hearts and brave spirits. You are a nuisance to me. Go home. I myself will save your people. Do not have the impertinence to ask me when. There is no time here. They are already saved."

'In that moment, while King Darzin and his soldiers were still jeering down the holes of the warren, confusion and terror came upon them in the falling darkness. The fields seemed full of huge rabbits with red eyes, stalking among the thistles. They turned and fled. They vanished in the night; and that is why no rabbit who tells the tales of El-ahrairah can say what kind of creatures they were or what they looked like. Not one of them has ever been seen, from that day to this.

'When at last El-ahrairah was able to rise to his feet, the Black Rabbit was gone and Rabscuttle was coming down the run, looking for him. Together they went out to the mountainside and made their way down the stone-rattling gully in the mist. They did not know where they were going, except that they were going away from the Black Rabbit's warren. But after a time it became plain that El-ahrairah was ill from shock and exhaustion. Rabscuttle dug a scrape and there they stayed for several days.

'Later, when El-ahrairah began to get better, they wandered on, but they could not find their way back. They were confused in their wits and had to beg help and shelter of other animals whom they met. Their journey home lasted three months and many adventures they had. Some of these, as you know, are stories in themselves. Once they lived with a lendri and found pheasants' eggs for him in the wood. And once they barely escaped from the middle of a hay-field when the hay was cutting. All the time, Rabscuttle looked after El-ahrairah, brought him fresh dock-leaves and kept the flies from his wounds until they healed.

'At last, one day, they came back to the warren. It was evening, and as the sun stretched out all the hills, they could see any number of rabbits at silflay, nibbling in the grass and playing over the ant-heaps. They stopped at the top of the field, sniffing the gorse and herb-robert on the wind.

'"Well, they look all right," said El-ahrairah. "A healthy lot, really. Let's just slip in quietly and see whether we can find one or two of the Owsla captains underground. We don't want a lot of fuss."

'They made their way along the hedgerow, but could not altogether get their bearings, because apparently the warren had grown bigger and there were more holes than before, both in the bank and in the field. They stopped to speak to a group of smart young bucks and does sitting under the elder bloom.

'"We want to find Loosestrife," said Rabscuttle. "Can you tell us where his burrow is?"

'"I never heard of him," answered one of the bucks. "Are you sure he's in this warren?"

'"Unless he's dead," said Rabscuttle. "But surely you must have heard of Captain Loosestrife? He was an officer of the Owsla in the fighting."

'"What fighting?" asked another buck.

'"The fighting against King Darzin," replied Rabscuttle.

'"Here, do me a favour, old fellow, will you?" said the buck. "That fighting – I wasn't born when it finished."

'"But surely you know the Owsla captains who were?" said Rabscuttle.

'"I wouldn't be seen dead with them," said the buck. "What, that white-whiskered old bunch? What do we want to know about them?"

'"What they did," said Rabscuttle.

'"That war lark, old fellow?" said the first buck. "That's all finished now. That's got nothing to do with us."

'"If this Loosestrife fought King What's-His-Name, that's his business," said one of the does. "It's not our business, is it?"

'"It was all a very wicked thing," said another doe. "Shameful, really. If nobody fought in wars there wouldn't be any, would there? But you can't get old rabbits to see that."

'"My father was in it," said the second buck. "He gets on about it sometimes. I always go out quick. 'They did this and then we did that' and all that caper. Makes you curl up, honest. Poor old geezer, you'd think he'd want to forget about it. I reckon he makes half of it up. And where did it get him, tell me that?"

'"If you don't mind waiting a little while, sir," said a third buck to El-ahrairah, "I'll go and see if I can find Captain Loosestrife for you. I don't actually know him myself, but then it's rather a big warren."

'"That's good of you," said El-ahrairah, "but I think I've got my bearings now and I can manage by myself."

'El-ahrairah went along the hedgerow to the wood and sat alone under a nut-bush, looking out across the fields. As the light began to fail, he suddenly realized that Lord Frith was close beside him, among the leaves.

'"Are you angry, El-ahrairah?" asked Lord Frith.

'"No, my lord," replied El-ahrairah, "I am not angry. But I have learned that with creatures one loves, suffering is not the only thing for which one may pity them. A rabbit who does not know when a gift has made him safe is poorer than a slug, even though he may think otherwise himself."

'"Wisdom is found on the desolate hillside, El-ahrairah, where none comes to feed, and the stony bank where the rabbit scratches a hole in vain. But speaking of gifts, I have brought a few trifles for you. A pair of ears, a tail and some whiskers. You may find the ears slightly strange at first. I put a little starlight in them, but it is really quite faint: not enough, I am sure, to give away a clever thief like you. Ah, there is Rabscuttle coming back. Good, I have something for him too. Shall we –"'

'Hazel! Hazel-rah!' It was Pipkin's voice from behind a clumb of burdock on the edge of the little circle of listeners. 'There's a fox coming up the combe!'

32. Across the Iron Road

Esprit de rivalité et de mésintelligence qui préserva plus d'une fois l'armée anglaise d'une défaite.

General Jourdan, *Mémoires Militaires*

SOME people have the idea that rabbits spend a good deal of their time running away from foxes. It is true that every rabbit fears the fox and will bolt if it smells one. But many rabbits go all their lives without seeing a fox and probably only a few actually fall victim to an enemy who smells strongly and cannot run as fast as they can. A fox trying to catch a rabbit usually creeps upwind under cover – perhaps through a patch of woodland to the edge. Then, if he succeeds in getting close to where the rabbits are at silflay along the bank or in the field, he lies still and watches his chance for a quick snatch. It is said that sometimes he fascinates them, as the weasel does, by rolling and playing in the open, coming closer little by little until he can make a grab. However this may be, it is certain that no fox hunts rabbits by going openly up a combe at sunset.

....ther Hazel nor any of the rabbits who had been ...stening to Dandelion's story had ever seen a fox. Nevertheless, they knew that a fox in the open, plain to be seen, is not dangerous as long as it is spotted in time. Hazel realized that he had been careless to allow everyone to gather round Dandelion and to have failed to post even one sentry. What wind there was, was from the north-east and the fox, coming up the combe from the west, might have broken in upon them without warning. But from this danger they had been saved by Fiver and Pipkin going into the open. Even in his flash of alarm as Pipkin spoke, it crossed Hazel's mind that Fiver, no doubt reluctant to advise him in front of the others, had probably seized the opportunity provided by Pipkin's fear to post himself as a sentry.

Hazel thought quickly. If the fox were not too close, all they had to do was run. There was woodland near-by and they could vanish into it, keeping more or less together, and simply continue on their way. He pushed through the burdocks.

'How close is it?' he asked. 'And where's Fiver?'

'I'm here,' replied Fiver, from a few yards away. He was squatting under the long briars of a dog-rose and did not turn his head as Hazel came up beside him. 'And there's the fox,' he added. Hazel followed his gaze.

The rough, weed-covered ground of the combe sloped away below them, a long dip bounded on the north by Caesar's Belt. The last of the setting sun shone straight up it through a break in the trees. The fox was below them and still some way off. Although it was almost directly downwind and therefore must be able to smell them, it did not look as though it were particularly interested in rabbits. It was trotting steadily up the combe like a dog, trailing its white-tipped brush. In colour it was sandy brown, with dark legs and ears. Even now, though obviously not hunting, it had a crafty, predatory look that made the watchers among the dog-roses shiver. As it passed behind a patch of thistles and disappeared from view, Hazel and Fiver returned to the others.

'Come on,' said Hazel. 'If you've never seen a fox don't bother to go and look now. Just follow me.'

He was about to lead the way up the south side of the combe, when suddenly a rabbit shouldered him roughly aside, pushed past Fiver and was gone into the open. Hazel stopped and looked round in amazement.

'Who was that?' he asked.

'Bigwig,' answered Fiver, staring.

Together they went quickly back to the briars and once more looked into the combe. Bigwig, in full view, was loping warily downhill, straight towards the fox. They watched him aghast. He drew near, but still the fox paid no attention.

'Hazel,' said Silver from behind, 'shall I –?'

'No one is to move,' said Hazel quickly. 'Keep still, all of you.'

At about thirty yards' distance the fox saw the approaching rabbit. It paused for a moment and then continued to trot forwards. It was almost upon him before Bigwig turned and began to limp up the north slope of the combe towards the trees of the Belt. The fox hesitated again and then followed him.

'What's he up to?' muttered Blackberry.

'Trying to draw it off, I suppose,' replied Fiver.

'But he didn't have to! We should have got away without that.'

'Confounded fool!' said Hazel. 'I don't know when I've been so angry.'

The fox had quickened its pace and was now some distance away from them. It appeared to be overtaking Bigwig. The sun had set and in the failing light they could just make him out as he entered the undergrowth. He disappeared and the fox followed. For several moments all was quiet. Then, horribly clear across the darkening, empty combe, there came the agonizing squeal of a stricken rabbit.

'O Frith and Inlé!' cried Blackberry, stamping. Pipkin turned to bolt. Hazel did not move.

'Shall we go, Hazel?' asked Silver. 'We can't help him now.'

As he spoke, Bigwig suddenly broke out of the trees, running very fast. Almost before they could grasp that he was alive, he had recrossed the entire upper slope of the combe in a single dash and bolted in among them.

'Come on,' said Bigwig, 'let's get out of here!'

'But what – what – are you wounded?' asked Bluebell in bewilderment.

'No,' said Bigwig, 'never better! Let's go!'

'You can wait until I'm ready,' said Hazel in a cold, angry tone. 'You've done your best to kill yourself and acted like a complete fool. Now hold your tongue and sit down!' He turned and, although it was rapidly becoming too dark to see any distance, made as though he were still looking out across the combe. Behind him, the rabbits fidgeted nervously. Several had begun to feel a dream-like sense of unreality. The long day above ground, the close, overgrown combe, the frightening story in which they had been absorbed, the sudden appearance of the fox, the shock of Bigwig's inexplicable adventure – all these, following one upon another, had flooded their spirits and left them dull and bemused.

'Get them out, Hazel,' whispered Fiver, 'before they all go tharn.' Hazel turned at once.

'Well, no fox,' he said cheerfully. 'It's gone and we'll go too. For goodness' sake keep close together, because if anyone gets lost in the dark we may not find him again. And remember, if we come upon any strange rabbits, you're to attack them at once and ask questions afterwards.'

They skirted the side of the wood that lay along the southern edge of the combe and then, in ones and twos, slipped across the empty road beyond. Little by little their spirits cleared. They found themselves in open farmland – indeed, they could both smell and hear the farm, not far away on the evening side – and the going was easy: smooth, wide pasture fields, sloping gently downhill and divided not by hedges but by broad, low banks, each as wide as a lane and overgrown with elder, dog-wood and spindle. It was true rabbit country, reassuring after the Belt and the tangled, goose-grassed combe; and when they had covered a good distance over the turf – halting continually to listen and sniff and running, now one and now another, from each piece of cover to the next – Hazel felt safe in giving them a rest. As soon as he had sent out Speedwell and Hawkbit as sentries, he led Bigwig to one side.

'I'm angry with you,' he said. 'You're the one rabbit we're not going to be able to do without and you have to go and run a silly risk like that. It wasn't necessary and it wasn't even clever. What were you up to?'

'I'm afraid I just lost my head, Hazel,' replied Bigwig. 'I've been strung up all day, thinking about this business at Efrafa – got me really on edge. When I feel like that I have to do something – you know, fight or run a risk. I thought if I could make that fox look a fool I wouldn't feel so worried about the other thing. What's more, it worked – I feel a lot better now.'

'Playing El-ahrairah,' said Hazel. 'You duffer, you might have thrown your life away for nothing – we all thought you had. Don't try it again, there's a good chap. You know everything's going to depend on you. But tell me, whatever happened in the trees? Why did you cry like that, if you were all right?'

'I didn't,' said Bigwig. 'It was very queer, what happened, and bad too, I'm afraid. I was going to lose the homba in the trees, you see, and then come back. Well, I went into the undergrowth, and I'd just stopped limping and was starting to run really fast, when suddenly I found myself face to face with a bunch of rabbits – strangers. They were coming towards me, as if they were going out into the open combe. Of course, I didn't have time to get a good look at them, but they seemed to be big fellows. "Look out – run!" I said as I dashed up to them, but all they did was try to stop me. One of them said, "You stay here!" or something like that, and then he got right in my way. So I knocked him down – I had to – and raced off: and the next thing I heard was this dreadful squealing. Of course, I went even faster then and I got clear of the trees and came back to you.'

'So the homba got this other rabbit?'

'It must have. After all, I led it right on to them, even though I didn't mean to. But I never saw what actually happened.'

'What became of the others?'

'I've no idea. They must have run, I suppose.'

'I see,' said Hazel thoughtfully. 'Well, perhaps it's all for the best. But look here, Bigwig, no more fancy tricks until the proper time – there's too much at stake. You'd better stay near Silver and me – we'll keep you in good heart.'

At that moment Silver came up to them.

'Hazel,' he said, 'I've just realized where we are and it's a lot too close to Efrafa. I think we ought to make off as soon as we can.'

'I want to go right round Efrafa – wide,' said Hazel. 'Do you think you can find the way to that iron road Holly told us about?'

'I think so,' replied Silver. 'But we can't make too big a circle or they'll be completely exhausted. I can't say I know the way, but I can tell the direction all right.'

'Well, we'll just have to take the risk,' said Hazel. 'If only we can get there by early morning, they can rest at the other end.'

They met with no more adventures that night, moving quietly along the edges of the fields under the dim light of a quarter-moon. The half-darkness was full of sounds and movement. Once Acorn put up a plover, which flew round them, calling shrilly, until at length they crossed a bank and left it behind. Soon after, somewhere near them, they heard the unceasing bubbling of a night-jar; a peaceful sound, without menace, which died gradually away as they pushed on. And once they heard a corncrake calling as it crept among the long grass of a path verge. (It makes a sound like a human finger-nail drawn down the teeth of a comb.) But elil they met none and although they were continually on the watch for signs of an Efrafan patrol, they saw nothing but mice, and a few hedgehogs hunting for slugs along the ditches.

At last, as the first lark rose towards the light that was still far up in the sky, Silver, his pale fur sodden dark with dew, came limping back to where Hazel was encouraging Bluebell and Pipkin.

'You can pluck up your spirits, Bluebell,' he said. 'I think we're close to the iron road.'

'I wouldn't care about my spirits,' said Bluebell, 'if my legs weren't so tired. Slugs are lucky not to have legs. I think I'll be a slug.'

'Well, I'm a hedgehog,' said Hazel, 'so you'd better get on!'

'You're not,' replied Bluebell. 'You haven't enough fleas. Now slugs don't have fleas, either. How comforting to be a slug, among the dandelions so snug –'

'And feel the blackbird's sudden tug,' said Hazel. 'All right, Silver, we're coming. But where *is* the iron road? Holly said a steep, overgrown bank. I can't make out anything like that.'

'No, that's away up by Efrafa. Down here, it runs in a sort of combe of its own. Can't you smell it?'

Hazel sniffed. In the cool damp, he picked up at once the unnatural smells of metal, coal-smoke and oil. They went forward and in a very short time found themselves looking down from among the bushes and undergrowth on the edge of the railway cutting. All was quiet, but as they paused at the top of the bank, a tussling pack of six or seven sparrows flew down to the line and began to peck about between the sleepers. Somehow, the sight was reassuring.

'Are we to cross, Hazel-rah?' asked Blackberry.

'Yes,' said Hazel, 'at once. Put it between us and Efrafa; then we'll feed.'

They went rather hesitantly down into the cutting, half-expecting the fiery, thundering angel of Frith to appear out of the twilight: but the silence remained unbroken. Soon they were all feeding in the meadow beyond, too tired to pay attention to concealment or to anything but the ease of resting their legs and nibbling the grass.

From above the larches Kehaar sailed down among them, alighted and folded his long, pale-grey wings.

'Meester 'Azel, vat you do? You no stay 'ere?'

'They're tired out, Kehaar. They've got to have a rest.'

'Ees not to rest 'ere. Ees rabbits come.'

'Yes, but not just yet. We can –'

'Ya, ya, ees coming for find you! Ees close!'

'Oh, curse these confounded patrols!' cried Hazel. 'Come on, all of you, get down the field into that wood! Yes, you too, Speedwell, unless you want to have your ears chewed off in Efrafa. Come on, move!'

They tottered over the pasture to the woodland beyond and lay completely exhausted on flat, bare ground under fir trees. Hazel and Fiver consulted Kehaar again.

'It's no good expecting them to go any farther, Kehaar,' said Hazel. 'They've been going all night, you know. We'll have to sleep here today. Did you actually see a patrol?'

'Ya, ya, come all along by udder side iron road. Yoost in time you go.'

'Well, then, you saved us. But look, Kehaar, could you go and see where they are now? If they're gone, I'm going to tell our lot to go to sleep – not that they need telling: look at them!'

Kehaar returned with the news that the Efrafan patrol had turned back without crossing the iron road. Then he offered to keep watch himself until the evening and Hazel, greatly relieved, at once told the rabbits to sleep. One or two had already fallen asleep, lying on their sides on the open ground. Hazel wondered whether he ought to wake them and tell them to get under thicker cover, but as he was thinking about it he fell asleep himself.

The day came on hot and still. Among the trees the wood-pigeons called drowsily and from time to time a late cuckoo stammered. In the fields, nothing moved except the constantly-swishing tails of the cows gathered flank to flank in the shade.

33. The Great River

Never in his life had he seen a river before – this sleek, sinuous, full-bodied animal ... All was a-shake and a-shiver – glints and gleams and sparkles, rustle and swirl, chatter and bubble.

Kenneth Grahame, *The Wind in the Willows*

WHEN Hazel woke, he started up at once, for the air around him was full of the sharp cries of some creature hunting. He looked quickly round, but could see no signs of alarm. It was evening. Several of the rabbits were already awake and feeding on the edge of the wood. He realized that the cries, urgent and startling though they were, were too small and shrill for any kind of elil. They came from above his head. A bat flittered through the trees and out again without touching a twig. It was followed by another. Hazel could sense that there were many all about, taking flies and moths on the wing and uttering their minute cries as they flew. A human ear would hardly have heard them, but to the rabbits the air was full of their calls.

Outside the wood, the field was still bright with evening sunshine, but among the firs the light was dusky and here the bats were coming and going thickly. Mixed with the resinous scent of the firs there came another smell, strong and fragrant, yet sharp – the perfume of flowers, but of some kind unknown to Hazel. He followed it to its source at the edge of the wood. It came from several thick patches of soapwort growing along the edge of the pasture. Some of the plants were not yet in bloom, their buds curled in pink, pointed spirals held in the pale-green calices: but most were already star-flowering and giving off their strong scent. The bats were hunting among the flies and moths attracted to the soapwort.

Hazel passed hraka and began to feed in the field. He was disturbed to find that his hind leg was troubling him. He had thought that it was healed, but the forced journey over the downs had evidently proved too much for the muscle torn by the shot-gun pellets. He wondered whether it was far to the river of which Kehaar had spoken. If it was, he was in for trouble.

'Hazel-rah,' said Pipkin, coming up from among the soapwort, 'are you all right? Your leg looks queer – you're dragging it.'

'No, it's all right,' said Hazel. 'Look, Hlao-roo, where's Kehaar? I want to talk to him.'

'He's flown out to see if there's a patrol anywhere near, Hazel-rah. Bigwig woke some time ago and he and Silver asked Kehaar to go. They didn't want to disturb you.'

Hazel felt irritated. It would have been better to be told at once which way to go, rather than to wait while Kehaar looked for patrols. They were going to cross a river and as far as he was concerned they could not do it too soon. Fretting, he waited for Kehaar. Soon he had become as tense and nervous as he had ever been in his life. He was beginning to believe that after all he might have been rash. It was clear that Holly had not under-rated their danger near Efrafa. He had little doubt that Bigwig, by sheer chance, had led the fox on to a Wide Patrol which had been following their trail. Then, in the morning, again by luck and the help of Kehaar, they had evidently just missed another at the crossing of the iron road. Perhaps Silver's fear was well-founded and a patrol had already spotted and reported them without their knowing? Had General Woundwort got some sort of Kehaar of his own? Perhaps a bat was at this moment talking to him? How was one to foresee and guard against everything? The grass seemed sour, the sunshine chilly. Hazel sat hunched under the firs, worrying dismally. He felt less annoyed, now, with Bigwig: he could understand his feelings. Waiting was bad. He fidgeted for some kind of action. Just as he had decided to wait no longer, but to collect everyone and go immediately, Kehaar came flying from the direction of the cutting. He flapped clumsily down among the firs, silencing the bats.

'Meester 'Azel, ees no rabbits. I t'ink maybe dey no like for go across iron road.'

'Good. Is it far to the river, Kehaar?'

'Na, na. Ees close, in vood.'

'Splendid. We can find this crossing in daylight?'

'Ya, ya. I show you pridge.'

The rabbits had gone only a short distance through the wood when they sensed that they were already near the river. The ground became soft and damp. They could smell sedge and water. Suddenly, the harsh, vibrating cry of a moorhen echoed through the trees, followed by a flapping of wings and a watery scuttering. The rustling of the leaves seemed also to echo, as though reflected distantly from hard ground. A little further on, they could distinctly hear the water itself – the low, continuous pouring of a shallow fall. A human being, hearing from a distance the noise of a crowd, can form an idea of its size. The sound of the river told the rabbits that it must be bigger than any they had known before – wide, smooth and swift. Pausing among the comfrey and ground elder, they stared at each other, seeking reassurance. Then they began to lollop hesitantly forward into more open ground. There was still no river to be seen, but in front they could perceive a flicker and dance of mirrored light in the air. Soon afterwards Hazel, limping ahead with Fiver near him, found himself on a narrow, green path that divided the wilderness from the river bank.

The path was almost as smooth as a lawn and clear of bushes and weeds, for it was kept cut for fishermen. Along its farther side the riparian plants grew thickly, so that it was separated from the river by a kind of hedge of purple loosestrife, great willow-herb, fleabane, figwort and hemp agrimony, here and there already in bloom. Two or three more of the rabbits emerged from the wood. Peering through the plant-clumps, they could catch glimpses of the smooth, glittering river, evidently much wider and swifter than the Enborne. Although there was no enemy or other danger to be perceived, they felt the apprehension and doubt of those who have come unawares upon some awe-inspiring place, where they themselves are paltry fellows of no account. When Marco Polo came at last to Cathay, seven hundred years ago, did he not feel – and did his heart not falter as he realized – that this great and splendid capital of an empire had had its being all the years of his life and far longer, and that he had been ignorant of it? That it was in need of nothing from him, from Venice, from Europe? That it was full of wonders beyond his understanding? That his arrival was a matter of no importance whatever? We know that he felt these things, and so has many a traveller in foreign parts who did not know what he was going to find. There is nothing that cuts you down to size like coming to some strange and marvellous place where no one even stops to notice that you stare about you.

The rabbits were uneasy and confused. They crouched on the grass, sniffing the water-smells in the cooling, sunset air: and moved closer together, each hoping not to see in the others the nervousness he felt in himself. As Pipkin reached the path a great, shimmering dragon-fly, four inches long, all emerald and sable, appeared at his shoulder; hovered, droning and motionless, and was gone like lightning into the sedge. Pipkin leapt back in alarm. As he did so there came a shrill, vibrant cry and he caught sight, between the plants, of a brilliant, azure bird flashing past over the open water. A few moments later there came, from close behind the plant-hedge, the sound of a fairly heavy splash: but what creature might have made it there was no telling.

Looking round for Hazel, Pipkin caught sight of Kehaar, a little way off, standing in a patch of shallow water between two clumps of willow-herb. He was stabbing and snapping at something in the mud and after a few moments pulled out a six-inch leech and swallowed it whole. Beyond him, some distance down the path, Hazel was combing the goose-grass out of his coat and evidently listening to Fiver as they sat together under a rhododendron. Pipkin ran along the bank and joined them.

'There's nothing wrong with the place,' Fiver was saying. 'There's no more danger here than anywhere else. Kehaar's going to show us where to get across, isn't he? The thing to do is to get on with it before it gets dark.'

'They'll never stop here,' replied Hazel. 'We can't stay and wait for Bigwig in a place like this. It's unnatural for rabbits.'

'Yes, we can – calm down. They'll get used to it quicker than you think. I tell you, it's better than one or two other places we've been in. Not all strange things are bad. Would you like *me* to take them over? Say it's because of your leg.'

'Fine,' said Hazel. 'Hlao-roo, can you get everyone along here?'

When Pipkin had gone, he said, 'I feel troubled, Fiver. I'm asking so much of them, and there are so many risks in this plan.'

'They're a better lot than you give them credit for,' replied Fiver. 'If you were to –'

Kehaar called raucously across, startling a wren out of the bushes.

'Meester 'Azel, vat for you vait?'

'To know where to go,' answered Fiver.

'Pridge near. You go on, you see.'

Where they were, the undergrowth stood close to the green path, but beyond – downstream, as they all intuitively felt – it gave way to open parkland. Out into this they went, Hazel following Fiver.

Hazel did not know what a bridge was. It was another of Kehaar's unknown words that he did not feel up to questioning. Despite his trust in Kehaar and his respect for his wide experience, he felt still more disturbed as they came into the open. Clearly, this was some sort of man-place, frequented and dangerous. A short way ahead was a road. He could see the smooth, unnatural surface stretching away over the grass. He stopped and looked at it. At length, when he was sure that there were no men anywhere near, he went cautiously up to the verge.

The road crossed the river on a bridge about thirty feet long. It did not occur to Hazel that there was anything unusual in this. The idea of a bridge was beyond him. He saw only a line of stout posts-and-rails on either side of the road. Similarly, simple African villagers, who have never left their remote homes, may not be particularly surprised by their first sight of an aeroplane: it is outside their comprehension. But their first sight of a horse pulling a cart will set them pointing and laughing at the ingenuity of the fellow who thought of that one. Hazel saw without surprise the road crossing the river. What worried him was that where it did so, there were only very narrow verges of short grass, offering no cover. His rabbits would be exposed to view and unable to bolt, except along the road.

'Do you think we can risk it, Fiver?' he asked.

'I can't see why you're bothered,' answered Fiver. 'You went into the farmyard and the shed where the hutch-rabbits were. This is much less dangerous. Come on – they're all watching while we hesitate.'

Fiver hopped out on the road. He looked round for a moment and then made his way to the nearer end of the bridge. Hazel followed him along the verge, keeping close beside the rail on the upstream side. Looking round, he saw Pipkin close behind. In the middle of the bridge Fiver, who was perfectly calm and unhurried, stopped and sat up. The other two joined him.

'Let's put on a bit of an act,' said Fiver. 'Make them inquisitive. They'll follow us just to see what we're looking at.'

There was no sill along the edge of the bridge: they could have walked off it into the water three feet below. From under the lowest rail they looked out, upstream, and now, for the first time, saw the whole river plainly. If the bridge had not startled Hazel, the river did. He remembered the Enborne, its surface broken by gravel spits and plant growth. The Test, a weed-cut, carefully tended trout stream, seemed to him like a world of water. A good ten yards wide it was, fast-flowing and smooth, spangling and dazzling in the evening sun. The tree-reflections on the even current were unbroken as on a lake. There was not a reed or a plant to be seen above the water. Close by, under the left bank, a bed of crowfoot trailed downstream, the wheel-like leaves all submerged. Darker still, almost black, were the mats of water-moss, their thick masses motionless on the bed of the river and only the trailing fronds waving slowly from side to side. Waving, too, were the wider expanses of pale-green cress-weed; but these rippled with the current, lightly and quickly. The water was very clear, with a bed of clean, yellow gravel, and even in the middle was hardly four feet deep. As the rabbits stared down they could discern, here and there, a very fine scour, like smoke – chalk and powdered gravel carried along by the river as dust is blown on the wind. Suddenly, from under the bridge, with a languid movement of its flat tail, swam a gravel-coloured fish as long as a rabbit. The watchers, immediately above, could see the dark, vivid spots along its sides. Warily it hung in the current below them, undulating from side to side. It reminded Hazel of the cat in the yard. As they stared, it swam upwards with a lithe flicker and stopped just below the surface. A moment later its blunt nose thrust clear of the stream and they saw the open mouth, pure white inside. Rhythmically, without haste, it sucked down a floating sedge-fly and sank back under water. A ripple spread outwards in subsiding circles, breaking both the reflections and the transparency. Gradually the stream grew smooth and once more they saw the fish below them waving its tail as it held its place in the current.

'A water-hawk!' said Fiver. 'So they hunt and eat down there too! Don't fall in, Hlao-roo. Remember El-ahrairah and the pike.'

'Would it eat me?' asked Pipkin, staring.

'There may be creatures in there that could,' said Hazel. 'How do we know? Come on, let's get across. What would you do if a hrududu came?'

'Run,' said Fiver simply, 'like this.' And he scurried off the farther end of the bridge into the grass beyond.

On this far side of the river, undergrowth and a grove of great horse-chestnuts extended almost down to the bridge. The ground was marshy but at least there was plenty of cover. Fiver and Pipkin began at once on some scrapes, while Hazel sat chewing pellets and resting his injured leg. Soon they were joined by Silver and Dandelion, but the other rabbits, more hesitant even than Hazel, remained crouching in the long grass on the right bank. At last, just before darkness fell, Fiver re-crossed the bridge and coaxed them to follow him back. Bigwig, to everyone's surprise, showed considerable reluctance, and only crossed in the end after Kehaar, returning from another flight over Efrafa, had asked whether he would like him to go and fetch a fox.

The night that followed seemed to all of them disorganized and precarious. Hazel, still conscious of being in man-country, was half-expecting either a dog or a cat. But although they heard owls more than once, no elil attacked them and by the morning they were in better spirits.

As soon as they had fed, Hazel set them to exploring the surroundings. It became even more plain that the ground near the river was too wet for rabbits. Indeed, in places it was almost bog. Marsh sedge grew there, pink, sweet-scented valerian and the drooping water-avens. Silver reported that it was drier up in the woodland away from the bank, and at first Hazel had the idea of picking a fresh spot and digging again. But presently the day grew so hot and humid that all activity was quenched. The faint breeze vanished. The sun drew up a torpid moisture from the watery thickets. The smell of water-mint filled all the hydrophanic air. The rabbits crept into the shade, under any cover that offered. Long before ni-Frith, all were drowsing in the undergrowth.

It was not until the dappled afternoon began to grow cool that Hazel woke suddenly, to find Kehaar beside him. The gull was strutting from side to side with short, quick steps and pecking impatiently in the long grass. Hazel sat up quickly.

'What is it, Kehaar? Not a patrol?'

'Na, na. Ees all fine for sleep like bloody owls. Maybe I go for Peeg Vater. Meester 'Azel, you getting mudders now soon? Vat for vait now?'

'No, you're right, Kehaar, we must start now. The trouble is, I can see how to start but not how to finish.'

Hazel made his way through the grass, roused the first rabbit he found – who happened to be Bluebell – and sent him to fetch Bigwig, Blackberry and Fiver. When they came, he took them to join Kehaar on the short grass of the river bank.

'This is the problem, Blackberry,' he said. 'You remember that when we were under the down that evening, I said we should have to do three things: get the does out of Efrafa, break up the pursuit and then get right away so that they wouldn't find us. This plan you've thought up is clever. It'll do the first two things all right, I'm sure of that. But what about the last one? The Efrafan rabbits are fast and savage. They'll find us if we're to be found and I don't believe we can run away faster than they can follow – especially with a lot of does who've never been out of Efrafa. We couldn't possibly stand and fight them to a finish – we're too few. And on top of that, my leg seems to be bad again. So what's to be done?'

'I don't know,' answered Blackberry. 'But obviously, we shall need to disappear. Could we swim the river? No scent then, you know.'

'It's too swift,' said Hazel. 'We'd be carried away. But even if we *did* swim it, we couldn't count on not being followed. From what I've heard of these Efrafans, they'd certainly swim the river if they thought *we* had. What it comes to is that with Kehaar to help us, we can break up a pursuit while we're getting the does out, but they'll know which way we've gone and they won't leave it at that. No, you're right, we've got to vanish without a trace, so that they can't even track us. But how?'

'I don't know,' said Blackberry again. 'Shall we go up the river a little way and have a look at it? Perhaps there's something we could use for a hiding-place. Can you manage that with your leg?'

'If we don't go too far,' replied Hazel.

'Can I come, Hazel-rah?' asked Bluebell, who had been waiting about, a little way off.

'Yes, all right,' said Hazel good-naturedly, as he began to limp along the bank upstream.

They soon realized that the woodland on this left bank was lonely, thick and overgrown – denser than the nut copses and bluebell woods of Sandleford. Several times they heard the drumming of a great woodpecker, the shyest of birds. As Blackberry was suggesting that perhaps they might look for a hiding-place somewhere in this jungle, they became aware of another sound – the falling water which they had heard on their approach the day before. Soon they reached a place where the river curved round in a bend from the east, and here they came upon the broad, shallow fall. It was no more than a foot high – one of those artificial falls, common on the chalk streams, made to attract trout. Several were already rising to the evening hatch of fly. Just above the fall a plank footbridge crossed the river. Kehaar flew up, circled the pool and perched on the hand-rail.

'This is more sheltered and lonely than the bridge we crossed last night,' said Blackberry. 'Perhaps we could make some use of it. You didn't know about this bridge, Kehaar, did you?'

'Na, not know, not see heem. But ees goot pridge – no von come.'

'I'd like to go across, Hazel-rah,' said Blackberry.

'Well, Fiver's the rabbit for that,' replied Hazel. 'He simply loves crossing bridges. You carry on. I'll come behind, with Bigwig and Bluebell here.'

The five rabbits hopped slowly along the planks, their great, sensitive ears full of the sound of the falling water. Hazel, who was not sure of his footing, had to stop several times. When at length he reached the further side, he found that Fiver and Blackberry had already gone a little way downstream below the fall, and were looking at some large object sticking out from the bank. At first he thought that it must be a fallen tree-trunk, but as he came closer he saw that although it was certainly wooden, it was not round, but flat, or nearly flat, with raised edges – some man-thing.

He remembered how once, long ago, sniffing over a farm rubbish-heap with Fiver, he had come upon a similar object – large, smooth and flat. (That had, in fact, been an old, discarded door.) It had been of no use to them and they had left it alone. His inclination was to leave this alone too.

One end of the thing was pressed into the bank, but along its length it diverged, sticking out slightly into the stream. There were ripples round it, for under the banks the current was as swift as in mid-stream, on account of weed-cutting and sound camp-sheeting. As Hazel came nearer, he saw that Blackberry had actually scrambled on the thing. His claws made a faint hollow sound on the wood, so there must be water underneath. Whatever it might be, the thing did not extend downwards to the bottom: it was lying on the water.

'What are you after, Blackberry?' he said rather sharply.

'Food,' replied Blackberry. 'Flayrah. Can't you smell it?'

Kehaar had alighted on the middle of the thing, and was snapping away at something white. Blackberry scuttered along the wood towards him and began to nibble at some kind of green-stuff. After a little while Hazel also ventured out on the wood and sat in the sunshine, watching the flies on the warm, varnished surface and sniffing the strange river smells that came up from the water.

'What is this man-thing, Kehaar?' he asked. 'Is it dangerous?'

'Na, no dangerous. You not know? Ees poat. At Peeg Vater is many, many poat. Men make dem, go on vater. Ees no harm.'

Kehaar went on pecking at the broken pieces of stale bread. Blackberry, who had finished the fragments of lettuce he had found, was sitting up and looking over the very low side, watching a stone-coloured, black-spotted trout swim up into the fall. The 'boat' was a miniature punt, used for reed-cutting – little more than a raft, with a single thwart amidships. Even when it was unmanned, as now, there were only a few inches of freeboard.

'You know,' said Fiver from the bank, 'seeing you sitting there reminds me of that other wooden thing you found, when the dog was in the wood and you got Pipkin and me over the river. Do you remember?'

'I remember shoving you along,' said Bigwig. 'It was jolly cold.'

'What puzzles me,' said Blackberry, 'is why this boat-thing doesn't go along. Everything in this river goes along, and fast too – see there.' He looked out at a piece of stick floating down on the even, two-mile-an-hour current. 'So what's stopping this thing from going?'

Kehaar had a 'short way with landlubbers' manner which he sometimes used to those of the rabbits that he did not particularly like. Blackberry was not one of his favourites: he preferred straightforward characters such as Bigwig, Buckthorn and Silver.

'Ees rope. You like bite heem, den you go damn' queek, all de vay.'

'Yes, I see,' said Fiver. 'The rope goes round that metal thing where Hazel's sitting: and the other end's fixed on the bank here. It's like the stalk of a big leaf. You could gnaw it through and the leaf – the boat – would drop off the bank.'

'Well, anyway, let's go back now,' said Hazel, rather dejectedly. 'I'm afraid we don't seem to be any nearer to finding what we're looking for, Kehaar. Can you possibly wait until tomorrow? I had the idea that we might all move to somewhere a bit drier before tonight – higher up in the wood, away from the river.'

'Oh, what a pity!' said Bluebell. 'Do you know, I'd quite decided to become a water-rabbit.'

'A what?' asked Bigwig.

'A water-rabbit,' repeated Bluebell. 'Well, there are water-rats and water-beetles and Pipkin says that last night he saw a water-hawk. So why not a water-rabbit? I shall float merrily along –'

'Great golden Frith on a hill!' cried Blackberry suddenly. 'Great jumping Rabscuttle! That's it! That's it! Bluebell, you *shall* be a water-rabbit!' He began leaping and skipping about on the bank and cuffing Fiver with his front paws. 'Don't you see, Fiver? Don't you see? We bite the rope and off we go: and General Woundwort doesn't know!'

Fiver paused. 'Yes, I *do* see,' he replied at length. 'You mean on the boat. I must say, Blackberry, you're a clever fellow. I remember now that after we'd crossed that other river, you said that that floating trick might come in handy again some time.'

'Here, wait a moment,' said Hazel. 'We're just simple rabbits, Bigwig and I. Do you mind explaining?'

Then and there, while the black gnats settled on their ears, by the plank bridge and the pouring waterfall, Blackberry and Fiver explained.

'Could you just go and try the rope, Hazel-rah?' added Blackberry, when he had finished. 'It may be too thick.'

They went back to the punt.

'No, it's not,' said Hazel, 'and it's stretched tight, of course, which makes it much easier to gnaw. I can gnaw that all right.'

'Ya, ees goot,' said Kehaar. 'You go fine. But you do heem queek, ya? Maybe somet'ing change. Man come, take poat – you know?'

'There's nothing more to wait for,' said Hazel. 'Go on, Bigwig, straight away: and may El-ahrairah go with you. And remember, you're the leader now. Send word by Kehaar what you want us to do; we shall all be here, ready to back you up.'

Afterwards, they all remembered how Bigwig had taken his orders. No one could say that he did not practise what he preached. He hesitated a few moments and then looked squarely at Hazel.

'It's sudden,' he said. 'I wasn't expecting it tonight. But that's all to the good – I hated waiting. See you later.'

He touched his nose to Hazel's, turned and hopped away into the undergrowth. A few minutes later, guided by Kehaar, he was running up the open pasture north of the river, straight for the brick arch in the overgrown railway embankment and the fields that lay beyond.

34. General Woundwort

Like an obelisk towards which the principal streets of a
town converge, the strong will of a proud spirit stands
prominent and commanding in the middle of the art of war.

Clausewitz, *On War*

DUSK was falling on Efrafa. In the failing light, General
Woundwort was watching the Near Hind Mark at
silflay along the edge of the great pasture field that lay
between the warren and the iron road. Most of the rabbits
were feeding near the Mark holes, which were close beside
the field, concealed among the trees and undergrowth
bordering a lonely bridle-path. A few, however, had
ventured out into the field, to browse and play in the last
of the sun. Further out still were the sentries of the Owsla,
on the alert for the approach of men or elil and also for any
rabbit who might stray too far to be able to get underground
quickly if there should be an alarm.

Captain Chervil, one of the two officers of the Mark,
had just returned from a round of his sentries and was

talking to some of the does near the centre of the Mark ground, when he saw the General approaching. He looked quickly about to see whether anything was at fault. Since all seemed to be well, he began nibbling at a patch of sweet vernal with the best air of indifference that he could manage.

General Woundwort was a singular rabbit. Some three years before, he had been born – the strongest of a litter of five – in a burrow outside a cottage garden near Cole Henley. His father, a happy-go-lucky and reckless buck, had thought nothing of living close to human beings, except that he would be able to forage in their garden in the early morning. He had paid dearly for his rashness. After two or three weeks of spoiled lettuces and nibbled cabbage-plants, the cottager had lain in wait and shot him as he came through the potato-patch at dawn. The same morning, the man set to work to dig out the doe and her growing litter. Woundwort's mother escaped, racing across the kale-field towards the downs, her kittens doing their best to follow her. None but Woundwort succeeded. His mother, bleeding from a shot-gun pellet, made her way along the hedges in broad daylight, with Woundwort limping beside her.

It was not long before a weasel picked up the scent of the blood and followed it. The little rabbit cowered in the grass while his mother was killed before his eyes. He made no attempt to run, but the weasel, its hunger satisfied, left him alone and made off through the bushes. Several hours later a kind old schoolmaster from Overton, walking through the fields, came upon Woundwort nuzzling the cold, still body and crying. He carried him home to his own kitchen and saved his life, feeding him with milk from a nasal dropper until he was old enough to eat bran and greenstuff. But Woundwort grew up very wild and, like Cowper's hare, would bite when he could. In a month he was big and strong and had become savage. He nearly killed the schoolmaster's cat, which had found him at liberty in the kitchen and tried to torment him. One night, a week later, he tore the wire from the front of his hutch and escaped to the open country.

Most rabbits in his situation, lacking almost all experience of wild life, would have fallen victim at once to the elil: but not Woundwort. After a few days' wandering, he came upon a small warren and, snarling and clawing, forced them to accept him. Soon he had become Chief Rabbit, having killed both the previous Chief and a rival named Fiorin. In combat he was terrifying, fighting entirely to kill, indifferent to any wounds he received himself and closing with his adversaries until his weight overbore and exhausted them. Those who had no heart to oppose him were not long in feeling that here was a leader indeed.

Woundwort was ready to fight anything except a fox. One evening he attacked and drove off a foraging Aberdeen puppy. He was impervious to the fascination of the mustelidae and hoped some day to kill a weasel, if not a stoat. When he had explored the limits of his own strength, he set to work to satisfy his longing for still more power in the only possible way – by increasing the power of the rabbits about him. He needed a bigger kingdom. Men were the great danger, but this could be circumvented by cunning and discipline. He left the small warren, taking his followers with him, and set out to look for a place suited to his purpose, where the very existence of rabbits could be concealed and extermination made very difficult.

Efrafa grew up round the crossing-point of two green bridle-paths, one of which (the east-to-west) was tunnel-like, bordered on both sides by a thick growth of trees and bushes. The immigrants, under Woundwort's direction, dug their holes between the roots of the trees, in the undergrowth and along the ditches. From the first the warren prospered. Woundwort watched over them with a tireless zeal that won their loyalty even while they feared him. When the does stopped digging, Woundwort himself went on with their work while they slept. If a man was coming, Woundwort spotted him half a mile away. He fought rats, magpies, grey squirrels and, once, a crow. When litters were kindled, he kept an eye on their growth, picked out the strongest youngsters for the Owsla and trained them himself. He would allow no rabbit to leave the warren. Quite early on, three who tried to do so were hunted down and forced to return.

As the warren grew, so Woundwort developed his system to keep it under control. Crowds of rabbits feeding at morning and evening were likely to attract attention. He devised the Marks, each controlled by its own officers and sentries, with feeding-times changed regularly to give all a share of early morning and sunset – the favourite hours for silflay. All signs of rabbit life were concealed as closely as possible. The Owsla had privileges in regard to feeding, mating and freedom of movement. Any failure of duty on their part was liable to be punished by demotion and loss of privileges. For ordinary rabbits, the punishments were more severe.

When it was no longer possible for Woundwort to be everywhere, the Council was set up. Some of the members came from the Owsla, but others were selected solely for their loyalty or their cunning as advisers. Old Snowdrop was growing deaf, but no one knew more than he about organizing a warren for safety. On his advice, the runs and burrows of the various Marks were not connected underground, so that disease or poison, if they came, would spread less readily. Conspiracy would also spread less readily. To visit the burrows of another Mark was not allowed without an officer's permission. It was on Snowdrop's advice, too, that Woundwort at length ordered that the warren was not to extend further, on account of the risk of detection and the weakening of central control. He was persuaded only with difficulty, for the new policy frustrated his restless desire of power after power. This now needed another outlet and soon after the warren had been stopped from growing, he introduced the Wide Patrols.

The Wide Patrols began as mere forays or raids, led by Woundwort, into the surrounding country. He would simply pick four or five of the Owsla and take them out to look for trouble. On the first occasion they were lucky enough to find and kill a sick owl that had eaten a mouse that had eaten poison-dressed seed-corn. On the next, they came upon two hlessil whom they compelled to return with them to join the warren. Woundwort was no mere bully. He knew how to encourage other rabbits and to fill them with a spirit of emulation. It was not long before his officers were asking to be allowed to lead patrols. Woundwort would give them tasks – to search for hlessil in a certain direction or to find out whether a particular ditch or barn contained rats which could later be attacked in force and driven out. Only from farms and gardens were they ordered to keep clear. One of these patrols, led by a certain Captain Orchis, discovered a small warren two miles to the east, beyond the Kingsclere–Overton road, on the outskirts of Nutley Copse. The General led an expedition against it and broke it up, the prisoners being brought back to Efrafa, where a few of them later rose to be Owsla members themselves.

As the months went on, the Wide Patrols became systematic; during summer and early autumn there were usually two or three out at a time. There came to be no other rabbits for a long way round Efrafa and any who might wander into the neighbourhood by chance were quickly picked up. Casualties in the Wide Patrols were high, for the elil got to know that they went out. Often, it would take all a leader's courage and skill to complete his task and bring his rabbits – or some of his rabbits – back to the warren. But the Owsla were proud of the risks they ran: and besides, Woundwort was in the habit of going out himself to see how they were getting on. A patrol leader, more than a mile from Efrafa, limping up a hedgerow in the rain, would come upon the General, squatting like a hare under a tussock of darnel, and find himself required then and there to report what he had been doing or why he was off his route. The patrols were the training-grounds of cunning trackers, swift runners and fierce fighters, and the casualties – although there might be as many as five or six in a bad month – suited Woundwort's purpose, for numbers needed keeping down and there were always fresh vacancies in the Owsla, which the younger bucks did their best to be good enough to fill. To feel that rabbits were competing to risk their lives at his orders gratified Woundwort, although he believed – and so did his Council and his Owsla – that he was giving the warren peace and security at a price which was modest enough.

Nevertheless, this evening, as he came out from among the ash-trees to talk to Captain Chervil, the General was feeling seriously concerned about several things. It was less and less easy to keep the size of the warren under control. Overcrowding was becoming a grave problem, and this despite the fact that many of the does were reabsorbing their litters before birth. While their doing so was all to the good in itself, some of them were growing restive and hard to manage. Not long ago, a group of does had come before the Council and asked to leave the warren. They had been peaceable at first, offering to go as far away as the Council wished: but when it had become plain that their request was not going to be granted on any terms, they had become first petulant and then aggressive and the Council had had to take strong measures. There was still a good deal of bad feeling over the business. Then in the third place, the Owsla had lately lost a certain amount of respect among the rank-and-file.

Four wandering rabbits – giving themselves out to be some kind of embassy from another warren – had been held and impressed into the Right Flank Mark. He had intended, later, to find out where they had come from. But they had succeeded in playing a very simple trick, bamboozling the Mark commander, attacking his sentries and escaping by night. Captain Bugloss, the officer responsible, had, of course, been demoted and expelled from the Owsla, but his disgrace, though very proper, only added to the General's difficulties. The truth was that Efrafa had become, for the moment, short of good officers. Ordinary Owsla – sentries – were not too hard to find, but officers were another matter and he had lost three in less than a month. Bugloss was as good as a casualty: he would never hold rank again. But worse, Captain Charlock – a brave and resourceful rabbit – while leading the pursuit of the fugitives, had been run down on the iron road by a train; a further proof, if any were needed, of the wicked malice of men. Worst of all, only two nights ago a patrol which had been out to the north had returned with the shocking news that its leader, Captain Mallow, an officer of exceptional prestige and experience, had been killed by a fox. It was an odd business. The patrol had picked up the scent of a fairly large party of rabbits evidently coming towards Efrafa from the north. They had been following it but had not yet sighted their quarry, when suddenly a strange rabbit had burst in upon them as they were nearing the edge of some woodland. They had, of course, tried to stop him and at that moment the fox, which had apparently been following him closely, had come from the open combe beyond and killed poor Mallow in an instant. All things considered, the patrol had come away in good order and

Groundsel, the second-in-command, had done well. But nothing more had been seen of the strange rabbit; and the loss of Mallow, with nothing to show for it, had upset and demoralized the Owsla a good deal.

Other patrols had been sent out at once, but all that they had established was that the rabbits from the north had crossed the iron road and disappeared southwards. It was intolerable that they should have passed so close to Efrafa and gone their way without being apprehended. Even now, they might possibly be caught, if only there were a really enterprising officer to put in charge of the search. It would certainly need an enterprising officer – Captain Campion perhaps – for patrols seldom crossed the iron road and the wet country beyond – the country near the river – was only partly known. He would have gone himself, but with the recent disciplinary troubles in the warren he could not take the risk; and Campion could hardly be spared just now. No – infuriating as it was, the strangers were best forgotten for the moment. The first thing was to replace the Owsla losses – and preferably with rabbits who knew how to deal ruthlessly with any further signs of dissension. They would simply have to promote the best they had got, draw their horns in for a time and concentrate on training until things got back to normal.

Woundwort greeted Captain Chervil rather abstractedly and went on turning the problem over in his mind.

'What are your sentries like, Chervil?' he asked at length. 'Do I know any of them?'

'They're a good lot, sir,' replied Chervil. 'You know Marjoram: he's been on patrol with you as a runner. And I think you know Moneywort.'

'Yes, I know them,' said Woundwort, 'but they wouldn't make officers. We need to replace Charlock and Mallow: that's what I'm getting at.'

'That's difficult, sir,' said Chervil. 'That sort of rabbit doesn't hop out of the grass.'

'Well, they've got to hop from somewhere,' said Woundwort. 'You'd better think about it and tell me any ideas that occur to you. Anyway, I want to go round your sentries now. Come with me, will you?'

They were about to set off when a third rabbit approached – none other than Captain Campion himself. It was Campion's principal duty to search the outskirts of Efrafa at morning and evening and to report anything new – the tyre-marks of a tractor in mud, the droppings of a sparrow-hawk or the spreading of fertilizer on a field. An expert tracker, he missed little or nothing and was one of the very few rabbits for whom Woundwort felt a genuine respect.

'Do you want me?' said Woundwort, pausing.

'Well, I think so, sir,' replied Campion. 'We've picked up a hlessi and brought him in.'

'Where was he?'

'Down by the arch, sir. Just this side of it.'

'What was he doing?'

'Well, sir, he says he's come a long way on purpose to join Efrafa. That's why I thought you might like to see him.'

'*Wants* to join Efrafa?' asked Woundwort, puzzled.

'That's what he says, sir.'

'Why can't the Council see him tomorrow?'

'Just as you like, sir, of course. But he strikes me as being a bit out of the ordinary. I'd say, a distinctly useful rabbit.'

'H'm,' said Woundwort, considering. 'Well, all right. I haven't got long, though. Where is he now?'

'At the Crixa, sir.' (Campion meant the crossing-point of the two bridle-paths, which was about fifty yards away, among the trees.) 'Two of my patrol are with him.'

Woundwort made his way back to the Crixa. Chervil, being on duty with his Mark, remained where he was. Campion accompanied the General.

At this hour the Crixa was all green shade, with red gleams of sun that winked through the moving leaves. The damp grass along the edges of the paths was dotted with spikes of mauve bugle, and the sanicles and yellow archangels flowered thickly. Under an elder bush, on the far side of the track, two Owslafa, or Council police, were waiting; and with them was the stranger.

Woundwort saw at once what Campion had meant. The stranger was a big rabbit, heavy but alert, with a rugged, seasoned appearance and the look of a fighter. He had a curious, thick growth of fur – a kind of top-knot – on the crown of his head. He stared at Woundwort with a detached, appraising air which the General had not encountered for a very long time.

'Who are you?' said Woundwort.

'My name is Thlayli,' replied the stranger.

'Thlayli, *sir*,' prompted Campion. The stranger said nothing.

'The patrol brought you in, I'm told. What were you doing?'

'I've come to join Efrafa.'

'Why?'

'I'm surprised you ask. It's your warren, isn't it? Is there anything odd about someone wanting to join?'

Woundwort was nonplussed. He was no fool and it was, he could not help feeling, extremely odd that any right-minded rabbit should choose to walk into Efrafa of his own accord. But he could hardly say so.

'What can you do?'

'I can run and fight and spoil a story telling it. I've been an officer in an Owsla.'

'Fight, can you? Could you fight him?' said Woundwort, looking at Campion.

'Certainly, if you wish.' The stranger reared up and aimed a heavy cuff at Campion, who leapt back just in time.

'Don't be a fool,' said Woundwort. 'Sit down. Where were you in an Owsla?'

'Far off. The warren was destroyed by men, but I escaped. I've been wandering some time. It won't surprise you that I heard of Efrafa. I've come a long way to join it. I thought you might have some use for me.'

'Are you alone?'

'I am now.'

Woundwort considered again. It was likely enough that this rabbit had been an officer in an Owsla. Any Owsla would want him. If he was speaking the truth, he had had wits enough to escape the destruction of his warren and survive a long journey through open country. It must have been a very long journey, for there was no warren within the normal range of the Efrafan patrols.

'Well,' he said at length, 'I dare say we might be able to find some use for you, as you put it. Campion here will look after you tonight and tomorrow morning you'll come before the Council. Meanwhile, don't start fighting, do you see? We can give you plenty to do without that.'

'Very well.'

The following morning, after the Council had discussed the predicament of the warren due to the recent losses, General Woundwort proposed that for a start, they might do worse than try the big newcomer as an officer in the Near Hind Mark, under the instruction of Captain Chervil. The Council, having seen him, agreed. By ni-Frith Thlayli, still bleeding from the Mark gash inflicted in his left haunch, had taken up his duties.

35. Groping

This world, where much is to be done, and little known ...

Dr Johnson

'—AND then before the Mark silflay,' said Chervil, 'I always have a look at the weather. The previous Mark send a runner, of course, to say when they're going down, and he reports on the weather, but I always go and have a look for myself as well. In moonlight we put the sentries fairly close in and keep on the move ourselves to make sure no one goes too far. But in rain or darkness we send the Mark up in small groups, one after the other, and each group has a sentry in charge. In absolutely desperate weather we ask the General's permission to postpone the silflay.'

'But do they often try to run away?' asked Bigwig. During the afternoon he had been up and down the runs and crowded burrows with Chervil and Avens, the other Mark officer, and had thought to himself that never in his life had he seen such a cheerless, dispirited lot of rabbits. 'They don't strike me as a very difficult bunch.'

'Most of them are no trouble, it's true,' said Avens, 'but you never know when trouble's coming. For instance, you'd have said there wasn't a more docile lot in Efrafa than the Right Flank. And then one day they get four hlessil wished on them by the Council and the next evening Bugloss isn't very quick in the uptake for some reason; and suddenly these hlessil play a trick on him and bunk. And that's the end of him – to say nothing of poor old Charlock killed on the iron road. When something like that happens, it happens like lightning and it isn't always planned: sometimes it's more like a frenzy. A rabbit tears away on impulse and if you don't knock him over quick, the next thing you know three more will be off after him. The only safe way is to watch all the time when they're above ground and do your own relaxing when you can. After all, that's what we're here for – that and the patrols.'

'Now, about burying hraka,' said Chervil, 'you can't be too strict. If the General finds any hraka in the fields he'll stuff your tail down your throat. They always try to dodge burying, though. They want to be natural, the anti-social little beasts. They just don't realize that everyone's good depends on everyone's cooperation. What I do is to set three or four of them to dig a new trough in the ditch every day, as a punishment. You can nearly always find someone to punish if you try hard enough. Today's squad fills up yesterday's trough and digs another. There are special runs leading into the bottom of the ditch and the Mark have got to use those and no others when they go out to pass hraka. We keep a hraka-sentry in the ditch to make sure they come back.'

'How do you check them in after silflay?' asked Bigwig.

'Well, we know them all by sight,' replied Chervil, 'and we watch them go down. There are only two entrance holes for the Mark and one of us sits at each hole. Every rabbit knows which hole he has to use and I should certainly miss any of mine who didn't go down. The sentries come in last of all – I only call them in when I'm quite sure that all the Mark are down. And once they're down, of course, they can't very well get out, with a sentry at each hole. Digging I should hear. You're not allowed to dig in Efrafa without permission from the Council. The only really dangerous time is when there's an alarm – say, a man or a fox. Then we all bolt for the nearest hole, of course. So far, it doesn't seem to have occurred to anyone that he could bolt the other way and have quite a long start before he was missed. Still, no rabbit will bolt towards elil, and that's the real safeguard.'

'Well, I admire your thoroughness,' said Bigwig, thinking to himself that his secret task seemed to be even more hopeless than he had expected. 'I'll get the hang of it all as soon as I can. When do we have the chance of a patrol?'

'I expect the General will take you on patrol himself to begin with,' said Avens. 'He did me. You may not be so keen when you've had a day or two with him – you'll be worn out. Still, I must admit, Thlayli, you're a fine size, and if you've been living rough for some time you'll probably manage it all right.'

At this moment a rabbit with a white scar across his throat came down the run.

'The Neck Mark's just going down, Captain Chervil, sir,' he said. 'It's a beautiful evening: I should make the most of it.'

'I was wondering when you were going to show up,' replied Chervil. 'Tell Captain Sainfoin I'm bringing my Mark up at once.'

Turning to one of his own sentries who was close by, Chervil told him to go round the burrows and send everyone up for silflay.

'Now,' he said, 'Avens, you go to the further hole as usual, and Thlayli can join me on the nearer one. We'll send four sentries out to the line to start with, and when the Mark have all gone out, we'll add four more and keep two in reserve. I'll see you in the usual place, by the big flint in the bank.'

Bigwig followed Chervil along the run, down which came the scents of warm grass, clover and hop trefoil. He had found most of the runs closer and stuffier than he was used to, no doubt because there were so few holes into the open air. The prospect of an evening silflay, even in Efrafa, was pleasant. He thought of the beech leaves rustling above the far-off Honeycomb, and sighed. 'I wonder how old Holly's getting on,' he thought, 'and whether I'll ever see him again: or Hazel either, for the matter of that. Well, I'll give these blighters something to think about before I've finished. I do feel lonely, though. How hard it is to carry a secret by yourself!'

They reached the mouth of the hole and Chervil went outside to look round. When he returned he took up station at the top of the run. As Bigwig found a place alongside, he noticed for the first time, in the opposite wall of the run, a kind of recess like an open cave. In this, three rabbits were squatting. Those on either side had the tough, stolid look of members of the Owslafa. But it was at the one in the middle that he stared. This rabbit had very dark fur – almost black. But this was not the most remarkable thing about him. He was dreadfully mutilated. His ears were nothing but shapeless shreds, ragged at the edges, seamed with ill-knit scars and beaded here and there with lumps of proud, bare flesh. One eyelid was misshapen and closed askew. Despite the cool, exciting air of the July evening, he seemed apathetic and torpid. He kept his gaze fixed on the ground and blinked continually. After a time, he lowered his head and rubbed his nose on his fore-paws in a listless manner. Then he scratched his neck and settled down in his former, drooping position.

Bigwig, his warm, impulsive nature stirred by curiosity and pity, went across the run.

'Who are you?' he asked.

'My name is Blackavar, sir,' replied the rabbit. He did not look up and spoke without expression, as though he had answered this question many times before.

'Are you going to silflay?' said Bigwig. No doubt, he thought, this was some hero of the warren, wounded in a great fight and now infirm, whose past services merited an honourable escort when he went out.

'No, sir,' answered the rabbit.

'Why ever not?' said Bigwig. 'It's a lovely evening.'

'I don't silflay at this time, sir.'

'Then why are you here?' asked Bigwig, with his usual directness.

'The Mark that has the evening silflay, sir,' began the rabbit. 'The Mark that has – they come – I –' He hesitated and fell silent.

One of the Owslafa spoke. 'Get on with it,' he said.

'I come here for the Mark to see me,' said the rabbit in his low, drained voice. 'Every Mark should see how I have been punished as I deserve for my treachery in trying to leave the warren. The Council were merciful – the Council were merciful – the Council – I can't remember it, sir, I really can't,' he burst out, turning to the sentry who had spoken. 'I can't seem to remember anything.'

The sentry said nothing. Bigwig, after staring in shocked silence for a few moments, rejoined Chervil.

'He's supposed to tell everybody who asks,' said Chervil, 'but he's getting sort of stupid after half a month of it. He tried to run away. Campion caught him and brought him back and the Council ripped up his ears and said he had to be shown at every morning and evening silflay, as an example to the others. But if you ask me, he won't last much longer. He'll meet a blacker rabbit than himself one of these nights.'

Bigwig shuddered, partly at Chervil's tone of callous indifference and partly at his own memories. The Mark were filing up now and he watched as they went past, each darkening the entrance for a moment before hopping out under the hawthorn. It was clear that Chevril prided himself on knowing his rabbits by name. He spoke to most of them and was at pains to show that he had some knowledge of their personal lives. It seemed to Bigwig that the answers he got were not particularly warm or friendly, but he did not know whether to put that down to dislike of Chervil or merely to the lack of spirit that seemed to be common to the rank-and-file in Efrafa. He was closely on the watch – as Blackberry had advised him to be – for any signs of disaffection or rebellion, but he could see little grounds for hope in the expressionless faces that went by. At the end came a little group of three or four does, talking among themselves.

'Well, are you getting on all right with your new friends, Nelthilta?' said Chervil to the first, as she passed him.

The doe, a pretty, long-nosed rabbit not more than three months old, stopped and looked at him.

'You'll get on yourself one day, Captain, I dare say,' she replied. 'Like Captain Mallow – he got on, you know. Why don't you send some does on Wide Patrol?'

She paused for Chervil to reply, but he made no answer and did not speak to the does who followed Nelthilta out into the field.

'What did she mean by that?' asked Bigwig.

'Well, there's been trouble, you know,' said Chervil. 'A bunch of does in the Near Fore started a row at a Council meeting. The General said they must be broken up and we had a couple sent to us. I've been keeping an eye on them. They're no trouble themselves but Nelthilta's taken up with them and it seems to have made her cheeky and resentful: sort of thing you saw just now. I don't really mind that – it shows they feel the Owsla's on top. If the young does became quiet and polite I should be much more worried: I should wonder what they were up to. All the same, Thlayli, I'd like you to do what you can to get to know those particular does, and bring them a bit more into line.'

'Right,' said Bigwig. 'By the way, what are the rules about mating?'

'Mating?' said Chervil. 'Well, if you want a doe you have one – any doe in the Mark, that is. We're not officers for nothing, are we? The does are under orders and none of the bucks can stop you. That just leaves you and me and Avens; and we shall hardly quarrel. There are plenty of does, after all.'

'I see,' said Bigwig. 'Well, I'll silflay now. Unless you've got any other ideas, I'll go and talk to some of the Mark and then go round the sentries and get the lie of the land. What about Blackavar?'

'Leave him,' said Chervil. 'He's none of our business. The Owslafa will keep him here until the Mark come back and after that they'll take him away.'

Bigwig made his way into the field, conscious of the wary glances of the rabbits he passed. He felt perplexed and apprehensive. How was he to begin his dangerous task? Begin he must, in one way or another, for Kehaar had made it clear that he was not ready to wait. There was nothing for it but to take a chance and trust somebody. But whom? A warren like this must be full of spies. Probably only General Woundwort knew who the spies were. Was there a spy watching him now?

'I shall just have to trust my feelings,' he thought. 'I'll go round the place a bit and see if I can make any friends. But I know one thing – if I *do* succeed in getting any does out of here, I'll take that poor wretched Blackavar with me as well. Frith on a bridge! It makes me angry just to think of him being forced to sit there like that. General Woundwort indeed! A gun's too good for him.'

Nibbling and pondering, he moved slowly over the open meadow in the evening sun. After a while he found that he was approaching a small hollow, much like the one on Watership Down where he and Silver had found Kehaar. In this hollow there were four does, with their backs to him. He recognized them as the little group who had gone out last. They had evidently finished the hungry, intent stage of feeding and were browsing and talking at leisure, and he could see that one of them had the attention of the other three. Even more than most rabbits, Bigwig loved a story and now he felt attracted by the prospect of hearing something new in this strange warren. He moved quietly up to the edge of the hollow just as the doe began to speak.

At once he realized that this was no story. Yet he had heard the like before, somewhere. The rapt air, the rhythmic utterance, the intent listeners – what was it they recalled? Then he remembered the smell of carrots, and Silverweed dominating the crowd in the great burrow. But these verses went to his heart as Silverweed's had not.

'Long ago
The yellow-hammer sang, high on the thorn.
He sang near a litter that the doe brought out to play,
He sang in the wind and the kittens played below.
Their time slipped by all under the elder bloom.
But the bird flew away and now my heart is dark
And time will never play in the fields again.

Long ago
The orange beetles clung to the rye-grass stems.
The windy grass was waving. A buck and doe
Ran through the meadow. They scratched a hole in the bank,
They did what they pleased all under the hazel leaves.
But the beetles died in the frost and my heart is dark;
And I shall never choose a mate again.
The frost is falling, the frost falls into my body.
My nostrils, my ears are torpid under the frost.
The swift will come in the spring, crying "News! News!
Does, dig new holes and flow with milk for your litters."
I shall not hear. The embryos return
Into my dulled body. Across my sleep
There runs a wire fence to imprison the wind.
I shall never feel the wind blowing again.'

The doe was silent and her three companions said nothing: but their stillness showed plainly enough that she had spoken for all of them. A flock of starlings passed overhead, chattering and whistling, and a liquid dropping fell into the grass among the little group, but none moved or startled. Each seemed taken up with the same melancholy thoughts – thoughts which, however sad, were at least far from Efrafa.

Bigwig's spirit was as tough as his body and quite without sentimentality, but like most creatures who have experienced hardship and danger, he could recognize and respect suffering when he saw it. He was accustomed to sizing up other rabbits and deciding what they were good for. It struck him that these does were not far from the end of their powers. A wild animal that feels that it no longer has any reason to live, reaches in the end a point when its remaining energies may actually be directed towards dying. It was this state of mind that Bigwig had mistakenly attributed to Fiver in the warren of the snares. Since then his judgement had matured. He felt that despair was not far from these does; and from all that he had heard of Efrafa, both from Holly and from Chervil, he could understand why. He knew that the effects of overcrowding and tension in a warren show themselves first in the does. They become infertile and aggressive. But if aggression cannot mend their troubles, then often they begin to drift towards the only other way out. He wondered what point of this dismal path these particular does had reached.

He hopped down into the hollow. The does, disturbed from their thoughts, looked at him resentfully and drew back.

'I know you're Nelthilta,' said Bigwig to the pretty young doe who had retorted to Chervil in the run. 'But what's your name?' he went on, turning to the doe beside her.

After a pause, she answered reluctantly, 'Thethuthinnang, sir.'*

'And yours?' said Bigwig, to the doe who had spoken the verses.

She turned to him a look of such wretchedness, so full of accusation and suffering, that it was all he could do not to beg her then and there to believe that he was her secret

---

* Thethuthinnang: Movement-of-leaves. The first and last syllables are stressed, as in the phrase 'Once in a way'.

friend and that he hated Efrafa and the authority which he represented. Nelthilta's rejoinder to Chervil in the run had been full of hatred, but this doe's gaze spoke of wrongs beyond her power to express. As Bigwig stared back at her, he suddenly recalled Holly's description of the great yellow hrududu that had torn open the earth above the destroyed warren. 'That might have met a look like this,' he thought. Then the doe answered, 'My name is Hyzenthlay, sir.'

'Hyzenthlay?' said Bigwig, startled out of his self-possession. 'Then it was you who –' He stopped. It might be dangerous to ask whether she remembered speaking to Holly. But whether she did or not, here, evidently, was the rabbit who had told Holly and his companions about the troubles of Efrafa and the discontent of the does. If he remembered Holly's story rightly, she had already made some sort of attempt to leave the warren. 'But,' he thought, as he met once more her desolate eyes, 'what is she good for now?'

'May we have permission to go, sir?' asked Nelthilta. 'The company of officers absolutely overpowers us, you see: we find a little of it goes an awfully long way.'

'Oh – yes – certainly – by all means,' replied Bigwig in confusion. He remained where he was as the does hopped away, Nelthilta raising her voice to remark, 'What a great oaf!' and half looking round in the evident hope that he would take her up.

'Oh well, there's one of them with some spirit left, anyway,' he thought, as he made his way out to the sentries.

He spent some time talking to the sentries and learning how they were organized. It was a depressingly efficient system. Each sentry could reach his neighbour in a matter of moments; and the appropriate stamping signal – for they had more than one – would bring out the officers and the reserves. If necessary, the Owslafa could be alerted in almost no time at all and so could Captain Campion, or whatever officer might be patrolling the outskirts of the warren. Since only one Mark fed at a time, there could hardly be any confusion about where to go if an alarm were given. One of the sentries, Marjoram, told him about the attempted escape by Blackavar.

'He pretended to feed his way out as far as he could,' said Marjoram, 'and then he made a dash. He actually managed to knock down two sentries who tried to stop him; and I doubt whether anyone on his own has ever done as much as that. He ran like mad, but Campion had got the alarm, you see, and he simply moved round and intercepted him further down the fields. Of course, if he hadn't smashed up the sentries the Council might have let him off more lightly.'

'Do you like the warren life?' asked Bigwig.

'It's not too bad now I'm in the Owsla,' answered Marjoram, 'and if I can get to be an officer it'll be better still. I've done two Wide Patrols now – they're the thing for getting yourself noticed. I can track and fight as well as most, but of course they want more than that from an officer. I think our officers are a strong bunch, don't you?'

'Yes, I do,' said Bigwig with feeling. It struck him that Marjoram evidently did not know that he himself was a newcomer to Efrafa. At any rate, he showed neither jealousy nor resentment. Bigwig was beginning to realize that in this place, nobody was told more than was good for him; or got to know much, except what was before his nose. Marjoram probably supposed that he, Bigwig, had been promoted out of another Mark.

As darkness fell, just before the end of the silflay, Captain Campion came up the field with a patrol of three and Chervil ran out to meet him on the sentry-line. Bigwig joined them and listened to the talk. He gathered that Campion had been out as far as the iron road but had found nothing unusual.

'Don't you ever go beyond the iron road?' he asked.

'Not very often,' answered Campion. 'It's wet, you know – bad rabbit country. I have been there, but on these ordinary circuit patrols I'm really looking nearer home. My job is partly to notice anything new that the Council ought to know about, and partly to make sure we pick up anyone who bolts. Like that miserable Blackavar – and he gave me a bite I shan't forget, before I got him down. On a fine evening like this, I generally go down as far as the bank of the iron road and then work along this side of it. Or sometimes I go out in the other direction, as far as the barn. It all depends what's wanted. By the way, I saw the General earlier this evening and I rather think he means to take you on patrol in two or three days' time, as soon as you've settled down and your Mark have come off the dawn and evening silflay.'

'Why wait for that?' said Bigwig with all the enthusiasm he could assume. 'Why not sooner?'

'Well, a Mark generally keeps a full Owsla when it's on dawn and evening silflay. The rabbits are more lively at those times, you see, and need more supervision. But a Mark that's on ni-Frith and fu-Inlé silflay can generally spare Owsla for a Wide Patrol. Now, I'll leave you here. I've got to take my lot to the Crixa and report to the General.'

As soon as the Mark had gone underground and Blackavar had been taken away by his escort, Bigwig excused himself to Chervil and Avens and went to his own burrow. Although the rank-and-file were cramped underground, the sentries had two large, roomy burrows to themselves, while each officer had a private burrow. By himself at last, Bigwig settled down to think over his problem.

The difficulties were bewildering. He was fairly certain that with Kehaar's help he himself could escape from Efrafa whenever he wished. But how in the world was he to bring a bunch of does out – supposing that any were ready to try it? If he took it upon himself to call the sentries in during a silflay, Chervil would see what he had done in a matter of moments. The only possibility, then, was to make the breakout during the day: to wait until Chervil was asleep and then order a sentry to leave his post at the mouth of one of the holes. Bigwig considered. He could see no flaw in this idea. Then the thought came to him, 'And what about Blackavar?' Blackavar presumably spent the day under guard in some special burrow. Probably hardly anyone knew where – no one knew anything in Efrafa – and certainly no one would tell. So he would have to leave Blackavar: no realistic plan could include him.

'I'll be jiggered if I leave him,' muttered Bigwig to himself. 'I know Blackberry would say I was a fool. Still, he's not here and I'm doing this myself. But suppose I wreck the whole thing because of Blackavar? Oh, Frith in a barn! What a business!'

He thought until he realized that he was thinking in circles. After a time, he fell asleep. When he woke, he could tell that it was moonlight outside, fine and still. It occurred to him that perhaps he might start his venture from the other end – by persuading some of the does to join him and working out a plan afterwards, perhaps with their help. He went down the run until he came upon a young rabbit sleeping as best he could outside an over-crowded burrow. He woke him.

'Do you know Hyzenthlay?' he asked.

'Oh yes, sir,' replied the rabbit, with a rather pathetic attempt to sound brisk and ready.

'Go and find her and tell her to come to my burrow,' said Bigwig. 'No one else is to come with her. Do you understand?'

'Yes, sir.'

When the youngster had scurried off, Bigwig returned to his burrow, wondering whether there would be any suspicion. It seemed unlikely. From what Chervil had said, it was common enough for Efrafan officers to send for does. If he were questioned he had only to play up. He lay down and waited.

In the dark, a rabbit came slowly up the run and stopped at the entrance to the burrow. There was a pause.

'Hyzenthlay?' said Bigwig.

'I am Hyzenthlay.'

'I want to talk to you,' said Bigwig.

'I am in the Mark, sir, and under your orders. But you have made a mistake.'

'No, I haven't,' replied Bigwig. 'You needn't be afraid. Come in here, close beside me.'

Hyzenthlay obeyed. He could feel her fast pulse. Her body was tense: her eyes were closed and her claws dug into the floor.

'Hyzenthlay,' whispered Bigwig in her ear, 'listen carefully. You remember that many days ago now, four rabbits came to Efrafa in the evening. One had very pale grey fur and one had a healed rat-bite in his foreleg. You talked with their leader – his name was Holly. I know what he told you.'

She turned her head in fear. 'How do you know?'

'Never mind. Only listen to me.'

Then Bigwig spoke of Hazel and Fiver; of the destruction of the Sandleford warren and the journey to Watership Down. Hyzenthlay neither moved nor interrupted.

'The rabbits who talked to you that evening,' said Bigwig, 'who told you about the warren that was destroyed and of how they had come to ask for does from Efrafa – do you know what became of them?'

Hyzenthlay's reply was no more than the faintest murmur in his ear.

'I know what I heard. They escaped the next evening. Captain Charlock was killed pursuing them.'

'And was any other patrol sent after them, Hyzenthlay? The next day, I mean?'

'We heard that there was no officer to spare, with Bugloss under arrest and Charlock dead.'

'Those rabbits returned to us safely. One of them is not far away now, with Hazel and Fiver and several more. They are cunning and resourceful. They are waiting for me to bring does out of Efrafa – as many as I can get to come. I shall be able to send them a message tomorrow morning.'

'How?'

'By a bird – if all goes well.' Bigwig told her about Kehaar. When he had finished, Hyzenthlay made no reply and he could not tell whether she was considering all that he had said or whether fear and disbelief had so troubled her that she did not know what to say. Did she think he was a spy trying to trap her? Did she perhaps wish only that he would let her go away? At last he said,

'Do you believe me?'

'Yes, I believe you.'

'Might I not be a spy sent by the Council?'

'You are not. I can tell.'

'How?'

'You spoke of your friend – the one who knew that that warren was a bad place. He is not the only such rabbit. Sometimes I can tell these things too: but not often now, for my heart is in the frost.'

'Then will you join me – and persuade your friends as well? We need you: Efrafa doesn't need you.'

Again she was silent. Bigwig could hear a worm moving in the earth nearby and faintly down the tunnel came the sound of some small creature pattering through the grass outside. He waited quietly, knowing that it was vital that he should not upset her.

At last she spoke again, so low in his ear that the words seemed barely more than broken cadences of breathing.

'We can escape from Efrafa. The danger is very great, but in that we can succeed. It is beyond that I cannot see. Confusion and fear at nightfall – and then men, men, it is all things of men! A dog – a rope that snaps like a dry branch. A rabbit – no, it is not possible! – a rabbit that rides in a hrududu! Oh, I have become foolish – tales for kittens on a summer evening. No, I cannot see as I did once: it is like the shapes of trees beyond a field of rain.'

'Well, you'd better come and meet this friend of mine,' said Bigwig. 'He talks just like that, and I've come to trust him, so I trust you too. If you feel we're going to succeed, that's fine. But what I'm asking is whether you'll bring your friends to join us.'

After another silence, Hyzenthlay said,

'My courage – my spirit: it's so much less than it was. I'm afraid to let you rely on me.'

'I can tell that. What is it that's worn you down? Weren't you the leader of the does who went to the Council?'

'There was myself and Thethuthinnang. I don't know what's happened to the other does who were with us. We were all in the Right Fore Mark then, you know. I've still got the Right Fore mark, but I've been marked again since. Blackavar – you saw him?'

'Yes, of course.'

'He was in that Mark. He was our friend and encouraged us. Only a night or two after the does went up to speak to the Council, he tried to run away, but he was caught. You've seen what they did to him. That was the same evening that your friends came: and the next night they escaped. After that, the Council sent for us does once more. The General said that no one else would have the chance to run away. We were to be split up among the Marks, no more than two to each Mark. I don't know why they left Thethuthinnang and me together. Perhaps they didn't stop to think. Efrafa's like that, you know. The order was "Two to each Mark", so as long as the order was carried out it didn't particularly matter which two. Now I'm frightened and I feel the Council are always watching.'

'Yes, but *I'm* here now,' said Bigwig.

'The Council are very cunning.'

'They'll need to be. We've got some rabbits who are far more cunning, believe me. El-ahrairah's Owsla, no less. But tell me – was Nelthilta with you when you went to the Council?'

'Oh no, she was born here, in the Near Hind. She's got spirit, you know, but she's young and silly. It excites her to let everyone see that she's a friend of rabbits who are thought of as rebels. She doesn't realize what she's doing or what the Council are really like. It's all a kind of game to her – to cheek the officers and so on. One day she'll go too far and get us into trouble again. She couldn't be trusted with a secret, on any account.'

'How many does in this Mark would be ready to join an escape?'

'Hrair. There's a great deal of discontent, you know. But Thlayli, they mustn't be told until a very short time before we run – not just Nelthilta, but all of them. No one can keep a secret in a warren and there are spies everywhere.

You and I must make a plan ourselves and tell no one but Thethuthinnang. She and I will get enough does to come with us when the time comes.'

Bigwig realized that he had stumbled, quite unexpectedly, upon what he needed most of all: a strong, sensible friend, who would think on her own account and help to bear his burden.

'I'll leave it to you to pick the does,' he said. 'I can make the chance to run if you'll have them ready to take it.'

'When?'

'Sunset will be best, and the sooner the better. Hazel and the others will meet us and fight any patrol that follows. But the main thing is that the bird will fight for us. Even Woundwort won't be expecting that.'

Hyzenthlay was silent again and Bigwig realized with admiration that she was going over what he had said and searching for flaws.

'But how many can the bird fight?' she said at last. 'Can he drive them *all* away? This is going to be a big break-out and make no mistake, Thlayli, the General himself will be after us with the best rabbits he has. We can't go on running away for ever. They won't lose track of us and sooner or later they'll overtake us.'

'I told you our rabbits were more cunning than the Council. I don't think you'd really understand this part, however carefully I explained. Have you ever seen a river?'

'What is a river?'

'Well, there you are. I can't explain. But I promise you we shan't have to run far. We shall actually disappear before the Owsla's eyes – if they're there to see. I must say I'm looking forward to that.'

She said nothing and he added, 'You must trust me, Hyzenthlay. Upon my life, we're going to vanish. I'm not deceiving you.'

'If you were wrong, those who died quickly would be the lucky ones.'

'No one's going to die. My friends have prepared a trick that El-ahrairah himself would be proud of.'

'If it is to be at sunset,' she said, 'it must be tomorrow or the next night. In two days the Mark loses the evening silflay. You know that?'

'Yes, I'd heard. Tomorrow then. Why wait longer? But there is one other thing. We're going to take Blackavar.'

'Blackavar? How? He is guarded by Council police.'

'I know. It adds very much to the risk, but I've decided that I can't leave him behind. What I mean to do is this. Tomorrow evening, when the Mark silflay, you and Thethuthinnang must keep the does near you – as many as you've got together – ready to run. I shall meet the bird a little way out in the meadow and tell him to attack the sentries as soon as he sees me go back into the hole. Then I shall come back and deal with Blackavar's guards myself. They won't be expecting anything of the sort. I'll have him out in a moment and join you. There'll be complete confusion and in that confusion we'll run. The bird will attack anyone who tries to follow us. Remember, we go straight down to the great arch on the iron road. My friends will be waiting there. You've only to follow me – I'll lead the way.'

'Captain Campion may be on patrol.'

'Oh, I do hope he is,' said Bigwig. 'I really do.'

'Blackavar may not run at once. He will be as startled as the guards.'

'Is it possible to warn him?'

'No. His guards never leave him and they take him out to silflay alone.'

'For how long will he have to live like that?'

'When he has been to every Mark in turn, the Council will kill him. We all feel sure of that.'

'Then that settles it. I *won't* go without him.'

'Thlayli, you are very brave. Are you cunning too? All our lives will depend on you tomorrow.'

'Well, can you see anything wrong with the plan?'

'No, but I am only a doe who has never been out of Efrafa. Suppose something unexpected happens?'

'Risk is risk. Don't you want to get out and come and live on the high downs with us? Think of it!'

'Oh, Thlayli! Shall we mate with whom we choose and dig our own burrows and bear our litters alive?'

'You shall: and tell stories in the Honeycomb and silflay whenever you feel like it. It's a fine life, I promise you.'

'I'll come! I'll run any risk.'

'What a stroke of luck that you should be in this Mark,' said Bigwig. 'Before this talk with you tonight, I was at my wits' end wondering whatever I was going to do.'

'I'll go back to the lower burrows now, Thlayli. Some of the other rabbits are bound to wonder why you sent for me. It's not mating time with me, you see. If I go now, we can say you made a mistake and were disappointed. Don't forget to say that.'

'I won't. Yes, go now, and have them ready at silflay tomorrow evening. I shan't fail you.'

When she had gone, Bigwig felt desperately tired and lonely. He tried to hold in his mind that his friends were not far off and that he would see them again in less than a day. But he knew that all Efrafa lay between himself and Hazel. His thoughts broke up into the dismal fancies of anxiety. He fell into a half-dream, in which Captain Campion turned into a seagull and flew screaming over the river, until he woke in panic; and dozed again, to see Captain Chervil driving Blackavar before him towards a shining wire in the grass. And over all, as big as a horse in a field, aware of all that passed from one end of the world to the other, brooded the gigantic figure of General Woundwort. At last, worn out with his apprehensions, he passed into a deep sleep where even his fear could not follow, and lay without sound or movement in the solitary burrow.

36. Approaching Thunder

We was just goin' ter scarper
When along comes Bill 'Arper,
So we never done nuffin' at all.

Musk Hall Song

BIGWIG wavered gradually up from sleep, like a bubble of marsh gas from the bed of a still stream. There was another rabbit beside him in the burrow – a buck. He started up at once and said, 'Who is it?'

'Avens,' replied the other. 'Time for silflay, Thlayli. Larks have gone up. You're a sound sleeper.'

'I dare say,' said Bigwig. 'Well, I'm ready.' He was about to lead the way down the run, but Avens's next words brought him to a halt.

'Who's Fiver?' said Avens.

Bigwig grew tense. 'What did you say?'

'I said, Who's Fiver?'

'How should I know?'

'Well, you were talking in your sleep. You kept saying, "Ask Fiver, ask Fiver." I wondered who he was.'

'Oh, I see. A rabbit I knew once. He used to foretell the weather and so on.'

'Well, he could do it now, then. Can you smell the thunder?'

Bigwig sniffed. Mixed with the scents of grass and cattle came the warm, thick smell of a heavy cloud-mass, still far off. He perceived it uneasily. Almost all animals are disturbed by the approach of thunder, which oppresses them with its mounting tension and breaks the natural rhythm by which they live. Bigwig's inclination was to go back to his burrow, but he had little doubt that no mere trifle like a thundery morning would be allowed to interfere with the time-table of an Efrafan Mark.

He was right. Chervil was already at the entrance, squatting opposite Blackavar and his escort. He looked round as his officers came up the run.

'Come on, Thlayli,' he said. 'Sentries are out already. Does the thunder worry you?'

'It does rather,' replied Bigwig.

'It won't break today,' said Chervil. 'It's a long way off yet. I'd give it until tomorrow evening. Anyway, don't let the Mark see it affects you. Nothing's to be altered unless the General says so.'

'Couldn't wake him up,' said Avens, with a touch of malice. 'There was a doe in your burrow last night, Thlayli, wasn't there?'

'Oh, was there?' said Chervil. 'Which one?'

'Hyzenthlay,' replied Bigwig.

'Oh, the *marli tharn*,'* said Chervil. 'Funny, I didn't think she was ready.'

'She wasn't,' said Bigwig. 'I made a mistake. But if you remember, you asked me to do what I could to get to know the awkward squad and bring them a bit more under control, so I kept her talking for a time, just the same.'

'Get anywhere?'

'Hard to say, really,' said Bigwig, 'but I'll keep at it.'

He spent the time while the Mark went out in deciding upon the best and quickest way to enter the hole and attack Blackavar's escort. He would have to put one of them out of action in no time at all and then go straight for the other, who would be that much less unprepared. If he had to fight him, it would be better to avoid doing it between Blackavar and the mouth of the hole, for Blackavar would be as bewildered as the rest and might bolt back down the run. If he was going to bolt anywhere he must bolt outwards. Of course, with any luck, the second guard might make off underground without fighting at all, but one could not count on that. Efrafan Owslafa were not given to running away.

As he went out into the field, he wondered whether he would be spotted by Kehaar. The arrangement had been that Kehaar would find him whenever he might come above ground on the second day.

He need not have worried. Kehaar had been over Efrafa since before dawn. As soon as he saw the Mark come up, he alighted a little way out in the field, half-way between

---

* *Marli* – a doe. *Tharn* – stupefied, distraught. In this particular context, the nearest translation might be 'the maiden all forlorn'.

the undergrowth and the sentry-line, and began pecking about in the grass. Bigwig nibbled his way slowly towards him and then settled down to feed without a glance in his direction. After a while, he sensed that Kehaar was behind him, a little to one side.

'Meester Pigvig, I t'ink ees not goot ve talk much. Meester 'Azel, 'e say vat you do? Vat you vant?'

'I want two things, Kehaar – both at sunset tonight. First, our rabbits must be down by the big arch. I shall come through that arch with the does. If we're pursued, you and Hazel and the rest must be ready to fight. The boat-thing, is it still there?'

'Ya, ya, men no take heem. I tell Meester 'Azel vat you say.'

'Good. Now listen, Kehaar, this is the second thing; and it's terribly important. You see those rabbits out beyond us, in the field? They're the sentries. At sunset, you meet me here. Then I shall run back to those trees and go down a hole. As soon as you see me go in, attack the sentries – terrify them, drive them away. If they won't run, hurt them. They *must* be driven off. You'll see me come out again almost at once and then the does – the mothers – will start running with me and we'll go straight down to the arch. But we may very well be attacked on the way. If that happens, can you pile in again?'

'Ya, ya. I fly at dem – dey no stop you.'

'Splendid. That's it, then. Hazel and the others – are they all right?'

'Fine – fine. Dey say you dam' good fella. Meester Pluebell, 'e say to pring one mudder for everyone else and two for 'im.'

Bigwig was trying to think of some appropriate reply to this when he saw Chervil running across the grass towards him. At once, without speaking again to Kehaar, he took a few hops in Chervil's direction and began biting busily at a patch of clover. As Chervil came up, Kehaar flew low above their heads and disappeared over the trees.

Chervil looked after the flying gull and then turned to Bigwig.

'Aren't you afraid of those birds?' he asked.

'Not particularly,' answered Bigwig.

'They sometimes attack mice, you know, and rabbit kittens too,' said Chervil. 'You were taking a risk, feeding there. Why were you so careless?'

For answer, Bigwig sat up and gave Chervil a playful cuff, hard enough to roll him over.

'That's why,' he said. Chervil got up with a sulky air.

'All right, so you're heavier than I am,' he said. 'But you've got to learn, Thlayli, that there's more than weight to being an Efrafan officer. And it doesn't alter the fact that those birds can be dangerous. Anyway, it's not the season for them and that's odd for a start. It'll have to be reported.'

'Whatever for?'

'Because it's unusual. Everything unusual has to be reported. If we don't report it and someone else does, nice fools we shall look when we have to say we saw it. We couldn't say we didn't – several of the Mark have seen it. In fact, I shall go and report it now. Silflay's nearly over, so if I'm not back in time, you and Avens had better see the Mark underground yourselves.'

As soon as Chervil had left him, Bigwig went to look for Hyzenthlay. He found her in the hollow with Thethuthinnang. Most of the Mark did not appear to be unduly affected by the thunder, which was still distant, as Chervil had said. The two does, however, were subdued and nervous. Bigwig told them what he had arranged with Kehaar.

'But will this bird really attack the sentries?' asked Thethuthinnang. 'I've never heard of anything like that.'

'It will, I promise you. Get the does together as soon as silflay begins this evening. When I come out with Blackavar, the sentries will be running for cover.'

'And which way do we run?' asked Thethuthinnang.

Bigwig took them well out into the field, so that they could see the distant arch in the embankment about four hundred yards away.

'We're bound to meet Campion,' said Thethuthinnang. 'You know that?'

'I believe he had some trouble stopping Blackavar,' replied Bigwig, 'so I'm sure he won't be good enough for me and the bird. Look, there's Avens bringing in the sentries – we'll have to go. Now, don't worry. Chew your pellets and get some sleep. If you can't sleep, sharpen up your claws: you may need them.'

The Mark went underground and Blackavar was taken away by the escort. Bigwig returned to his burrow and tried to put the coming evening out of his mind. After some time he gave up the idea of spending the day alone. He made a round of the lower burrows, joined a game of bob-stones, heard two stories and told one himself, passed hraka in the ditch and then, on an impulse, went to Chervil and obtained his consent to visit another Mark. He wandered across the Crixa, found himself in the middle of the ni-Frith silflay with the Left Flank Mark and went underground with them. Their officers shared a single large burrow and here he met some experienced veterans and listened with interest to their stories of Wide Patrols and other exploits. In the mid-afternoon he came back to the Near Hind relaxed and confident, and slept until one of the sentries woke him for silflay.

He went up the run. Blackavar was already slumped in his alcove. Squatting beside Chervil, Bigwig watched the Mark go out. Hyzenthlay and Thethuthinnang passed him without a glance. They looked tense but steady. Chervil followed the last rabbit.

Bigwig waited until he was sure that Chervil had had time to get well away from the hole. Then, with a last, quick look to where Blackavar was sitting, he went out himself. The bright sunset dazzled him and he sat up on his hind legs, blinking and combing the fur along one side of his face as his eyes got accustomed to the light. A few moments later, he saw Kehaar come flying across the field.

'This is it, then,' he said to himself. 'Here we go.'

At that moment a rabbit spoke from behind him.

'Thlayli, I want a few words with you. Just come back under the bushes, will you?'

Bigwig dropped on his front paws and looked round.

It was General Woundwort.

37. The Thunder Builds Up

Youk'n hide de fier, but w'at you gwine do wid de smoke?
Joel Chandler Harris, *Proverbs of Uncle Remus*

BIGWIG'S first impulse was to fight Woundwort on the spot. He realized immediately that this would be futile and would only bring the whole place round his ears. There was nothing to do but obey. He followed Woundwort through the undergrowth and into the shade of the bridle-path. Despite the sunset, the evening seemed heavy with cloud and among the trees it was sultry and grey. The thunder was building up. He looked at Woundwort and waited.

'You were out of the Near Hind burrows this afternoon?' began Woundwort.

'Yes, sir,' replied Bigwig. He still disliked addressing Woundwort as 'sir', but since he was supposed to be an Efrafan officer, he could not very well do otherwise. However, he did not add that Chervil had given him permission. He had not been accused of anything as yet.

'Where did you go?'

Bigwig swallowed his annoyance. No doubt Woundwort knew perfectly well where he had been.

'I went to the Left Flank Mark, sir. I was in their burrows.'

'Why did you go?'

'To pass the time and learn something from listening to the officers.'

'Did you go anywhere else?'

'No, sir.'

'You met one of the Left Flank Owsla – a rabbit named Groundsel.'

'Very likely, I didn't learn all their names.'

'Have you ever seen that rabbit before?'

'No, sir. How could I?'

There was a pause.

'May I ask what this is all about, sir?' said Bigwig.

'I'll ask the questions,' said Woundwort. 'Groundsel has seen *you* before. He knew you by the fur on your head. Where do you think he saw you?'

'I've no idea.'

'Have you ever run from a fox?'

'Yes, sir, a few days ago, while I was coming here.'

'You led it on to some other rabbits and it killed one of them. Is that correct?'

'I didn't intend to lead it on to them. I didn't know they were there.'

'You didn't tell us anything about this?'

'It never occurred to me. There's nothing wrong in running from a fox.'

'You've caused the death of an Efrafan officer.'

'Quite by accident. And the fox might have got him anyway, even if I'd not been there.'

'It wouldn't,' said Woundwort. 'Mallow wasn't the rabbit to run on to a fox. Foxes aren't dangerous to rabbits who know their business.'

'I'm sorry the fox got him, sir. It was a stroke of very bad luck.'

Woundwort stared at him out of his great, pale eyes.

'Then one more question, Thlayli. That patrol was on the track of a band of rabbits – strangers. What do you know about them?'

'I saw their tracks too, about that time. I can't tell you any more than that.'

'You weren't with them?'

'If I'd been with them, sir, would I have come to Efrafa?'

'I told you I'd ask the questions. You can't tell me where they might have gone?'

'I'm afraid I can't, sir.'

Woundwort stopped staring and sat silent for some time. Bigwig felt that the General was waiting for him to ask if that was all and whether he could now go. He determined to remain silent himself.

'Now there's another thing,' said Woundwort at last. 'About this white bird in the field this morning. You're not afraid of these birds?'

'No, sir. I've never heard of one hurting a rabbit.'

'But they have been known to, for all your wide experience, Thlayli. Anyway, why did you go near it?'

Bigwig thought quickly. 'To tell you the truth, sir, I think I may have been trying to make an impression on Captain Chervil.'

'Well, you could have a worse reason. But if you're going to impress anyone, you'd better start with me. The day after tomorrow, I'm taking out a Wide Patrol myself. It will cross the iron road and try to pick up traces of those rabbits – the rabbits Mallow would have found if you hadn't gone and blundered into him. So you'd better come along and show us how good you are then.'

'Very well, sir; I shall be glad to.'

There was another silence. This time Bigwig decided to make as if to go. He did so, and immediately a fresh question stopped him short.

'When you were with Hyzenthlay, did she tell you why she was put into the Near Hind Mark?'

'Yes, sir.'

'I'm not at all sure the trouble's over there, Thlayli. Keep an eye on it. If she'll talk to you, so much the better. Perhaps those does are settling down and perhaps they aren't. I want to know.'

'Very well, sir,' said Bigwig.

'That's all,' said Woundwort. 'You'd better get back to your Mark now.'

Bigwig made his way into the field. The silflay was almost over, the sun had set and it was growing dark. Heavy clouds dimmed the after-light. Kehaar was nowhere to be seen. The sentries came in and the Mark began to go underground. Sitting alone in the grass, he waited until the last rabbit had disappeared. There was still no sign of Kehaar. He hopped slowly to the hole. Entering, he knocked into one of the police escort, who was blocking the mouth to make sure that Blackavar did not try to bolt as he was taken down.

'Get out of my way, you dirty little tale-bearing bloodsucker,' said Bigwig. 'Now go and report that,' he added over his shoulder, as he went down to his burrow.

As the light faded from the thick sky, Hazel slipped once more across the hard, bare earth under the railway arch, came out on the north side and sat up to listen. A few moments later Fiver joined him and they crept a little way into the field, towards Efrafa. The air was close and warm and smelt of rain and ripening barley. There was no sound close by, but behind and below them, from the water-meadow on the nearer bank of the Test, came faintly the shrill, incessant fussing of a pair of sandpipers. Kehaar flew down from the top of the embankment.

'You're sure he said tonight?' asked Hazel for the third time.

'Ees bad,' said Kehaar. 'Maybe dey catch 'im. Ees finish Meester Pigvig. You t'ink?'

Hazel made no reply.

'I can't tell,' said Fiver. 'Clouds and thunder. That place up the field – it's like the bottom of a river. Anything could be happening in there.'

'Bigwig's there. Suppose he's dead? Suppose they're trying to make him tell them –'

'Hazel,' said Fiver. 'Hazel-rah, you won't help him by staying here in the dark and worrying. Quite likely there's nothing wrong. He's just had to sit tight for some reason.

Anyway, he won't come tonight – that's certain now – and our rabbits are in danger here. Kehaar can go up tomorrow at dawn and bring us another message.'

'I dare say you're right,' said Hazel, 'but I hate to go. Just suppose he were to come. Let Silver take them back and I'll stay here.'

'You couldn't do any good by yourself, Hazel, even if your leg was all right. You're trying to eat grass that isn't there. Why don't you give it a chance to grow?'

They returned under the arch and as Silver came out of the bushes to meet them, they could hear the other rabbits stirring uneasily among the nettles.

'We'll have to give it up for tonight, Silver,' said Hazel. 'We must get them back over the river now, before it's completely dark.'

'Hazel-rah,' said Pipkin, as he slipped by, 'it – it is going to be all right, isn't it? Bigwig will come tomorrow, won't he?'

'Of course he will,' said Hazel, 'and we'll all be here to help him. And I'll tell you something else, Hlao-roo. If he doesn't come tomorrow, I'm going into Efrafa myself.'

'I'll come with you, Hazel-rah,' said Pipkin.

Bigwig crouched in his burrow, pressed against Hyzenthlay. He was trembling, but not with cold: the stuffy runs of the Mark were dense with thunder: the air felt like a deep drift of leaves. Bigwig was close to utter nervous exhaustion. Since leaving General Woundwort, he had become more and more deeply entangled in all the age-old terrors of the conspirator. How much had Woundwort discovered? Clearly, there was no information that failed to reach him.

He knew that Hazel and the rest had come from the north and crossed the iron road. He knew about the fox. He knew that a gull, which should have been far away at this time of year, was hanging round Efrafa and that he, Bigwig, had deliberately been near it. He knew that Bigwig had made a friend of Hyzenthlay. How long could it be before he took the final step of fitting all these things together? Perhaps he had already done so and was merely waiting to arrest them in his own time?

Woundwort had every advantage. He sat secure at the junction of all paths, seeing clearly down each, while he, Bigwig, ludicrous in his efforts to measure up to him as an enemy, clambered clumsily and ignorantly through the undergrowth, betraying himself with every movement He did not know how to get in touch with Kehaar again. Even if he managed to do so, would Hazel be able to bring the rabbits a second time? Perhaps they had already been spotted by Campion on patrol? To speak to Blackavar would be suspect. To go near Kehaar would be suspect. Through more holes than he could possibly stop, his secret was leaking – pouring – out.

There was worse to come.

'Thlayli,' whispered Hyzenthlay, 'do you think you and I and Thethuthinnang could get away tonight? If we fought the sentry at the mouth of the run we might be able to get clear before a patrol could start after us.'

'Why?' asked Bigwig. 'What makes you ask that?'

'I'm frightened. We told the other does, you see, just before the silflay. They were ready to run when the bird attacked the sentries, and then nothing happened. They all know about the plan – Nelthilta and the rest – and it can't be long before the Council find out. Of course we've told them that their lives depend on keeping quiet and that you're going to try again. Thethuthinnang's watching them now: she says she'll do her best not to sleep. But no secret can be kept in Efrafa. It's even possible that one of the does is a spy, although Frith knows we chose them as carefully as we could. We may all be arrested before tomorrow morning.'

Bigwig tried to think clearly. He could certainly succeed in getting out with a couple of resolute, sensible does. But the sentry – unless he could kill him – would raise the alarm at once and he could not be sure of finding the way to the river in the dark. Even if he did, it was possible that the pursuit might follow him over the plank bridge and into the middle of his unprepared, sleeping friends. And at the best he would have come out of Efrafa with no more than a couple of does, because his nerve had failed. Silver and the others would not know what he had had to endure. They would know only that he had run away.

'No, we mustn't give up yet,' he said, as gently as he could. 'It's the thunder and the waiting that make you feel so much upset. Listen, I promise you that by this time tomorrow you'll be out of Efrafa for ever and the others with you. Now go to sleep here for a little while and then go back and help Thethuthinnang. Keep thinking of those high downs and all that I told you. We'll get there – our troubles won't last much longer.'

As she fell asleep beside him, Bigwig wondered how on earth he was going to fulfil this promise and whether they would be woken by the Council police. 'If we are,' he thought, 'I'll fight until they tear me to bits. They'll make no Blackavar out of me.'

When he woke, he found that he was alone in the burrow. For a moment he wondered whether Hyzenthlay had been arrested. Then he felt sure that the Owslafa could not have removed her while he slept. She must have woken and slipped back to Thethuthinnang without disturbing him.

It was a little before dawn, but the oppression in the air had not lessened. He slipped up the run to the entrance. Moneywort, the sentry on duty, was peering uneasily out of the mouth of the hole, but turned as he approached.

'I wish it would rain, sir,' he said. 'The thunder's enough to turn the grass sour, but not much hope of it breaking before the evening, I'd say.'

'It's bad luck for the Mark's last day on dawn and evening,' replied Bigwig. 'Go and wake Captain Chervil. I'll take your place here until the Mark come up.'

When Moneywort had gone, Bigwig sat in the mouth of the hole and sniffed the heavy air. The sky seemed as close as the tops of the trees, covered with still cloud and flushed on the morning side with a lurid, foxy glow. Not a lark was up, not a thrush singing. The field before him was empty and motionless. The longing to run came over him. In less than no time he could be down to the arch. It was a safe bet that Campion and his patrol would not be out in weather like this. Every living creature up and down the fields and copses must be muted, pressed down as though under a great, soft paw. Nothing would be moving, for the day was unpropitious and instincts were blurred and not to be trusted. It was a time to crouch and be silent. But a fugitive would be safe. Indeed, he could not hope for a better chance.

'Lord with the starlight ears, send me a sign!' said Bigwig.

He heard movement in the run behind him. It was the Owslafa bringing up the prisoner. In the thundery twilight, Blackavar looked more sick and dejected than ever. His nose was dry and the whites of his eyes showed. Bigwig went out into the field, pulled a mouthful of clover and brought it back.

'Cheer up,' he said to Blackavar. 'Have some clover.'

'That's not allowed, sir,' said one of the escort.

'Oh, let him have it, Bartsia,' said the other. 'There's no one to see. It's hard enough for everyone on a day like this, let alone the prisoner.'

Blackavar ate the clover and Bigwig took up his usual place as Chervil arrived to watch the Mark go out.

The rabbits were slow and hesitant and Chervil himself seemed unable to rise to his usual brisk manner. He had little to say as they passed him. He let both Thethuthinnang and Hyzenthlay go by in silence. Nelthilta, however, stopped of her own accord and stared impudently at him.

'Under the weather, Captain?' she said. 'Brace up, now. You may have a surprise soon, who knows?'

'What do you mean?' answered Chervil sharply.

'Does might grow wings and fly,' said Nelthilta, 'and before very much longer, too. Secrets go faster than moles underground.'

She followed the other does into the field. For a moment Chervil looked as though he were going to call her back.

'I wonder whether you could have a look at my off hind foot?' said Bigwig. 'I think I've got a thorn in it.'

'Come on, then,' said Chervil, 'outside: not that we'll be able to see much better there.'

But whether because he was still thinking about what Nelthilta had said, or for some other reason, he did not make a particularly thorough search for the thorn: which was perhaps as well, for there was no thorn there.

'Oh, confound it!' he said, looking up, 'There's that dratted white bird again. What's it keep coming here for?'

'Why does it worry you?' asked Bigwig. 'It's not doing any harm – only looking for snails.'

'Anything out of the ordinary is a possible source of danger,' replied Chervil, quoting Woundwort. 'And you keep away from it today, Thlayli, d'you see? That's an order.'

'Oh, very well,' said Bigwig. 'But surely you know how to get rid of them? I thought all rabbits knew that.'

'Don't be ridiculous. You're not suggesting attacking a bird that size, with a beak as thick as my front paw?'

'No, no – it's a sort of charm-thing that my mother taught me. You know, like "Ladybird, ladybird, fly away home". That works and so does this: or it always used to with my mother.'

'The ladybird thing only works because all ladybirds crawl to the top of the stem and then fly.'

'Well, all right,' said Bigwig, 'have it your own way. But you don't like the bird and I've offered to get rid of it for you. We had a lot of these charms and sayings in my old warren. I only wish we'd had one to get rid of men.'

'Well, what is the charm?' said Chervil.

'You say,

> 'O fly away, great bird so white,
> And don't come back until tonight.

'Of course, you have to use hedgerow talk. No use expecting them to understand Lapine. Let's have a go, anyway. If it doesn't work, we're none the worse and if it does, the Mark will think it was you who drove the bird away. Where's it got to? I can hardly see anything in this light. Oh, there it is, look, behind those thistles. Well, you run like this. Now you have to hop to this side, then to the other side, scratch with your legs – that's right, splendid – cock your ears and then go straight on until – ah! Here we are; now then:

> 'O fly away, great bird so white,
> And don't come back until tonight.

'There you are, you see. It *did* work. I think there's more than we know to some of these old rhymes and spells. Of course, it might have been just going to fly away anyway. But you must admit it's gone.'

'Probably all that prancing about as we came up to it,' said Chervil sourly. 'We must have looked completely mad. What on earth will the Mark think? Anyway, now we're out here, we may as well go round the sentries.'

'I'll stop and feed, if you don't mind,' said Bigwig. 'I didn't get much last night, you know.'

*

Bigwig's luck was not altogether out. Later that morning, quite unexpectedly, he came upon a chance to talk to Blackavar alone. He had been through the sweltering burrows, finding everywhere quick breathing and feverish pulses; and he was just wondering whether he could not plausibly go and press Chervil to ask the Council's permission for the Mark to spend part of the day in the bushes above ground – for that might very well bring some sort of opportunity with it – when he began to feel the need to pass hraka. No rabbit passes hraka underground: and like schoolchildren, who know that they cannot very well be refused a request to go to the lavatory – as long as it is not too soon after the last time – the Efrafan rabbits used to slip into the ditch for a breath of air and a change of scene. Although they were not supposed to be allowed to go more often than was necessary, some of the Owsla were easier than others. As Bigwig approached the hole that led into the ditch, he found two or three young bucks loitering in the run and as usual, set himself to act his part as convincingly as he could.

'Why are you hanging about here?' he asked.

'The prisoner's escort are up at the hole and they turned us back, sir,' answered one. 'They're not letting anyone out for the moment.'

'Not to pass hraka?' said Bigwig.

'No, sir.'

Indignant, Bigwig made his way to the mouth of the hole. Here he found Blackavar's escort talking to the sentry on duty.

'I'm afraid you can't go out for the moment, sir,' said Bartsia. 'The prisoner's in the ditch, but he won't be long.'

'Neither shall I,' said Bigwig. 'Just get out of the way, will you?' He pushed Bartsia to one side and hopped into the ditch.

The day had become even more lowering and overcast. Blackavar was squatting a little way off, under an overhanging plume of cow-parsley. The flies were walking on his shreds of ears, but he seemed not to notice them. Bigwig went along the ditch and squatted beside him.

'Blackavar, listen,' he said quickly. 'This is the truth, by Frith and the Black Rabbit. I am a secret enemy of Efrafa. No one knows this but you and a few of the Mark does. I'm going to escape with them tonight and I'm going to take you as well. Don't do anything yet. When the time comes I'll be there to tell you. Just brace up and get yourself ready.'

Without waiting for an answer, he moved away as though to find a better spot. Even so, he was back at the hole before Blackavar, who evidently meant to stay outside for as long as the escort – clearly in no hurry themselves – would allow.

'Sir,' said Bartsia, as Bigwig came in, 'that's the third time, sir, that you've disregarded my authority. Council police can't be treated in this way. I'm afraid I shall have to report it, sir.'

Bigwig made no reply and returned up the run.

'Wait a bit longer if you can,' he said as he passed the bucks. 'I don't suppose that poor fellow will get out again today.'

He wondered whether to go and look for Hyzenthlay, but decided that it would be prudent to keep away from her. She knew what to do, and the less they were seen together the better. His head ached in the heat and he wanted only to be alone and quiet. He went back to his burrow and slept.

38. The Thunder Breaks

Why, now, blow wind, swell billow and swim bark!
The storm is up and all is on the hazard!

Shakespeare, *Julius Caesar*

LATE in the afternoon it came on dark and very close.
It was plain that there would be no true sunset. On the
green path by the river bank, Hazel sat fidgeting as he tried
to imagine what might be going on in Efrafa.

'He told you he wanted you to attack the sentries while
the rabbits were feeding, didn't he,' he said to Kehaar, 'and
that he'd bring the mothers out in the confusion?'

'Ya, say dis, but not 'appen. Den 'e say go away, come
again tonight.'

'So that's still what he means to do. The question is,
when *will* they be feeding? It's getting dark already. Silver,
what do you think?'

'If I know them, they won't alter anything they usually
do,' said Silver. 'But if you're worried in case we're not
there in time, why not go now?'

'Because they're always patrolling. The longer we wait up there, the greater the risk. If a patrol finds us before Bigwig comes, it won't be just a matter of getting ourselves away. They'll realize we're there for some purpose and give the alarm: and that'll be the end of any chance he's got.'

'Listen, Hazel-rah,' said Blackberry. 'We ought to reach the iron road at the same time as Bigwig and not a moment before. Why don't you take them all over the river now and wait in the undergrowth, near the boat? Once Kehaar's attacked the sentries, he can fly back and tell us.'

'Yes, that's it,' answered Hazel. 'But once he's told us, we must get up there in no time at all. Bigwig's going to need us as well as Kehaar.'

'Well, *you* won't be able to dash up to the arch,' said Fiver, 'with your leg. The best thing you can do is to get on the boat and have the rope gnawed half through by the time we come back. Silver can look after the fighting, if there's going to be any.'

Hazel hesitated. 'But some of us are probably going to get hurt. I can't stay behind.'

'Fiver's right,' said Blackberry. 'You *will* have to wait on the boat, Hazel. We can't risk your being left to be picked up by the Efrafans. Besides, it's very important that the rope should be half-gnawed – that's a job for someone sensible. It mustn't break too soon or we're all finished.'

It took them some time to persuade Hazel. When at last he agreed, he was still reluctant.

'If Bigwig doesn't come tonight,' he said, 'I shall go and find him, wherever he is. Frith knows what may have happened already.'

As they set off up the left bank, the wind began to blow in fitful, warm gusts, with a multifoliate rustling through the sedges. They had just reached the plank bridge when there came a rumble of thunder. In the intense, strange light, the plants and leaves seemed magnified and the fields beyond the river very near. There was an oppressive stillness.

'You know, Hazel-rah,' said Bluebell, 'this really is the funniest evening I've ever gone looking for a doe.'

'It's going to get a lot funnier soon,' said Silver. 'There'll be lightning and pouring rain. For goodness' sake, all of you, don't panic, or we'll never see our warren again. I think this is going to be a rough business,' he added quietly to Hazel. 'I don't like it much.'

Bigwig woke to hear his name repeated urgently.

'Thlayli! Thlayli! Wake up! *Thlayli!*'

It was Hyzenthlay.

'What is it?' he said. 'What's the matter?'

'Nelthilta's been arrested.'

Bigwig leapt to his feet.

'How long ago? How did it happen?'

'Just now. Moneywort came down to our burrow and told her to come up to Captain Chervil at once. I followed them up the run. When she got to Chervil's burrow, there were two Council police waiting just outside and one of them said to Chervil, "Well, as quick as you can, and don't be long." And then they took her straight out. They must have gone to the Council. Oh Thlayli, what shall we do? She'll tell them everything –'

'Listen to me,' said Bigwig. 'There's not a moment to lose. Go and get Thethuthinnang and the others and bring them up to this burrow. I shan't be here, but you must wait quietly until I come back. It won't be long. Quick now! Everything depends on it.'

Hyzenthlay had hardly disappeared down the run when Bigwig heard another rabbit approaching from the opposite direction.

'Who's there?' he said, turning swiftly.

'Chervil,' answered the other. 'I'm glad you're awake. Listen, Thlayli, there's going to be a whole lot of trouble. Nelthilta's been arrested by the Council. I was sure she would be, after my report to Vervain this morning. Whatever it was she was talking about, they'll get it out of her. I dare say the General will be here himself as soon as he knows what's what. Now look here, I've got to go over to the Council burrow at once. You and Avens are to stay here and get the sentries on duty immediately. There'll be no silflay and no one is to go outside for any reason whatever. All the holes are to be double-guarded. Now, you understand these orders, don't you?'

'Have you told Avens?'

'I haven't time to go looking for Avens; he's not in his burrow. Go and alert the sentries yourself. Send someone to find Avens and someone else to tell Bartsia that Blackavar won't be wanted this evening. Then sit on those holes – and the hraka holes too – with every sentry you've got. For all I know there may be some plot to make a break-out. We arrested Nelthilta as quietly as we could, but the Mark are bound to realize what's happened. If necessary you're to get rough, do you see? Now I'm off.'

'Right,' said Bigwig. 'I'll get busy at once.'

He followed Chervil to the top of the run. The sentry at the hole was Marjoram. As he stood clear to let Chervil pass, Bigwig came up behind him and looked out into the overcast.

'Did Chervil tell you?' he said. 'Silflay's early tonight, on account of the weather. The orders are that we're to get on with it at once.'

He waited for Marjoram's reply. If Chervil had already told him that no one was to go out, it would be necessary to fight him. But after a moment, Marjoram said, 'Have you heard any thunder yet?'

'Get on with it at once, I said,' answered Bigwig. 'Go down and get Blackavar and the escort up, and be quick, too. We'll need to get the Mark out immediately if they're to feed before the storm breaks.'

Marjoram went and Bigwig hurried back to his own burrow. Hyzenthlay had lost no time. Three or four does were crammed into the burrow itself and near-by, in a side run, Thethuthinnang was crouching with several more. All were silent and frightened and one or two were close to the stupefaction of terror.

'This is no time to go tharn,' said Bigwig. 'Your lives depend on doing as I say. Listen, now. Blackavar and the police guards will be up directly. Marjoram will probably come up behind them and you must find some excuse to keep him talking. Soon after, you'll hear fighting, because I'm going to attack the police guards. When you hear that, come up as fast as you can and follow me out into the field. Don't stop for anything.'

As he finished speaking, he heard the unmistakable sound of Blackavar and the guards approaching. Blackavar's weary, dragging gait was like that of no other rabbit. Without waiting for the does to reply, Bigwig returned to the mouth of the run. The three rabbits came up in single file, Bartsia leading.

'I'm afraid I've brought you up here for nothing,' said Bigwig. 'I've just been told that silflay's cancelled for this evening. Have a look outside and you'll see why.'

As Bartsia went to look out of the hole, Bigwig slipped quickly between him and Blackavar.

'Well, it looks very stormy, certainly,' said Bartsia, 'but I shouldn't have thought –'

'*Now*, Blackavar!' cried Bigwig, and leapt on Bartsia from behind.

Bartsia fell forwards out of the hole with Bigwig on top of him. He was not a member of the Owslafa for nothing and was reckoned a good fighter. As they rolled over on the ground, he turned his head and sunk his teeth in Bigwig's shoulder. He had been trained to get a grip at once and to hold it at all costs. More than once in the past this had served him well. But in fighting a rabbit of Bigwig's strength and courage it proved a mistake. His best chance would have been to keep clear and use his claws. He retained his hold like a dog and Bigwig, snarling, brought both his own back legs forward, sank his feet in Bartsia's side and then, ignoring the pain in his shoulder, forced himself upwards. He felt Bartsia's closed teeth come tearing out through his flesh and then he was standing above him as he fell back on the ground, kicking helplessly. Bigwig leapt clear. It was plain that Bartsia's haunch was injured. He struggled, but could not get up.

'Think yourself lucky,' said Bigwig, bleeding and cursing, 'that I don't kill you.'

Without waiting to see what Bartsia would do, he jumped back into the hole. He found Blackavar grappling with the other guard. Just beyond them, Hyzenthlay was coming up the run with Thethuthinnang behind her. Bigwig gave the guard a tremendous cuff on the side of the head, which knocked him clear across the run and into the prisoner's alcove. He picked himself up, panting, and stared at Bigwig without a word.

'Don't move,' said Bigwig. 'There'll be worse to come if you do. Blackavar, are you all right?'

'Yes, sir,' said Blackavar, 'but what do we do now?'

'Follow me,' said Bigwig, 'all of you. Come on!'

He led the way out again. There was no sign of Bartsia, but as he looked back to make sure that the others were following, he caught a glimpse of the astonished face of Avens peering out of the other hole.

'Captain Chervil wants you!' he called, and dashed away into the field.

As he reached the clump of thistles where he had spoken to Kehaar that morning, a long roll of thunder sounded from across the valley beyond. A few great, warm drops of rain were falling. Along the western horizon the lower clouds formed a single, purple mass, against which distant trees stood out minute and sharp. The upper edges rose into the light, a far land of wild mountains. Copper-coloured, weightless and motionless, they suggested a glassy fragility like that of frost. Surely, when the thunder struck them again they would vibrate, tremble and shatter, till warm shards, sharp as icicles, fell flashing down from the ruins. Racing through the ochre light, Bigwig was impelled by a frenzy of tension and energy. He did not feel the wound in his shoulder. The storm was his own. The storm would defeat Efrafa.

He was well out into the great field and looking for a sight of the distant arch when he felt along the ground the first stamping thuds of the alarm. He pulled up and looked about him. There did not seem to be any stragglers. The does – however many there were – were well up with him, but scattered to either side. Rabbits in flight tend to keep away from each other and the does had opened out as they left the hole. If there was a patrol between him and the iron road they would not get past it without loss unless they came closer together. He would have to collect them, despite the delay. Then another thought came to him. If they could get out of sight, their pursuers might be puzzled, for the rain and the failing light would make tracking difficult.

The rain was falling faster now and the wind was rising. Over on the evening side, a hedge ran down the length of the field towards the iron road. He saw Blackavar near-by and ran across to him.

'I want everyone the other side of that hedge,' he said. 'Can you get hold of some of them and bring them that way?'

Bigwig remembered that Blackavar knew nothing except that they were on the run. There was no time to explain about Hazel and the river.

'Go straight to that ash tree in the hedge,' he said, 'and take all the does you can pick up on the way. Get through to the other side and I'll be there as soon as you are.'

At this moment Hyzenthlay and Thethuthinnang came running towards them, followed by two or three other does. They were plainly confused and uncertain.

'The stamping, Thlayli!' panted Thethuthinnang. 'They're coming!'

'Well, run, then,' said Bigwig. 'Keep near me, all of you.'

They were better runners than he had dared to hope. As they made for the ash tree, more does fell in with them and it seemed to him that they ought now to be a match for a patrol, unless it were a very strong one. Once through the hedge he turned south and, keeping close beside it, led them down the slope. There, ahead of him, was the arch in the overgrown embankment. But would Hazel be there? And where was Kehaar?

'Well, and what was to happen after that, Nelthilta?' asked General Woundwort. 'Make sure you tell us everything, because we know a good deal already. Let her alone, Vervain,' he added. 'She can't talk if you keep cuffing her, you fool.'

'Hyzenthlay said – oh! oh! – she said a big bird would attack the Owsla sentries,' gasped Nelthilta, 'and we would run away in the confusion. And then –'

'She said a *bird* would attack the sentries?' interrupted Woundwort, puzzled. 'Are you telling the truth? What sort of a bird?'

'I don't – I don't know,' panted Nelthilta. 'The new officer – she said he had told the bird –'

'What do *you* know about a bird?' said Woundwort, turning to Chervil.

'I reported it, sir,' replied Chervil. 'You'll not forget, sir, that I reported the bird –'

There was a scuffling outside the crowded Council burrow and Avens came pushing his way in.

'The new officer, sir!' he cried. 'He's gone! Taken a crowd of the Mark does with him. Jumped on Bartsia and broke his leg, sir! Blackavar's cut and run too. We never had a chance to stop them. Goodness knows how many have joined him. Thlayli – it's Thayli's doing!'

'Thlayli?' cried Woundwort. 'Embleer Frith, I'll *blind* him when I catch him! Chervil, Vervain, Avens – yes and you two as well – come with me. Which way has he gone?'

'He was going downhill, sir,' answered Avens.

'Lead the way you saw him take,' said Woundwort.

As they came out from the Crixa, two or three of the Efrafan officers checked at the sight of the murky light and increasing rain. But the sight of the General was more alarming still. Pausing only to stamp the escape alarm, they set out behind him towards the iron road.

Very soon they came upon traces of blood which the rain had not yet washed away, and these they followed towards the ash tree in the hedge to the west of the warren.

Bigwig came out from the farther side of the railway arch, sat up and looked round him. There was no sign either of Hazel or of Kehaar. For the first time since he had attacked Bartsia he began to feel uncertain and troubled. Perhaps, after all, Kehaar had not understood his cryptic message that morning? Or had some disaster overtaken Hazel and the rest? If they were dead – scattered – if there was no one left alive to meet him? He and his does would wander about the fields until the patrols hunted them down.

'No, it shan't come to that,' said Bigwig to himself. 'At the worst we can cross the river and try to hide in the woodland. Confound this shoulder! It's going to be more nuisance than I thought. Well, I'll try to get them down to the plank bridge at least. If we're not overtaken soon, perhaps the rain will discourage whoever's after us; but I doubt it.'

He turned back to the does waiting under the arch. Most of them looked bewildered. Hyzenthlay had promised that they were to be protected by a great bird and that the new officer was going to work a secret trick to evade the pursuit – a trick which would defeat even the General. These things had not happened. They were wet through. Runnels of water were trickling through the arch from the uphill side, and the bare earth was beginning to turn into mud. Ahead of them, there was nothing to be seen but a track leading through the nettles into another wide and empty field.

'Come on,' said Bigwig. 'It's not far now and then we'll all be safe. This way.'

All the rabbits obeyed him at once. There was something to be said for Efrafan discipline, thought Bigwig grimly, as they left the arch and met the force of the rain.

Along one side of the field, beside the elms, farm tractors had pounded a broad, flat path downhill towards the water-meadow below – that same path up which he had run three nights before, after he had left Hazel by the boat. It was turning muddy now – unpleasant going for rabbits –

but at least it led straight to the river and was open enough for Kehaar to spot them if he should turn up.

He had just begun to run once more when a rabbit overtook him.

'Stop, Thlayli! What are you doing here? Where are you going?'

Bigwig had been half-expecting Campion to appear and had made up his mind to kill him if necessary. But now that he actually saw him at his side, disregarding the storm and the mud, self-possessed as he led his patrol, no more than four strong, into the thick of a pack of desperate runaways, he could feel only what a pity it was that the two of them should be enemies and how much he would have liked to have taken Campion with him out of Efrafa.

'Go away,' he said. 'Don't try to stop us, Campion. I don't want to hurt you.'

He glanced to his other side. 'Blackavar, get the does to close up. If there are any stragglers the patrol will jump on them.'

'You'd do better to give in now,' said Campion, still running beside him. 'I shan't let you out of my sight, wherever you go. There's an escape patrol on the way – I heard the signal. When they get here you won't stand a chance. You're bleeding badly now.'

'Curse you!' cried Bigwig, striking at him. 'You'll bleed too, before I've done.'

'Can I fight him, sir?' said Blackavar. 'He won't beat me a second time.'

'No,' answered Bigwig, 'he's only trying to delay us. Keep running.'

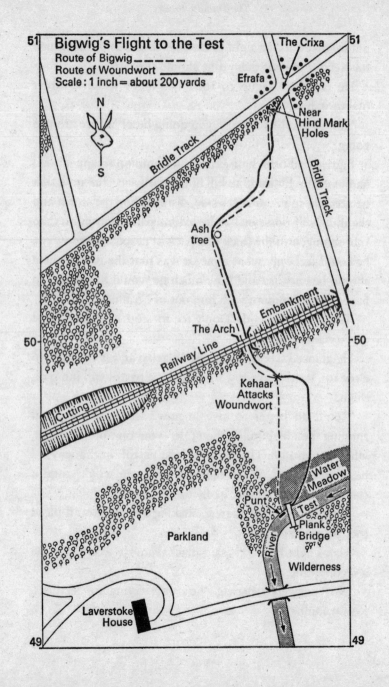

Bigwig's Flight to the Test
Route of Bigwig _ _ _ _ _
Route of Woundwort _____
Scale : 1 inch = about 200 yards

N
S

The Crixa

Efrafa

Near
Hind Mark
Holes

Bridle Track

Bridle Track

Ash
tree

Embankment

The Arch

Railway Line

Kehaar
Attacks
Woundwort

Cutting

Water
Meadow

Punt

Test

Plank
Bridge

Parkland

River

Wilderness

Laverstoke
House

'Thlayli!' cried Thethuthinnang suddenly, from behind him. 'The General! The General! Oh, what shall we do?'

Bigwig looked back. It was indeed a sight to strike terror into the bravest heart. Woundwort had come through the arch ahead of his followers and was running towards them by himself, snarling with fury. Behind him came the patrol. In one quick glance Bigwig recognized Chervil, Avens and Groundsel. With them were several more, including a heavy, savage-looking rabbit whom he guessed to be Vervain, the head of the Council police. It crossed his mind that if he were to run, immediately and alone, they would probably let him go as he had come, and feel glad to be so easily rid of him. Certainly the alternative was to be killed. At this moment Blackavar spoke.

'Never mind, sir,' he said. 'You did your very best and it nearly came off. We may even be able to kill one or two of them before it's finished. Some of these does can fight well when they're put to it.'

Bigwig rubbed his nose quickly against Blackavar's mutilated ear and sat back on his haunches as Woundwort came up to them.

'You dirty little beast,' said Woundwort. 'I hear you've attacked one of the Council police and broken his leg. We'll settle with you here. There's no need to take you back to Efrafa.'

'You crack-brained slave-driver,' answered Bigwig. 'I'd like to see you try.'

'All right,' said Woundwort, 'that's enough. Who have we got? Vervain, Campion, put him down. The rest of you, start getting these does back to the warren. The prisoner you can leave to me.'

'Frith sees you!' cried Bigwig. 'You're not fit to be called a rabbit! May Frith blast you and your foul Owsla full of bullies!'

At that instant a dazzling claw of lightning streaked down the length of the sky. The hedge and the distant trees seemed to leap forward in the brilliance of the flash. Immediately upon it came the thunder; a high, tearing noise, as though some huge thing were being ripped to pieces close above, which deepened and turned to enormous blows of dissolution. Then the rain fell like a waterfall. In a few seconds the ground was covered with water and over it, to a height of inches, rose a haze formed of a myriad minute splashes. Stupefied with the shock, unable even to move, the sodden rabbits crouched inert, almost pinned to the earth by the rain.

A small voice spoke in Bigwig's mind.

'Your storm, Thlayli-rah. Use it.'

Gasping, he struggled up and pushed Blackavar with his foot.

'Come on,' he said, 'get hold of – Hyzenthlay. We're going.'

He shook his head, trying to blink the rain out of his eyes. Then it was no longer Blackavar who was crouching in front of him but Woundwort, drenched in mud and rain, glaring and scrabbling in the silt with his great claws.

'I'll kill you myself,' said Woundwort.

His long front teeth were bared like the fangs of a rat. Afraid, Bigwig watched him closely. He knew that Woundwort, with all the advantage of weight, would jump and try to close with him. He must try to avoid him and rely on his claws. He shifted his ground uneasily and felt himself slipping in the mud. Why did Woundwort not jump? Then he realized that Woundwort was no longer looking at him, but staring over his head at something beyond, something that he himself could not see. Suddenly, Woundwort leapt backwards and in the same moment, through the all-enveloping sound of the rain, there sounded a raucous clamour.

'Yark! Yark! Yark!'

Some big, white thing was striking at Woundwort, who was cowering and guarding his head as best he could. Then it was gone, sailing upwards and turning in the rain.

'Meester Pigvig, ees rabbits come!'

Sights and feelings swirled through Bigwig as though in a dream. The things that were happening no longer seemed connected by anything except his own dazed senses. He heard Kehaar screaming as he dived again to attack Vervain. He felt the rain pouring cold into the open gash in his shoulder. Through the curtain of rain he glimpsed Woundwort dodging among his officers and urging them back into the ditch on the edge of the field. He saw Blackavar striking at Campion and Campion turning to run. Then someone beside him was saying, 'Hullo, Bigwig. Bigwig! Bigwig! What do you want us to do?' It was Silver.

'Where's Hazel?' he said.

'Waiting at the boat. I say, you're wounded! What –'

'Then get these does down there,' said Bigwig.

All was confusion. In ones and twos the does, utterly bemused and scarcely able to move or to understand what was said to them, were urged into getting up and stumbling their way down the field. Other rabbits began to appear through the rain: Acorn, clearly frightened, but determined not to run; Dandelion encouraging Pipkin; Speedwell and Hawkbit making towards Kehaar – the only creature visible above the ground-haze. Bigwig and Silver brought them together as best they could and made them understand that they were to help to get the does away.

'Go back to Blackberry, go back to Blackberry,' Silver kept repeating. 'I left three of our rabbits in different places to mark the way back,' he explained to Bigwig. 'Blackberry's first, then Bluebell, then Fiver – he's quite near the river.'

'And there *is* Blackberry,' said Bigwig.

'You did it then, Bigwig,' said Blackberry, shivering. 'Was it very bad? Good heavens, your shoulder –'

'It's not finished yet,' said Bigwig. 'Has everyone passed you?'

'You're the last,' said Blackberry. 'Can we go? This storm's terrifying me!'

Kehaar alighted beside them.

'Meester Pigvig,' he said, 'I fly on dose dam' rabbits, but dey no run, dey get in ditch. I no catch 'em in dere. Dey coming all along beside you.'

'They'll never give up,' said Bigwig. 'I warn you, Silver, they'll be at us before it's done. There's thick cover in the water-meadow – they'll use that. Acorn, come back, keep away from that ditch!'

'Go back to Bluebell! Go back to Bluebell!' repeated Silver, running from side to side.

They found Bluebell by the hedge at the bottom of the field. He was white-eyed and ready to bolt.

'Silver,' he said, 'I saw a bunch of rabbits – strangers, Efrafans, I suppose – come out of the ditch over there and slip across into the water-meadow. They're behind us now. One of them was the biggest rabbit I've ever seen.'

'Then don't stay here,' said Silver. 'There goes Speedwell. And who's that? Acorn and two does with him. That's everyone. Come on, quick as you can.'

It was only a short distance now to the river, but among the sodden patches of rushes, the bushes and sedge and deep puddles, they found it next to impossible to tell their direction. Expecting to be attacked at any moment, they scattered and floundered through the undergrowth, finding here a doe and there one of their own rabbits and forcing them on. Without Kehaar they would certainly have lost all touch with each other and perhaps never reached the river. The gull kept flying backwards and forwards along the direct line to the bank, only alighting now and then to guide Bigwig towards some straggling doe whom he had spotted going the wrong way.

'Kehaar,' said Bigwig, as they waited for Thethuthinnang to struggle up to them through a half-flattened clump of nettles, 'will you go and see whether you can spot the Efrafans? They can't be far away. But why haven't they attacked us? We're all so scattered that they could easily do us a lot of harm. I wonder what they're up to?'

Kehaar was back in a very short time.

'Dey hiding at pridge,' he said, 'all under pushes. I come down, dat peeg fella 'e make for fight me.'

'Did he?' said Bigwig. 'The brute's got courage, I'll give him that.'

'Dey t'ink you got to cross river dere or else go all along pank. Dey not know heem poat. You near poat now.'

Fiver came running through the undergrowth.

'We've been able to get some of them on the boat, Bigwig,' he said, 'but most of them won't trust me. They just keep asking where *you* are.'

Bigwig ran behind him and came out on the green path by the bank. All the surface of the river was winking and plopping in the rain. The level did not appear to have risen much as yet. The boat was just as he remembered it – one end against the bank, the other a little way out in the stream. On the raised part at the near end Hazel was crouching, his ears drooping on either side of his head and his flattened fur completely black with rain. He was holding the taut rope in his teeth. Acorn, Hyzenthlay and two more were crouching near him on the wood, but the rest were huddled here and there along the bank. Blackberry was trying unsuccessfully to persuade them to get out on the boat.

'Hazel's afraid to leave the rope,' he said to Bigwig. 'Apparently he's bitten it very thin already. All these does will say is that you're their officer.'

Bigwig turned to Thethuthinnang.

'This is the magic trick now,' he said. 'Get them over there, where Hyzenthlay's sitting, do you see? All of them – quickly.'

Before she could reply, another doe gave a squeal of fear. A little way downstream, Campion and his patrol had emerged from the bushes and were coming up the path. From the opposite direction Vervain, Chervil and Groundsel were approaching. The doe turned and darted for the undergrowth immediately behind her. Just as she reached it, Woundwort himself appeared in her way, reared up and dealt her a great, raking blow across the face. The doe turned once more and ran blindly across the path and on to the boat.

Bigwig realized that since the moment when Kehaar had attacked him in the field, Woundwort had not only retained control over his officers but had actually made a plan and put it into effect. The storm and the difficult going had upset the fugitives and disorganized them. Woundwort, on the other hand, had taken his rabbits into the ditch and then made use of it to get them down to the water-meadow, unexposed to further attack from Kehaar. Once there, he must have gone straight for the plank bridge – which he evidently knew about – and set an ambush under cover. But as soon as he had grasped that for some reason the runaways were not making for the bridge after all, he had instantly sent Campion to make his way round through the undergrowth, regain the bank downstream and cut them off: and Campion had done this without error or delay. Now Woundwort meant to fight them, here on the bank. He knew that Kehaar could not be everywhere and that the bushes and undergrowth provided enough cover, at a pinch, to dodge him. It was true that the other side had twice his numbers, but most of them were afraid of him and none was a trained Efrafan officer. Now that he had them pinned against the river, he would split them up and kill as many as possible. The rest could run away and come to grief as they might.

Bigwig began to understand why Woundwort's officers followed him and fought for him as they did.

'He's not like a rabbit at all,' he thought. 'Flight's the last thing he ever thinks of. If I'd known three nights ago what I know now, I don't believe I'd ever have gone into Efrafa. I suppose he hasn't realized about the boat too? It wouldn't surprise me.' He dashed across the grass and jumped on the planking beside Hazel.

The appearance of Woundwort had achieved what Blackberry and Fiver could not. Every one of the does ran from the bank to the boat. Blackberry and Fiver ran with them. Woundwort, following them close, reached the edge of the bank and came face to face with Bigwig. As he stood his ground, Bigwig could hear Blackberry just behind him, speaking urgently to Hazel.

'Dandelion's not here,' said Blackberry. 'He's the only one.'

Hazel spoke for the first time. 'We shall have to leave him,' he answered. 'It's a shame, but these fellows will be at us in a moment and we can't stop them.'

Bigwig spoke without taking his eyes from Woundwort. 'Just a few more moments, Hazel,' he said. 'I'll keep them off. We can't leave Dandelion.'

Woundwort sneered up at him. 'I trusted you, Thlayli,' he said. 'You can trust me now. You'll either go into the river or be torn to pieces here – the whole lot of you. There's nowhere left to run.'

Bigwig had caught sight of Dandelion looking out of the undergrowth opposite. He was plainly at a loss.

'Groundsel! Vervain!' said Woundwort. 'Come over here beside me. When I give the word, we'll go straight into them. As for that bird, it's not dangerous –'

'There it is!' cried Bigwig. Woundwort looked up quickly and leapt back. Dandelion shot out of the bushes, crossed the path in a flash and was on the boat beside Hazel. In the same moment the rope parted and immediately the little punt began to move along the bank in the steady current. When it had gone a few yards, the stern swung slowly outwards, until it was broadside on to the stream. In this position it drifted to the middle of the river and into the southward bend.

Looking back, the last thing Bigwig saw was the face of General Woundwort staring out of the gap in the willow-herb where the boat had lain. It reminded him of the kestrel on Watership Down, which had pounced into the mouth of the hole and missed the mouse.

PART FOUR

Hazel-Rah

39. The Bridges

Boatman dance, boatman sing,
Boatman do most anything,
Dance, boatman, dance.
    Dance all night till the broad daylight,
    Go home with the girls in the morning.
Hey, ho, boatman row,
    Sailing down the river on the Ohio.

American Folk Song

O N ALMOST any other river, Blackberry's plan would not have worked. The punt would not have left the bank or if it had, would have run aground or been fouled by weeds or some other obstruction. But here, on the Test, there were no submerged branches and no gravel spits or beds of weed above the surface at all. From bank to bank the current, regular and unvaried, flowed as fast as a man strolling. The punt slipped downstream smoothly, without any alteration of the speed which it had gained within a few yards of leaving the bank.

Most of the rabbits had very little idea of what was happening. The Efrafan does had never seen a river and it would certainly have been beyond Pipkin or Hawkbit to explain to them that they were on a boat. They – and nearly all the others – had simply trusted Hazel and done as they were told. But all – bucks and does alike – realized that Woundwort and his followers had vanished. Wearied by all they had gone through, the sodden rabbits crouched without talking, incapable of any feeling but a dull relief and without even the energy to wonder what was going to happen next.

That they should feel any relief – dull or otherwise – was remarkable in the circumstances and showed both how little they understood their situation and how much fear Woundwort could inspire, for their escape from him seemed to be their only good fortune. The rain was still falling. Already so wet that they no longer felt it, they were nevertheless shivering with cold and weighted with their drenched fur. The punt was holding over half an inch of rainwater. There was one small, slatted floorboard and this was floating. Some of the rabbits, in the first confusion of boarding the punt, had found themselves in this water, but now all had got clear of it – most either to bows or stern, though Thethuthinnang and Speedwell were hunched on the narrow thwart, amidships. In addition to their discomfort, they were exposed and helpless. Finally, there was no way of controlling the punt and they did not know where they were going. But these last were troubles beyond the understanding of everyone but Hazel, Fiver and Blackberry.

Bigwig had collapsed beside Hazel and lay on his side, exhausted. The feverish courage had gone which had brought him from Efrafa to the river and his wounded shoulder had begun to hurt badly. In spite of the rain and the throbbing pulse down his foreleg, he felt ready to sleep where he was, stretched upon the planking. He opened his eyes and looked up at Hazel.

'I couldn't do it again, Hazel,' he said.

'You haven't got to,' replied Hazel.

'It was touch and go, you know,' said Bigwig. 'A chance in a thousand.'

'Our children's children will hear a good story,' answered Hazel, quoting a rabbit proverb. 'How did you get that wound? It's a nasty one.'

'I fought a member of the Council police,' said Bigwig.

'A what?' The term 'Owslafa' was unknown to Hazel.

'A dirty little beast like Hufsa,' said Bigwig.

'Did you beat him?'

'Oh yes – or I shouldn't be here. I should think he'll stop running. I say, Hazel, we've got the does. What's going to happen now?'

'I don't know,' said Hazel. 'We need one of these clever rabbits to tell us. And Kehaar – where's he gone? He's supposed to know about this thing we're sitting on.'

Dandelion, crouching beside Hazel, got up at the mention of 'clever rabbits', made his way across the puddled floor and returned with Blackberry and Fiver.

'We're all wondering what to do next,' said Hazel.

'Well,' said Blackberry, 'I suppose we shall drift into the bank before long and then we can get out and find cover.

479

There's no harm, though, in going a good long way from those friends of Bigwig's.'

'There is,' said Hazel. 'We're stuck here in full view and we can't run. If a man sees us we're in trouble.'

'Men don't like rain,' said Blackberry. 'Neither do I, if it comes to that, but it makes us safer just now.'

At this moment Hyzenthlay, sitting just behind him, started and looked up.

'Excuse me, sir, for interrupting you,' she said, as though speaking to an officer in Efrafa, 'but the bird – the white bird – it's coming towards us.'

Kehaar came flying up the river through the rain and alighted on the narrow side of the punt. The does nearest to him backed away nervously.

'Meester 'Azel,' he said, 'pridge come. You see 'im pridge?'

It had not occurred to any of the rabbits that they were floating beside the path up which they had come earlier that evening before the storm broke. They were on the opposite side of the hedge of plants along the bank and the whole river looked different. But now they saw, not far ahead, the bridge which they had crossed when they first came to the Test four nights before. This they recognized at once, for it looked the same as it had from the bank.

'Maybe you go under 'im, maybe not,' said Kehaar. 'But you sit dere, ees trouble.'

The bridge stretched from bank to bank between two low abutments. It was not arched. Its under-side, made of iron girders, was perfectly straight – parallel with the surface and about eight inches above it. Just in time Hazel saw what Kehaar meant. If the punt did pass under the bridge without sticking, it would do so by no more than a claw's breadth. Any creature above the level of the sides would be struck and perhaps knocked into the river. He scuttered through the warm bilge-water to the other end and pushed his way up among the wet, crowded rabbits.

'Get down in the bottom! Get down in the bottom!' he said. 'Silver, Hawkbit – all of you. Never mind the water. You, and you – what's your name? Oh, Blackavar, is it? – get everyone into the bottom. Be quick.'

Like Bigwig, he found that the Efrafan rabbits obeyed him at once. He saw Kehaar fly up from his perch and disappear over the wooden rails. The concrete abutments projected from each bank, so that the narrowed river ran slightly faster under the bridge. The punt had been drifting broadside on, but now one end swung forward, so that Hazel lost his bearings and found that he was no longer looking at the bridge but at the bank. As he hesitated, the bridge seemed to come at him in a dark mass, like snow sliding from a bough. He pressed himself into the bilge. There was a squeal and a rabbit tumbled on top of him. Then a heavy blow vibrated along the length of the punt and its smooth movement was checked. This was followed by a hollow sound of scraping. It grew dark and a roof appeared, very low above him. For a moment Hazel had the vague idea that he was underground. Then the roof vanished, the punt was gliding on and he heard Kehaar calling. They were below the bridge and still drifting downstream.

The rabbit who had fallen on him was Acorn. He had been struck by the bridge and the blow had sent him flying.

However, though dazed and bruised, he seemed to have escaped injury.

'I wasn't quick enough, Hazel-rah,' he said. 'I'd better go to Efrafa for a bit.'

'You'd be wasted,' said Hazel. 'But I'm afraid there's someone at the other end who hasn't been so lucky.'

One of the does had held back from the bilge-water and the upstream girder under the bridge had caught her across the back. It was plain that she was injured, but how badly Hazel could not tell. He saw Hyzenthlay beside her and it seemed to him that since there was nothing he could do to help, it would probably be best to let them alone. He looked round at his bedraggled, shivering comrades and then at Kehaar, spruce and brisk on the stern.

'We ought to get back on the bank, Kehaar,' he said. 'How can we do it? Rabbits weren't meant for this, you know.'

'You not stop poat. But again is nudder pridge more. 'E stop 'im.'

There was nothing to be done but wait. They drifted on and came to a second bend, where the river curved westwards. The current did not slacken and the punt came round the bend almost in the middle of the stream, revolving as it did so. The rabbits had been frightened by what had happened to Acorn and to the doe, and remained squatting miserably, half in and half out of the bilge. Hazel crept back to the raised bow and looked ahead.

The river broadened and the current slackened. He realized that they had begun to drift more slowly. The nearer bank was high and the trees stood close and thick, but on the farther bank the ground was low and open. Grassy, it stretched away, smooth as the mown gallops on Watership Down. Hazel hoped that they might somehow drop out of the current and reach that side, but the punt moved quietly on, down the very centre of the broad pool. The open bank slipped by and now the trees towered on both sides. Downstream, the pool was closed by the second bridge, of which Kehaar had spoken.

It was old, built of darkened bricks. Ivy trailed over it and the valerian and creeping mauve toadflax. Well out from either bank stood four low arches – scarcely more than culverts, each filled by the stream to within a foot of the apex. Through them, thin segments of daylight showed from the downstream side. The piers did not project, but against each lay a little accumulation of flotsam, from which driftweed and sticks continually broke away to be carried through the bridge.

It was plain that the punt would drift against the bridge and be held there. As it approached, Hazel dropped back into the bilge-water. But this time there was no need. Broadside on, the punt struck gently against two of the piers and stopped, pinned squarely across the mouth of one of the central culverts. It could go no further.

They had floated not quite half a mile in just over fifteen minutes.

Hazel put his forepaws on the low side and looked gingerly over upstream. Immediately below, a shallow ripple spread all along the water-line, where the current met the woodwork. It was too far to jump to the shore and both banks were steep. He turned and looked upwards. The brickwork was sheer, with a projecting course half-way between him and the parapet. There was no scrambling up that.

'What's to be done, Blackberry?' he asked, making his way to the bolt fixed on the bow, with its ragged remnant of painter. 'You got us on this thing. How do we get off?'

'I don't know, Hazel-rah,' replied Blackberry. 'Of all the ways we could finish up, I never thought of this. It looks as though we'll have to swim.'

'Swim?' said Silver. 'I don't fancy it, Hazel-rah. I know it's no distance, but look at those banks. The current would take us down before we could get out: and that means into one of these holes under the bridge.'

Hazel tried to look through the arch. There was very little to be seen. The dark tunnel was not long – perhaps not much longer than the punt itself. The water looked smooth. There seemed to be no obstructions and there was room for the head of a swimming animal between the surface of the water and the apex of the arch. But the segment was so narrow that it was impossible to see exactly what lay on the other side of the bridge. The light was failing. Water, green leaves, moving reflections of leaves, the splashing of the raindrops and some curious thing that appeared to be standing in the water and to be made of vertical, grey lines – these were all that could be made out. The rain echoed dismally up the culvert. The hard, ringing noise from under the soffit, so much unlike any sound to be heard in an earth tunnel, was disturbing. Hazel returned to Blackberry and Silver.

'This is as bad a fix as we've been in,' he said. 'We can't stay here, but I can't see any way out.'

Kehaar appeared on the parapet above them, flapped the rain out of his wings and dropped down to the punt.

'Ees finish poat,' he said. 'Not vait more.'

'But how can we get to the bank, Kehaar?' said Hazel.

The gull was surprised. 'Dog sveem, rat sveem. You no sveem?'

'Yes, we can swim as long as it's not very far. But the banks are too steep for us, Kehaar. We wouldn't be able to stop the current taking us down one of these tunnels and we don't know what's at the other end.'

'Ees goot – you get out fine.'

Hazel felt at a loss. What exactly was he to understand from this? Kehaar was not a rabbit. Whatever the Big Water was like, it must be worse than this and Kehaar was used to it. He never said much in any case and what he did say was always restricted to the simplest, since he spoke no Lapine. He was doing them a good turn because they had saved his life but, as Hazel knew, he could not help despising them for timid, helpless, stay-at-home creatures who could not fly. He was often impatient. Did he mean that he had looked at the river and considered it as if he were a rabbit? That there was slack water immediately below the bridge, with a low, shelving bank where they could get out easily? That seemed too much to hope for. Or did he simply mean that they had better hurry up and take a chance on being able to do what he himself could do without difficulty? This seemed more likely. Suppose one of them did jump out of the boat and go down with the current – what would that tell the others, if he did not come back?

Poor Hazel looked about him. Silver was licking Bigwig's wounded shoulder. Blackberry was fidgeting on and off the thwart, strung-up, able to feel only too clearly all that

Hazel felt himself. As he still hesitated, Kehaar let out a squawk.

'Yark! Dam' rabbits no goot. Vat I do, I show you.'

He tumbled clumsily off the raised bow. There was no gap between the punt and the dark mouth of the culvert. Sitting low in the water like a mallard, he floated into the tunnel and vanished. Peering after him, Hazel could at first see nothing. Then he made out Kehaar's shape black against the light at the far end. It floated into daylight, turned sideways and passed out of the restricted view.

'What does that prove?' said Blackberry, his teeth chattering. 'He may have flown off the surface or put his great webbed feet down. It's not he that's soaked through and shivering and twice as heavy with wet fur.'

Kehaar reappeared on the parapet above.

'You go now,' he said shortly.

Still the wretched Hazel hung back. His leg had begun to hurt again. The sight of Bigwig – Bigwig of all rabbits – at the end of his tether, half-unconscious, playing no part in this desperate exploit, lowered his courage still more. He knew that he had not got it in him to jump into the water. The horrible situation was beyond him. He stumbled on the slippery planking and as he sat up found Fiver beside him.

'I'll go, Hazel,' said Fiver quietly. 'I think it'll be all right.'

He put his front paws on the edge of the bow. Then, on the instant, all the rabbits froze motionless. One of the does stamped on the puddled floor of the punt. From above came the sounds of approaching footsteps and men's voices, and the smell of a burning white stick.

Kehaar flew away. Not a rabbit moved. The footsteps grew nearer, the voices louder. They were on the bridge above, no farther away than the height of a hedge. Every one of the rabbits was seized by the instinct to run, to go underground. Hazel saw Hyzenthlay looking at him and returned her stare, willing her with all his might to keep still. The voices, the smell of men's sweat, of leather, of white sticks, the pain in his leg, the damp, chuckling tunnel at his very ear – he had known them all before. How could the men not see him? They must see him. He was lying at their feet. He was wounded. They were coming to pick him up.

Then the sound and smells were receding into the distance, the thudding of the footsteps diminished. The men had crossed the bridge without looking over the parapet. They were gone.

Hazel came to. 'That settles it,' he said. 'Everyone's got to swim. Come on, Bluebell, you say you're a water-rabbit. Follow me.' He got on the thwart and went along it to the side.

But it was Pipkin that he found next to him.

'Quick, Hazel-rah,' said Pipkin, twitching and trembling. 'I'll come too. Only be quick.'

Hazel shut his eyes and fell over the side into the water.

As in the Enborne, there was an instant shock of cold. But more than this, and at once, he felt the pull of the current. He was being drawn away by a force like a high wind, yet smooth and silent. He was drifting helplessly down a suffocating, cold run, with no hold for his feet. Full of fear, he paddled and struggled, got his head up and took a breath, scrabbled his claws against rough bricks underwater and lost them again as he was dragged on. Then the current slackened, the run vanished, the dark became light and there were leaves and sky above him once more. Still struggling, he fetched up against something hard, bumped off it, struck it again and then for a moment touched soft ground. He floundered forwards and found that he was dragging himself through liquid mud. He was out on a clammy bank. He lay panting for several moments and then wiped his face and opened his eyes. The first thing he saw was Pipkin, plastered with mud, crawling to the bank a few feet away.

Full of elation and confidence, all his terrors forgotten, Hazel crawled over to Pipkin and together they slipped into the undergrowth. He said nothing and Pipkin did not seem to expect him to speak. From the shelter of a clump of purple loosestrife they looked back at the river.

The water came out from the bridge into a second pool. All round, on both banks, trees and undergrowth grew close. There was a kind of swamp here and it was hard to tell where water ended and woodland began. Plants grew in clumps both in and out of the muddy shallows. The bottom was covered with fine silt and mud that was half water and in this the two rabbits had made furrows as they dragged themselves to shore. Running diagonally across the pool, from the brickwork of the bridge near the opposite bank to a point a little below them on their own side, was a grating of thin, vertical iron rods. In the cutting season the river weed, drifting in tangled mats from the fishing reaches above, was held against this grating and raked out of the pool by men in waders, who piled it to be used as compost. The left bank was a great rubbish-heap of rotting weed among the trees. It was a green, rank-smelling place, humid and enclosed.

'Good old Kehaar!' said Hazel, gazing with satisfaction round the foetid solitude. 'I should have trusted him.'

As he spoke, a third rabbit came swimming out from under the bridge. The sight of him, struggling in the current like a fly in a spider's web, filled them both with fear. To watch another in danger can be almost as bad as sharing it. The rabbit fetched up against the grating, drifted a little way along it, found the bottom and crawled out of the turbid water. It was Blackavar. He lay on his side and seemed unaware of Hazel and Pipkin when they came up to him. After a little while, however, he began to cough, vomited some water and sat up.

'Are you all right?' asked Hazel.

'More or less,' said Blackavar. 'But have we got to do much more tonight, sir? I'm very tired.'

'No, you can rest here,' said Hazel. 'But why did you risk it on your own? We might already have gone under for all you knew.'

'I thought you gave an order,' replied Blackavar.

'I see,' said Hazel. 'Well, at that rate you're going to find us a sloppy lot, I'm afraid. Was there anyone else who looked like coming when you jumped in?'

'I think they're a bit nervous,' answered Blackavar. 'You can't blame them.'

'No, but the trouble is that anything can happen,' said Hazel, fretting. 'They may all go tharn, sitting there. The men may come back. If only we could tell them it's all right –'

'I think we can, sir,' said Blackavar. 'Unless I'm wrong, it's only a matter of slipping up the bank there and down the other side. Shall I go?'

Hazel was disconcerted. From what he had gathered, this was a disgraced prisoner from Efrafa – not even a member of the Owsla, apparently; and he had just said that he felt exhausted. He was going to take some living up to.

'We'll both go,' he said. 'Hlao-roo, can you stay here and keep a look-out? With any luck, they'll start coming through to you. Help them if you can.'

Hazel and Blackavar slipped through the dripping undergrowth. The grass track which crossed the bridge ran above them, at the top of a steep bank. They climbed the bank and looked out cautiously from the long grass at the verge. The track was empty and there was nothing to be heard or smelt. They crossed it and reached the end of the bridge on the upstream side. Here the bank dropped almost sheer to the river, some six feet below. Blackavar scrambled down without hesitation, but Hazel followed more slowly. Just above the bridge, between it and a thorn-bush upstream, was a ledge of turf which overhung the water. Out in the river, a few feet away, the punt lay against the weedy piers.

'Silver!' said Hazel. 'Fiver! Come on, get them into the water. It's all right below the bridge. Get the does in first, if you can. There's no time to lose. The men may come back.'

It was no easy matter to rouse the torpid, bewildered does and make them understand what they had to do.

Silver went from one to another. Dandelion, as soon as he saw Hazel on the bank, went at once to the bow and plunged in. Speedwell followed, but as Fiver was about to go Silver stopped him.

'If all our bucks go, Hazel,' he said, 'the does will be left alone and I don't think they'll manage it.'

'They'll obey Thlayli, sir,' said Blackavar, before Hazel could reply. 'I think he's the one to get them started.'

Bigwig was still lying in the bilge water, in the place he had taken up when they came to the first bridge. He seemed to be asleep, but when Silver nuzzled him he raised his head and looked about in a dazed manner.

'Oh, hullo, Silver,' he said. 'I'm afraid this shoulder of mine's going to be a bother. I feel awfully cold, too. Where's Hazel?'

Silver explained. Bigwig got up with difficulty and they saw that he was still bleeding. He limped to the thwart and climbed on it.

'Hyzenthlay,' he said, 'your friends can't be any wetter, so we'll get them to jump in now. One by one, don't you think? Then there'll be no risk of them scratching or hurting each other as they swim.'

In spite of what Blackavar had said, it was a long time before everyone had left the boat. There were in fact ten does altogether – though none of the rabbits knew the number – and although one or two responded to Bigwig's patient urging, several were so much exhausted that they remained huddled where they were, or looked stupidly at the water until others were brought to take their place. From time to time Bigwig would ask one of the bucks to give a lead and in this way Acorn, Hawkbit and Bluebell all scrambled over the side. The injured doe, Thrayonlosa, was clearly in a bad way and Blackberry and Thethuthinnang swam through together, one in front of her and one behind.

As darkness closed in the rain stopped. Hazel and Blackavar went back to the bank of the pool below the bridge. The sky cleared and the oppression lifted as the thunder moved away eastwards. But it was fu Inlé before Bigwig himself came through the bridge with Silver and Fiver. It was much as ever he could keep afloat and when he reached the grating he rolled over in the water, belly uppermost, like a dying fish. He drifted into the shallows and, with Silver's help, pulled himself out. Hazel and several of the others were waiting for him, but he cut them short with a flash of his old, bullying manner.

'Come on, get out of the way,' he said, 'I'm going to sleep now, Hazel, and Frith help you if you say I'm not.'

'That's how *we* go on, you see,' said Hazel to the staring Blackavar. 'You'll get used to it after a bit. Now, let's look for somewhere dry that no one else has found and then perhaps we can sleep too.'

Every dry spot among the undergrowth seemed to be crowded with exhausted, sleeping rabbits. After searching for a time they found a fallen tree-trunk, from the under side of which the bark had pulled away. They crept beneath the twigs and leaves, settled themselves in the smooth, curved trough – which soon took on some of the warmth of their bodies – and slept at once.

40. The Way Back

Dame Hickory, Dame Hickory
Here's a wolf at your door,
His teeth grinning white,
And his tongue wagging sore!
'Nay,' said Dame Hickory, 'Ye False Faerie!'
But a wolf t'was indeed, and famished was he.

Walter de la Mare, *Dame Hickory*

THE FIRST thing that Hazel learned the next morning was that Thrayonlosa had died during the night. Thethuthinnang was distressed, for it was she who had picked Thrayonlosa as one of the more sturdy and sensible does in the Mark and persuaded her to join in the escape. After they had come through the bridge together, she had helped her ashore and fallen asleep beside her in the undergrowth, hoping that she might have recovered by the next day. But she had woken to find Thrayonlosa gone and, searching, had found her in a clump of reeds downstream. Evidently the poor creature had felt that she was going to die and, in the manner of animals, had slipped away.

The news depressed Hazel. He knew that they had been lucky to get so many does out of Efrafa and to escape from Woundwort without having to stand and fight. The plan had been a good one, but the storm and the frightening efficiency of the Efrafans had nearly defeated it. For all the courage of Bigwig and of Silver, they would have failed without Kehaar. Now Kehaar was going to leave them. Bigwig was wounded and his own leg was none too good. With the does to look after, they would not be able to travel in the open as fast or as easily as they had on the way down from Watership. He would have liked to stay where they were for a few days, so that Bigwig could recover his strength and the does find their feet and get used to life outside a warren. But the place, he realized, was hopelessly inhospitable. Although there was good cover, it was too wet for rabbits. Besides, it was evidently close to a road busier than any they had known. Soon after daylight they began to hear and smell hrududil passing, not so far away as the breadth of a small field. There was continual disturbance and the does in particular were startled and uneasy. Thrayonlosa's death made matters worse. Worried by the noise and vibration and unable to feed, the does kept wandering downstream to look at the body and whisper together about the strange and dangerous surroundings.

He consulted Blackberry, who pointed out that probably it would not be long before men found the boat; then very likely several would be close by for some time. This decided Hazel that they had better set out at once and try to reach somewhere where they could rest more easily. He could hear and smell that the swamp extended a long way downstream. With the road lying to the south, the only way seemed to be northwards, over the bridge, which was in any case the way home.

Taking Bigwig with him, he climbed the bank to the grass track. The first thing they saw was Kehaar, picking slugs out of a clump of hemlock near the bridge. They came up to him without speaking and began to nibble the short grass nearby.

After a little while Kehaar said, 'Now you getting mudders, Meester 'Azel. All go fine, eh?'

'Yes. We'd never have done it without you, Kehaar. I hear you turned up just in time to save Bigwig last night.'

'Dis bad rabbit, pig fella, 'e go fight me. Plenty clever too.'

'Yes. He got a shock for once, though.'

'Ya, ya. Meester 'Azel, soon is men come. Vat you do now?'

'We're going back to our warren, Kehaar, if we can get there.'

'Ees finish here now for me. I go to Peeg Vater.'

'Shall we see you again, Kehaar?'

'You go back hills? Stay dere?'

'Yes, we mean to get there. It's going to be hard going with so many rabbits, and there'll be Efrafan patrols to dodge, I expect.'

'You get dere, later on ees vinter, plenty cold, plenty storm on Peeg Vater. Plenty bird come in. Den I come back, see you vere you live.'

'Don't forget, then, Kehaar, will you?' said Bigwig. 'We shall be looking out for you. Come down suddenly, like you did last night.'

'Ya, ya, frighten all mudders und liddle rabbits, all liddle Pigvigs run avay.'

Kehaar arched his wings and rose into the air. He flew over the parapet of the bridge and upstream. Then he turned in a circle to the left, came back over the grass track and flew straight down it, skimming just over the rabbits' heads. He gave one of his raucous cries and was gone to the southward. They gazed after him as he disappeared above the trees.

'Oh, fly away, great bird so white,' said Bigwig. 'You know, he made me feel I could fly too. That Big Water! I wish I could see it.'

As they continued to look in the direction where Kehaar had gone, Hazel noticed for the first time a cottage at the far end of the track, where the grass sloped up to join the road. A man, taking care to keep still, was leaning over the hedge and watching them intently. Hazel stamped and bolted into the undergrowth of the swamp, with Bigwig hard on his heels.

'You know what he's thinking about?' said Bigwig. 'He's thinking about the vegetables in his garden.'

'I know,' replied Hazel. 'And we shan't be able to keep this lot away from them once they get the idea into their heads. The quicker we push on the better.'

Shortly afterwards the rabbits set out across the park to the north. Bigwig soon found that he was not up to a long journey. His wound was painful and the shoulder muscle would not stand hard use. Hazel was still lame and the does, though willing and obedient, showed that they knew little about the life of hlessil. It was a trying time.

In the days that followed – days of clear sky and fine weather – Blackavar proved his worth again and again, until Hazel came to rely on him as much as on any of his veterans. There was a great deal more to him than anyone could have guessed. When Bigwig had determined not to come out of Efrafa without Blackavar, he had been moved entirely by pity for a miserable, helpless victim of Woundwort's ruthlessness. It turned out, however, that Blackavar, when not crushed by humiliation and ill-treatment, was a good cut above the ordinary. His story was an unusual one. His mother had not been born an Efrafan. She had been one of the rabbits taken prisoner when Woundwort attacked the warren at Nutley Copse. She had mated with an Efrafan captain and had had no other mate. He had been killed on Wide Patrol. Blackavar, proud of his father, had grown up with the resolve to become an officer in the Owsla. But together with this – and paradoxically – there had come to him from his mother a certain resentment against Efrafa and a feeling that they should have no more of him than he cared to give them. Captain Mallow, to whose Mark – the Right Fore – he had been sent on trial, had praised his courage and endurance but had not failed to notice the proud detachment of his nature. When the Right Flank needed a junior officer to help Captain Chervil, it was Avens and not Blackavar who had been selected by the Council. Blackavar, who knew his own worth, felt convinced that his mother's blood had prejudiced the Council against him. While still full of his wrongs he had met Hyzenthlay and made himself a secret friend and adviser of the discontented does in the Right

Fore. He had begun by urging them to try to get the Council's consent to their leaving Efrafa. If they had succeeded they would have asked for him to be allowed to go with them. But when the does' deputation to the Council failed, Blackavar turned to the idea of escape. At first he had meant to take the does with him but his nerve, strained to the limit, as Bigwig's had been, by the dangers and uncertainties of conspiracy, had given way and in the end he had simply made a dash on his own, to be caught by Campion. Under the punishment inflicted by the Council his mercurial spirit had fallen low and he had become the apathetic wretch the sight of whom had so much shocked Bigwig. Yet at the whispered message in the hraka-pit this spirit had flickered up again where another's might well have failed to do so, and he had been ready to set all on the hazard and have another shot. Now, free among these easy-going strangers, he saw himself as a trained Efrafan, using his skill to help them in their need. Although he did all that he was told, he did not hesitate to make suggestions as well, particularly when it came to reconnoitring and looking for signs of danger. Hazel, who was ready to accept advice from anybody when he thought it was good, listened to most of what he said and was content to leave it to Bigwig – for whom, naturally, Blackavar entertained a tremendous respect – to see that he did not over-reach himself in his warm-hearted, rather candid zeal.

After two or three days of slow, careful journeying, with many halts in cover, they found themselves, late one afternoon, once more in sight of Caesar's Belt, but further west than before, close to a little copse at the top of some rising ground. Everyone was tired and when they had fed – 'Evening silflay every day, just as you promised,' said Hyzenthlay to Bigwig – Bluebell and Speedwell suggested that it might be worth while to dig some scrapes in the light soil under the trees and live there for a day or two. Hazel felt willing enough, but Fiver needed persuasion.

'I know we can do with a rest, but somehow I don't altogether like it, Hazel-rah,' he said. 'I suppose I've got to try to think why?'

'Not on my account,' answered Hazel. 'But I doubt you'll shift the others this time. One or two of these does are "ready for mudder", as Kehaar would say, and that's the real reason why Bluebell and the rest are prepared to be at the trouble of digging scrapes. Surely it'll be all right at that rate, won't it? You know what they say – "Rabbit underground, rabbit safe and sound".'

'Well, you may be right,' said Fiver. 'That Vilthuril's a beautiful doe. I'd like a chance to get to know her better. After all, it's not natural to rabbits, is it? – on and on day after day.'

Later, however, when Blackavar returned with Dandelion from a patrol they had undertaken on their own initiative, he came out more strongly against the idea.

'This is no place to stop, Hazel-rah,' he said. 'No Wide Patrol would bivouac here. It's fox country. We ought to try to get further before dark.'

Bigwig's shoulder had been hurting him a good deal during the afternoon and he felt low and surly. It seemed to him that Blackavar was being clever at other people's expense. If he got his way they would have to go on, tired as they were, until they came to somewhere which was suitable by Efrafan standards. There they would be as safe – no more and no less – than they would have been if they had stayed at this copse; but Blackavar would be the clever fellow who had saved them from a fox that had never existed outside his own fancy. His Efrafan scoutcraft act was getting to be a bore. It was time someone called his bluff.

'There are likely to be foxes anywhere about the downs,' said Bigwig sharply. 'Why is this fox country more than anywhere else?'

Tact was a quality which Blackavar valued about as much as Bigwig did; and now he made the worst possible reply.

'I can't exactly tell you why,' he said. 'I've formed a strong impression, but it's hard to explain quite what it's based on.'

'Oh, an impression, eh?' sneered Bigwig. 'Did you see any hraka? Pick up any scent? Or was it just a message from little green mice singing under a toadstool?'

Blackavar felt hurt. Bigwig was the last rabbit he wanted to quarrel with.

'Ye think I'm a fool, then,' he answered, his Efrafan accent becoming more marked. 'No, there was neether hraka ner scent, but I still think that this is a place where a fox comes. On these patrols we used to do, ye know, we –'

'Did *you* see or smell anything?' said Bigwig to Dandelion.

'Er – well, I'm not really quite sure,' said Dandelion. 'I mean, Blackavar seems to know an awful lot about patrolling and he asked me whether I didn't feel a sort of –'

'Well, we can go on like this all night,' said Bigwig. 'Blackavar, do you know that earlier this summer, before we had the benefit of your experience, we went for days across every kind of country – fields, heather, woods, downs – and never lost one rabbit?'

'It's the idea of scrapes, that's all,' said Blackavar apologetically. 'New scrapes get noticed; and digging can be heard a surprisingly long way, ye know.'

'Let him alone,' said Hazel, before Bigwig could speak again. 'You didn't get him out of Efrafa to bully him. Look, Blackavar, I suppose I've got to decide this. I think you're probably right and there is a certain amount of risk. But we're at risk all the time until we get back to our warren and everyone's so tired that I think we might just as well stop here for a day or two. We shall be all the better for it.'

Enough scrapes were finished by soon after sunset and next day, sure enough, all the rabbits felt a great deal better for a night underground. As Hazel had foreseen, there was some mating and a scuffle or two, but no one was hurt. By the evening a kind of holiday spirit prevailed. Hazel's leg was stronger and Bigwig felt fitter than at any time since he went into Efrafa. The does, harassed and bony two days before, were beginning to look quite sleek.

On the second morning, silflay did not begin until some time after dawn. A light wind was blowing straight into the north bank of the copse, where the scrapes had been dug, and Bluebell, when he came up, swore he could smell rabbits on it.

'It's old Holly pressing his chin glands for us, Hazel-rah,' he said. 'A rabbit's sneeze on the morning breeze sets homesick hearts aglow –'

'Sitting with his rump in a chicory clump and longing for a nice plump doe,' replied Hazel.

'That won't do, Hazel-rah,' said Bluebell. 'He's got two does up there.'

'Only hutch-does,' replied Hazel. 'I dare say they're fairly tough and fast by now, but all the same they'll never be quite like our own kind. Clover, for instance – she'd never go far from the hole on silflay, because she knew she couldn't run as fast as we can. But these Efrafan does, you see – they've been kept in by sentries all their lives. Yet now there aren't any, they wander about quite happily. Look at those two, right away under the bank there. They feel they can – oh great Frith!'

As he spoke a tawny shape, dog-like, sprang out of the overhanging nut-bushes as silently as light from behind a cloud. It landed between the two does, grabbed one by the neck and dragged her up the bank in a flash. The wind veered and the reek of fox came over the grass. With stamping and flashing of tails every rabbit on the slope dashed for cover.

Hazel and Bluebell found themselves crouched with Blackavar. The Efrafan was matter-of-fact and detached.

'Poor little beast,' he said. 'You see, their instincts are weakened by life in the Mark. Fancy feeding under bushes on the windward side of a wood! Never mind, Hazel-rah, these things happen. But look, I tell you what. Unless there are two hombil, which would be very bad luck, we've got till ni-Frith at least to get away. That homba won't be hunting any more for some time. I suggest we all move on as soon as we can.'

With a word of agreement, Hazel went out to call the rabbits together. They made a scattered but swift run to the north-east, along the edge of a field of ripening wheat. No one spoke of the doe. They had covered more than three-quarters of a mile before Bigwig and Hazel halted to rest and to make sure that no one had fallen behind. As Blackavar came up with Hyzenthlay, Bigwig said,

'You told us how it would be, didn't you? And I was the one who wouldn't listen.'

'Told you?' said Blackavar. 'I don't understand.'

'That there was likely to be a fox.'

'I don't remember, I'm afraid. But I don't see that any of us could possibly have known. Anyway, what's a doe more or less?'

Bigwig looked at him in astonishment but Blackavar, apparently unconcerned either to stress what he had said or to break off the talk, simply began to nibble the grass. Bigwig, puzzled, moved away and himself began to feed a little distance off, with Hyzenthlay and Hazel.

'What's he getting at?' he asked after a while. 'You were all there when he warned us, two nights ago, that there was likely to be a fox. I treated him badly.'

'In Efrafa,' said Hyzenthlay, 'if a rabbit gave advice and the advice wasn't accepted, he immediately forgot it and so did everyone else. Blackavar thought what Hazel decided;

and whether it turned out later to be right or wrong was all the same. His own advice had never been given.'

'I can believe that,' said Bigwig. 'Efrafa! Ants led by a dog! But we're not in Efrafa now. Has he really forgotten that he warned us?'

'Probably he really has. But whether or not, you'd never get him to admit that he warned you or to listen while you told him he'd been right. He could no more do that than pass hraka underground.'

'But you're an Efrafan. Do you think like that too?'

'I'm a doe,' said Hyzenthlay.

During the early afternoon they began to approach the Belt and Bigwig was the first to recognize the place where Dandelion had told the story of the Black Rabbit of Inlé.

'It was the same fox, you know,' he said to Hazel. 'That's almost certain. I ought to have realized how likely it was that –'

'Look here,' said Hazel, 'you know very well what we owe to you. The does all think El-ahrairah sent you to get them out of Efrafa. They believe no one else could have done it. As for what happened this morning, it was my fault as much as yours. But I never supposed we *would* get home without losing some rabbits. In fact we've lost two and that's better than I expected. We can get back to the Honeycomb tonight if we press on. Let's forget about the homba now, Bigwig – it can't be altered – and try to – Hullo, who's this?'

They were coming to a thicket of juniper and dog-roses, tangled at ground level with nettles and trails of bryony on which the berries were now beginning to ripen and turn red. As they stopped to pick a line into the undergrowth, four big rabbits appeared out of the long grass and sat looking down at them. One of the does, coming up the slope a little way behind, stamped and turned to bolt. They heard Blackavar check her sharply.

'Well, why don't you answer his question, Thlayli?' said one of the rabbits. 'Who am I?'

There was a pause. Then Hazel spoke.

'I can see they're Efrafans because they're marked,' he said. 'Is that Woundwort?'

'No,' said Blackavar, at his shoulder. 'That's Captain Campion.'

'I see,' said Hazel. 'Well, I've heard of you, Campion. I don't know whether you mean us any harm, but the best thing you can do is to let well alone. As far as we're concerned our dealings with Efrafa are finished.'

'You may think that,' replied Campion, 'but you'll find it's otherwise. That doe behind you must come with us; and so must any others that are with you.'

As he spoke, Silver and Acorn appeared lower down the slope, followed by Thethuthinnang. After a glance at the Efrafans, Silver spoke quickly to Thethuthinnang, who slipped back through the burdocks. Then he came up to Hazel.

'I've sent for the white bird, Hazel,' he said quietly.

As a piece of bluff it was effective. They saw Campion look upwards nervously and another of the patrol glanced back to the cover of the bushes.

'What you're saying is stupid,' said Hazel to Campion. 'There are a lot of us here and unless you've got more rabbits than I can see, we're too many for you.'

Campion hesitated. The truth was that for once in his life he had acted rashly. He had seen Hazel and Bigwig approaching, with Blackavar and one doe behind them. In his eagerness to have something really worthwhile to show on his return to the Council, he had jumped to the conclusion that they were alone. The Efrafans usually kept fairly close together in the open and it had not occurred to Campion that other rabbits might straggle more widely. He had seen a golden opportunity to attack – perhaps kill – the detestable Thlayli and Blackavar, together with their one companion – who seemed to be lame – and bring the doe back to the Council. This he could certainly have done; and he had decided to confront rather than ambush them, in the hope that the bucks would surrender without fighting. But now, as more rabbits began to appear in ones and twos, he realized that he had made a mistake.

'I have a great many more rabbits,' he said. 'The does must stay here. The rest of you can go. Otherwise we shall kill you.'

'Very well,' said Hazel. 'Bring your whole patrol into the open and we'll do as you say.'

By this time a considerable number of rabbits was coming up the slope. Campion and his patrol looked at them in silence but made no move.

'You'd better stay where you are,' said Hazel at length. 'If you try to interfere with us it will be the worse for you. Silver and Blackberry, take the does and go on. The rest of us will join you.'

'Hazel-rah,' whispered Blackavar, 'the patrol must be killed – all of them. They mustn't report back to the General.'

This had also occurred to Hazel. But as he thought of the dreadful fight and the four Efrafans actually torn to pieces – for that was what it would mean – he could not find it in his heart to do it. Like Bigwig, he felt a reluctant liking for Campion. Besides, it would take some doing. Quite probably some of his own rabbits would be killed – certainly wounded. They would not reach the Honeycomb that night and they would leave a fresh blood trail wherever they went. Apart from his dislike of the whole idea, there were disadvantages that might be fatal.

'No, we'll let them alone,' he replied firmly.

Blackavar was silent and they sat watching Campion as the last of the does disappeared through the bushes.

'Now,' said Hazel, 'take your patrol and go the same way that you saw us come. Don't speak – go.'

Campion and the patrol made off downhill and Hazel, relieved to be rid of them so easily, hurried after Silver, with the others close behind.

Once through the Belt they made excellent progress. After the rest of a day and a half the does were in good shape. The promise of an end to the journey that night and the thought that they had escaped both the fox and the patrol made them eager and responsive. The only cause of delay was Blackavar, who seemed uneasy and kept hanging about in the rear. At last, in the late afternoon, Hazel sent for him and told him to go ahead, on the line of the path they were following, and look out for the long strip of the beech hanger in the dip on the morning side. Blackavar had not been gone very long before he came racing back.

'Hazel-rah, I've been quite close to that wood you spoke of,' he said, 'and there are two rabbits playing about on a patch of short grass just outside it.'

'I'll come and see,' said Hazel. 'Dandelion, you come too, will you?'

As they ran down the hill to the right of the track, Hazel fairly skipped to recognize the beech hanger. He noticed one or two yellow leaves and a faint touch of bronze here and there in the green boughs. Then he caught sight of Buckthorn and Strawberry running towards them across the grass.

'Hazel-rah!' cried Buckthorn. 'Dandelion! What happened? Where are the others? Did you get any does? Is everyone all right?'

'They'll be here very soon,' said Hazel. 'Yes, we've got a lot of does and everyone who went has come back. This is Blackavar, who's come out of Efrafa.'

'Good for him,' said Strawberry. 'Oh, Hazel-rah, we've watched at the end of the wood every evening since you went. Holly and Boxwood are all right – they're back at the warren: and what do you think? Clover's going to kindle. That's fine, isn't it?'

'Splendid,' said Hazel. 'She'll be the first. My goodness, we've had a time, I can tell you. And so I will – what a story! – but it must wait a bit. Come on – let's go and bring the others in.'

By sunset the whole party – twenty rabbits all told – had made their way up the length of the beech hanger and reached the warren. They fed among the dew and the long shadows, with twilight already fallen in the fields below.

Then they crowded down into the Honeycomb to hear Hazel and Bigwig tell the story of their adventures to those who had waited so eagerly and so long to hear it.

As the last rabbits disappeared underground the Wide Patrol, which had followed them from Caesar's Belt with superlative skill and discipline, veered away in a half-circle to the east and then turned for Efrafa. Campion was expert at finding a night's refuge in the open. He planned to rest until dawn and then cover the three miles back by evening of the following day.

41. The Story of Rowsby Woof
and the Fairy Wogdog

Be not merciful unto them that offend of malicious
wickedness. They grin like a dog and run about through the
city. But thou, O Lord, shalt have them in derision. Thou
shalt laugh all the heathen to scorn.

Psalm 59

NOW came the dog days – day after day of hot, still
summer, when for hours at a time light seemed the
only thing that moved; the sky – sun, clouds and breeze –
awake above the drowsing downs. The beech leaves grew
darker on the boughs and fresh grass grew where the old
had been nibbled close. The warren was thriving at last and
Hazel could sit basking on the bank and count their
blessings. Above and under ground, the rabbits fell
naturally into a quiet, undisturbed rhythm of feeding,
digging and sleeping. Several fresh runs and burrows were
made. The does, who had never dug in their lives before,

enjoyed the work. Both Hyzenthlay and Thethuthinnang told Hazel that they had had no idea how much of their frustration and unhappiness in Efrafa had been due simply to not being allowed to dig. Even Clover and Haystack found that they could manage pretty well and boasted that they would bear the warren's first litters in burrows that they had dug for themselves. Blackavar and Holly became close friends. They talked a great deal about their different ideas of scouting and tracking, and made some patrols together, more for their own satisfaction than because there was any real need. One early morning they persuaded Silver to come with them and travelled over a mile to the outskirts of Kingsclere, returning with a tale of mischief and feasting in a cottage garden. Blackavar's hearing had weakened since the mutilation of his ears: but Holly found that his power of noticing and drawing conclusions from anything unusual was almost uncanny and that he seemed to be able to become invisible at will.

Sixteen bucks and ten does made a happy enough society for a warren. There was some bickering here and there, but nothing serious. As Bluebell said, any rabbits who felt discontented could always go back to Efrafa; and the thought of all that they had faced together was enough to take the sting out of anything that might have made a real quarrel. The contentment of the does spread to everyone else, until one evening Hazel remarked that he felt a perfect fraud as Chief Rabbit, for there were no problems and hardly a dispute to be settled.

'Have you thought about the winter yet?' asked Holly.

Four or five of the bucks, with Clover, Hyzenthlay and Vilthuril, were feeding along the sunny west side of the hanger about an hour before sunset. It was still hot and the down was so quiet that they could hear the horses tearing the grass in the paddock of Cannon Heath Farm, more than half a mile away. It certainly did not seem a time to think of winter.

'It'll probably be colder up here than any of us have been used to,' said Hazel. 'But the soil's so light and the roots break it up so much that we can dig a lot deeper before the cold weather comes. I think we ought to be able to get below the frost. As for the wind, we can block some of the holes and sleep warm. Grass is poor in winter, I know; but anyone who wants a change can always go out with Holly here and try his luck at pinching some green-stuff or cattle-roots. It's a time of year to be careful of the elil, though. Myself, I shall be quite happy to sleep underground, play bob-stones and hear a few stories from time to time.'

'What about a story now?' said Bluebell. 'Come on, Dandelion. "How I nearly missed the boat." What about that?'

'Oh, you mean "Woundwort Dismayed",' said Dandelion. 'That's Bigwig's story – I wouldn't presume to tell it. But it makes a change to be thinking about winter on an evening like this. It reminds me of a story I've listened to but never tried to tell myself. So some of you may know it and perhaps some won't. It's the story of Rowsby Woof and the Fairy Wogdog.'

'Off you go,' said Fiver, 'and lay it on thick.'

'There was a big rabbit,' said Dandelion. 'There was a small rabbit. There was El-ahrairah; and he had the frost in his fine new whiskers. The earth up and down the runs of the warren was so hard that you could cut your paws on it and the robins answered each other across the bare, still copses, "This is my bit here. You go and starve in your own."

'One evening, when Frith was sinking huge and red in a green sky, El-ahrairah and Rabscuttle limped trembling through the frozen grass, picking a bite here and there to carry them on for another long night underground. The grass was as brittle and tasteless as hay and although they were hungry, they had been making the best of the miserable stuff so long that it was as much as they could do to get it down. At last Rabscuttle suggested that they might take a risk for once in a way and slip across the fields to the edge of the village, where there was a big vegetable garden.

'This particular garden was bigger than any of the others round about. The man who worked in it lived in a house at one end and he used to dig or cut great quantities of vegetables, put them into a hrududu and drive them away. He had put wire all round the garden to keep rabbits out. All the same, El-ahrairah could usually find a way in if he wanted to; but it was dangerous, because the man had a gun and often shot jays and pigeons and hung them up.

'"It isn't only the gun we'd be risking, either," said El-ahrairah thinking it over. "We'd have to keep an eye open for that confounded Rowsby Woof as well."

'Now Rowsby Woof was the man's dog; and he was the most objectionable, malicious, disgusting brute that ever licked a man's hand. He was a big, woolly sort of animal with hair all over his eyes and the man kept him to guard the vegetable garden, especially at night. Rowsby Woof, of course, did not eat vegetables himself and anyone might have thought that he would be ready to let a few hungry animals have a lettuce or a carrot now and then and no questions asked. But not a bit of it. Rowsby Woof used to run loose from evening till dawn the next day; and not content with keeping men and boys out of the garden, he would go for any animals he found there – rats, rabbits, hares, mice, even moles – and kill them if he could. The moment he smelt anything in the nature of an intruder he would start barking and kicking up a shine, although very often it was only this foolish noise which warned a rabbit and enabled him to get away in time. Rowsby Woof was reckoned to be a tremendous ratter and his master had boasted about this skill of his so often and showed him off so much, that he had become revoltingly conceited. He believed himself to be the finest ratter in the world. He ate a lot of raw meat (but not in the evening, because he was left hungry at night to keep him active) and this made it rather easier to smell him coming. But even so, he made the garden a dangerous place.

'"Well, let's chance Rowsby Woof for once," said Rabscuttle. "I reckon you and I ought to be able to give him the slip if we have to."

'El-ahrairah and Rabscuttle made their way across the fields to the outskirts of the garden. When they got there, the first thing they saw was the man himself, with a white stick burning away in his mouth, cutting row after row of frosted cabbages. Rowsby Woof was with him, wagging his tail and jumping about in a ridiculous manner. After a time the man piled as many of the cabbages as he could into a wheel-thing and pushed them away to the house. He came back several times and when he had taken all the cabbages to the door of the house he began carrying them inside.

'"What's he doing that for?" asked Rabscuttle.

'"I suppose he wants to get the frost out of them tonight," replied El-ahrairah, "before he takes them away in the hrududu tomorrow."

'"They'd be much better to *eat* with the frost out of them, wouldn't they?" said Rabscuttle. "I wish we could get at them while they're in there. Still, never mind. Now's our chance. Let's see what we can do up this end of the garden while he's busy down there."

'But hardly had they crossed the top of the garden and got among the cabbages than Rowsby Woof had winded them and down he came, barking and yelping, and they were lucky to get out in time.

'"Dirty little beasts," shouted Rowsby Woof. "How – how! How – how dare you come snou – snou – snouting round here? Get out – out! Out – out!"

'"Contemptible brute!" said El-ahrairah, as they scurried back to the warren with nothing to show for all their trouble. "He's really annoyed me. I don't know yet how it's going to be done, but by Frith and Inlé! before this frost thaws, we'll eat his cabbages inside the house and make him look a fool into the bargain."

'"That's saying too much, master," said Rabscuttle. "A pity to throw your life away for a cabbage, after all we've done together."

'"Well, I shall be watching my chance," said El-ahrairah. "I shall just be watching my chance, that's all."

'The following afternoon Rabscuttle was out, nosing along the top of the bank beside the lane, when a hrududu came by. It had doors at the back and these doors had somehow come open and were swinging about as the hrududu went along. There were things wrapped up in bags like the ones men sometimes leave about the fields; and as the hrududu passed Rabscuttle, one of these bags fell out into the lane. When the hrududu had gone Rabscuttle, who hoped that the bag might have something to eat inside, slipped down into the lane to have a sniff at it. But he was disappointed to find that all it contained was some kind of meat. Later, he told El-ahrairah about his disappointment.

'"Meat?" said El-ahrairah. "Is it still there?"

'"How should I know?" said Rabscuttle. "Beastly stuff."

'"Come with me," said El-ahrairah. "Quickly, too."

'When they got to the lane the meat was still there. El-ahrairah dragged the bag into the ditch and they buried it.

'"But what good will this be to us, master?" said Rabscuttle.

'"I don't know yet," said El-ahriarah. "But some good it will surely be, if the rats don't get it. Come home now, though. It's getting dark."

'As they were going home, they came on an old, black wheel-covering thrown away from a hrududu, lying in the ditch. If you've ever seen these things, you'll know that they're something like a huge fungus – smooth and very strong, but pad-like and yielding too. They smell unpleasant and are no good to eat.

'"Come on," said El-ahrairah immediately. "We have to gnaw off a good chunk of this. I need it."

'Rabscuttle wondered whether his master was going mad, but he did as he was told. The stuff had grown fairly rotten and before long they were able to gnaw off a lump about as big as a rabbit's head. It tasted dreadful, but El-ahrairah carried it carefully back to the warren. He spent a lot of time that night nibbling at it and after morning silflay the next day he continued. About ni-Frith he woke Rabscuttle, made him come outside and put the lump in front of him.

'"What does that look like?" he said. "Never mind the smell. What does it *look* like?"

'Rabscuttle looked at it. "It looks rather like a dog's black nose, master," he answered, "except that it's dry."

'"Splendid," said El-ahrairah, and went to sleep.

'It was still frosty – very clear and cold – that night, with half a moon, but fu Inlé, when all the rabbits were keeping warm underground, El-ahrairah told Rabscuttle to come with him. El-ahrairah carried the black nose himself and on the way he pushed it well into every nasty thing he could find. He found a –'

'Well, never mind,' said Hazel. 'Go on with the story.'

'In the end' (continued Dandelion), 'Rabscuttle kept well away from him, but El-ahrairah held his breath and still carried the nose somehow, until they got to the place where they had buried the meat.

'"Dig it up," said El-ahrairah. "Come on."

'They dug it up and the paper came off. The meat was all bits joined together in a kind of trail like a spray of bryony, and poor Rabscuttle was told to drag it along to the bottom of the vegetable garden. It was hard work and he was glad when he was able to drop it.

'"Now," said El-ahrairah, "we'll go round to the front."

'When they got to the front, they could tell that the man had gone out. For one thing, the house was all dark but besides, they could smell that he had been through the gate a little while before. The front of the house had a flower garden and this was separated from the back and the vegetable garden by a high, close-boarded fence that ran right across and ended in a big clump of laurels. Just the other side of the fence was the back door that led into the kitchen.

'El-ahrairah and Rabscuttle went quietly through the front garden and peeped through a crack in the fence. Rowsby Woof was sitting on the gravel path, wide awake and shivering in the cold. He was so near that they could see his eyes blink in the moonlight. The kitchen door was shut but near-by, along the wall, there was a hole above the drain where a brick had been left out. The kitchen floor was made of bricks and the man used to wash it with a rough broom and sweep the water out through the hole. The hole was plugged up with an old cloth to keep out the cold.

'After a little while, El-ahrairah said in a low voice,

'"Rowsby Woof! O Rowsby Woof!"

'Rowsby Woof sat up and looked about him, bristling.

'"Who's there?" he said. "Who are you?"

'"O Rowsby Woof!" said El-ahrairah, crouching on the other side of the fence, "Most fortunate, most blessed Rowsby Woof! Your reward is at hand! I bring you the best news in the world!"

'"What?" said Rowsby Woof. "Who's that? None of your tricks, now!"

'"Tricks, Rowsby Woof?" said El-ahrairah. "Ah, I see you do not know me. But how should you? Listen, faithful, skilful hound. I am the Fairy Wogdog, messenger of the great dog-spirit of the East, Queen Dripslobber. Far, far in the East her palace lies. Ah, Rowsby Woof, if only you could see her mighty state, the wonders of her kingdom! The carrion that lies far and wide upon the sands! The manure, Rowsby Woof! The open sewers! Oh, how you would jump for joy and run nosing all about!"

'Rowsby Woof got to his feet and looked about in silence. He could not tell what to make of the voice, but he was suspicious.

'"Your fame as a ratter has come to the ears of the Queen," said El-ahrairah. "We know you – and honour you – as the greatest ratter in the world. That is why I am here. But poor, bewildered creature! I see you are perplexed, and well you may be. Come here, Rowsby Woof! Come close to the fence and know me better!"

'Rowsby Woof came up to the fence and El-ahrairah pushed the rubber nose into the crack and moved it about. Rowsby Woof stood close, sniffing.

'"Noble rat-catcher," whispered El-ahrairah, "it is indeed I, the Fairy Wogdog, sent to honour you!"

'"Oh, Fairy Wogdog!" cried Rowsby Woof, dribbling and piddling all over the gravel. "Ah, what elegance! What aristocratic distinction! Can that really be decayed cat that I smell? With a delicate overtone of rotten camel! Ah, the gorgeous East!"

('What on earth's "camel"?' said Bigwig.

'I don't know,' replied Dandelion. 'But it was in the story when I heard it, so I suppose it's some creature or other.')

'"Happy, happy dog!" said El-ahrairah. "I must tell you that Queen Dripslobber her very self has expressed her gracious wish that you should meet her. But not yet, Rowsby Woof, not yet. First you must be found worthy. I am sent to bring you both a test and a proof. Listen, Rowsby Woof. Beyond the far end of the garden there lies a long rope of meat. Ay, real meat, Rowsby Woof, for though we are fairy dogs yet we bring real gifts to noble, brave animals such as you. Go now – find and eat that meat. Trust me, for I will guard the house until you return. That is the test of your belief."

'Rowsby Woof was desperately hungry and the cold had got into his stomach, but still he hesitated. He knew that his master expected him to guard the house.

'"Ah well," said El-ahrairah, "never mind. I will depart. In the next village there lives a dog –"

'"No, no," cried Rowsby Woof. "No, Fairy Wogdog, do not leave me! I trust you! I will go at once! Only guard the house and do not fail me!"

'"Have no fear, noble hound," said El-ahrairah. "Only trust the word of the great Queen."

'Rowsby Woof went bounding away in the moonlight and El-ahrairah watched him out of sight.

'"Are we to go into the house now, master?" asked Rabscuttle. "We shall have to be quick."

'"Certainly not," said El-ahrairah. "How could you suggest such double-dealing? For shame, Rabscuttle! We will guard the house."

'They waited silently and after a while Rowsby Woof returned, licking his lips and grinning. He came sniffing up to the fence.

'"I perceive, honest friend," said El-ahrairah, "that you found the meat as swiftly as though it had been a rat. The house is safe and all is well. Now hark. I shall return to the

Queen and tell her of all that has passed. It was her gracious purpose that if you showed yourself worthy tonight, by trusting her messenger, she would herself send for you and honour you. Tomorrow night she will be passing through this land on her way to the Wolf Festival of the North and she means to break her journey in order that you may appear before her. Be ready, Rowsby Woof!"

'"Oh, Fairy Wogdog!" cried Rowsby Woof. "What joy it will be to grovel and abase myself before the Queen! How humbly I shall roll upon the ground! How utterly shall I make myself her slave! What menial cringing will be mine! I will show myself a true dog!"

'"I do not doubt it," said El-ahrairah. "And now, farewell. Be patient and await my return!"

'He withdrew the rubber nose and very quietly they crept away.

'The following night was, if anything, still colder. Even El-ahrairah had to pull himself together before he could set out over the fields. They had hidden the rubber nose outside the garden and it took them some time to get it ready for Rowsby Woof. When they had made sure that the man had gone out, they went cautiously into the front garden and up to the fence. Rowsby Woof was padding up and down outside the back door, his breath steaming in the frosty air. When El-ahrairah spoke, he put his head on the ground between his front paws and whined for joy.

'"The Queen is coming, Rowsby Woof," said El-ahrairah from behind the nose, "with her noble attendants, the fairies Postwiddle and Sniffbottom. And this is her wish. You know the cross-roads in the village, do you not?"

'"Yes, yes!" whined Rowsby Woof. "Yes, yes! Oh let me show how abject I can be, dear Fairy Wogdog. I will –"

'"Very well," said El-ahrairah. "Now, O fortunate dog, go to the crossroads and await the Queen. She is coming on the wings of night. It is far that she must come, but wait patiently. Only wait. Do not fail her and great blessing will be yours."

'"Fail her? No, no!" cried Rowsby Woof. "I will wait like a worm upon the road. Her beggar am I, Fairy Wogdog! Her mendicant, her idiot, her –"

'"Quite right, most excellent," said El-ahrairah. "Only make haste."

'As soon as Rowsby Woof had gone, El-ahrairah and Rabscuttle went quickly through the laurels, round the end of the fence and along to the back door. El-ahrairah pulled the cloth out of the hole above the drain with his teeth and led the way into the kitchen.

'The kitchen was as warm as this bank and at one end was a great pile of vegetables ready for the hrududu in the morning – cabbages, brussels-sprouts and parsnips. They were thawed out and the delicious smell was quite overpowering. El-ahrairah and Rabscuttle began at once to make amends for the past days of frozen grass and tree-bark.

'"Good, faithful fellow," said El-ahrairah with his mouth full. "How grateful he will be to the Queen for keeping him waiting. He will be able to show her the full extent of his loyalty, won't he? Have another parsnip, Rabscuttle."

'Meanwhile, down at the cross-roads, Rowsby Woof waited eagerly in the frost, listening for the coming of

Queen Dripslobber. After a long time he heard footsteps. They were not the steps of a dog but of a man. As they came near, he realized that they were the steps of his own master. He was too stupid to run away or hide, but merely remained where he was until his master – who was returning home – came up to the crossroads.

'"Why, Rowsby Woof," said his master, "what are you doing here?"

'Rowsby Woof looked foolish and nosed about. His master was puzzled. Then a thought came to him.

'"Why, good old chap," he said, "you came to meet me, did you? Good fellow, then! Come on, we'll go home together."

'Rowsby Woof tried to slip away, but his master grabbed him by the collar, tied him by a bit of string he had in his pocket and led him home.

'Their arrival took El-ahrairah by surprise. In fact, he was so busy stuffing cabbage that he heard nothing until the door-handle rattled. He and Rabscuttle had only just time to slip behind a pile of baskets before the man came in, leading Rowsby Woof. Rowsby Woof was quiet and dejected and did not even notice the smell of rabbit, which anyway was all mixed up with the smell of the fire and the larder. He lay on the mat while the man made some sort of drink for himself.

'El-ahrairah was watching his chance to dash out of the hole in the wall. But the man, as he sat drinking and puffing away at a white stick, suddenly looked round and got up. He had noticed the draught coming in through the open hole. To the rabbits' horror, he picked up a sack and plugged the hole up very tightly indeed. Then he finished his drink, made up the fire and went away to sleep, leaving Rowsby Woof shut in the kitchen. Evidently he thought it too cold to turn him out for the night.

'At first, Rowsby Woof whined and scratched at the door, but after a time he came back to the mat by the fire and lay down. El-ahrairah moved very quietly along the wall until he was behind a big, metal box in the corner under the sink. There were sacks and old papers here too and he felt fairly sure that Rowsby Woof could not manage to see behind it. As soon as Rabscuttle had joined him, he spoke.

'"O Rowsby Woof!" whispered El-ahrairah.

'Rowsby Woof was up in a flash.

'"Fairy Wogdog!" he cried. "Is that you I hear?"

'"It is indeed," said El-ahrairah. "I am sorry for your disappointment, Rowsby Woof. You did not meet the Queen."

'"Alas, no," said Rowsby Woof; and he told what had happened at the cross-roads.

'"Never mind," said El-ahrairah. "Do not be downhearted, Rowsby Woof. There was good reason why the Queen did not come. She received news of danger – ah, great danger, Rowsby Woof! – and avoided it in time. I myself am here at the risk of my own safety to warn you. You are lucky indeed that I am your friend, for otherwise your good master must have been stricken with mortal plague."

'"With plague?" cried Rowsby Woof. "Oh how, good fairy?"

'"Many fairies and spirits there are in the animal kingdoms of the East," said El-ahrairah. "Some are friends and there are those – may misfortune strike them down – who are our deadly enemies. Worst of them all, Rowsby Woof, is the great Rat-Spirit, the giant of Sumatra, the curse of Hamelin. He dares not openly fight our noble Queen, but he works by stealth, by poison, by disease. Soon after you left me, I learned that he has sent his hateful rat-goblins through the clouds, carrying sickness. I warned the Queen; but still I remained here, Rowsby Woof, to warn you. If the sickness falls – and the goblins are very near – it will harm not you, but your master it will slay – and me too, I fear. You can save him and you alone. I cannot."

'"Oh, horror!" cried Rowsby Woof. "There is no time to be lost! What must I do, Fairy Wogdog?"

'"The sickness works by a spell," said El-ahrairah. "But if a real dog, of flesh and blood, could run four times round the house, barking as loudly as he could, then the spell would be broken and the sickness would have no power. But alas! I forgot! You are shut in, Rowsby Woof. What is to be done? I fear that all is lost!"

'"No, no!" said Rowsby Woof. "I will save you, Fairy Wogdog, and my dear master too. Leave it to me!"

'Rowsby Woof began to bark. He barked to raise the dead. The windows shook. The coal fell in the grate. The noise was terrifying. They could hear the man upstairs, shouting and cursing. Still Rowsby Woof barked. The man came stamping down. He flung open the window and listened for thieves, but he could hear nothing, partly because there was nothing to hear and partly because of the ceaseless barking. At last he picked up his gun, flung open the door and went cautiously out to see what was the matter. Out shot Rowsby Woof, bellowing like a bull, and tore round the house. The man followed him at a run, leaving the door wide.

'"Quick!" said El-ahrairah. "Quicker than Wogdog from the Tartar's bow! Come on!"'

'El-ahrairah and Rabscuttle dashed into the garden and disappeared through the laurels. In the field beyond they paused for a moment. From behind came the sounds of yelping and woofing, mixed with shouts and angry cries of "Come 'ere, damn you!"

'"Noble fellow," said El-ahrairah. "He has saved his master, Rabscuttle. He has saved us all. Let us go home and sleep sound in our burrow."

'For the rest of his life Rowsby Woof never forgot the night when he had waited for the great Dog-Queen. True, it was a disappointment, but this, he felt, was a small matter, compared with the recollection of his own noble conduct and of how he had saved both his master and the good Fairy Wogdog from the wicked Rat-Spirit.'

42. News at Sunset

You will be sure to prove that the act is unjust and hateful to
 the gods?
Yes, indeed, Socrates; at least, if they will listen to me.

Plato, *Euthyphro*

AS HE came to the end of his story, Dandelion
remembered that he was supposed to be relieving Acorn
as sentry. The post was a little way away, near the eastern
corner of the wood, and Hazel – who wanted to see how
Boxwood and Speedwell were getting on with a hole they
were digging – went with Dandelion along the foot of the
bank. He was just going down the new hole when he noticed
that some small creature was pattering about in the grass. It
was the mouse that he had saved from the kestrel. Pleased to
see that he was still safe and sound, Hazel turned back to
have a word with him. The mouse recognized him and sat up,
washing his face with his front paws and chattering effusively.

'Is a good a days, a hot a days. You like? Plenty for eata,
keepa warm is a no trouble. Down in a bottom a hill is a

harvest. I go for a corn a but is a long a way. I tink a you go away, is a not a long a you come a back, yes?'

'Yes,' said Hazel. 'A lot of us went away, but we found what we were looking for and now we've come back for good.'

'Is a good. Is a lots of rabbits a now, keepa grass a short.'

'What difference does it make to him if the grass is short?' said Bigwig who, with Blackavar, was lolloping and nibbling close by. 'He doesn't eat it.'

'Is a good a for get about, you know?' said the mouse in a familiar tone which made Bigwig shake his ears with irritation. 'Is a run along a queek – but is a no seeds a from a short a grass. Now is a warren a here and now a today is a new a rabbits a come, soon is another warren a more. New a rabbits is a your friends a too?'

'Yes, yes, all friends,' said Bigwig, turning away. 'There was something I wanted to say, Hazel, about the new-born rabbits, when they're ready to come above ground.'

Hazel, however, had remained where he was, looking intently at the mouse.

'Wait a moment, Bigwig,' he said. 'What did you say, mouse, about another warren? Where is there going to be another warren?'

The mouse was surprised. 'You not a know? Not a your friends?'

'I don't know until you tell me. What did you mean about new rabbits and another warren soon?'

His tone was urgent and inquisitive. The mouse became nervous and, after the manner of his kind, began to say what he thought the rabbits would like to hear.

'Maybe is a no warren. Is a plenty good a rabbits 'ere, is all a my friends. Is a no more a rabbits. Not a for want other rabbits.'

'But what other rabbits?' persisted Hazel.

'No, sir, no, sir, no other rabbits, is a not a go for soon a rabbits, all stay 'ere are my friends, a save a me a very good a my life, zen 'ow can I if a she mek me?' twittered the mouse.

Hazel considered this lot briefly, but it beat him.

'Oh, come on, Hazel,' said Bigwig. 'Let the poor little beast alone. I want to talk to you.'

Hazel ignored him. Going close to the mouse, he bent his head and spoke quietly and firmly.

'You've often said you're our friend,' he said. 'If you are, tell me, and don't be afraid, what you know about other rabbits coming.'

The mouse looked confused. Then he said, 'I not a see other rabbits, sir, but a my brother 'e say a yellow-hammer say is a new rabbits, plenty, plenty rabbits, a come to combe over on a morning side. Maybe is a lots a rubbish. I tell you a wrong, you no like a mouse for more, not a friend a more.'

'No, that's all right,' said Hazel. 'Don't worry. Just tell me again. Where did the bird say these new rabbits were?'

''E say is a come a justa now on a morning side. I not a see.'

'Good fellow,' said Hazel. 'That's very helpful.' He turned back to the others. 'What d'you make of this, Bigwig?' he asked.

'Not much,' answered Bigwig. 'Long-grass rumours. These little creatures say anything and change it five times a day. Ask him again fu Inlé – he'll tell you something else.'

'If you're right, then I'm wrong and we can all forget it,' said Hazel. 'But I'm going to get to the bottom of this. Someone must go and see. I'd go myself, but I've got no speed with this leg.'

'Well, leave it for tonight, anyway,' said Bigwig. 'We can –'

'Someone must go and see,' repeated Hazel firmly. 'A good patroller, too. Blackavar, go and get Holly for me, will you?'

'I'm here, as it happens,' said Holly, who had come along the top of the bank while Hazel was speaking. 'What's the trouble, Hazel-rah?'

'There's a rumour of strangers on the down, on the morning side,' replied Hazel, 'and I wish I knew more. Can you and Blackavar run over that way – say as far as the top of the combe – and find out what's going on?'

'Yes, of course, Hazel-rah,' said Holly. 'If there really are some other rabbits there, we'd better bring them back with us, hadn't we? We could do with a few more.'

'It depends who they are,' said Hazel. 'That's what I want to find out. Go at once, Holly, will you? Somehow it worries me not to know.'

Holly and Blackavar had hardly set off when Speedwell appeared above ground. He had an excited, triumphant look which attracted everyone's attention immediately. He squatted in front of Hazel and looked round him in silence, to make sure of his effect.

'You've finished the hole?' asked Hazel.

'Never mind the hole,' answered Speedwell. 'I didn't come up to say that. Clover's had her litter. All good, healthy kittens. Three bucks and three does, she says.'

'You'd better go up in the beech tree and sing that,' said Hazel. 'See that everybody knows! But tell them not to go crowding down disturbing her.'

'I shouldn't think they would,' said Bigwig. 'Who'd be a kitten again, or even want to see one – blind and deaf and no fur?'

'Some of the does may want to see them,' said Hazel. 'They're excited, you know. But we don't want Clover disturbed into eating them or anything miserable like that.'

'It looks as though we really are going to live a natural life again at last, doesn't it?' said Bigwig, as they browsed their way along the bank. 'What a summer it's been! What a – what a desperate lark! I keep dreaming I'm back in Efrafa, you know; but it'll pass off, I suppose. One thing I brought back out of that place, though, and that's the value of keeping a warren hidden. As we get bigger, Hazel, we ought to take care of that. We'll do better than Efrafa, though. When we've reached the right size, rabbits can be encouraged to leave.'

'Well, don't *you* leave,' said Hazel, 'or I'll tell Kehaar to bring you back by the scruff of the neck. I'm relying on you to produce us a really good Owsla.'

'It's certainly something to look forward to,' said Bigwig. 'Take a pack of young fellows across to the farm and chase the cats out of the barn to get an appetite. Well, it'll come. I say, this grass is as dry as horse-hair on barbed wire, isn't it? What about a run down the hill to the fields – just you and I and Fiver? Corn's been cut, you know, and there should be good pickings. I expect they're going to burn off the field, but they haven't done it yet.'

'No, we must wait a bit,' said Hazel. 'I want to hear what Holly and Blackavar have to say when they come in.'

'That needn't keep you long,' replied Bigwig. 'Here they come already, unless I'm much mistaken. Straight down the open track, too! Not bothered about keeping hidden, are they? What a rate they're going!'

'There's something wrong,' said Hazel, staring at the approaching rabbits.

Holly and Blackavar reached the long shadow of the wood at top speed, as though they were being pursued. The watchers expected them to slow down as they came to the bank, but they kept straight on and appeared actually to be going to run underground. At the last moment Holly stopped, looked about him and stamped twice. Blackavar disappeared down the nearest hole. At the stamping, all the rabbits above ground ran for cover.

'Here, wait a minute,' said Hazel, pushing past Pipkin and Hawkbit as they came across the grass. 'Holly, what's the alarm? Tell us something, instead of stamping the place to pieces. What's happened?'

'Get the holes filled in!' gasped Holly. 'Get everyone underground! There's not a moment to lose.' His eyes rolled white and he panted foam over his chin.

'Is it men, or what? There's nothing to be seen, heard or smelt. Come on, tell us something and stop gibbering, there's a good chap.'

'It'll have to be quick, then,' said Holly. 'That combe – it's full of rabbits from Efrafa.'

'From Efrafa? Fugitives, do you mean?'

'No,' said Holly, 'not fugitives. Campion's there. We ran right into him and three or four more that Blackavar recognized. I believe Woundwort's there himself. They've come for us – don't make any mistake about that.'

'You're sure it's more than a patrol?'

'I'm certain,' answered Holly. 'We could smell them; and we heard them, too – below us in the combe. We wondered what so many rabbits could be doing there and we were going down to see when we suddenly came face to face with Campion. We looked at him and he looked at us and then I realized what it must mean and we turned and ran. He didn't follow us – probably because he'd had no orders. But how long will it take them to get here?'

Blackavar had returned from underground, bringing Silver and Blackberry.

'We ought to leave at once, sir,' he said to Hazel. 'We might be able to get quite a long way before they come.'

Hazel looked about him. 'Anyone who wants to go can go,' he said. 'I shan't. We made this warren ourselves and Frith only knows what we've been through on account of it. I'm not going to leave it now.'

'Neither am I,' said Bigwig. 'If I'm for the Black Rabbit there's one or two from Efrafa will come with me.'

There was a short silence.

'Holly's right to want to stop the holes,' went on Hazel. 'It's the best thing to do. We fill the holes in, good and thorough. Then they have to dig us out. The warren's deep. It's under a bank, with tree roots all through it and over the top. How long can all those rabbits stay on the down without attracting elil? They'll have to give it up.'

'You don't know these Efrafans,' said Blackavar. 'My mother used to tell me what happened at Nutley Copse. It would be better to go now.'

'Well, go on then,' answered Hazel. 'I'm not stopping you. And I'm not leaving this warren. It's my home.' He looked at Hyzenthlay, heavy with young, who was sitting in the mouth of the nearest hole and listening to the talk. 'How far do you think *she'll* get? And Clover – do we leave her or what?'

'No, we must stay,' said Strawberry. 'I believe El-ahrairah will save us from this Woundwort; and if he doesn't, I'm not going back to Efrafa, I'll tell you that.'

'Fill in the holes,' said Hazel.

As the sun set, the rabbits fell to clawing and scrabbling in the runs. The sides were hard with the hot weather. It was not easy to get started and when the soil began to fall, it was light and powdery and did little to block the holes. It was Blackberry who hit upon the idea of working outwards from inside the Honeycomb itself, scratching down the ceilings of the runs where they came into the meeting hall and blocking the holes by breaking the underground walls into them. One run, leading up into the wood, was left open for coming and going. It was the one where Kehaar used to shelter and the lobby at the mouth was still cluttered with guano. As Hazel passed the place, it occurred to him that Woundwort did not know that Kehaar had left them. He dug out as much of the mess as he could and scattered it about. Then, as the work went on below, he squatted on the bank and watched the darkening eastern sky-line.

His thoughts were very sad. Indeed, they were desperate. Although he had spoken resolutely in front of the others, he knew only too well how little hope there was of saving the warren from the Efrafans. They knew what they were doing. No doubt they had their methods of breaking into a closed warren. It was the faintest of chances that elil would disperse them. Most of the Thousand hunted rabbits for food. A stoat or a fox took a rabbit and took no more until it was ready to hunt again. But the Efrafans were accustomed to a death here and there. Unless General Woundwort himself were killed, they would stay until the job was done. Nothing would stop them, short of some unexpected catastrophe.

But suppose that he himself were to go and talk to Woundwort? Might there not just possibly be a chance of getting him to see sense? Whatever had happened at Nutley Copse, the Efrafans could not fight to the finish against rabbits like Bigwig, Holly and Silver without losing lives – probably a good many lives. Woundwort must know this. Perhaps it might not be too late, even now, to persuade him to agree to a new plan – a plan that would be as good for one warren as the other.

'And perhaps it might be,' thought Hazel grimly. 'But it's a possible chance and so I'm afraid the Chief Rabbit has got to take it. And since this savage brute is probably not to be trusted, I suppose the Chief Rabbit must go alone.'

He returned to the Honeycomb and found Bigwig.

'I'm off to talk to General Woundwort, if I can get hold of him,' he said. 'You're Chief Rabbit until I come back. Keep them at it.'

'But Hazel,' said Bigwig, 'wait a moment. It's not safe –'

'I shan't be long,' said Hazel. 'I'm just going to ask him what he's up to.'

A moment later he was down the bank and limping up the track, pausing from time to time to sit up and look about him for an Efrafan patrol.

43. The Great Patrol

What is the world, O soldiers?
It is I.
I, this incessant snow,
This northern sky;
Soldiers, this solitude
Through which we go
Is I.

Walter de la Mare, *Napoleon*

WHEN the punt floated down the river in the rain, part of General Woundwort's authority went with it. He could not have appeared more openly and completely at a loss if Hazel and his companions had flown away over the trees. Until that very moment he had shown up strongly, a most formidable adversary. His officers had been demoralized by Kehaar's unexpected attack. He had not. On the contrary, he had kept up the pursuit in spite of Kehaar and had actually carried out a scheme to cut off the fugitives' retreat. Cunning and resourceful in adversity, he had nearly succeeded in hurting the gull when he leapt at him out of the close cover by the plank bridge. Then, when he had his quarry cornered in a place where Kehaar could not have done a great deal to help them, they had suddenly shown their own cunning greater than his, and left him bewildered on the bank. He had overheard the very word – tharn – spoken by one of his officers to another as they returned to Efrafa through the rain. Thlayli, Blackavar and the does of the Near Hind had vanished. He had tried to stop them and he had conspicuously failed.

For a great part of that night Woundwort remained awake, considering what was best to be done. The following day he called a Council meeting. He pointed out that it would be no good taking an expedition down the river to look for Thlayli unless it were strong enough to defeat him if it found him. That would mean taking several officers and a number of the Owsla. There would be the risk of trouble at home while they were away. There might be another break-out. The odds were that they would not find Thlayli at all, for there would be no trail and they did not know where to search for him. If they did not find him, they would look even bigger fools when they came back.

'And fools we look now,' said Woundwort. 'Make no mistake about that. Vervain will tell you what the Marks are saying – that Campion was chased into the ditch by the white bird and Thlayli called down lightning from the sky and Frith knows what besides.'

'The best thing,' said old Snowdrop, 'will be to say as little about it as possible. Let it blow over. They've got short memories.'

'There's one thing I think worth doing,' said Woundwort. 'We know now that there was one place where we *did* find Thlayli and his gang, only nobody realized it at the time. That was when Mallow was after them with his patrol, just before he was killed by the fox. Something tells me that where they were once, there they'll be again, sooner or later.'

'But we can hardly stay out there with enough rabbits to fight them, sir,' said Groundsel, 'and it would mean digging in and living there for some time.'

'I agree with you,' replied Woundwort. 'A patrol will be stationed there continuously until further notice. They'll dig scrapes and live there. They'll be relieved every two days. If Thlayli comes, he's to be watched and followed secretly. When we know where he's taken the does, then we may be able to deal with him. And I'll tell you this,' he ended, glaring round at them with his great, pale eyes. 'If we *do* find out where he is, I shall be ready to go to a great deal of trouble. I told Thlayli I'd kill him myself. He may have forgotten that, but I haven't.'

Woundwort led the first patrol in person, taking Groundsel to show him where Mallow had picked up the strangers' southward trail. They dug scrapes among the scrub along the edge of Caesar's Belt and waited. After two days their hopes were lower. Vervain relieved Woundwort. He was relieved two days later by Campion. By this time there were captains in the Owsla who said privately to each other that the General was in the grip of an obsession. Some way would have to be found of getting him to drop it before it went too far. At the Council meeting the next evening it was suggested that the patrol should be discontinued in two days' time. Woundwort, snarling, told them to wait and see. An argument began, behind which he sensed more opposition than he had ever encountered before. In the middle of this, with a dramatic effect that could not have been better timed from the General's point of view, Campion and his patrol came in, dead-beat, with the report that they had met Thlayli and his rabbits exactly where Woundwort had said they would. Unseen, they had followed them to their warren which, though a long way off, was not too distant to be attacked, especially since no time would have to be spent in searching for it. It did not appear to be very large and could probably be surprised.

The news put an end to all opposition and brought both Council and Owsla back under Woundwort's undisputed control. Several of the officers were for starting at once but Woundwort, now that he was sure of his followers and his enemy, took his time. Having learned from Campion that he had actually come face to face with Thlayli, Blackavar and the rest, he decided to wait some little while, in case they might be on their guard. Besides, he wanted time both to reconnoitre the way to Watership and to organize the expedition. His idea was that if possible they should make the journey in one day. This would forestall any possible rumours of their approach. To satisfy himself that they could do this and still be fit to fight when they arrived, he took Campion and two others, and himself covered the three and a half miles to the down east of Watership. Here, he grasped at once the best way to approach the beech hanger without being seen or smelt. The prevailing wind was westerly, as at Efrafa. They would arrive at evening and then assemble and rest in the combe south of Cannon Heath Down. As soon as twilight fell and Thlayli and his rabbits had gone underground, they would come along the ridge and attack the warren. With luck, there would be no warning whatever. They would be safe for the night in the captured warren and the following day he himself and Vervain would be able to return to Efrafa. The remainder, under Campion, could have a day's rest and then make their way back with the does and any other prisoners there might be. The whole thing could be finished in three days.

It would be best not to take too many rabbits. Anyone not strong enough to go the distance and then fight would only be a nuisance. In the event, speed might turn out to be everything. The slower the journey, the more dangerous it would be and stragglers would attract elil and discourage the rest. Besides, as Woundwort very well knew, his leadership was going to be vital. Every rabbit would need to feel that he was close to the General; and if he felt himself one of a picked band as well, that would be all to the good.

The rabbits to go were chosen most carefully. There were in fact about twenty-six or seven of them, half Owsla and the rest promising youngsters recommended by their Mark officers. Woundwort believed in emulation and he let it be known that there would be plenty of chances to win rewards. Campion and Chervil were kept busy taking out endurance patrols, and tussles and training fights were organized at morning silflay. The members of the expedition were excused all sentry duties and allowed to silflay whenever they wished.

They started before dawn one clear August morning, going due north in groups along the banks and hedges. Before they had reached the Belt, Groundsel's party was attacked by a pair of stoats, one old and the other a yearling. Woundwort, hearing the squealing from behind him, covered the distance in a few moments and set upon the veteran stoat with slashing teeth and great kicks from his needle-clawed back paws. With one of its forelegs ripped to the shoulder, it turned and made off, the younger one following.

'You ought to be able to see to these things yourself,' said Woundwort to Groundsel. 'Stoats aren't dangerous. Come on.'

Shortly after ni-Frith, Woundwort went back to pick up stragglers. He found three, one injured by a piece of glass. He stopped the bleeding, brought the three up to rejoin their groups and then called a halt to rest and feed, himself keeping a watch round about. It was very hot and some of the rabbits were showing signs of exhaustion. Woundwort formed these into a separate group and took charge of it himself.

By the early evening – about the same time as Dandelion was beginning the story of Rowsby Woof – the Efrafans had skirted an enclosure of pigs east of Cannon Heath Farm and were slipping into the combe south of Cannon Heath Down. Many were tired and, in spite of their tremendous respect for Woundwort, there was a certain feeling that they had come a long way from home. They were ordered to take cover, feed, rest and wait for sunset.

The place was deserted, except for yellow-hammers and a few mice pattering about in the sun. Some of the rabbits went to sleep in the long grass. The slope was already in shadow when Campion came running down with the news that he had come face to face with Blackavar and Holly in the upper part of the combe.

Woundwort was annoyed. 'What made them come trapesing over here, I wonder?' he said. 'Couldn't you have killed them? Now we've lost surprise.'

'I'm sorry, sir,' said Campion. 'I wasn't really alert at the time and I'm afraid they were a bit too quick for me. I didn't pursue them because I wasn't sure whether you'd want me to.'

'Well, it may not make much difference,' said Woundwort. 'I don't see what they can do. But they'll try to do something, I suppose, now they know we're here.'

As he went among his rabbits, looking them over and encouraging them, Woundwort considered the situation. One thing was clear – there was no longer the chance of catching Thlayli and the rest off their guard. But perhaps they were already so much frightened that they would not fight at all? The bucks might give up the does to save their own lives. Or they might already be on the run, in which case they must be followed and caught at once, for they were fresh and his own rabbits were tired and could not pursue them far. He ought to find out quickly. He turned to a young rabbit of the Neck Mark, who was feeding close at hand.

'Your name's Thistle, isn't it?' he asked.

'Thistle, sir,' answered the rabbit.

'Well, you're the very fellow I want,' said Woundwort. 'Go and find Captain Campion and tell him to meet me up there, by that juniper – do you see where I mean? – at once. You'd better come there too. Be quick: there's no time to lose.'

As soon as Campion and Thistle had joined him, Woundwort took them up to the ridge. He meant to see what was happening over at the beech hanger. If the enemy were already in flight, Thistle could be sent back with a message to Groundsel and Vervain to bring everyone up immediately. If they were not, he would see what threats could do.

They reached the track above the combe and began to make their way along it with some caution, since the sunset was in their eyes. The light west wind carried a fresh smell of rabbits.

'If they *are* running they haven't gone far,' said Woundwort. 'But I don't think they *are* running: I think they're still in their warren.'

At that moment a rabbit came out of the grass and sat up in the middle of the track. He paused for a few moments and then moved towards them. He was limping and had a strained, resolute look.

'You're General Woundwort, aren't you?' said the rabbit. 'I've come to talk to you.'

'Did Thlayli send you?' asked Woundwort.

'I'm a friend of Thlayli,' replied the rabbit. 'I've come to ask why you're here and what it is you want.'

'Were you on the river bank in the rain?' said Woundwort.

'Yes, I was.'

'What was left unfinished there will be finished now,' said Woundwort. 'We are going to destroy you.'

'You won't find it easy,' replied the other. 'You'll take home fewer rabbits than you brought. We should both do better to come to terms.'

'Very well,' said Woundwort. 'These are the terms. You will give back all the does who ran from Efrafa and you will hand over the deserters Thlayli and Blackavar to my Owsla.'

'No, we can't agree to that. I've come to suggest something altogether different and better for us both. A rabbit has two ears; a rabbit has two eyes, two nostrils. Our two warrens ought to be like that. They ought to be together – not fighting. We ought to make other warrens between us – start one between here and Efrafa, with rabbits from both sides. You wouldn't lose by that, you'd gain. We both would. A lot of your rabbits are unhappy now and it's all you can do to control them, but with this plan you'd soon see a difference. Rabbits have enough enemies as it is. They ought not to make more among themselves. A mating between free, independent warrens – what do you say?'

At that moment, in the sunset on Watership Down, there was offered to General Woundwort the opportunity to show whether he was really the leader of vision and genius which he believed himself to be, or whether he was no more than a tyrant with the courage and cunning of a pirate. For one beat of his pulse the lame rabbit's idea shone clearly before him. He grasped it and realized what it meant. The next, he had pushed it away from him. The sun dipped into the cloud-bank and now he could see clearly the track along the ridge, leading to the beech hanger and the bloodshed for which he had prepared with so much energy and care.

'I haven't time to sit here talking nonsense,' said Woundwort. 'You're in no position to bargain with us. There's nothing more to be said. Thistle, go back and tell Captain Vervain I want everyone up here at once.'

'And this rabbit, sir,' asked Campion. 'Shall I kill him?'

'No,' replied Woundwort. 'Since they've sent him to ask our terms, he'd better take them back. Go and tell Thlayli that if the does aren't waiting outside your warren, with him and Blackavar, by the time I get down there, I'll tear the throat out of every buck in the place by ni-Frith tomorrow.'

The lame rabbit seemed about to reply, but Woundwort had already turned away and was explaining to Campion what he was to do. Neither of them bothered to watch the lame rabbit as he limped back by the way he had come.

44. A Message from El-Ahrairah

The enforced passivity of their defence, the interminable waiting, became insupportable. Day and night they heard the muffled thud of the picks above and dreamt of the collapse of the grotto and of every ghastly eventuality. They were subject to 'castle-mentality' in its most extreme form.

Robin Fedden, *Crusader Castles*

'THEY'VE stopped digging, Hazel-rah,' said Speedwell. 'As far as I can tell, there's no one in the hole.'

In the close darkness of the Honeycomb, Hazel pushed past three or four of his rabbits crouching among the tree roots and reached the higher shelf where Speedwell lay listening for sounds from above. The Efrafans had reached the hanger at early twilight and at once begun a search along the banks and among the trees to find out how big the warren was and where its holes were. They had been surprised to find so many holes in such a small area, for not many of them had had experience of any warren but Efrafa, where very few holes served the needs of many rabbits. At first they had supposed that there must be a large number of rabbits underground. The silence and emptiness of the open beech-wood made them suspicious, and most kept outside, nervous of an ambush. Woundwort had to reassure them. Their enemies, he explained, were fools who made more runs than any properly organized warren needed. They would soon discover their mistake, for every one would be opened, until the place became impossible to defend. As for the droppings of the white bird, scattered in the wood, it was plain that they were old. There were no signs whatever that the bird was anywhere near. Nevertheless, many of the rank-and-file continued to look cautiously about them. At the sudden cry of a peewit on the down, one or two bolted and had to be brought back by their officers. The story of the bird which had fought for Thlayli in the storm had lost nothing in the telling up and down the burrows of Efrafa.

Woundwort told Campion to post sentries and keep a patrol round about, while Vervain and Groundsel tackled the blocked holes. Groundsel set to work along the bank, while Vervain went into the wood, where the mouths of the holes lay between the tree roots. He came at once upon the open run. He listened, but all was quiet. Vervain (who was more used to dealing with prisoners than with enemies) ordered two of his rabbits to make their way down it. The discovery of the silent, open run gave him the hope that he might be able to seize the warren by a sudden dash to the very centre. The wretched rabbits, obeying his orders, were met by Silver and Buckthorn at a point where the run opened out. They were cuffed and mauled and barely got out with their lives. The sight of them did nothing to encourage Vervain's party, who were reluctant to dig and made little headway during the darkness before moonrise.

Groundsel, who felt that he ought to set an example, himself dug his way into the loose, fallen soil of one of the bank runs. Ploughing over the soft earth like a fly on summer butter and holding his head clear, he suddenly found himself face to face with Blackavar, who sank his front teeth into his throat. Groundsel, with no freedom to use his weight, screamed and kicked out as best he could. Blackavar hung on and Groundsel – a heavy rabbit, like all the Efrafan officers – dragged him forward a short distance before he could rid himself of his grip. Blackavar spat out a mouthful of fur and jumped clear, clawing with his front paws. But Groundsel had already gone. He was lucky not to have been more severely wounded.

It became clear to Woundwort that it was going to be extremely difficult, if not impossible, to take the warren by attack down the defended runs. There would be a good chance of success if several runs could be opened and then tackled at the same time, but he doubted whether his rabbits would attempt it, after what they had seen. He realized that he had not given enough thought, earlier on, to what he would have to do if he lost surprise and had to force an entry: he had better give it some thought now. As the moon rose, he called Campion in and talked it over with him.

Campion's suggestion was they should simply starve the warren out. The weather was warm and dry and they could easily stay two or three days. This Woundwort rejected impatiently. In his own mind, he was not altogether certain that daylight might not bring the white bird down upon them. They ought to be underground by dawn. But apart from this secret anxiety, he felt that his reputation depended on a fighting victory. He had brought his Owsla to get at these rabbits, knock them down and beat them. A siege would be a miserable anticlimax. Also, he wanted to get back to Efrafa as soon as he could. Like most war-lords, he was never very confident about what was going on behind his back.

'If I remember rightly,' he said, 'after the main part of the warren at Nutley Copse was taken and the fighting was as good as over, there were a few rabbits who shut themselves into a smaller burrow where it was difficult to get at them. I said they were to be dealt with and then I went back to Efrafa with the prisoners. How *were* they dealt with and who did it, do you know?'

'Captain Mallow did it,' said Campion. 'He's dead, of course; but I expect there's someone here who was with him. I'll go and find out.'

He returned with a heavy, stolid Owsla sentry named Ragwort, who at first had some difficulty in understanding what it was that the General wanted to know. At last, however, he said that when he had been with Captain Mallow, more than a year ago, the captain had told them to dig a hole straight down into the ground. In the end the earth had given way under them and they had fallen down among some rabbits whom they had fought and beaten.

'Well, that's about the only way it *can* be done,' said Woundwort to Campion. 'And if we get them all on to it, relieving each other in shifts, we should have a way into the place before dawn. You'd better get your sentries out again – not more than two or three – and we'll make a start at once.'

Soon after, Hazel and his rabbits, below in the Honeycomb, heard the first sounds of scratching above. It was not long before they realized that the digging was going on at two points. One was at the north end of the Honeycomb, above the place where the tree roots formed a kind of cloister in the burrow. Here the roof, latticed through and through with fine roots, was very strong. The other seemed to be more or less above the open centre of the Honeycomb, but rather nearer to the south end, where the hall broke up into bays and runs with columns of earth between. Beyond these runs lay several of the warren's burrows. One, lined with fur torn from her own belly, contained Clover and the pile of grass and leaves, covered over with earth, in which her new-born litter were sleeping.

'Well, we seem to be putting them to a great deal of trouble,' said Hazel. 'That's all to the good. It'll blunt their claws and I should think they'll be tired out before they've done. What do you make of it, Blackberry?'

'I'm afraid it's a bad look-out, Hazel-rah,' replied Blackberry. 'It's true they're in trouble up at the top end. There's a lot of ground above us there and the roots will hold them up for a long time. But down this end it's easier for them. They're bound to dig through fairly soon. Then the roof will come in; and I can't see that we can do anything to stop them.'

Hazel could feel him trembling as he spoke. As the sounds of digging continued, he sensed fear spreading all through the burrow. 'They'll take us back to Efrafa,' whispered Vilthuril to Thethuthinnang. 'The warren police –'

'Be quiet,' said Hyzenthlay. 'The bucks aren't talking like that and why should we? I'd rather be here now, as we are, than never have left Efrafa.'

It was bravely said, but Hazel was not the only one who could tell her thoughts. Bigwig remembered the night in Efrafa when he had calmed her by talking of the high downs and the certainty of their escape. In the dark, he nuzzled Hazel's shoulder and pressed him over to one side of the wide burrow.

'Listen, Hazel,' he said, 'we're not finished yet. Not by a long way. When the roof breaks, they'll come down into this end of the Honeycomb. But we can get everybody back into the sleeping burrows behind and block the runs that lead to them. They'll be no better off.'

'Well, if we do that it'll last a bit longer,' said Hazel. 'But they'll soon be able to break into the sleeping burrows, once they're in here.'

'They'll find me there when they do,' said Bigwig, 'and one or two more besides. I shouldn't wonder if they didn't decide to go home.'

With a kind of wry envy, Hazel realized that Bigwig was actually looking forward to meeting the Efrafan assault. He knew he could fight and he meant to show it. He was not thinking of anything else. The hopelessness of their chances had no important place in his thoughts. Even the sound of the digging, clearer already, only set him thinking of the best way to sell his life as dearly as he could. But what else was there for any of them to do? At least Bigwig's preparations would keep the others busy and perhaps do something to dispel the silent fear that filled all the warren.

'You're quite right, Bigwig,' he said. 'Let's prepare a little reception. Will you tell Silver and the others what you want and get them started?'

As Bigwig began to explain his plan to Silver and Holly, Hazel sent Speedwell to the north end of the Honeycomb to listen to the digging and keep reporting what he could make out about its progress. As far as he could see, it would make little difference whether the roof-fall came there or in the centre, but at least he ought to try to show the others that he was keeping his wits about him.

'We can't break these walls down to stop the run between, Bigwig,' said Holly. 'They hold the roof up at this end, you know.'

'I know that,' answered Bigwig. 'We'll dig into the walls of the sleeping burrows behind. They'll need to be bigger anyway, if we're all going to get in there together. Then kick the loose earth back into the spaces between the columns. Stop the whole thing right up.'

Since he had come out of Efrafa Bigwig's standing was very high. Seeing him in good heart, the others set aside their fear as best they could and did as he told them, enlarging the burrows beyond the south end of the Honeycomb and piling up the soft earth in the entry runs until what had been a colonnade began to become a solid wall. It was during a pause in this work that Speedwell reported that the digging above the north end had stopped. Hazel went and crouched beside him, listening for some time. There was nothing to be heard. He went back to where Buckthorn sat guarding the foot of the single open run – Kehaar's run, as it was called.

'You know what's happened?' he said. 'They've realized they're all among the beech roots up there, so they've chucked it. They'll be going harder at the other end now.'

'I suppose so, Hazel-rah,' replied Buckthorn. After a little he said, 'D'you remember the rats in the barn? We got out of that all right, didn't we? But I'm afraid we shan't get out of this. It's a pity, after all we've done together.'

'Yes, we shall,' said Hazel, with all the conviction he could muster. But he knew that if he stayed he would not be able to keep up the pretence. Buckthorn – a decent, straightforward fellow if ever there was one – where would he be by ni-Frith tomorrow? And he himself – where had he led them, with all his clever schemes? Had they come over the common, among the shining wires, through the thunderstorm, the culverts on the great river, to die at the claws of General Woundwort? It was not the death they deserved; it was not the right end of the clever track they had run. But what could stop Woundwort? What could save them now? Nothing, he knew – unless some tremendous blow were to fall upon the Efrafans from outside: and of that there was no chance. He turned away from Buckthorn.

Scratch, scratch; scratch, scratch came the sound of the digging above. Crossing the floor in the dark, Hazel found himself beside another rabbit, who was crouching silently on the near side of the new-piled wall. He stopped, sniffing. It was Fiver.

'Aren't you working?' he asked listlessly.

'No,' replied Fiver. 'I'm listening.'

'To the digging, you mean?'

'No, not the digging. There's something I'm trying to hear – something the others can't hear. Only I can't hear it either. But it's close. Deep. Leaf-drift, deep. I'm going away, Hazel – going away.' His voice grew slow and drowsy. 'Falling. But it's cold. Cold.'

The air in the dark burrow was stifling. Hazel bent over Fiver, pushing the limp body with his nose.

'Cold,' muttered Fiver. 'How – how. How – how cold!'

There was a long silence.

'Fiver?' said Hazel. 'Fiver? Can you hear me?'

Suddenly a terrible sound broke from Fiver; a sound at which every rabbit in the warren leapt in dreadful fear; a sound that no rabbit had ever made, that no rabbit had the power to make. It was deep and utterly unnatural. The rabbits working on the far side of the wall crouched terrified. One of the does began to squeal.

'Dirty little beasts,' yelped Fiver. 'How – how dare you? Get out – out! Out – out!'

Bigwig burst through the piled earth, twitching and panting.

'In the name of Frith, stop him!' he gasped. 'They'll all go mad!'

Shuddering, Hazel clawed at Fiver's side.

'Wake! Fiver, wake!'

But Fiver was lying in a deep stupor.

In Hazel's mind, green branches were straining in the wind. Up and down they swayed, thresh and ply. There was something – something he could glimpse between them. What was it? Water he sensed; and fear. Then suddenly he saw clearly, for an instant, a little huddle of rabbits on the bank of a stream at dawn, listening to the sound of yelping in the wood above and the scolding of a jay.

'If I were you, I shouldn't wait until ni-Frith. I should go now. In fact, I think you'll have to. There's a large dog loose in the wood. There's a large dog loose in the wood.'

The wind blew, the trees shook their myriads of leaves. The stream was gone. He was in the Honeycomb, facing Bigwig in the dark, across the motionless body of Fiver. The scratching from above was louder and closer.

'Bigwig,' said Hazel, 'do as I say at once, there's a good fellow. We've got hardly any time. Go and get Dandelion and Blackberry and bring them to me at the foot of Kehaar's run, quickly.'

At the foot of the run Buckthorn was still in his place. He had not moved at Fiver's cry, but his breath was short and his pulse very quick. He and the other three rabbits gathered about Hazel without a word.

'I've got a plan,' said Hazel. 'If it works, it'll finish Woundwort for good and all. But I've no time to explain. Every moment counts now. Dandelion and Blackberry, you come with me. You're to go straight up out of this run and through the trees to the down. Then northwards, over the edge and down to the fields. Don't stop for anything. You'll go faster than I shall. Wait for me by the iron tree at the bottom.'

'But, Hazel –' said Blackberry.

'As soon as we've gone,' said Hazel, turning to Bigwig, 'you're to block this run and get everyone back behind the wall you've made. If they break in, hold them up as long as you can. Don't give in to them on any account. El-ahrairah has shown me what to do.'

'But where are you going, Hazel?' asked Bigwig.

'To the farm,' said Hazel, 'to gnaw another rope. Now, you two, follow me up the run; and don't forget, you stop for nothing until you're down the hill. If there are rabbits outside, don't fight – run.'

Without another word he dashed up the tunnel and out into the wood, with Blackberry and Dandelion on his heels.

45. Nuthanger Farm Again

Cry Havoc! And let slip the dogs of war.

Shakespeare, Julius Caesar

AT THAT moment General Woundwort, out on the open grass below the bank, was facing Thistle and Ragwort in the chequered, yellow moonlight of the small hours.

'You weren't put at the mouth of that run to listen,' he said. 'You were put there to stop anyone breaking out. You had no business to leave it. Get back at once.'

'I give you my word, sir,' said Thistle, querulously, 'there's some animal down there that is not a rabbit. We both heard it.'

'And did you smell it?' asked Woundwort.

'No, sir. No tracks or droppings either. But we both heard an animal and it was no rabbit.'

Several of the diggers had left their work and were gathered nearby, listening. A muttering began.

'They had a homba that killed Captain Mallow. My brother was there. He saw it.'

'They had a great bird that turned into a shaft of lightning.'

'There was another animal that took them away down the river.'

'Why can't we go home?'

'Stop that!' said Woundwort. He went up to the group. 'Who said that? You, was it? Very well, go home. Go on, hurry up. I'm waiting. That's the way – over there.'

The rabbit did not move. Woundwort looked slowly round.

'Right,' he said. 'Anyone else who wants to go home can get on with it. It's a nice long way and you'll have no officers, because they'll all be busy digging, including myself. Captain Vervain, Captain Groundsel, will you come with me? You, Thistle, go out there and fetch Captain Campion. And you, Ragwort, get back to the mouth of that run you had no business to leave.'

Very soon, the digging was resumed. The hole was deep now – deeper than Woundwort had expected and still there was no sign of a fall. But all three rabbits could sense that not far below them there lay a hollow space.

'Keep at it,' said Woundwort. 'It won't take long now.'

When Campion came in, he reported that he had seen three rabbits running away over the down to the north. One appeared to be the lame rabbit. He had been about to pursue them but had returned in response to the order brought by Thistle.

'It doesn't matter,' said Woundwort. 'Let them go. There'll be three less when we get in. What, you again?' he snapped, as Ragwort appeared beside him. 'What is it this time?'

'The open run, sir,' said Ragwort. 'It's been broken in and stopped from down below.'

'Then you can start doing something useful,' said Woundwort. 'Get that root out. No, that one, you fool.'

The digging continued, as the first streaks of light began to come into the east.

The great field at the foot of the escarpment had been reaped, but the straw had not yet been burned and lay in long, pale rows upon the darker stubble, tenting over the bristling stalks and the weeds of harvest – knot-grass and pimpernel, fluellen and speedwell, heartsease and persicary – colourless and still in the old moonlight. Between the lines of straw the expanse of stubble was as open as the down.

'Now,' said Hazel, as they came out from the belt of hawthorn and dogwood where the pylon stood, 'are you both sure you understand what we're going to do?'

'It's a tall order, isn't it, Hazel-rah?' answered Dandelion. 'But we've got to try it, that's certain. There's nothing else that'll save the warren now.'

'Come on, then,' said Hazel. 'The going's easy, anyway – half as far now the field's been cut. Don't bother about cover – just run in the open. Keep with me, though. I'll go as fast as I can.'

They crossed the field easily enough, Dandelion running ahead. The only alarm came when they startled four partridges, which whirred away over the hedge to the west and sailed down, spread-winged, into the field beyond. Soon they reached the road and Hazel halted among the quickset on top of the nearer bank.

'Now, Blackberry,' he said, 'this is where we leave you. Lie close and don't move. When the time comes, don't break too soon. You've got the best head of any of us. Use it – and keep it, too. When you get back, go to ground in Kehaar's run and stay there till things are safe. Have you got your line clear?'

'Yes, Hazel-rah,' replied Blackberry. 'But as far as I can see, I may have to run from here to the iron tree without a check. There's no cover.'

'I know,' said Hazel. 'It can't be helped. If the worst comes to the worst, you'll have to turn for the hedge and then keep popping in and out of it. Do whatever you like. There's no time for us to stay and work it out. Only make sure you get back to the warren. It all depends on you.'

Blackberry burrowed his way into the moss and ivy round the base of the thorn. The other two crossed the road and made uphill towards the sheds beside the lane.

'Good roots they keep there,' said Hazel, as they passed them and reached the hedge. 'Pity we've no time just now. When this is over we'll have a nice, quiet raid on the place.'

'I hope we do, Hazel-rah,' said Dandelion. 'Are you going straight up the lane? What about cats?'

'It's the quickest way,' said Hazel. 'That's all that matters now.'

By this time the first light was clear and several larks were up. As they approached the great ring of elm trees, they heard once more the quick sighing and rustling above them and one yellow leaf came spinning down to the edge of the ditch. They reached the top of the slope and saw before them the barns and the farmyard. Bird-song was breaking out all round and the rooks were calling from high in the elms, but nothing – not even a sparrow – moved on the ground. Straight in front, on the other side of the farmyard, close to the house, stood the dog-kennel. The dog was not to be seen, but the rope, tied to the eye-bolt on the flat roof, trailed over the edge and disappeared across the straw-covered threshold.

'We're in time,' said Hazel. 'The brute's still asleep. Now Dandelion, you mustn't make any mistake. You lie in the grass just there, opposite the kennel. When the rope's gnawed through you'll see it fall. Unless the dog's ill or deaf, it'll alert by then; probably before, I'm afraid, but that's my look-out. It's up to you to attract it and make it chase you all the way down to the road. You're very fast. Take care it doesn't lose you. Use the hedges if you want to: but remember it'll be trailing the rope. Get it down to Blackberry. That's all that matters.'

'If we ever meet again, Hazel-rah,' said Dandelion, as he took cover in the grass verge, 'we ought to have the makings of the best story ever.'

'And you'll be the chap to tell it,' said Hazel.

He moved away in a half-circle to the morning side and reached the wall of the farmhouse. Then he began to hop cautiously along the wall, in and out of the narrow flowerbed. His head was a tumult of smells – phlox in bloom, ashes, cow-dung, dog, cat, hens, stagnant water. He came to the back of the kennel, reeking of creosote and of rank straw. A half-used bale of straw stood against it – no doubt clean bedding which, in the dry weather, had not been put back under cover. Here at least was one piece of luck, for he had expected to have trouble in getting on the roof. He scrambled up the straw. Across part of the felted roof lay a torn piece of old blanket, wet with dew. Hazel sat up, sniffing, and put his fore-paws on it. It did not slip. He pulled himself up.

How much noise had he made? How strong was his scent over the tar and straw and farmyard? He waited, tense to jump, expecting movement below. There was no sound. In a terrible miasma of dog-smell, which gripped him with fear and called 'Run! Run!' down every nerve, he crept forward to where the eye-bolt was screwed into the roof. His claws scraped slightly and he stopped again. Still there was no movement. He crouched down and began to nibble and gnaw at the thick cord.

It was easier than he had thought it would be. It was a good deal easier than the cord on the punt, though about as thick. The punt-cord had been drenched through with rain, pliant, slippery and fibrous. This, though dewy on the outside, was dry-cored and light. In very little time the clean inside was showing. His chisel-like fore-teeth bit steadily and he felt the dry strands rip. The cord was as good as half through already.

At that moment he felt the heavy weight of the dog move beneath him. It stretched, shuddered and yawned. The rope moved a little and the straw rustled. The foul smell of it came strong, in a cloud.

'It doesn't matter if it hears me now,' thought Hazel. 'If only I can get the rope bitten through quickly, it doesn't matter. The dog'll go to Dandelion, if only I can be quick enough to make sure that the rope breaks when it begins to tug.'

He ripped at the cord again and sat back for a quick breath, looking across the track to where Dandelion was waiting. Then he froze and stared. A short distance behind Dandelion, in the grass, was the white-chested tabby, wide-eyed, tail-lashing, crouching. It had seen both himself and Dandelion. As he watched, it crept a length nearer. Dandelion was lying still, watching the front of the kennel intently, as he had been told. The cat tensed itself to spring.

Before he knew what he was doing, Hazel stamped on the hollow roof. Twice he stamped and then turned to leap to the ground and run. Dandelion, reacting instantly, shot out of the grass to the open gravel. In the same moment, the cat jumped and landed exactly where he had been lying. The dog gave two quick, sharp barks and rushed out of the kennel. It saw Dandelion at once and ran to the full extent of the rope. The rope went taut, held for an instant and then parted at the point where Hazel had gnawed it to a thread. The kennel jerked forward, tilted, fell back and struck the ground with a jolt. Hazel, already off balance, clawed at the blanket, missed his footing and fell over the edge. He landed heavily on his weak leg and lay kicking. The dog was gone.

Hazel stopped kicking and lay still. There was a spurt of pain along his haunch but he knew that he could move. He remembered the raised floor of the barn across the farmyard. He could limp the short distance, get under the floor and then make his way to the ditch. He raised himself on his fore-legs.

On the instant he was knocked sideways and felt himself pressed down. There was a light but sharp pricking beneath the fur across his back. He lashed out with his hind legs but struck nothing. He turned his head. The cat was on him, crouched half across his body. Its whiskers brushed his ear. Its great, green eyes, the pupils contracted to vertical, black slits in the sunshine, were staring into his own.

'Can you run?' hissed the cat. 'I think not.'

46. Bigwig Stands His Ground

Hard pounding this, gentlemen. Let's see who will pound longest.

The Duke of Wellington (at Waterloo)

GROUNDSEL scrambled up the steep slope of the shaft and rejoined Woundwort in the pit at the top.

'There's nothing left to dig, sir,' he said. 'The bottom will fall in if anyone goes down there now.'

'Can you make out what's below?' asked Woundwort. 'Is it a run or a burrow we shall be into?'

'I'm fairly sure it's a burrow, sir,' answered Groundsel. 'In fact, it feels to me as though there's an unusually big space underneath.'

'How many rabbits are in it, do you think?'

'I couldn't hear any at all. But they may be keeping quiet and waiting to attack us when we break in.'

'They haven't done much attacking up to now,' said Woundwort. 'A poor lot, I'd say – skulking underground, and some of them running away in the night. I don't fancy we'll have much trouble.'

'Unless, sir –' said Groundsel.

Woundwort looked at him and waited.

'Unless the – the animal attacks us, sir,' said Groundsel. 'Whatever it is. It's not like Ragwort to imagine anything. He's very stolid. I'm only trying to think ahead,' he added, as Woundwort still said nothing.

'Well,' said Woundwort at last, 'if there *is* an animal, it'll find out that *I'm* an animal too.' He came out on the bank, where Campion and Vervain were waiting with a number of the other rabbits.

'We've done all the hard work now,' he said. 'We'll be able to take our does home as soon as we've finished down below. The way we'll go about it is this. I'm going to break the bottom of the hole in and go straight down into the burrow underneath. I want only three others to follow, otherwise there'll be complete confusion and we shall all be fighting each other. Vervain, you come behind me and bring two more. If there's any trouble we'll deal with it. Groundsel, you follow. But you're to stay in the shaft, understand? Don't jump down until I tell you. When we know where we are and what we're doing, you can bring a few more in.'

There was not a rabbit in the Owsla but had confidence in Woundwort. As they heard him preparing to go first into the depths of the enemy warren as calmly as though he were looking for dandelions, his officers' spirits rose. It seemed to them quite likely that the place would be given up without any fighting at all. When the General had led the final assault at Nutley Copse he had killed three rabbits underground and no more had dared to oppose him, although there had been some hard tussles in the outer runs the day before.

'Very well,' said Woundwort. 'Now, I don't want anyone straying away. Campion, you see to that. As soon as we get one of the blocked runs opened from inside you can fill the place up. Keep them together here till I let you know and then send them in fast.'

'Best of luck, sir,' said Campion.

Woundwort jumped into the pit, flattened his ears and went down the shaft. He had already decided that he was not going to stop to listen. There was no point, since he meant to break in at once whether there was anything to be heard or not. It was more important that he should not seem to hesitate or cause Vervain to do so; and that the enemy, if they were there, should have the shortest possible time in which to hear him coming. Below, there would be either a run or a burrow. Either he would have to fight immediately or else there would first be a chance to look round and sense where he was. It did not matter. What mattered was finding rabbits and killing them.

He came to the bottom of the shaft. As Groundsel had said, it was plainly thin – brittle as ice on a puddle – chalk, pebbles and light soil. Woundwort scored it across with his fore-claws. Slightly damp, it held a moment and then fell inwards, crumbling. As it fell, Woundwort followed it.

He fell about the length of his own body – far enough to tell him that he was in a burrow. As he landed he kicked out with his hind legs and then dashed forward, partly to be out of Vervain's way as he followed and partly to reach the wall and face about before he could be attacked from behind.

He found himself against a pile of soft earth – evidently the end of a blocked run leading out of the burrow – and turned. A moment later Vervain was beside him. The third rabbit, whoever he was, seemed to be in difficulties. They could both hear him scrabbling in the fallen soil.

'Over here,' said Woundwort sharply.

The rabbit, a powerful, heavy veteran by the name of Thunder, joined them, stumbling.

'What's the matter?' asked Woundwort.

'Nothing, sir,' answered Thunder, 'only there's a dead rabbit on the floor and it startled me for a moment.'

'A dead rabbit?' said Woundwort. 'Are you sure he's dead? Where is he?'

'Over there, sir, by the shaft.'

Woundwort crossed the burrow quickly. On the far side of the rubble that had fallen in from the shaft was lying the inert body of a buck. He sniffed at it and then pressed it with his nose.

'He's not been dead long,' he said. 'He's nearly cold but not stiff. What do you make of it, Vervain? Rabbits don't die underground.'

'It's a very small buck, sir,' answered Vervain. 'Didn't fancy the idea of fighting us, perhaps, and the others killed him when he said so.'

'No, that won't do. There's not a scratch on him. Well, leave him, anyway. We've got to get on, and a rabbit this size isn't going to make any difference, dead or alive.'

He began to move along the wall, sniffing as he went. He passed the mouths of two blocked runs, came to an opening between thick tree-roots, and stopped. The place was evidently very big – bigger than the Council burrow at Efrafa. Since they were not being attacked, he could turn the space to his own advantage by getting some more rabbits in at once. He went back quickly to the foot of the shaft. By standing on his hind legs he could just rest his fore-paws on the ragged lip of the hole.

'Groundsel?' he said.

'Yes, sir?' answered Groundsel from above.

'Come on,' said Woundwort, 'and bring four others with you. Jump to this side' – he moved slightly – 'there's a dead rabbit on the floor – one of theirs.'

He was still expecting to be attacked at any moment, but the place remained silent. He continued to listen, sniffing the close air, while the five rabbits dropped one by one into the burrow. Then he took Groundsel over to the two blocked runs along the eastern wall.

'Get these open as quick as you can,' he said, 'and send two rabbits to find out what's behind the tree roots beyond. If they're attacked you're to go and join in at once.'

'You know, there's something strange about the wall at the other end, sir,' said Vervain, as Groundsel began setting his rabbits to work. 'Most of it's hard earth that's never been dug. But in one or two places there are piles of much softer stuff. I'd say that runs leading through the wall have been filled up very recently – probably since yesterday evening.'

Woundwort and Vervain went carefully along the south wall of the Honeycomb, scratching and listening.

'I believe you're right,' said Woundwort. 'Have you heard any movement from the other side?'

'Yes, sir, just about here,' said Vervain.

'We'll get this pile of soft earth down,' said Woundwort. 'Put two rabbits on it. If I'm right and Thlayli's on the other side, they'll run into trouble before long. That's what we want – to force him to attack them.'

As Thunder and Thistle began to dig, Woundwort crouched silently behind them, waiting.

Even before he heard the roof of the Honeycomb fall in, Bigwig knew that it could be only a matter of time before the Efrafans found the soft places in the south wall and set to work to break through one of them. That would not take long. Then he would have to fight – probably with Woundwort himself: and if Woundwort closed with him and used his weight he would have little chance. Somehow, he must manage to hurt him at the outset, before he expected it. But how?

He put the problem to Holly.

'The trouble is this warren wasn't dug to be defended,' said Holly. 'That was what the Slack Run was for, back at home, so the Threarah once told me. It was made so that if we ever had to, we could get down beneath an enemy and come up where he wasn't expecting us.'

'That's it!' cried Bigwig. 'That's the idea! Look, I'm going to dig myself into the floor of the run just behind this blocked opening. Then you cover me with earth. It won't be noticed – there's so much digging and mess in the place already. I know it's a risk, but it'll be better than just trying to stand up in front of a rabbit like Woundwort.'

'But suppose they break through the wall somewhere else?' said Holly.

'You must try to make them do it here,' replied Bigwig. 'When you hear them on the other side, make a noise – do a bit of scratching or something – just above where I am. Anything to get them interested. Come on, help me to dig. And Silver, get everyone back out of the Honeycomb now and close this wall completely.'

'Bigwig,' said Pipkin, 'I can't wake Fiver. He's still lying out there in the middle of the floor. What's to be done?'

'I'm afraid there's nothing we can do now,' replied Bigwig. 'It's a great pity, but we'll have to leave him.'

'Oh, Bigwig,' cried Pipkin, 'let me stay out there with him! You'll never miss me, and I can go on trying –'

'Hlao-roo,' said Holly as kindly as he could, 'if we lose no one but Fiver before this business is ended, then the Lord Frith himself will be fighting for us. No, I'm sorry, old chap, not another word. We need you, we need everyone. Silver, see that he goes back with the others.'

When Woundwort dropped through the roof of the Honeycomb, Bigwig was already lying under a thin covering of soil on the other side of the south wall, not far from Clover's burrow.

Thunder sunk his teeth into a piece of broken root and pulled it out. There was an instant fall of earth and a gap opened where he had been digging. The soil no longer reached to the roof. It was only a broad pile of soft earth, half-filling the run. Woundwort, still waiting silently, could smell and hear a considerable number of rabbits on the far side. He hoped that now they might come into the open burrow and try to attack him. But they made no move.

When it came to fighting, Woundwort was not given to careful calculation. Men, and larger animals such as wolves, usually have an idea of their own numbers and those of the enemy and this affects their readiness to fight and how they go about it. Woundwort had never had any need to think like this. What he had learned from all his experience of fighting was that nearly always there are those who want to fight and those who do not but feel they cannot avoid it. More than once he had fought alone and imposed his will on crowds of other rabbits. He held down a great warren with the help of a handful of devoted officers. It did not occur to him now – and if it had, he would not have thought it mattered – that most of his rabbits were still outside; that those who were with him were fewer than those on the other side of the wall and that until Groundsel had got the runs open they could not get out even if they wanted to. This sort of thing does not count among fighting rabbits. Ferocity and aggression are everything. What Woundwort knew was that those beyond the wall were afraid of him and that on this account he had the advantage.

'Groundsel,' he said, 'as soon as you've got those runs open, tell Campion to send everyone down here. The rest of you, follow me. We'll have this business finished by the time the others get in to join us.'

Woundwort waited only for Groundsel to bring back the two rabbits who had been sent to search among the tree roots at the north end of the burrow. Then, with Vervain behind him, he climbed the pile of fallen earth and thrust his way into the narrow run. In the dark he could hear and smell the rustling and crowding of rabbits – both bucks and does – ahead of him. There were two bucks directly in his path but they fell back as he ploughed through the loose soil. He plunged forward and felt the ground suddenly turn beneath him. The next moment a rabbit started up from the earth at his feet and sank his teeth in the pit of his near foreleg, just where it joined the body.

Woundwort had won almost every fight of his life by using his weight. Other rabbits could not stop him and once they went down they seldom got up. He tried to push now, but his back legs could get no purchase in the pile of loose, yielding soil behind him. He reared up, and as he did so realized that the enemy beneath him was crouching in a scooped-out trench the size of his own body. He struck out and felt his claws score deeply along the back and haunch. Then the other rabbit, still keeping his grip under Woundwort's shoulder, thrust upwards with his hind legs braced against the floor of the trench. Woundwort, with both forefeet off the ground, was thrown over on his back on the earth pile. He lashed out, but the enemy had already loosed his hold and was beyond his reach.

Woundwort stood up. He could feel the blood running down the inside of his near foreleg. The muscle was wounded. He could not put his full weight on it. But his own claws, too, were bloody and this blood was not his.

'Are you all right, sir?' asked Vervain, behind him.

'Of course I'm all right, you fool,' said Woundwort. 'Follow me close.'

The other rabbit spoke from in front of him.

'You told me once to start by impressing you, General. I hope I have.'

'I told you once that I would kill you myself,' replied Woundwort. 'There is no white bird here, Thlayli.' He advanced for the second time.

Bigwig's taunt had been deliberate. He hoped that Woundwort would fly at him and so give him a chance to bite him again. But as he waited, pressed to the ground, he realized that Woundwort was too clever to be drawn. Always quick to size up any new situation, he was coming forward slowly, keeping close to the ground himself. He meant to use his claws. Afraid, listening to Woundwort's approach, Bigwig could hear the uneven movement of his forepaws, almost within striking distance. Instinctively he drew back and as he did so the thought came with the sound. 'The near forepaw's dragging. He can't use it properly.' Leaving his right flank exposed, he struck out on his near side.

His claws found Woundwort's leg, ripping sideways; but before he could draw back, Woundwort's whole weight came down on him and the next moment his teeth had met in his right ear. Bigwig squealed, pressed down and thrashing from side to side. Woundwort, feeling his enemy's fear and helplessness, loosed his hold of the ear and rose above him, ready to bite and tear him across the back of the neck. For an instant he stood above the helpless Bigwig, his shoulders filling the run. Then his injured foreleg gave way and he lurched sideways against the wall. Bigwig cuffed him twice across the face and felt the third blow pass through his whiskers as he sprang back. The sound of his heavy breathing came plainly from the top of the earth pile. Bigwig, the blood oozing from his back and ear, stood his ground and waited. Suddenly he realized that he could see the dark shape of General Woundwort faintly outlined, where he crouched above him. The first traces of daylight were glimmering through the broken roof of the Honeycomb behind.

47. The Sky Suspended

Ole bull he comes for me, wi's head down. But I didn't
flinch . . . I went for 'e. 'Twas him as did th' flinchin'.

Flora Thompson, *Lark Rise to Candleford*

WHEN Hazel stamped, Dandelion leapt instinctively
from the grass verge. If there had been a hole he would
have made for it. For the briefest instant he looked up and
down the gravel. Then the dog was rushing upon him and he
turned and made for the raised barn. But before he reached it
he realized that he must not take refuge under the floor. If he
did the dog would check: very likely a man would call it back.
He had to get it out of the farmyard and down to the road. He
altered direction and raced up the lane towards the elms.

He had not expected the dog to be so close behind him.
He could hear its breath and the loose gravel flying under
its paws.

'It's too fast for me!' he thought. 'It's going to catch me!'
In another moment it would be on him and then it would
roll him over, snapping his back and biting out his life. He

knew that hares, when overtaken, dodge by turning more quickly and neatly than the pursuing dog and doubling back on their track. 'I shall have to double,' he thought desperately. 'But if I do it will hunt me up and down the lane and the man will call it off, or else I shall have to lose it by going through the hedge: then the whole plan will fail.'

He tore over the crest and down towards the cattle-shed. When Hazel had told him what he was to do it had seemed to him that his task would consist of leading the dog on and persuading it to follow him. Now he was running simply to save his life, and that at a speed he had never touched before, a speed he knew he could not keep up.

In actual fact Dandelion covered three hundred yards to the cattle-shed in a good deal less than half a minute. But as he reached the straw at the entrance it seemed to him that he had run for ever. Hazel and the farmyard were long, long ago. He had never done anything in his life but run in terror down the the lane, feeling the dog's breath at his haunches. Inside the gate a big rat ran across in front of him and the dog checked at it for a moment. Dandelion gained the nearest shed and went headlong between two bales of straw at the foot of a pile. It was a narrow place and he turned round only with some difficulty. The dog was immediately outside, scratching eagerly, whining and throwing up loose straw as it sniffed along the foot of the bales.

'Sit tight,' said a young rat, from the straw close beside him. 'It'll be off in a minute. They're not like cats, you know.'

'That's the trouble,' said Dandelion, panting and rolling the whites of his eyes. 'It mustn't lose me; and time's everything.'

'What?' said the rat, puzzled. 'What you say?'

Without answering, Dandelion slipped along to another crack, gathered himself a moment and then broke cover, running across the yard to the opposite shed. It was open-fronted and he went straight through to the boarding along the back. There was a gap under the broken end of a board and here he crept into the field beyond. The dog, following, thrust its head into the gap and pushed, barking with excitement. Gradually the loose board levered open like a trap-door until it was able to force its way through.

Now that he had a better start, Dandelion kept in the open and ran down the field to the hedge beside the road. He knew he was slower but the dog seemed slower too. Choosing a thick part, he went through the hedge and crossed the road. Blackberry came to meet him, scuttering down the further bank. Dandelion dropped exhausted in the ditch. The dog was not twenty feet away on the other side of the hedge. It could not find a big enough gap.

'It's faster than ever I thought,' gasped Dandelion, 'but I've taken the edge off it. I can't do any more. I must go to ground. I'm finished.'

It was plain that Blackberry was frightened.

'Frith help me!' he whispered. 'I'll never do it!'

'Go on, quick,' said Dandelion, 'before it loses interest. I'll overtake you and help if I can.'

Blackberry hopped deliberately into the road and sat up. Seeing him, the dog yelped and thrust its weight against the hedge. Blackberry ran slowly along the road towards a pair of gates that stood opposite each other further down. The dog stayed level with him. As soon as he was sure that it had seen the gate on its own side and meant to go to it, Blackberry turned and climbed the bank. Out in the stubble he waited for the dog to reappear.

It was a long time coming; and when at last it pushed its way between the gate-post and the bank into the field, it paid him no attention. It nosed along the foot of the bank, put up a partridge and bounced after it and then began to scratch about in a clump of dock-plants. For some time Blackberry felt too terrified to move. Then, in desperation, he hopped slowly towards it, trying to act as though he had not noticed that it was there. It dashed after him, but almost at once seemed to lose interest and returned to its nosing and sniffing over the ground. Finally, when he was utterly at a loss, it set off over the field of its own accord, padding easily along – beside one of the rows of threshed straw, trailing the broken cord and pouncing in and out at every squeak and rustle. Blackberry, sheltering behind a parallel row, kept level with it. In this manner they covered the distance to the pylon line, half way to the foot of the down. It was here that Dandelion caught up with him.

'It's not fast enough, Blackberry! We *must* get on. Bigwig may be dead.'

'I know, but at least it's going the right way. I couldn't get it to move at all to start with. Can't we –'

'It's got to come up the down at speed or there'll be no surprise. Come on, we'll draw it together. We'll have to get ahead of it first, though.'

They ran fast through the stubble until they neared the trees. Then they turned and crossed the dog's line in full view. This time it pursued instantly and the two rabbits reached the undergrowth at the bottom of the steep with no more than ten yards to spare. As they began to climb they heard the dog crashing through the brittle elders. It barked once and then they were out on the open slope with the dog running mute behind them.

The blood ran over Bigwig's neck and down his foreleg. He watched Woundwort steadily where he crouched on the earth pile, expecting him to leap forward at any moment. He could hear a rabbit moving behind him but the run was so narrow that he could not have turned even if it had been safe to do so.

'Everyone all right?' he asked.

'They're all right,' replied Holly. 'Come on, Bigwig, let me take your place now. You need a rest.'

'Can't,' panted Bigwig. 'You couldn't get past me here – no room – and if I go back that brute'll follow – next thing you'd know he'd be loose in the burrows. You leave it to me. I know what I'm doing.'

It had occurred to Bigwig that in the narrow run even his dead body would be a considerable obstacle. The Efrafans would either have to get it out or dig round it and this would mean more delay. In the burrow behind him he could hear Bluebell, who was apparently telling the does a story. 'Good idea,' he thought. 'Keep 'em happy. More than I could do if I had to sit there.'

'So then El-ahrairah said to the fox, "Fox you may smell and fox you may be, but I can tell your fortune in the water."

Suddenly Woundwort spoke.

'Thlayli,' he said, 'why do you want to throw your life away? I can send one fresh rabbit after another into this run if I choose. You're too good to be killed. Come back to Efrafa. I promise I'll give you the command of any Mark you like. I give you my word.'

'*Silflay hraka, u embleer rah*,' replied Bigwig.

'"Ah ha," said the fox, "tell my fortune, eh? And what do you see in the water, my friend? Fat rabbits running through the grass, yes, yes?"'

'Very well,' said Woundwort. 'But remember, Thlayli, you yourself can stop this nonsense whenever you wish.'

'"No," replied El-ahrairah, "it is not fat rabbits that I see in the water, but swift hounds on the scent and my enemy flying for his life."'

Bigwig realized that Woundwort also knew that in the run his body would be nearly as great a hindrance dead as alive. 'He wants me to come out on my feet,' he thought. 'But it's Inlé, not Efrafa, that I shall go to from here.'

Suddenly Woundwort leapt forward in a single bound and landed full against Bigwig like a branch falling from a tree. He made no attempt to use his claws. His great weight was pushing, chest to chest, against Bigwig's. With heads side by side they bit and snapped at each other's shoulders. Bigwig felt himself sliding slowly backwards. He could not resist the tremendous pressure. His back legs, with claws extended, furrowed the floor of the run as he gave ground. In a few moments he would be pushed bodily into the burrow behind. Putting his last strength into the effort to remain where he was, he loosed his teeth from Woundwort's shoulder and dropped his head, like a cart-horse straining at a load. Still he was slipping. Then, very gradually it seemed, the terrible pressure began to slacken. His claws had a hold of the ground. Woundwort, teeth sunk in his back, was snuffling and choking. Though Bigwig did not know it, his earlier blows had torn Woundwort across the nose. His nostrils were full of his own blood and with jaws closed in Bigwig's fur he could not draw his breath. A moment more and he let go his hold. Bigwig, utterly exhausted, lay where he was. After a few moments he tried to get up, but a faintness came over him and a feeling of turning over and over in a ditch of leaves. He closed his eyes. There was silence and then, quite clearly, he heard Fiver speaking in the long grass. 'You are closer to death than I. You are closer to death than I.'

'The wire!' squealed Bigwig. He jerked himself up and opened his eyes. The run was empty. General Woundwort was gone.

Woundwort clambered out into the Honeycomb, now dimly lit, down the shaft, by the daylight outside. He had never felt so tired. He saw Vervain and Thunder looking at him uncertainly. He sat on his haunches and tried to clean his face with his front paws.

'Thlayli won't give any more trouble,' he said. 'You'd better just go in and finish him off, Vervain, since he won't come out.'

'You're asking *me* to fight him, sir?' asked Vervain.

'Well, just take him on for a few moments,' answered Woundwort. 'I want to start them getting this wall down in one or two other places. Then I'll come back.'

Vervain knew that the impossible had happened. The General had come off worst. What he was saying was, 'Cover up for me. Don't let the others know.'

'What in Frith's name happens now?' thought Vervain. 'The plain truth is that Thlayli's had the best of it all along, ever since he first met him in Efrafa. And the sooner we're back there the better.'

He met Woundwort's pale stare, hesitated a moment and then climbed on the earth pile. Woundwort limped across to the two runs, half-way down the eastern wall, which Groundsel had been told to get open. Both were now clear at the entrances and the diggers were out of sight in the tunnels. As he approached. Groundsel backed down the farther tunnel and began cleaning his claws on a projecting root.

'How are you getting on?' asked Woundwort.

'This run's open, sir,' said Groundsel, 'but the other will take a bit longer, I'm afraid. It's heavily blocked.'

'One's enough,' said Woundwort, 'as long as they can come down it. We can bring them in and start getting that end wall down.'

He was about to go up the run himself when he found Vervain beside him. For a moment he thought that he was going to say that he had killed Thlayli. A second glance showed him otherwise.

'I've – er – got some grit in my eye, sir,' said Vervain. 'I'll just get it out and then I'll have another go at him.'

Without a word Woundwort went back to the far end of the Honeycomb. Vervain followed.

'You coward,' said Woundwort, in his ear. 'If my authority goes, where will yours be in half a day? Aren't you the most hated officer in Efrafa? That rabbit's *got* to be killed.'

Once more he climbed on the earth pile. Then he stopped. Vervain and Thistle, raising their heads to peer past him from behind, saw why. Thlayli had made his way up the run and was crouching immediately below. Blood had matted the great thatch of fur on his head and one ear, half-severed, hung down beside his face. His breathing was slow and heavy.

'You'll find it much harder to push me back from here, General,' he said.

With a sort of weary, dull surprise, Woundwort realized that he was afraid. He did not want to attack Thlayli again. He knew, with flinching certainty, that he was not up to it. And who was? he thought. Who could do it? No, they would have to get in by some other way and everyone would know why.

'Thlayli,' he said, 'we've unblocked a run out here. I can bring in enough rabbits to pull down this wall in four places. Why don't you come out?'

Thlayli's reply, when it came, was low and gasping, but perfectly clear.

'My Chief Rabbit has told me to defend this run and until he says otherwise I shall stay here.'

'His Chief Rabbit?' said Vervain, staring.

It had never occurred to Woundwort or any of his officers that Thlayli was not the Chief Rabbit of his warren. Yet what he said carried immediate conviction. He was speaking the truth. And if he was not the Chief Rabbit, then somewhere close by there must be another, stronger rabbit who was. A stronger rabbit than Thlayli. Where was he? What was he doing at this moment?

Woundwort became aware that Thistle was no longer behind him.

'Where's that young fellow gone?' he said to Vervain.

'He seems to have slipped away, sir,' answered Vervain.

'You should have stopped him,' said Woundwort. 'Fetch him back.'

But it was Groundsel who returned to him a few moments later.

'I'm sorry, sir,' he said, 'Thistle's gone up the opened run. I thought you'd sent him or I'd have asked him what he was up to. One or two of my rabbits seem to have gone with him – I don't know what for, I'm sure.'

'I'll give them what for,' said Woundwort. 'Come with me.'

He knew now what they would have to do. Every rabbit he had brought must be sent underground to dig and every blocked gap in the wall must be opened. As for Thlayli, he could simply be left where he was and the less said about him the better. There must be no more fighting in narrow runs and when the terrible Chief Rabbit finally appeared he would be pulled down in the open, from all sides.

He turned to recross the burrow, but remained where he was, staring. In the faint patch of light below the ragged hole in the roof, a rabbit was standing – no Efrafan, a rabbit unknown to the General. He was very small and was looking tensely about him – wide-eyed as a kitten above ground for the first time – as though by no means sure where he might be. As Woundwort watched, he raised a trembling fore-paw and passed it gropingly across his face. For a moment some old, flickering, here-and-gone feeling stirred in the General's memory – the smell of wet cabbage leaves in a cottage garden, the sense of some easy-going, kindly place, long forgotten and lost.

'Who the devil's that?' asked General Woundwort.

'It – it must be the rabbit that's been lying there, sir,' answered Groundsel. 'The rabbit we thought was dead.'

'Oh, is that it?' said Woundwort. 'Well, he's just about your mark, isn't he, Vervain? That's one of them you might be able to tackle, at all events. Hurry up,' he sneered, as Vervain hesitated, uncertain whether the General were serious, 'and come on out as soon as you've finished.'

Vervain advanced slowly across the floor. Even he could derive little satisfaction from the prospect of killing a tharn rabbit half his own size, in obedience to a contemptuous taunt. The small rabbit made no move whatever, either to retreat or to defend himself, but only stared at him from great eyes which, though troubled, were certainly not those of a beaten enemy or a victim. Before his gaze, Vervain stopped in uncertainty and for long moments the two faced each other in the dim light. Then, very quietly and with no trace of fear, the strange rabbit said:

'I am sorry for you with all my heart. But you cannot blame us, for you came to kill us if you could.'

'Blame you?' answered Vervain. 'Blame you for what?'

'For your death. Believe me, I am sorry for your death.'

Vervain in his time had encountered any number of prisoners who, before they died, had cursed or threatened him, not uncommonly with supernatural vengeance, much as Bigwig had cursed Woundwort in the storm. If such things had been liable to have any effect on him, he would not have been head of the Owslafa. Indeed, for almost any utterance that a rabbit in this dreadful situation could find to make, Vervain was unthinkingly ready with one or other of a stock of jeering rejoinders. Now, as he continued to meet the eyes of this unaccountable enemy – the only one he had faced in all the long night's search for bloodshed – horror came upon him and he was filled with a sudden fear of his words, gentle and inexorable as the falling of bitter snow in a land without refuge. The shadowy recesses of the strange burrow seemed full of whispering, malignant ghosts and he recognized the forgotten voices of rabbits done to death months since in the ditches of Efrafa.

'Let me alone!' cried Vervain. 'Let me go! Let me go!'

Stumbling and blundering, he found his way to the opened run and dragged himself up it. At the top he came upon Woundwort, listening to one of Groundsel's diggers, who was trembling and white-eyed.

'Oh, sir,' said the youngster, 'they say there's a great Chief Rabbit bigger than a hare: and a strange animal they heard –'

'Shut up!' said Woundwort. 'Follow me, come on.'

He came out on the bank, blinking in the sunlight. The rabbits scattered about the grass stared at him in horror, several wondering whether this could really be the General. His nose and one eyelid were gashed and his whole face was masked with blood. As he limped down from the bank his near fore-leg trailed and he staggered sideways. He scrambled into the open grass and looked about him.

'Now,' said Woundwort, 'this is the last thing we have to do, and it won't take long. Down below, there's a kind of wall.' He stopped, sensing all around him reluctance and fear. He looked at Ragwort, who looked away. Two other rabbits were edging off through the grass. He called them back.

'What do you think you're doing?' he asked.

'Nothing, sir,' replied one. 'We only thought that –'

All of a sudden Captain Campion dashed round the corner of the hanger. From the open down beyond came a single, high scream. At the same moment two strange rabbits, running together, leapt the bank into the wood and disappeared down one of the blocked tunnels.

'Run!' cried Campion, stamping. 'Run for your lives!'

He raced through them and was gone over the down. Not knowing what he meant or where to run, they turned one way and another. Five bolted down the opened run and a few more into the wood. But almost before they had begun to scatter, into their midst bounded a great, black dog, snapping, biting and chasing hither and thither like a fox in a chicken-run.

Woundwort alone stood his ground. As the rest fled in all directions he remained where he was, bristling and snarling, bloody-fanged and bloody-clawed. The dog, coming suddenly upon him face to face among the rough tussocks, recoiled a moment, startled and confused. Then it sprang forward; and even as they ran, his Owsla could hear the General's raging, squealing cry, 'Come back, you fools! Dogs aren't dangerous! Come back and fight!'

48. Dea Ex Machina

And as I was green and carefree, famous among the barns
About the happy yard and singing as the farm was home,
In the sun that is young once only . . .

                    Dylan Thomas, 'Fern Hill'

WHEN Lucy woke, the room was already light. The curtains were not drawn and the pane of the open casement reflected a gleam of sun which she could lose and find by moving her head on the pillow. A wood-pigeon was calling in the elms. But it was some other sound, she knew, that had woken her – a sharp sound, a part of the dream which had drained away, as she woke, like water out of a wash-basin. Perhaps the dog had barked. But now everything was quiet and there was only the flash of sun from the window-pane and the sound of the wood-pigeon, like the first strokes of a paint-brush on a big sheet of paper when you were still not sure how the picture was going to go. The morning was fine. Would there be any mushrooms yet? Was it worth getting up now and going down the field to see? It was still too dry and hot – not good mushroom weather. The mushrooms were like the blackberries – both wanted a drop of rain before they'd be any good. Soon there'd be damp mornings and the big spiders would come in the hedges – the ones with a white cross on their backs. Jane Pocock running off to the back of the school bus when she brought one in a matchbox to show Miss Tallant.

> Spider, spider on the bus
> Soppy Jane that made a fuss,
> Spider got th' eleven-plus.

Now she couldn't catch the reflection in her eyes any more. The sun had moved. What was going to happen today? Thursday – market day in Newbury. Dad would be going in. Doctor was coming to see Mum. Doctor had funny glasses that pinched on his nose. They'd made a mark each side. If he wasn't in a hurry he'd talk to her. Doctor was a bit funny-like when you didn't know him but when you did he was nice.

Suddenly there was another sharp sound. It ripped through the still, early morning like something spilt across a clean floor – a squealing – something frightened, something desperate. Lucy jumped out of bed and ran across to the window. Whatever it was, it was only just outside. She leaned well out, with her feet off the floor and the sill pressing breathlessly across her stomach. Tab was down below, right by the kennel. He'd got something: rat it must be, squealing like that.

'Tab!' called Lucy sharply. 'Tab! Wha' you got?'

At the sound of her voice the cat looked up for a moment and immediately looked back again at its prey. ''Tweren't no rat, though; 'twas rabbit, layin' on its side by the kennel. It looked proper bad. Kickin' out an' all.' Then it squealed again.

Lucy ran down the stairs in her night-dress and opened the door. The gravel made her hobble and she left it and went on up the flower-bed. As she reached the kennel the cat looked up and spat at her, keeping one paw pressed down on the rabbit's neck.

'Git out, Tab!' said Lucy. 'Grool thing! Let'n alone!'

She cuffed the cat, which tried to scratch her, ears laid flat. She raised her hand again and it growled, ran a few feet and stopped, looking back in sulky rage. Lucy picked up the rabbit. It struggled a moment and then held itself tense in her firm grip.

''Old still!' said Lucy. 'I ain't gon' urtcher!'

She went back to the house, carrying the rabbit.

'What you bin up to, eh?' said her father, boots scratch scratch over the tiles. 'Look at yore feet! En I told you – Wha' got there then?'

'Rabbit,' said Lucy, defensively.

'In yer night-dress an' all, catch yore bloomin' death! Wha' want with 'im, then?'

'Goner keep 'im.'

'You ain't!'

'Ah, Dad. 'E's nice.'

''E won't be n' bloomin' good t' yer. You put 'im in 'utch 'e'll only die. You can't keep woild rabbit. 'N if 'e gets out 'e'll do all manner o' bloomin' 'arm.'

'But 'e's bad, Dad. Cat's bin at 'im.'

'Cat was doin' 'is job then. Did oughter've let 'im finish be roights.'

'I wanner show 'im to Doctor.'

'Doctor's got summin' better to do than bide about wi' old rabbit. You jus' give 'im 'ere now.'

Lucy began to cry. She had not lived all her life on a farm for nothing and she knew very well that everything her father had said was right. But she was upset by the idea of killing the rabbit in cold blood. True, she did not really know what she could do with it in the long run. What she wanted was to show it to Doctor. She knew that Doctor thought of her as a proper farm girl – a country girl. When she showed him things she had found – a goldfinch's egg, a Painted Lady fluttering in a jam-jar or a fungus that looked exactly like orange peel – he took her seriously and talked to her as he would to a grown-up person. To ask his advice about a damaged rabbit and discuss it with him would be very grown-up. Meanwhile, her father might give way or he might not.

'I on'y just wanted to show 'im to Doctor, Dad. I won't let 'im do no 'arm, honest. On'y it's nice talking to Doctor.'

Although he never said so, her father was proud of the way Lucy got on with Doctor. She was a proper bright kid – very likely goin' to grammar school an' all, so they told him. Doctor had said once or twice she was real sensible with these things she picked up what she showed him. Comin' to somethin', though, bloody rabbits. All same, would'n' 'urt, long's she didn' let 'un go on the place.

'Why don' you do somethin' sensible,' he said, ''stead o' bidin' there 'ollerin' and carryin' on like you was skimmish?

593

You wants go'n get some cloze on, then you c'n go'n put 'im in that old cage what's in shed. One what you 'ad for they budgies.'

Lucy stopped crying and went upstairs, still carrying the rabbit. She shut it in a drawer, got dressed and went out to get the cage. On the way back she stopped for some straw from behind the kennel. Her father came across from the long barn.

'Did y'see Bob?'

'Never,' said Lucy. 'Where's 'e gone then?'

'Bust 'is rope an' off. I know'd that old rope were gett'n on like, but I didn't reckon 'e could bust 'im. Anyways, I go' go in to Newbury s'mornin'. 'F'e turns up agen you'd best tie 'im up proper.'

'I'll look out fer 'im, Dad,' said Lucy. 'I'll ge' bi' o' breakfast up to Mum now.'

'Ah, that's good girl. I reckon she'll be right's a trivet to-morrer.'

Doctor Adams arrived soon after ten. Lucy, who was making her bed and tidying her room later than she should have been, heard him stop his car under the elms at the top of the lane and went out to meet him, wondering why he had not driven up to the house as usual. He had got out of the car and was standing with his hands behind his back, looking down the lane, but he caught sight of her and called in the rather shy, abrupt way she was used to.

'Er – Lucy.'

She ran up. He took off his pince-nez and put them in his waistcoat pocket.

'Is that your dog?'

The Labrador was coming up the lane, looking decidedly tired and trailing its broken rope. Lucy laid hold of it.

''E's bin off, Doctor. 'Bin ever so worried 'bout 'im.'

The Labrador began to sniff at Doctor Adams' shoes.

'Something's been fighting with him, I think,' said Doctor Adams. 'His nose is scratched quite badly, and that looks like some kind of a bite on his leg.'

'What d'you reckon 'twas then, Doctor?'

'Well, it might have been a big rat, I suppose, or perhaps a stoat. Something he went for, that put up a fight.'

'I got a rabbit s'mornin', Doctor. Woild one. 'E's aloive. I took 'un off o' the cat. On'ly I reckon 'e's urt. Joo like see 'im?'

'Well, I'd better go and see Mrs Cane first, I think.' (Not 'Your mother,' thought Lucy.) 'And then if I've got time I'll have a look at the chap.'

Twenty minutes later Lucy was holding the rabbit as quiet as she could, while Doctor Adams pressed it gently here and there with the balls of two fingers.

'Well, there doesn't seem to be much the matter with him, as far as I can see,' he said at last. 'Nothing's broken. There's something funny about this hind leg, but that's been done some time and it's more or less healed – or as much as it ever will. The cat's scratched him across here, you see, but that's nothing much. I should think he'll be all right for a bit.'

'No good to keep 'im, though, Doctor, would it? In 'utch, I mean.'

'Oh no, he wouldn't live shut up in a box. If he couldn't get out he'd soon die. No, I should let the poor chap go – unless you want to eat him.'

Lucy laughed. 'Dad'd be ever s'woild, though, if I was to let 'im go anywheres round 'ere. 'E always says one rabbit means 'undred an' one.'

'Well, I'll tell you what,' said Doctor Adams, taking his thin fob watch on the fingers of one hand and looking down at it as he held it at arm's length – for he was long-sighted – 'I've got to go a few miles up the road to see an old lady at Cole Henley. If you like to come along in the car, you can let him go on the down and I'll bring you back before dinner.'

Lucy skipped. 'I'll just go'n ask Mum.'

On the ridge between Hare Warren Down and Watership Down, Doctor Adams stopped the car.

'I should think this would be as good as anywhere,' he said. 'There's not a lot of harm he can do here, if you come to think about it.'

They walked a short distance eastwards from the road and Lucy set the rabbit down. It sat stupefied for nearly half a minute and then suddenly dashed away over the grass.

'Yes, he *has* got something the matter with that leg, you see,' said Doctor Adams, pointing. 'But he could perfectly well live for years, as far as that goes. Born and bred in a briar patch, Brer Fox.'

49. Hazel Comes Home

> Well, we've been lucky devils both
> And there's no need of pledge or oath
> To bind our lovely friendship fast,
> > By firmer stuff
> > Close bound enough.
>
> Robert Graves, *Two Fusiliers*

ALTHOUGH Woundwort had shown himself at the last to be a creature virtually mad, nevertheless what he did proved not altogether futile. There can be little doubt that if he had not done it, more rabbits would have been killed that morning on Watership Down. So swiftly and silently had the dog come up the hill behind Dandelion and Blackberry that one of Campion's sentries, half asleep under a tussock after the long night, was pulled down and killed in the instant that he turned to bolt. Later – after it had left Woundwort – the dog beat up and down the bank and the open grass for some time, barking and dashing at every bush and clump of weeds. But by now the Efrafans had had time to scatter and hide, as best they could. Besides, the dog, unexpectedly scratched and bitten, showed a certain reluctance to come to grips. At last, however, it succeeded in putting up and killing the rabbit who had been wounded by glass the day before, and with this it made off by the way it had come, disappearing over the edge of the escarpment.

There could be no question now of the Efrafans renewing their attack on the warren. None had any idea beyond saving his own life. Their leader was gone. The dog had been set on them by the rabbits they had come to kill – of this they were sure. It was all one with the mysterious fox and the white bird. Indeed Ragwort, the most unimaginative rabbit alive, had actually heard it underground. Campion, crouching in a patch of nettles with Vervain and four or five more, met with nothing but shivering agreement when he said that he was sure that they ought to leave at once this dangerous place, where they had already stayed far too long.

Without Campion, probably not one rabbit would have got back to Efrafa. As it was, all his skill as a patroller could not bring home half of those who had come to Watership. Three or four had run and strayed too far to be found and what became of them no one ever knew. There were probably fourteen or fifteen rabbits – no more – who set off with Campion, some time before ni-Frith, to try to retrace the long journey they had made only the previous day. They were not fit to cover the distance by nightfall: and before long they had worse to face than their own fatigue and low spirits. Bad news travels fast. Down to the Belt and beyond, the rumour spread that the terrible

General Woundwort and his Owsla had been cut to pieces on Watership Down and that what was left of them was trailing southwards in poor shape, with little heart to keep alert. The Thousand began to close in – stoats, a fox, even a tom-cat from some farm or other. At every halt yet another rabbit was not to be found and no one could remember seeing what had happened to him. One of these was Vervain. It had been plain from the start that he had nothing left and indeed there was little reason for him to return to Efrafa without the General.

Through all the fear and hardship Campion remained steady and vigilant, holding the survivors together, thinking ahead and encouraging the exhausted to keep going. During the afternoon of the following day, while the Off-Fore Mark were at silflay, he came limping through the sentry-line with a straggling handful of six or seven rabbits. He was close to collapse himself and scarcely able to give the Council any account of the disaster.

Only Groundsel, Thistle and three others had the presence of mind to dart down the opened run when the dog came. Back in the Honeycomb, Groundsel immediately surrendered himself and his fugitives to Fiver, who was still bemused from his long trance and scarcely restored to his senses sufficiently to grasp what was toward. At length, however, after the five Efrafans had remained crouching for some time in the burrow, listening to the sounds of the dog hunting above, Fiver recovered himself, made his way to the mouth of the run where Bigwig still lay half-conscious, and succeeded in making Holly and Silver understand that the siege was ended. There was no lack of helpers to tear open the blocked gaps in the south wall. It so happened that Bluebell was the first through into the Honeycomb; and for many days afterwards he was still improving upon his imitation of Captain Fiver at the head of his crowd of Efrafan prisoners – 'like a tom-tit rounding up a bunch of moulting jackdaws', as he put it.

No one was inclined to pay them much attention at the time, however, for the only thoughts throughout the warren were for Hazel and Bigwig. Bigwig seemed likely to die. Bleeding in half a dozen places, he lay with closed eyes in the run he had defended and made no reply when Hyzenthlay told him that the Efrafans were defeated and the warren was saved. After a time, they dug carefully to broaden the run and as the day wore on the does, each in turn, remained beside him, licking his wounds and listening to his low, unsteady breathing.

Before this, Blackberry and Dandelion had burrowed their way in from Kehaar's run – it had not been blocked very heavily – and told their story. Dandelion could not say what might have happened to Hazel after the dog broke loose, and by the early afternoon everyone feared the worst. At last Pipkin, in great anxiety and distress, insisted on setting out for Nuthanger. Fiver at once said that he would go with him and together they left the wood and set off northwards over the down. They had gone only a short distance when Fiver, sitting up on an ant-hill to look about, saw a rabbit approaching over the high ground to the west. They both ran nearer and recognized Hazel. Fiver went to meet him while Pipkin raced back to the Honeycomb with the news.

As soon as he had learned all that had happened – including what Groundsel had to tell – Hazel asked Holly to take two or three rabbits and find out for certain whether the Efrafans had really gone. Then he himself went into the run where Bigwig was lying. Hyzenthlay looked up as he came.

'He was awake a little while ago, Hazel-rah,' she said. 'He asked where you were; and then he said his ear hurt very much.'

Hazel nuzzled the matted fur cap. The blood had turned hard and set into pointed spikes that pricked his nose.

'You've done it, Bigwig,' he said. 'They've all run away.'

For several moments Bigwig did not move. Then he opened his eyes and raised his head, pouching out his cheeks and sniffing at the two rabbits beside him. He said nothing and Hazel wondered whether he had understood. At last he whispered, 'Ees finish Meester Voundvort, ya?'

'Ya,' replied Hazel. 'I've come to help you silflay. It'll do you good and we can clean you up a lot better outside. Come on: it's a lovely afternoon, all sun and leaves.'

Bigwig got up and tottered forward into the devastated Honeycomb. There he sank down, rested, got up again and reached the foot of Kehaar's run.

'I thought he'd killed me,' he said. 'No more fighting for me – I've had enough. And you – your plan worked, Hazel-rah, did it? Well done. Tell me what it was. And how did you get back from the farm?'

'A man brought me in a hrududu,' said Hazel, 'nearly all the way.'

'And you flew the rest, I suppose,' said Bigwig, 'burning a white stick in your mouth? Come on, Hazel-rah, tell me sensibly. What's the matter, Hyzenthlay?'

'Oh!' said Hyzenthlay, staring. 'Oh!'

'What is it?'

'He did!'

'Did what?'

'He *did* ride home in a hrududu. And I saw him as he came – that night in Efrafa, when I was with you in your burrow. Do you remember?'

'I remember,' said Bigwig. 'I remember what I said, too. I said you'd better tell it to Fiver. That's a good idea – let's go and do it. And if he'll believe you, Hazel-rah, then I will.'

50. And Last

Professing myself, moreover, convinced that the General's unjust interference, so far from being really injurious to their felicity, was perhaps rather conducive to it, by improving their knowledge of each other, and adding strength to their attachment, I leave it to be settled by whomsoever it may concern ...

Jane Austen, *Northanger Abbey*

IT WAS a fine, clear evening in mid-October, about six weeks later. Although leaves remained on the beeches and the sunshine was warm, there was a sense of growing emptiness over the wide space of the down. The flowers were sparser. Here and there a yellow tormentil showed in the grass, a late harebell or a few shreds of purple bloom on a brown, crisping tuft of self-heal. But most of the plants still to be seen were in seed. Along the edge of the wood a sheet of wild clematis showed like a patch of smoke, all its sweet-smelling flowers turned to old man's beard. The songs of the insects were fewer and intermittent. Great stretches of the long grass, once the teeming jungle of summer, were almost deserted, with only a hurrying beetle or a torpid spider left out of all the myriads of August. The gnats still danced in the bright air, but the swifts that had swooped for them were gone and instead of their screaming cries in the sky, the twittering of a robin sounded from the top of a spindle tree. The fields below the hill were all cleared. One had already been ploughed and the polished edges of the furrows caught the light with a dull glint, conspicuous from the ridge above. The sky too was void, with a thin clarity like that of water. In July the still blue, thick as cream, had seemed close above the green trees, but now the blue was high and rare, the sun slipped sooner to the west and once there, foretold a touch of frost, sinking slow and big and drowsy, crimson as the rosehips that covered the briar. As the wind freshened from the south, the red and yellow beech leaves rasped together with a brittle sound, harsher than the fluid rustle of earlier days. It was a time of quiet departures, of the sifting away of all that was not staunch against winter.

Many human beings say that they enjoy the winter, but what they really enjoy is feeling proof against it. For them there is no winter food problem. They have fires and warm clothes. The winter cannot hurt them and therefore increases their sense of cleverness and security. For birds and animals, as for poor men, winter is another matter. Rabbits, like most wild animals, suffer hardship. True, they are luckier than some, for food of a sort is nearly always to be had. But under snow they may stay underground for days at a time, feeding only by chewing pellets. They are more subject to disease in winter and the cold lowers their vitality. Nevertheless, burrows can be snug and warm, especially when crowded. Winter is a more active mating season than the late summer and the autumn, and the time of greatest fertility for the does starts about February. There are fine days when silflay is still enjoyable. For the adventurous, garden raiding has its charms. And underground, there are stories to be told and games to be played – bob-stones and the like. For rabbits, winter remains what it was for men in the Middle Ages – hard, but bearable by the resourceful and not altogether without compensations.

On the west side of the beech hanger, in the evening sun, Hazel and Fiver were sitting with Holly, Silver and Groundsel. The Efrafan survivors had been allowed to join the warren and after a shaky start, when they were regarded with dislike and suspicion, were settling down pretty well, largely because Hazel was determined that they should.

Since the night of the siege, Fiver had spent much time alone and even in the Honeycomb, or at morning and evening silflay, was often silent and preoccupied. No one resented this – 'He looks right through you in such a nice, friendly way' as Bluebell put it – for each in his own manner recognized that Fiver was now more than ever governed, whether he would or no, by the pulse of that mysterious world of which he had once spoken to Hazel during the late June days they had spent together at the foot of the down. It was Bigwig who said – one evening when Fiver was absent from the Honeycomb at story-time – that Fiver was one who had paid more dearly than even himself for the night's victory over the Efrafans. Yet to his doe, Vilthuril, Fiver was devotedly attached, while she had come to understand him almost as deeply as ever Hazel had.

Just outside the beech hanger, Hyzenthlay's litter of four young rabbits were playing in the grass. They had first been brought up to graze about seven days before. If Hyzenthlay had had a second litter she would by this time have left them to look after themselves. As it was, however, she was grazing close by, watching their play and every now and then moving in to cuff the strongest and stop him bullying the others.

'They're a good bunch, you know,' said Holly. 'I hope we get some more like those.'

'We can't expect many more until towards the end of the winter,' said Hazel, 'though I dare say there'll be a few.'

'We can expect anything, it seems to me,' said Holly. 'Three litters born in autumn – have *you* ever heard of such a thing before? Frith didn't mean rabbits to mate in the high summer.'

'I don't know about Clover,' said Hazel. 'She's a hutch rabbit: it may be natural to her to breed at any time, for all I know. But I'm sure that Hyzenthlay and Vilthuril started their litters in the high summer because they'd had no natural life in Efrafa. For all that, they're the only two who *have* had litters, as yet.'

'Frith never meant us to go on fighting in the high summer, either, if that comes to that,' said Silver. 'Everything that's happened is unnatural – the fighting, the breeding – and all on account of Woundwort. If he wasn't unnatural, who was?'

'Bigwig was right when he said he wasn't like a rabbit at all,' said Holly. 'He was a fighting animal – fierce as a rat or a dog. He fought because he actually felt safer fighting than running. He was brave all right. But it wasn't natural; and that's why it was bound to finish him in the end. He was trying to do something that Frith never meant any rabbit to do. I believe he'd have hunted like the elil if he could.'

'He isn't dead, you know,' broke in Groundsel.

The others were silent.

'He hasn't stopped running,' said Groundsel passionately. 'Did you see his body? No. Did anyone? No. Nothing could kill him. He made rabbits bigger than they've ever been – braver, more skilful, more cunning. I know we paid for it. Some gave their lives. It was worth it, to feel we were Efrafans. For the first time ever, rabbits didn't go scurrying away. The elil feared us. And that was on account of Woundwort – him and no one but him. We weren't good enough for the General. Depend upon it, he's gone to start another warren somewhere else. But no Efrafan officer will ever forget him.'

'Well, now I'll tell you something,' began Silver. But Hazel cut him short.

'You mustn't say you weren't good enough,' he said. 'You did everything for him that rabbits could do and a great deal more. And what a lot we learnt from you! As for Efrafa, I've heard it's doing well under Campion, even if some things aren't quite the same as they used to be. And listen – by next spring, if I'm right, we shall have too many rabbits here for comfort. I'm going to encourage some of the youngsters to start a new warren between here and

Efrafa: and I think you'll find Campion will be ready to send some of his rabbits to join them. You'd be just the right fellow to start that scheme off.'

'Won't it be difficult to arrange?' asked Holly.

'Not when Kehaar comes,' said Hazel, as they began to hop easily back towards the holes at the north-east corner of the hanger. 'He'll turn up one of these days, when the storms begin on that Big Water of his. He can take a message to Campion as quickly as you'd run to the iron tree and back.'

'By Frith in the leaves, and I know someone who'll be glad to see him!' said Silver. 'Someone not so very far away.'

They had reached the eastern end of the trees and here, well out in the open where it was still sunny, a little group of three young rabbits – bigger than Hyzenthlay's – were squatting in the long grass, listening to a hulking veteran, lop-eared and scarred from nose to haunch – none other than Bigwig, captain of a very free-and-easy Owsla. These were the bucks of Clover's litter and a likely lot they looked.

'Oh no, no, no, no,' Bigwig was saying. 'Oh, my wings and beak, that won't do! You – what's your name? – Scabious – look, I'm a cat and I see you down at the bottom of my garden chewing up the lettuces. Now, what do I do? Do I come walking up the middle of the path waving my tail? Well, do I?'

'Please, sir, I've never seen a cat,' said the young rabbit.

'No, you haven't yet,' admitted the gallant captain. 'Well, a cat is a horrible thing with a long tail. It's covered with fur and has bristling whiskers and when it fights it makes fierce, spiteful noises. It's cunning, see?'

'Oh yes, sir,' answered the young rabbit. After a pause, he said politely, 'Er – you lost your tail?'

'Will you tell us about the fight in the storm, sir,' asked one of the other rabbits, 'and the tunnel of water?'

'Yes, later on,' said the relentless trainer. 'Now look, I'm a cat, right? I'm asleep in the sun, right? And you're going to get past me, right? Now then –'

'They pull his leg, you know,' said Silver, 'but they'd do anything for him.' Holly and Groundsel had gone underground and Silver and Hazel moved out once more into the sun.

'I think we all would,' replied Hazel. 'If it hadn't been for him that day, the dog would have come too late. Woundwort and his lot wouldn't have been above ground. They'd have been down below, finishing what they'd come to do.'

'He beat Woundwort, you know,' said Silver. 'He had him beat before the dog came. That was what I was going to say just now, but it was as well I didn't, I suppose.'

'I wonder how they're getting on with that winter burrow down the hill,' said Hazel. 'We're going to need it when the hard weather comes. That hole in the roof of the Honeycomb doesn't help at all. It'll close up naturally one day, I suppose, but meanwhile it's a confounded nuisance.'

'Here come the burrow-diggers, anyway,' said Silver.

Pipkin and Bluebell came over the crest, together with three or four of the does.

'Ah ha, ah ha, O Hazel-rah,' said Bluebell. 'The burrow's snug, it hath been dug, 'tis free from beetle, worm and slug. And in the snow, when down we go –'

'Then what a lot to you we'll owe,' said Hazel. 'I mean it, too. The holes are concealed, are they?'

'Just like Efrafa, I should think,' said Bluebell. 'As a matter of fact, I brought one up with me to show you. You can't see it, can you? No – well, there you are. I say, just look at old Bigwig with those youngsters over there. You know, if he went back to Efrafa now they couldn't decide which Mark to put him in, could they? He's got them all.'

'Come over to the evening side of the wood with us, Hazel-rah?' said Pipkin. 'We came up early on purpose to have a bit of sunshine before it gets dark.'

'All right,' answered Hazel good-naturedly. 'We've just come back from there, Silver and I, but I don't mind slipping over again for a bit.'

'Let's go out to that little hollow where we found Kehaar that morning,' said Silver. 'It'll be out of the wind. D'you remember how he cursed at us and tried to peck us?'

'And the worms we carried?' said Bluebell. 'Don't forget them.'

As they came near the hollow they could hear that it was not empty. Evidently some of the other rabbits had had the same idea.

'Let's see how close we can get before they spot us,' said Silver. 'Real Campion style – come on.'

They approached very quietly, up wind from the north. Peeping over the edge, they saw Vilthuril and her litter of four lying in the sun. Their mother was telling the young rabbits a story.

'So after they had swum the river,' said Vilthuril, 'El-ahrairah led his people on in the dark, through a wild, lonely place. Some of them were afraid, but he knew the way and in the morning he brought them safely to some green fields, very beautiful, with good, sweet grass. And here they found a warren; a warren that was bewitched. All the rabbits in this warren were in the power of a wicked spell. They wore shining collars round their necks and sang like the birds and some of them could fly. But for all they looked so fine, their hearts were dark and tharn. So then El-ahrairah's people said, "Ah see, these are the wonderful rabbits of Prince Rainbow. They are like princes themselves. We will live with them and become princes too." '

Vilthuril looked up and saw the newcomers. She paused for a moment and then went on.

'But Frith came to Rabscuttle in a dream and warned him that the warren was enchanted. And he dug into the ground to find where the spell was buried. Deep he dug, and hard was the search, but at last he found that wicked spell and dragged it out. So they all fled from it, but it turned into a great rat and flew at El-ahrairah. Then El-ahrairah fought the rat, up and down, and at last he held it, pinned under his claws, and it turned into a great, white bird which spoke to him and blessed him.'

'I seem to know this story,' whispered Hazel, 'but I can't remember where I've heard it.'

Bluebell sat up and scratched his neck with his hind leg. The little rabbits turned round at the interruption and in a moment had tumbled up the side of the hollow, squeaking

'Hazel-rah! Hazel-rah!' and jumping on Hazel from all sides.

'Here, wait a minute,' said Hazel, cuffing them off. 'I didn't come here to get mixed up in a fight with a lot of roughs like you! Let's hear the rest of the story.'

'But there's a man coming on a horse, Hazel-rah,' said one of the young rabbits. 'Oughtn't we to run into the wood?'

'How can you tell?' asked Hazel. 'I can't hear anything.'

'Neither can I,' said Silver, listening with his ears up.

The little rabbit looked puzzled.

'I don't know how, Hazel-rah,' he answered, 'but I'm sure I'm not mistaken.'

They waited for some little time, while the red sun sank lower. At last, just as Vilthuril was about to go on with the story, they heard hooves on the turf and the horseman appeared from the west, cantering easily along the track towards Cannon Heath Down.

'*He* won't bother us,' said Silver. 'No need to run: he'll just go by. You're a funny chap, though, young Threar, to spot him so far off.'

'He's always doing things like that,' said Vilthuril. 'The other day he told me what a river looked like and said he'd seen it in a dream. It's Fiver's blood, you know. It's only to be expected with Fiver's blood.'

'Fiver's blood?' said Hazel. 'Well, as long as we've got some of that I dare say we'll be all right. But you know, it's turning chilly here, isn't it? Come on, let's go down, and hear the rest of that story in a good, warm burrow. Look, there's Fiver over on the bank now. Who's going to get to him first?'

A few minutes later there was not a rabbit to be seen on the down. The sun sank below Ladle Hill and the autumn stars began to shine in the darkening east – Perseus and the Pleiades, Cassiopeia, faint Pisces and the great square of Pegasus. The wind freshened, and soon myriads of dry beech leaves were filling the ditches and hollows and blowing in gusts across the dark miles of open grass. Underground, the story continued.

Epilogue

He did look far
Into the service of the time, and was
Discipled of the bravest: he lasted long,
But on us both did haggish age steal on,
And wore us out of act . . .

Shakespeare, *All's Well That Ends Well*

He was part of my dream, of course – but then I was part
of his dream, too.

Lewis Carroll, *Through the Looking-Glass*

'AND what happened in the end?' asks the reader,
who has followed Hazel and his comrades in all
their adventures and returned with them at last to the
warren where Fiver brought them from the fields of
Sandleford. The wise Mr Lockley has told us that wild
rabbits live for two or three years. He knows everything
about rabbits; but all the same, Hazel lived longer than
that. He lived a tidy few summers – as they say in that part

of the world – and learned to know well the changes of the downs to spring, to winter and to spring again. He saw more young rabbits than he could remember. And sometimes, when they told tales on a sunny evening by the beech trees, he could not clearly recall whether they were about himself or about some other rabbit hero of days gone by.

The warren prospered and so, in the fullness of time, did the new warren on the Belt, half Watership and half Efrafan – the warren that Hazel had first envisaged on that terrible evening when he set out alone to face General Woundwort and try to save his friends against all odds. Groundsel was the first Chief Rabbit; but he had Strawberry and Buckthorn to give him advice and he had learned better than to mark anyone or to order more than a very occasional Wide Patrol. Campion readily agreed to send some rabbits from Efrafa and the first party was led by none other than Captain Avens, who acted sensibly and made a very good job of it.

General Woundwort was never seen again. But it was certainly true, as Groundsel said, that no one ever found his body, so it may perhaps be that after all, that extraordinary rabbit really did wander away to live his fierce life somewhere else and to defy the elil as resourcefully as ever. Kehaar, who was once asked if he would look out for him in his flights over the downs, merely replied, 'Dat dam' rabbit – I no see 'im, I no vant I see 'im.' Before many months had passed, no one on Watership knew or particularly cared to know whether he himself or his mate was descended from one or two Efrafan parents or from none at all. Hazel was glad that it should be so. And yet there endured the legend that somewhere, out over the Down, there lived a great and solitary rabbit, a giant who drove the elil like mice and sometimes went to silflay in the sky. If ever great danger arose, he would come back to fight for those who honoured his name. And mother rabbits would tell their kittens that if they did not do as they were told, the General would get them – the General who was first cousin to the Black Rabbit himself. Such was Woundwort's monument: and perhaps it would not have displeased him.

One chilly, blustery morning in March, I cannot tell exactly how many springs later, Hazel was dozing and waking in his burrow. He had spent a good deal of time there lately, for he felt the cold and could not seem to smell or run so well as in days gone by. He had been dreaming in a confused way – something about rain and elder bloom – when he woke to realize that there was a rabbit lying quietly beside him – no doubt some young buck who had come to ask his advice. The sentry in the run outside should not really have let him in without asking first. Never mind, thought Hazel. He raised his head and said, 'Do you want to talk to me?'

'Yes, that's what I've come for,' replied the other. 'You know me, don't you?'

'Yes, of course,' said Hazel, hoping he would be able to remember his name in a moment. Then he saw that in the darkness of the burrow, the stranger's ears were shining with a faint, silver light. 'Yes, my lord,' he said. 'Yes, I know you.'

'You've been feeling tired,' said the stranger, 'but I can do something about that. I've come to ask whether you'd care to join my Owsla. We shall be glad to have you and you'll enjoy it. If you're ready, we might go along now.'

They went out past the young sentry, who paid the visitor no attention. The sun was shining and in spite of the cold there were a few bucks and does at silflay, keeping out of the wind as they nibbled the shoots of spring grass. It seemed to Hazel that he would not be needing his body any more, so he left it lying on the edge of the ditch, but stopped for a moment to watch his rabbits and to try to get used to the extraordinary feeling that strength and speed were flowing inexhaustibly out of him into their sleek young bodies and healthy senses.

'You needn't worry about them,' said his companion. 'They'll be all right – and thousands like them. If you'll come along, I'll show you what I mean.'

He reached the top of the bank in a single, powerful leap. Hazel followed; and together they slipped away, running easily down through the wood, where the first primroses were beginning to bloom.

WATERSHIP
DOWN

NOW A
MAJOR TV
MINI-SERIES

RICHARD ADAMS

1920 *Born 9 May in Newbury, Berkshire*

1926 *Attends Horris Hill Preparatory School*

1933 *Attends Bradfield College boarding school*

1938 *Enrols at Worcester College, Oxford, to study Modern History*

1940 *Called up to join the British Army in World War Two*

1946 *After the war he returns to Worcester College to finish his studies*

1948 *Joins the Civil Service*

1972 *Watership Down is published; in the same year it wins the Carnegie Medal and the Guardian Children's Fiction prize*

1974 *Shardik, his second novel is published, and he becomes a full-time writer*

1982	*Serves one year as President of the RSPCA*
1996	*The Tales of Watership Down is published, a sequel to his most famous novel*
2016	*Dies 24 December, aged 96*

INTERESTING FACTS

Richard Adams claims the rabbit from *Watership Down* he identifies with most is Hazel, but he has a high opinion of Dandelion. He values Shakespeare more highly than anybody or anything, and his favourite flavour of ice cream is strawberry!

David Parkins is a British cartoonist and illustrator. He didn't take up art until he was in the sixth form at school, when he began drawing caricatures of his teachers. At Lincoln College of Art he specialized in illustration. Since graduating in 1979 he has worked for The Beano *and* The Dandy *but now illustrates children's books, including the works of Dick King-Smith.*

ABOUT THE ILLUSTRATOR

DAVID PARKINS

WHERE DID THE
STORY COME FROM?

Richard Adams says that his inspiration for Watership
Down came from his love of nature, and from the
experiences he had during the war. He made up the
story for his two little girls — initially to pass the time
on a long car journey — and gradually expanded it until
his daughter Juliet told him it was too good to waste
and that he should write it down!

GUESS WHO?

A

Although he was a **yearling** and still below full weight, he had not the harassed look of most '**outskirters**'.

B

He had a curious, heavy growth of **fur** on the **crown of his head**, which gave him an odd appearance, as though he were wearing a kind of cap.

C

'He's almost as big as a hare and there's something about his mere presence that frightens you, as if blood and fighting and killing were all just part of the day's work to him.'

ANSWERS: A) *Hazel* B) *Bigwig* C) *General Woundwort*

WORDS GLORIOUS WORDS!

Lots of words have several different meanings — here are a few you'll find in this Puffin book. Use a **dictionary** or look them up online to find other definitions.

odyssey
a long, adventurous journey

prophesying
to foretell or predict

maverick
an independent individual

docile
easily handled

desolate *without comfort or hope*

scut
the short tail of a hare or rabbit

ubiquitous
being present everywhere at the same time

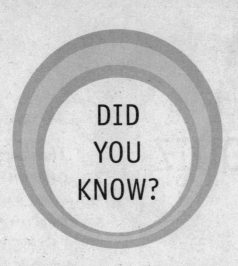

DID YOU KNOW?

Watership Down is set in the **Berkshire** and **Hampshire** countryside, eleven miles away from where Richard Adams still lives today.

Watership Down *was* **rejected** *by several agents and publishers — some of them thought it was* **'too grown-up for children'.**

If he could write it again, Richard Adams said he would give more attention to **Woundwort's** *character, making him a more* **heroic anti-hero**.

QUIZ

Thinking caps on – let's see how much you can remember! Answers are at the bottom of the opposite page. (No peeking!)

1 *In the beginning which rabbit predicts that something terrible will happen to the warren?*

a) *Bigwig*

b) *Hazel*

c) *Fiver*

d) *Holly*

HOLLY SAYS:
'Men will never rest till they've spoiled the earth and destroyed the animals.'

2 *What was the name of the warren they left?*

a) *Cowslip's warren*

b) *Watership Down*

c) *Sandleford warren*

d) *Efrafra*

3 Who is the leader of the Efrafan warren?

a) *Campion*

b) *Blackthorn*

c) *Hyzenthlay*

d) *Woundwort*

STRAWBERRY SAYS:

'Animals don't behave like men . . . They have dignity and animality.'

4 What is Bigwig saying when he tells Woundwort to 'Silflay hraka'?

a) *Get out of here*

b) *Eat rabbit droppings outside*

c) *Fight a dog*

d) *Go away before something bad happens to you*

5 Who has the first kittens at the new warren?

a) *Hyzenthlay*

b) *Haystack*

c) *Clover*

d) *Laurel*

RABBIT-Y FACTS

Rabbits have excellent senses of **smell**, **hearing** and **vision**. They can even see everything behind them and only have a small blind spot in front of their noses.

Rabbits have extremely **strong hind legs**, which allow them to leap great distances. They can jump up to **one metre high** and **three metres long**.

A rabbit's **expression of joy** is called a **'binky'**. They will run, jump into the air, twist their body and flick their feet.

Rabbits **stand upright** on their hind legs to give themselves a better chance of seeing **potential predators**.

If rabbits are spotted by a **predator**, they flee from them in a **zigzag pattern**. They can reach speeds of up to **18mph**!

Rabbits' **ears** can grow up to **10cm in length**. They use their ears to detect predators in their habitat.

Rabbits are popular in **mythology** and culture. Many people believe carrying a rabbit's foot will bring **good luck**.

PUFFIN WRITING TIP

Change your scenery and see something you've never seen before.

BIGWIG SAYS:
'Who knows why men do anything?'

MAKE AND DO

How to **draw a rabbit**

YOU WILL NEED:

* a sheet of plain paper
* a pencil
* an eraser
* colouring pencils or felt-tip pens

1 Draw three circles as shown – they don't have to be perfect.

2 Join up the circles with 2 lines as shown and add some ears.

3 Pencil in some twinkly eyes and a fluffy tail.

4 A little V will make a twitchy nose.

5 Draw on the front and back legs – don't forget the front paws!

6 Finally draw around the shapes with a darker pencil – make the line quite raggedy so your rabbit looks furry.

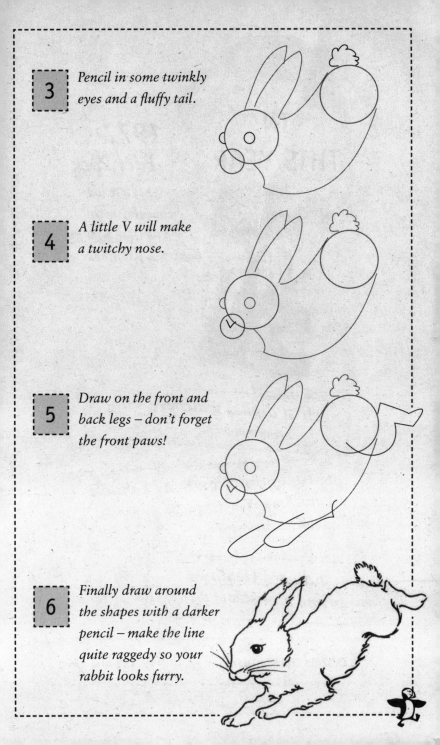

IN THIS YEAR

1972
Fact Pack

What else was happening in the world when this Puffin book was published?

The **first digital watches** are introduced.

The Eurovision Song Contest was held in Edinburgh and the winner was Luxembourg.

Edward Heath was **prime minister** of the UK.

Leeds United won the FA Cup for the first time.

FROM THE ARCHIVE

Here is a **sonnet** *written many years ago by* **Richard Adams**.

An Antarctic Sonnet

A trim, luxurious ship upon the ocean,
Controlled, secure in its magnificence,
Sure upon course, unfaltering in motion,
Your well-found heart's replete with confidence.
Zig-zag astern, I am your albatross,
Wing-tip to wave, hour after hour. Perhaps
There'll be some bits. I veer, cross and re-cross,
Stared at, admired; and hungry for your scraps.

The wake foams white at nightfall. Gaze at me
Once more, before you laugh and dine with friends.
i'll glide all right on my accustomed sea,
This solitude where love begins and ends.
Annie upon the deck, you never heard
That famished love's tenacious as a bird?

Richard Adams
1981.

If you have enjoyed *Watership Down* you may like to read *Tarka the Otter* – the incredible story of a young otter cub's survival against the odds.

CHAPTER ONE

TWILIGHT over meadow and water, the eve-star shining above the hill, and Old Nog the heron crying *kra-a-ark!* as his slow dark wings carried him down to the estuary. A whiteness drifting above the sere reeds of the riverside, for the owl had flown from under the middle arch of the stone bridge that once had carried the canal across the river.

Below Canal Bridge, on the right bank, grew twelve great trees, with roots awash. Thirteen had stood there – eleven oaks and two ash trees – but the oak nearest the North Star had never thriven, since first a pale green hook had pushed out of a swelled black acorn left by floods on the bank more than three centuries before. In its second year a bullock's hoof had crushed the seedling, breaking its two ruddy leaves, and the sapling grew up crooked. The cleft of its fork held the rains of two hundred years, until frost made a wedge of ice that split the trunk; another century's weather wore it hollow, while every flood took more earth and stones from under it. And one rainy night, when salmon and peal from the sea were swimming against the brown rushing water, the tree had suddenly groaned. Every root carried the groans of the moving trunk, and the voles ran in fear from their tunnels. It rocked until dawn; and when the wind left the land it gave a loud cry, scaring the white owl from its roost, and fell into the river as the sun was rising.

Now the water had dropped back, and dry sticks lodged on the branches marked the top of the flood. The river flowed slowly through the pool, a-glimmer with the clear green western sky. At the tail of the pool it quickened smoothly into paws of water with star-streaming claws. The water murmured against the stones. Jets and rills ran fast and shallow to an island, on which grew a leaning willow tree. Down from here the river moved swift and polished. Alder and sallow grew on its banks. Round a bend it hastened, musical over many stretches of shillet; at the end of the bend it merged into a dull silence of deep salt-water, and its bright spirit was lost. The banks below were mud, channered by the sluices of guts draining the marsh. Every twelve hours the sea passed an arm under Halfpenny Bridge, a minute's heron-flight below, and the spring tides felt the banks as far as the bend. The water moved down again immediately, for the tide's-head had no rest.

The tree lay black in the glimmering salmon-pool. Over the meadow a mist was moving, white and silent as the fringe of down on the owl's feathers. Since the fading of shadows it had been straying from the wood beyond the mill-leat, bearing in its breath the scents of the day, when bees had blended bluebell and primrose. Now the bees slept, and mice were running through the flowers. Over the old year's leaves the vapour moved, silent and wan, the wraith of waters once filling the ancient wide river-bed – men say that the sea's tides covered all this land, when the Roman galleys drifted up under the hills.